ACCIDENTAL HUSBAND

CRYSTAL KASWELL

Also by Crystal Kaswell

Sinful Serenade

Sing Your Heart Out - Miles

Strum Your Heart Out - Drew

Rock Your Heart Out - Tom

Play Your Heart Out - Pete

Sinful Ever After – series sequel

Dangerous Noise

Dangerous Kiss - Ethan

Dangerous Crush – Kit

Dangerous Rock – Joel

Dangerous Fling – Mal

Dangerous Encore - series sequel

Inked Hearts

Tempting - Brendon

Hooking Up - Walker

Pretend You're Mine - Ryan

Hating You, Loving You - Dean

Breaking the Rules - Hunter

Losing It - Wes

Accidental Husband - Griffin

more coming in 2019

Standalones

Broken - Trent & Delilah

Come Undone - A Love Triangle

Dirty Rich

Dirty Deal - Blake

Dirty Boss - Nick

Sign up for the Crystal Kaswell mailing list

About This Book

It's all fun and games in Vegas... until you accidentally marry your best friend.

Last night, I married Jules.

That's right, I married the girl who thought I had cooties in fourth grade.

Yeah, we drank a few too many shots of tequila. Sure, we danced a little too close. But nothing prepared me for the taste of her soft lips.

All of a sudden, we were in a borrowed limo (don't ask), ripping each other's clothes off, whispering dirty promises.

Then I was on one knee, asking her to make it forever, accepting her yes.

This morning, everything changed.

She wants to erase our night. Go back to normal.

Only there's no more normal. I'm acutely aware of her long legs, her soft curves, her sweet moan.

Mistakes be damned.

She's my wife. I'm not about to let her go.

Chapter One

JULIETTE

"This is our night, right?" he asks. "One perfect night in Vegas?"

"Exactly." Tonight is magic and fairy tales and fireworks. Tonight is everything.

Griffin reaches into his back pocket. "We're missing one part of the Vegas experience."

"What?"

He opens his hand.

It's sitting there, in the center of his palm:

A massive rock.

"Griff—"

"Marry me, Jules." He drops to one knee.

"But—" Fuck, that ring is huge. "We're drunk." It seems like a salient point.

"I know how I feel."

"How do you know?"

"I just do." His voice is steady. Sure. But Griff's voice is always sure. He's been my best friend since third grade. I know his voice, and this tone means *hell yes.* "I want to do this tonight." His dark eyes bore into mine. "I want to marry you tonight."

"Uh…" What the fuck? "What if you change your mind?"

"I won't."

"I…"

"It's a simple question, Jules." He holds up the ring. "Do you want to marry me or not?"

Chapter Two

GRIFFIN

Three Days Ago

J*ules: The wedding is off.*

That's it. That's the entire message.

I stare at my cell for a full minute, waiting for my best friend to offer a follow up.

She doesn't.

Those four words stay on my screen.

The wedding is off.

No explanation. No detail. No insight to her feelings.

Only four words that change everything.

My best friend is calling off her wedding. She's no longer marrying Jackson Jones, the most boring man in the history of the world.

She's no longer in a relationship with the most boring man in the history of the world.

She's single.

Not that it matters. Jules and I are friends. Just friends. Jackson didn't believe that—he was always giving me dirty looks, like he was sure I was only hanging around her to get in her pants—but that doesn't change the facts.

I've known Jules since I was in third grade. I barely register her as a girl. I don't want to fuck her.

If I did, I'd wrap my arms around her and whisper *take off your jeans, I want to feel you come. How do you want it? On my hands? My face? My cock? I'll grab a toy if that's what turns you on.*

I don't beat around the bush. I don't sugar coat. I don't bullshit.

When I want something, I demand it.

Right now, I need a fucking explanation.

"Griff? You okay?" Wes interrupts my train of thought. His blue eyes fix on me. Fill with that Wes-like *I'm fucking with you, but it's for your own good* playfulness.

I appreciate it, I do. Wes is a good friend. My best friend, after Jules. But, right now, I don't have time for the banter.

"Your plaything dump you?" he asks.

"No." My current fuck buddy and I texted plenty last night. Explicit shit. Explicit shit that made me hard enough to bust out of my jeans. Not that it matters at the moment.

"Then what's with the face?" he asks.

I shrug my shoulders, but it's not all that convincing. Which is ridiculous. There's no reason to be upset. This is a good thing. Jules is better off. Even if Jackson was the only thing keeping her in Southern California.

My heart thuds against my chest as I check our text history for clues to the timeline of her breakup. We were talking last night (after I finished with my fuck buddy).

She gushed about her current YA book—a *Sleeping Beauty* retelling that's making her believe in fairy tales again—and went on and on about the boys in blue. God, her love of the Dodgers is comical. And it's pure Jules too.

"Griff? You there?" Wes asks.

Right. I'm at work. With fifteen minutes until my next appointment.

Inked Hearts is a great shop. A Venice Beach institution. I'm lucky to have a gig here, with some of the best tattoo artists around.

I need to keep my head in the game. Stay professional. Stay out of the shop gossip.

We can talk after this. Or maybe never. It doesn't feel right sharing details.

Jules and I have always existed in our own universe. A place that belongs to us and only us.

I roll my shoulders back. Perfect my poker face. This needs to be calm, cool, convincing. "She called off the wedding."

"You two fucked."

"No." Why does everyone think that?

"She finally realize she's in love with you?"

I shoot him a *get real* look.

"You realized you're in love with her. She wanted time to process that, so she asked Mr. Boring to put things on pause."

"Seriously?" I ask.

"You're gonna realize it one day."

"Fat chance."

He nods *hell yes*.

It's ridiculous, but I'm not going to argue. It only encourages him.

Wes has been pushing this *you're in love with Jules thing* for ages. I appreciate the intention—I always want to hear the truth, even if it hurts—but he's dead wrong.

"Explain something to me, Griff." He rests his ass against the wall separating my suite and Brendon's.

"Yeah?" I stare at my cell, but it doesn't conjure a text from my best friend.

"Mr. Boring was a snooze."

"What do you need explained? Seems like you have it figured out."

"Your best friend is free of the weight around her neck. How is this a bad thing?"

It's a fair question. I appreciate that. I should have an answer.

I should go with my first impulse.

The truth, the whole truth, and nothing but the truth. No matter how badly it hurts. That's my motto. It serves me well, even if it convinces some people I'm a tactless asshole.

Right now…

What the hell can I say?

This isn't a bad thing. It's a great thing. Jules is free. It might hurt for a while—she was with Jackson forever—but it's a good thing.

Shit. That's it. "She's probably not happy about it."

"You're worried about her?"

"No shit, Sherlock." My teeth sink into my lip. I'm worried about my best friend. That's all this is.

I hurt when Jules hurts.

Fuck, nothing hurts more than her hurt.

"Griff?" He leans in to whisper. "This shop is full of nosy assholes."

"Yourself included." I try to find lightness, but my shoulders stay heavy.

Wes laughs as he flips me off. "Maybe you should get out of here. Go to her place. Talk to her."

"No shit." My phone buzzes against my thigh. The screen flashes with that pic of me and Jules at the beach.

We've got orange wedges in our mouths and we're making stupid faces. We're happy. She's happy.

Wes shakes his head *you're so into her*.

I ignore him. Focus every ounce of my attention on her message.

Jules: You want to get out of town for a few days?

There isn't a single mention of her breakup. Her mood. Her living arrangements.

Just a simple request.

Griffin: Where are you?

Jules: My mom's place. You?

Griffin: Work.

Jules: I'll text when you're free.

Griffin: I can be free now.

I can move my appointment. Or ask someone to fill in. It's an easy stencil. And this—

Jules is the most important person in my life. She comes before work, before play, before everything.

Jules: It's not a big deal.

Bullshit.

Griffin: You call off your wedding and it's not a big deal?

Jules: Who says I called it off?

Griffin: Me.

Mr. Boring (I have to hand it to Wes—that is the perfect way to describe Jackson) is an idiot, but he's not stupid enough to dump her. She's way too good for him.

Jules: Can we discuss it from some beach in Hawaii? The honeymoon is paid for. No reason why I can't use it.

Griffin: It's next week.

Jules: I can wait.

I can't.

I look up at Wes.

He's staring at me expectantly. Like I'm going to come up with some magical idea that fixes everything.

Although—

Fuck, that's it.

That's perfect.

Chapter Three

JULIETTE

Except for the tap tap of Mom's heels and the low murmur of her voice—she's in the kitchen, making calls—the house is quiet. I can't make out her words, but I can hear the tone.

Curt. Professional. All business.

It's amazing, really. My mother is the most passionate person I know, but she can steel herself in the blink of an eye. She snaps her fingers and goes from *oh my God, I love it, I love you, I want to marry you and have your babies* to *we really need to discuss quarter three projections* in seconds.

I do my best at keeping my feelings to myself, but I'm not as good at turning off the faucet.

Once it's running—

UGH.

I roll over. Bury my face in my pillowcase. The one with Princess Jasmine on it.

One of the many "strong role models" Mom adopted for me.

She had this phase where she tried, hard, to find good non-white role models, so I'd feel beautiful and normal and competent. As if there's any way to feel normal about inheriting features from the Colombian father I've never met.

Or her refusing to answer a single question about him.

I know they worked together twenty-something years ago. I assumed he was tall—I tower over her—and that he had dark hair and the recessive gene for green eyes.

Other than that, I don't have a clue.

Don't get me wrong. I love her. I love my step-dad too. I see him as my dad, I do. But there's something about not knowing my biological father, about looking in the mirror and seeing a reflection that clearly doesn't fit into the family.

Princess Jasmine is great. So is Mulan and Pocahontas and any character portrayed by America Ferrara.

But "role models" don't make up for that feeling of abandonment.

My father didn't want to be in my life.

Nothing makes up for that.

Disney heroines are great, but they exist in a fairy-tale world full of magic and happy endings.

I used to believe that.

After the way shit went with Jackson—

I see those movies for what they are. Fantasies.

There's no magic in the world. No one is coming to rescue me. Or bust me out of my prison. Or tell me I'm the chosen one.

My phone sings with text alerts.

Ugh. I have to talk to these people. I have to assure them I'm fine. And apologize for the inconvenience of canceling my wedding.

Yes, it must be so hard for everyone else that my fiancé was fucking his co-worker.

Ding.

I pick up my cell. Stare at the messages from people who aren't really friends.

I'm so sorry to hear about your wedding.

Omg, Juliette, are you okay?

Jackson never deserved you.

I already have the tickets to LA. How about I come and distract you?

Everyone means well. They want to help. But they also want me to tell them it's okay.

It's not okay.

I'm not telling them it is.

There's only one person I want right now. My best friend knows how to comfort me. He's obsessed with cheering me up.

Griffin: How about Vegas?

Jules: How about it?

Griffin: We should go.

Jules: Isn't Wes going?

Griffin: Yeah. He's taking his virgin. We can carpool.

My teeth sink into my lip. Usually, I love hearing the Inked Hearts gossip. It fills in the, um, gaps in my sex life. But that's a whole other conversation.

Jules: Wes is annoying.

Griffin: Exactly. He makes me look like a charmer.

My lips curl into a smile. I can't help it. Griff always knows exactly what to say. He just gets me.

Jules: Why hasn't he done it yet?

Griffin: You know how it is. You have to savor these things.

Jules: Do you?

Griffin: Fuck yeah.

Jules: TOO MUCH INFORMATION.

Griffin: I'm just getting started.

Jules: Please don't tell me how many women you've deflowered.

Griffin: Were you Jackson's first or not?

Jules: He was mine too. That doesn't count. And what about "too much information" makes you think I want to discuss this?

Griffin: When has that ever stopped me?

Jules: You're right. Your complete lack of manners is disgusting.

Griffin: Yet you're here.

Jules: You really want to go to Vegas with Wes and his fuck buddy?

Griffin: Dean and Chloe invited themselves too.

Jules: Oh.

Griffin: I'll tell them to get lost.

He should. We should get in my car and drive to Vegas right now. We can drink too much, cough as we attempt to smoke, lose a ton of money gambling.

Or I can stay home with my Kindle and a dozen pints of matcha ice cream and hide from the entire world.

A night at home with a strong cup of tea and a great book is as close to fairy-tale magic as it gets.

Jules: I'll consider it.

Griffin: Pretty sure they're doing it with or without us.

Jules: You should go.

Griffin: The point is to take you.

Jules: I'll take myself to Hawaii.

Griffin: With who?

Jules: With my other best friend.

Griffin: Oh yeah?

Jules: Hell yeah.

It's a bluff and we both know it. There's no second best friend. There's no one but Griff.

I push myself up. Let my gaze dart around the room.

It's still adorned with the trappings of high school.

Aladdin sheets. Dodgers blue desk. Paramore lyrics scribbled in silver sharpie.

Jules: You do realize it's August?

Griffin: I do.

Jules: It's going to be a hundred degrees in Vegas.

Griffin: Would you rather stay in your mom's air-conditioned house?

Jules: Better than dealing with your bullshit.

Griffin: You saying I shouldn't come over after work?

Jules: Here?

Griffin: I'll use the ladder in the backyard.

Like he did when we were kids. When Mom decided it was no longer appropriate for a boy and a girl to hang out with the door closed.

Which was ridiculous.

I don't see him that way. He doesn't see me that way. He may as well be a Ken doll. Not that I'd be friends with a Ken doll. But, uh, the point stands.

I don't think about Griffin's anatomy. As far as I'm concerned, he's another one of the girls. Not that he's in any way girly.

He's an incredibly masculine person what with the whole tall, dark, and handsome situation. I'm not blind. I do realize he's attractive. I just don't find him attractive.

It's an important distinction.

We're just friends.

Completely and totally platonic friends.

Jules: No. I need to get out of here. Let's meet somewhere.

Griffin: I know just the place.

Chapter Four

JULIETTE

"Is this really necessary?" I climb onto the lifeguard stand.

"Five bucks says you're listening to one of those whiny assholes." He reaches into his back pocket, pulls out his leather wallet, holds up a five-dollar bill.

I take his money. "Listen and weep."

He moves closer. His shoulder bumps mine. Then his arm. His hip. His leg.

His fingers brush my neck as he grabs an earbud.

His lips curl into a smile. "Let me guess—"

At the same time, we say, "this isn't a whiny asshole. It's a pissed goddess."

I flip him off.

He smiles. It's a big, wide smile. A real smile. Not that any of Griffin's smiles are fake. He doesn't fake anything, including politeness.

It's a marvel he has a job, honestly. I'm not sure what he does to convince his clients to work with him. Maybe it's the gorgeous dark eyes or the dimple on his cheek or the strong shoulders.

Or, um, well, he is a good artist. And some people appreciate a guy who tells it like it is. Even if it hurts. I certainly do.

And I don't appreciate the dimple. I mean, I do, because it's my best friend's dimple. But it's not like I *like like* his dimple. It's not like my heart is pounding against my chest from his proximity.

From the jog to the lifeguard stand, yeah? But the proximity is whatever.

Ahem.

I lean against the half-wall. Watch the setting sun turn the sky orange. It's a beautiful night. And it feels like summer. Warm air. Cool breeze. Ocean for miles.

This far south, the beach is quiet (well, quiet ish. It is August). It's just me, and Griffin, and my favorite band.

He closes his eyes. Mouths the chorus. Catches himself. Blushes.

It's a cute blush. It really is. Not because he's cute (he's attractive, but more in a hot way). Because it's rare.

Nothing rattles Griff.

His eyes meet mine. "Why don't you listen to a pissed goddess who writes quality shit?"

"Hmm, it's almost like I listen to what I enjoy."

"That's the problem."

"Is it?"

"You skipped the development stage where you acquired taste in music."

"And you skipped the one where you stopped complaining about music you hated in middle school."

"Got me there." His laugh lights up his dark eyes. Makes it easier to see the flecks of amber and honey that break up the deep coffee hue.

Not that it matters.

Yes, Griffin has gorgeous, deep, soulful eyes, but it's a simple fact.

Griffin is six feet of pure muscle. He has soulful brown eyes and lush waves every bit as beautiful as Kit Harrington's. His strong arms are covered in ink. And he's incredibly dirty.

Those are facts. They don't matter to me one way or another.

Griff chuckles. "You have to hand it to Haley." He refers to Haley Williams, the lead singer of my favorite band, by her first name. "She makes some of those guys look like Boyfriend of the Year."

"Which guys are these?" I fold his five-dollar bill.

"I'm gonna let you have that 'cause I feel sorry for you."

"Thank you for the charity." I slide the bill into my shorts. "It will buy an entire matcha latte."

"Not by my count."

I swat him.

Griff's fingers brush my neck as he pauses the song. "If you only listened to Paramore, I wouldn't worry so much."

"You worry about me?"

He nods.

I tap the band logo on his hoodie. The Black Keys. Of course. "This guy sounds like he's about to OD on Xanax."

"Maybe he is. That's good shit."

"Oh my God, really?"

He nods *really*. "I know you've swiped your mom's stash."

I shake my head. "You're the one who swiped it." I was terrified. Hell, I'm still terrified she's going to realize it and send me to therapy. She's an anxious flier, not a drug addict. She's not exactly popping pills like they're candy.

"You led me into her bathroom and opened the medicine cabinet."

"And you opened the bottle."

He shakes his head. "This inability to take responsibility is pathetic."

"Uh-huh." I turn my headphones off and slide them into the back pocket of my backpack.

"You still have that?" Griff points to the sharpie scribbles on the bright blue fabric. Well, the once bright blue fabric. It's more of a faded denim now.

His fingers trace the lines of a design—a rose with a knife through its blossoming petals (he insists it's not a sex thing).

"Yeah." I cross my legs and press my outer knees into the blanket. "I found it in the back of my closet."

His gaze shifts back to the design.

Neither one of us mentions that he drew it. That he used to hang out on the floor, doodling on my backpack, jeans, skin, while I read. That it was our normal, everyday routine until Mom freaked out.

We started cutting our hang out sessions short, so he'd be out of the house by the time she got home from Pilates.

Then I started dating Jackson and… we knew things had to be different. He stopped sleeping in my bed. I stopped offering my skin as a canvas. We sat at opposite ends of the couch.

It was different. There was a line. An *I know we're totally not into each other, and we never would be, but it so obviously doesn't matter, because I have a boyfriend* line.

Now…

He's closer than he's been in a long time.

"I brought you something." He rifles through his backpack. Pulls out a folded piece of paper. Hands it to me.

It's hard to see the details in the dim light, but I recognize it right away. The design he did for me. For us. When he first started tattooing. When I promised I'd never fall back into ugly habits.

This Too Shall Pass in a thin, cursive script, surrounded by peonies.

The tattoo on my wrist.

The one he traces every time he sees me.

"Come to Vegas," he says. "It's only a few days. It will be fun."

"Maybe." There's so much in this design. Things I can't handle right now. Promises I failed to keep.

"Jules—"

"Yeah?"

"You're being fucking stupid. Jackson is an asshole who never deserved you." His expression softens. "But I have heard stories about relationships."

"Have you?"

He nods, takes the paper, slips it into his backpack, stands. "I hear they fucking suck." He offers me his hand and nods to the beach. *Let's walk.*

He helps me collect my stuff and climb down the lifeguard stand.

It's freezing on the sand. Or maybe I'm underdressed. I've lived in Southern California my entire life, but I'm still not used to the temperature dropping thirty degrees between afternoon and evening.

Without a word, Griffin shrugs his hoodie off his shoulders and drapes it around mine.

My nose scrunches with distaste. "Do I really need to advertise your shitty taste in music?"

"Of course." He moves closer. And drops his voice to something that barely competes with the wind and the surf. "He didn't deserve you."

Yeah, but I'm not ready to discuss that yet. "Seriously, Griff. Don't."

"I won't. Not again. But it has to be said."

"Thank you." I swallow hard.

He nods *sure thing*. "He'd want you to ditch Vegas."

Probably true, but—"Are you going to use my ex as some card to manipulate me for the rest of my life?"

"If it works, yeah."

I can't help but laugh. He's so honest about being an asshole. "Seriously, why do I talk to you?"

He motions to his face. "It's the beautiful mug."

"I've seen better."

"Oh yeah?" He raises a brow. "Should we ask around?"

"Ask who?"

He motions to the boardwalk a hundred feet away. It's ramping down, but it's still thronged with tourists, merchants, skateboarders.

Plenty of people to assess Griffin's attractiveness. Which is stupid. And vain.

We both know he's conventionally attractive. There's nothing to prove.

Still, I shrug. "Eh, you're just okay. No Chris Hemsworth."

"You want to play with Thor's hammer, huh?"

"Oh my God, please do not tell me you're into that."

"I won't tell you." He wraps his fingers around my wrist. Pulls me toward the boardwalk. Hard. And fast.

Way, way too much information.

Gross.

So gross.

I try to push that mental image away as we cross the basketball court and approach a group of twenty-something girls, but it doesn't go.

Griffin in a blond wig and a red cape. Only a red cape. Pointing to his cock and whispering, 'baby, you want to play with my hammer?'

That's so wrong.

And I'm so curious if he's as big as—

He had a reputation for being well-endowed. Not that I care. I totally don't care.

It's just, I like knowing if gossip is accurate.

In a sociological kind of way.

"Excuse me." Griffin steps forward. "My friend and I want to settle something."

A cute brunette bats her eyelashes. "Of course." She steps forward. Arches her back to show off her massive boobs.

Women are always like this with Griffin. It's the tattooed arms that do it. Or maybe the shoulders. Or the chest.

Griffin flashes a cheeky smile. "She says I'm just okay. I think I'm—"

"God's gift to women," I say.

"Men can enjoy beautiful men too," Griffin says.

The brunette giggles. "You don't think your boyfriend is cute?"

"He's not." I break our touch. Press my hand to my side. "We're just friends."

"Really?" She chews on her lower lip. Stares at me with disbelief.

Which is ridiculous. "Do you think he's hot or what?" I ask.

"Well, yeah." She gives Griffin a long, slow once-over. "But I'm not really into being a third wheel."

Griffin's eyes light up. His smile widens. "Damn, Jules. That ruins our plans. I was really hoping—what's your name sweetie?"

"Alex," she says.

"Was hoping Alex could watch us come together.

Maybe another time, Alex." He winks, takes my hand, pulls me away.

"I hate you so much," I whisper under my breath.

"You should hate slower and move faster. The way she's watching—she's totally into it."

She is staring.

At him.

And at me.

At my ass.

Oh my God.

"I really hate you." I dart past a group of tourists. Then around a block of buildings. Into an alley.

"It's all right. If I was you, I'd be jealous of my beauty too."

I shake my head *you're ridiculous*.

He nods *hell yeah* and takes my hand. "Come on. I'll walk you home."

"What's in it for me?"

"A six-dollar matcha."

"Deal."

Chapter Five

JULIETTE

Is there anything better than a strong matcha latte?

I think not.

I swallow another sip. Let a sigh fall off my lips.

For a moment, I forget that I called off my wedding.

My world is green tea, milk, and honey.

"Fuck, Jules, you're gonna get us arrested." Griffin swallows a sip of his iced latte. Lets out an equally needy sigh.

"And you?"

"I can talk my way out of it."

I can't help but laugh. Griff is a lot of things. Lacking confidence is not on that list.

"You should stop teasing." I reach for his drink. The plastic is cold and wet against my fingers. "Or I'll steal this."

"What if that's my goal?" He offers me his drink.

"Why would that be your goal?"

"Maybe I want you over-caffeinated." Joy streaks his expression.

It makes my stomach flutter. "You're enjoying my misery, aren't you?"

"You're the fuckup for once."

I flip him off.

He returns the gesture.

I hide my smile behind my drink. He's doing a good job of cheering me up. "I'm not talking about it."

"I know."

"No, I mean, that's one of my terms. I'm not talking about him." I swallow another sip. Mmm. This drink really is creamy perfection. It's too much this late at night, but I don't care. Bliss is better than sleep anyway.

"There are terms?" He perks up.

"Yeah."

"So you're going?"

"Considering it." I pull my legs onto my chair and fold them over each other. "If you agree to my terms."

"Name them." His lips curl around the straw.

God, his lips really are full. Soft.

I bet he's a good kisser.

I've always wondered. As a friend.

I wonder about people. If their personalities out of the bedroom match their personalities in the bedroom.

"Jules?" He sets his drink down. Wipes a drop of coffee from his lips. "Your terms?"

Right. Terms. Not imagining my best friend's kissing skills. "No discussion of Jackson."

"Unless you bring him up."

I stare back at Griff.

"I know you, Jules. You're gonna get drunk and start crying and you're gonna want to talk about him."

I bite my lip. I know he means that in a loving way, but it still feels like an insult.

It's not like Griff is any better at handling his feelings. His liquor, sure. But his feelings?

No way.

His gaze passes over me slowly. "You're thinking something."

"That I enjoy the decor." I motion to the matcha shop's clean white walls. The framed photos of tea leaves and swirled soft serve in every shade of pastel. Matcha green, yuzu orange, sweet potato purple.

"It's conditioning," he says. "You love everything that comes with your caffeine high."

"And you?" I motion to his latte. This place specializes in matcha, but they have coffee too. And Griffin insists the iced lattes are to die for.

"There's a big difference between the two of us."

"Is there?"

He nods *hell yeah.*

I stare back at him, waiting.

He doesn't budge.

Okay, fine. "Which is…"

"Caffeine is your main source of pleasure. Whereas I have…" He motions to his crotch.

Gross. "You realize I'm as capable of masturbation as you are?"

He chuckles. "Not talking about masturbation."

I make a show of rolling my eyes, but it's all show. He's right. Jackson and I weren't having sex the last few months. And the sex before that was bad. Really bad. "Yes. Your skill as a lover so transcends mine, that I'm incapable of reaching the heights of bliss that you are." I take another sip. Make a point of moaning as loudly as I can. "This is all I have. Green tea and honey."

"I know," he deadpans. "It's sad. But I can solve that problem."

"Uh-huh."

"You know why single people go to Vegas?"

"To get one of those alcohol filled containers shaped like the Eiffel Tower," I say.

"Yeah, and you know what they do after they get wasted?"

"I don't need your help getting laid."

He shakes his head *you do.*

"I thought this was on my terms."

"Our terms." He leans back in his seat. Spreads his legs a few inches. Like he's inviting me to stare at his crotch.

My gaze flits there for a second, yeah, but only because of angles. It's not like I notice how perfectly his jeans fit his hips. And how the denim bulges over his—

Ahem.

"I'm going to show you a good time, Jules." He folds one leg over the other, so his limbs make a four. Which is basically an arrow pointing to his crotch.

Not that I'm looking. "My idea of a good time."

"So we're going to listen to emo music and read YA?"

"Yeah." I fold my arms over my chest. "I'm in the middle of a really great series."

"Bring it." He looks me in the eyes, dead serious. "You can fall asleep to the comfort of your teen fantasies. Hell, you can drag me to your hotel room and play Paramore's entire discography."

"I can?"

He nods. "We'll drive to the sounds of Haley Williams's whine."

"She doesn't whine."

He shoots me an *uh-huh, sure.* "Whatever you want to call her vocal style."

I want to call it awesome, but I don't need to have this discussion again. "Your friends will agree to my soundtrack?"

"I'll get them to agree." His voice is teasing, but there's nothing funny about this. If Griffin is willing to listen to music he hates for hours—

He really wants me to come. And he really wants me to have fun.

Which is sweet. And completely unacceptable.

I can't handle his expectations. No matter how good his intentions are.

If I want to spend my breakup miserable and alone, drinking my bodyweight in matcha lattes, reading YA romance, and listening to whiny singers curse their exes, I will.

And the singers aren't whiny. Why does everyone describe people who express emotion as whiny?

Yeah, they might be a little needy or clumsy with their professions of anger, but at least they're capable of getting it out.

That's more than I can say.

"Okay. I lead the conversation. We listen to emo music. And you read my YA romance with me," I say.

He looks at me like I'm crazy. "Why?"

"You're showing me your kind of good time. I'm showing you mine."

His nose scrunches with distaste. "What's the book we're reading?"

I set my backpack in my lap, dig until I find my Kindle, then show Griff the cover of our read. A gorgeous tiara on a pastel pink background.

Griffin groans. "Really?"

"That is a beautiful cover."

He shrugs *I guess*.

"Look me in the eyes and tell me you think it's poorly designed."

"Covers aren't really my thing."

"You design tattoos."

"Is that a tattoo?"

"You've never done a book cover tattoo?" I ask.

He groans. "That's a bullshit technicality."

"Hmm. Maybe it is. Or maybe you should admit you're wrong."

"It's a beautiful design, yeah. But it's also a fucking tiara."

"Do you have a problem with princesses?" I ask.

"Is this book really about a teenage girl finding out she's a princess?"

I shrug like it is. Really, the crown is a metaphor. Yes, the book is a modern day Cinderella story, but there's no actual royalty. Or fairy godmother. Or magic.

Only a midnight deadline and cruel stepparents. The ugly parts of the fairy tale without the magic.

Like life.

When I'm satisfied by his level of dread, I explain the plot.

He tries to hide his smile behind his latte, but he doesn't quite get there. "I will read this." He pulls out his cell, opens up the Kindle app, finds the book. "If you let me plan the entire trip."

"And our Paramore and YA romance afternoons?"

"I'll slot those in."

"All right." This is a win. Usually, he won't even discuss YA romance (beyond mocking my love).

He smiles that same *I'm getting exactly what I want* smile and offers his hand. "Trust me, Jules. By the time we're back in Los Angeles, you won't even remember Jackson's name."

"You're not supposed to bring him up."

He mimes zipping his lips then returns his hand to shaking position.

I take it.
Shake.
I feel like I'm making a deal with the devil.
But I kinda like it.

Chapter Six

GRIFFIN

Honestly, the Cinderella retelling isn't bad. It's better than the shitty action movies I watch with Wes. It's a hell of a lot better than the Barbie pink cover suggests.

The heroine is caring, loving, and tough as nails. She deals with a shitty, abusive father without cracking.

She could bail. Disappear somewhere else.

But she stays for her little sister.

She spends her days taking care of her family. Spends her nights disappearing into her fantasy life, talking to her online crush.

She has no idea who he is, she only loves him for his sweet personality. Of course, he's Hollywood royalty. A rich, handsome actor with a hundred thousand screaming fangirls.

And he's tall. Ridiculously tall for a sixteen-year-old.

I've read a few books with Jules. The guys are always handsome and tall. Even when they're fifteen.

What's with the height obsession?

I don't get it. I'm exactly six feet tall. Jules is five ten.

We're practically eye to eye. When we hug—

There's something about bodies connecting in the right places.

Not that I think about Jules that way.

More that I've fucked a lot of women who were her height. Or taller. Or shorter. It never really makes a difference.

Yeah, there are some positions that work better with certain proportions, but I can make anything work.

Jules is taller than Jackson, yeah, but it's not like the height difference is why he's a bad lay.

It's 'cause he's boring and selfish.

She can play coy about it if she wants, but I'm not buying it. That twitch in her lip gives her away.

She thinks she's a good liar. Maybe she is, but not when it's the two of us.

I know her tells.

Besides, I know what a satisfied woman looks like.

The only time Jules is satisfied is after she finishes a matcha latte.

No wonder the powdered green tea makes her groan like she's coming. She's not finding bliss in other places.

It's sad, really.

But it's got nothing to do with height.

I discuss sex with a lot of women. I always ask about the nights burnt into their memories.

No one ever mentions their partner's height. It's not like a woman gets going on a story: *oh my God, this make up sex with my ex was crazy. We were in Vegas and we were sharing one of those balloon shaped cups from The Paris. Then we snuck into the bathroom at the steakhouse, and he pressed my dress to my waist, and you know what? It was only a little hot, because he's five nine. I'm five four, sure, but I need a guy who's six feet tall, minimum.*

It's ridiculous. Like a guy who needs big tits or a small

waist.

Women are gorgeous. Doesn't matter if they're tall, short, thick, thin, white, black, Hispanic, Asian, loud, quiet, bossy, obedient—

There's something good about every flavor.

Fuck, I sound like my dad. I'm a slut, yeah, but I'm not a pig. I don't treat women like ice cream.

I'm upfront with every woman I fuck. It's a short-term arrangement. Maybe a night. Maybe a few weeks. Maybe a regular thing.

Depends on the woman. Depends how well she understands my inability to fall in love.

I make women come.

I'm good at it. Really fucking good at it.

Hell, after tattoos, it's probably my biggest skill.

What a résumé. *Excellent tattoo artist and skilled fuck. I want to make you come, sweet thing. I don't care if it's on my face, my hands, or my cock, so long as you're screaming my name when it happens.*

Shit. I'm losing track of my point.

My head is off today. Maybe it's all the coffee—I insisted on buying Jules a matcha for the road, but she'd only agree if she could buy me a latte.

Maybe it's the late dinner—I went straight to the beach after work.

Maybe it's the book.

Cinderella hits a little too close to home. Her asshole father is the spitting image of mine.

Jules must notice.

But she wouldn't do that to me. She wouldn't recommend this book to make some bullshit point. She knows I don't appreciate that kind of… I'll be generous and call it subtlety.

Yeah, she appreciates themes. She's always trying to get

me to see the messages in works of fiction. But not because she wants to brainwash me into discussing my philandering father.

Because she loves books more than she loves breathing.

Fuck, it's one of my favorite things about her. She lights up when she talks about her current read. It's what makes her happy.

The last time I saw her happy, really happy, was when she was applying to MFA programs. She applied to a dozen, got into most of them.

She never told me what happened. Only that she and Jackson agreed it was best if she go to the program at UCLA.

I'm sure the asshole decided he couldn't stomach her being away from him for months at a time. I'm sympathetic, really. I don't like it any more than he does.

But fuck him for clipping her wings.

Nobody is clipping her wings. Not on my watch.

This trip—I've been texting Wes and Dean all night, arranging details—is for her. To cheer her up. Help her figure out her shit.

I'm making sure she soars. Even if it means she leaves me behind.

Fuck. That's a problem for tomorrow. Next week, at the earliest. Right now, I'm teasing her about this book.

I grab my cell, shoot Jules a text about how evil she is for torturing me with YA, drop my phone on the bed.

It buzzes with her response.

Shit.

That's not her response. It's a cunt. Close up and in full definition.

Oh. It's a message from Lee Ann, my current fling. She's hot. And kinky. But this picture of her cunt isn't doing shit for me.

I skim our last week of texts.

Lee Ann: Yeah, give it to me hard.

Griffin: I'm going to bend you over, pin you to the bed, and spank you like the bad girl you are.

Lee Ann: Have I been bad?

Griffin: Very fucking bad.

Lee Ann: What did I do?

Griffin: You promised you wouldn't wear panties.

There's a picture of her thong-clad ass.

Lee Ann: I thought you'd like it.

Griffin: I do like it, sweet thing. But you can't disobey a direct order.

Lee: Yes, Griff. Spank me hard.

Griffin: Show me.

Lee: Show you what?

Griffin: Lose the panties and show me.

And there it is.

And I don't give a fuck.

When I asked for this picture, I was hard enough to cut granite.

Right now…

I really don't care.

Yeah, punishment isn't my thing. I don't get off on issuing orders. Or on giving spankings.

I'm open-minded. I'll try anything interesting. If a woman needs a rough hand, I'm not about to deny her.

Lee Ann was into being told she was a bad girl and begging for my cock. If she wants to beg me to come in her mouth—

That's just win-win.

It was fun. More fun than I'd had in a while. The novelty of growling *you don't get to take my cock unless you're a good girl* did shit to me.

But that thrill is gone. It disappeared sometime between the demand I sent her last night and that picture.

Nothing of note happened in the last day.

Nothing but Jules's news.

But that has nothing to do with this.

Jules: You can say I'm stuck in high school because I keep reading books about sixteen-year-olds. But who's the one hung up on what he hated in high school?

And there it is. That spark that's missing with Lee Ann.

It's not that I want to fuck Jules. It's her banter. Her smile. Her laugh.

Her laugh is better than anyone's groan.

I send my fuck buddy an *I've had fun, but I'm moving on. Take care* text (yeah, I could sugar coat it, but it's crueler giving her hope), then turn my attention to Jules.

We read the book together. One chapter. A flurry of texts. Rinse and repeat.

The more I read, the more I get why she loves this shit. It's sweet. Honest.

Even though they've been through a lot, these kids are innocent.

When they finally kiss, the clouds part, the birds sing, the Earth moves. They feel it in their bones, their hearts, their souls.

I wish I could believe in that kind of love, but I've seen the real thing. It destroys people, bit by bit, until they're shells of themselves.

Until they disappear completely.

THE NEXT DAY, I FINALIZE ARRANGEMENTS. THEN I POUR myself into the day's clients—a couple getting a heart and lock, a guy finishing his ocean-themed sleeve, a woman who wants *Carpe Diem* on her wrist.

With her hot pink hair and her The Cure t-shirt, she's a Goth version of Jules (who is way too lazy to commit to any sort of style). Tattooing her wrist brings me back to the day I adorned my best friend's skin.

I try to push the memory away, but it lingers. It's too loaded. It dissolves all my defenses. Disables my judgment.

All day—through work, the gym, a long shower, dinner, a night of texting Jules—I buzz with fury.

Only two things make me angry. Assholes who hurt my mom and assholes who hurt Jules.

Even when I'm the asshole.

When she's the asshole.

When some sort of abstract misery is the asshole.

This…

We don't talk about it. Not anymore. But every so often, it hits me. I wonder if she's still okay. If she's honoring her promise. If she's lying to me again.

I can't stand liars.

She knows that.

But I know—

Fuck, I'm not thinking about that. There's way too much to do.

I distract myself. Debate playlist details with Jules. I have no ground to stand on—I agreed to give her free rein—but I still put up a fight. Get her to include more Joy Division and less All Time Low.

She waits until midnight to admit that she hasn't packed.

I set my alarm for six a.m. Rise early, shower, pick up drinks on the way to her place.

But we don't have nearly enough time.

This place is a fucking disaster.

Chapter Seven

GRIFFIN

A yawn falls from Jules's lips. "I thought we were leaving at nine?"

"Eight."

Her gaze shifts from her messy room to the pristine hallway. To her parents' master bedroom. "Mom is still asleep." *She wouldn't want you in my room alone.*

"You're twenty-two."

"You're twenty-three."

"Fuck, I didn't realize that. Thanks for the update."

She takes a long sip of her matcha. Her low sigh of pleasure fades into a yawn. It's adorable. And hot as fuck.

I mean, it would be. If it was someone else.

"You must be tired." My fingers brush her shoulder. They trace the Angels logo. The t-shirt is thin. I can feel the heat of her skin beneath it. "Thought you burned this."

"All my good clothes are packed."

"Right."

"They are." She stretches her arms over her head, pulling her t-shirt (well, my t-shirt) up her torso.

My gaze shifts to the sliver of skin on display. The small of her back.

She thinks she's lacking curves, but she's not.

Her figure is gorgeous.

Not that I care.

Even if I wanted to fuck her—and I don't—I don't discriminate against women with a higher waist hip ratio.

I'm observing facts. Not stating preferences.

There are plenty of men fixed on conventional beauty standards. Jules is gorgeous, but she doesn't always play to her strengths.

If I want to help her get laid, I need to help her highlight her perky tits and her fantastic ass.

And that long, dark hair.

In high school, guys were always talking about her "exotic beauty." Which is fucking stupid. Her biological father was from Colombia—her mom had an affair with a senior VP at her company.

Jules doesn't know his name. She doesn't know anything about him except his ethnicity.

It bothers her. It always has.

I hate my dad. He's the scum of the Earth. But I'm glad I know he's the scum of the Earth. I can't imagine what it would be like going through life, not knowing the person who provided half my DNA.

Especially when said person was a married man who wanted nothing to do with his knocked up mistress.

Men really are shit. I don't know why women put up with us.

It's hard for her, not knowing anything about half her heritage. It's never mattered to me. It's never affected us, not beyond that phase in high school where she learned to make arepas. Or the idiotic guys who approached her to tell her how exotic she looked or ask "where are you from, no not Los Angeles, where are you really from?"

I just…

I really fucking hate those guys.

I hate everyone who hurts her. Even when it's a minor offense.

Still, I have to admit, her unique set of features is gorgeous.

The long dark hair she inherited from her father—

It's hot as hell. That's all that matters for our purposes.

It would look fucking fantastic between my fingers.

I don't care.

I don't think about her like that.

Ever.

Fuck, she really does have nice tits.

I bet they're responsive too.

She probably purrs like a pussycat when a guy toys with her nipples.

No. She's only been with Jackson. And there's no fucking way he knows his way around her body.

"Griff?" A yawn interrupts my name. "Are you just going to stand there?" She steps into her messy bedroom. Motions to her mom's room. *Get in here before she notices us.*

"She'd care less if you were dressed."

"Am I naked?"

Fuck, now that's in my head. Those dark curls fall to her shoulders. They frame her face perfectly. Stop right at her shoulders. Do nothing to cover her tits.

If she was naked—

What the fuck is wrong with me? I'm not thinking about my best friend naked. No matter how badly I want her to come.

I need to get her in a dress and heels and a little red lipstick.

Some guys don't appreciate a woman in an Angels t-shirt and boxers.

Fuck, she's swimming in my t-shirt. It's adorable. Even better 'cause she hates the Angels.

Which is silly. How can anyone hate the poor, neglected Angels? They got the short end of the stick when they became The Los Angeles Angels of Anaheim (what idiot thought it was a good idea to call a team The The Angels Angels?)

They're rarely competitive. Nowhere near as good as the boys in blue. Not that I'd ever admit that to her.

"See." She motions to the crumbled clothes in her royal blue suitcase. (She's like a parody of herself with her love of Dodgers blue). "I'm packed."

"That's packing?"

"It's almost done." She stifles a yawn. Takes another sip of her matcha. Sets her takeout cup on her dresser.

Her room is a mess, as usual. Notebooks and paperbacks cover the desk. Pens are everywhere. The floor is covered in clothes.

"What?" She folds her arms over her chest. "It's not too late for me to cancel."

"You have a closet."

"I'm aware."

"That's where most people keep their clothes."

"Is it really?"

"I know, it's shocking information."

She flips me off.

I smile as I return the gesture. It's been our thing since we learned the meaning of the middle finger.

Some things just stick. Like her love of music they played at middle school dances.

"You're going to fuck up my apartment, aren't you?" I kneel to sort through the pile next to the bed. T-shirts.

Shorts. Cotton bikini panties. Red with lace trim. Sexy and innocent at once. Not what I expect from her.

"Oh my God, Griff." She kicks my hand just hard enough to say *drop it*. "What is wrong with you?"

"Are these dirty?"

"No, but they could be."

"Then put them in the fucking suitcase."

"It's a three-day trip. How many pairs of panties do I need?"

"Depends."

"Does it?" she asks.

I nod. "Are you gonna listen to my dirty stories?"

She makes a show of rolling her eyes. "You're right. I better pack an entire suitcase of panties. Your tales of anonymous sex are just that hot. I have no access to erotica or porn or my own imagination. I can only get off on your words."

"Glad you realize it." I toss two pairs of panties into her suitcase.

"I packed underwear."

"Sexy underwear?"

"Why do I need sexy underwear?"

I stand. "I'm on your side here."

She raises a brow. "Which side is that?"

"You think I care about a woman's underwear?" Sure, I appreciate leather and lace. But I appreciate a cotton bikini just as much. Innocence is fucking hot.

"Apparently."

"You want to get laid or not?"

"I don't need your help getting laid."

"All right, we'll go to Victoria's Secret when we get in."

"I'm not going to Victoria's Secret with you."

"Then pack a thong."

Her nose scrunches in distaste. "I don't need floss in my crack."

"Damn, Jules, you're gonna make me hard."

"Gross." She moves to her dresser. Pulls open her top drawer. The one packed with panties in every color of the rainbow.

Most are classic cotton things. Comfortable and sexy in their own way.

But there's something. White scraps of lace. And a sheer white robe.

Fuck, between her curls and the chiffon fabric, she'd be pure angel. Innocent. Corruptible. Irresistible.

"That's perfect." I motion to the lingerie.

She swallows hard. "No, um, that was a gift. For my shower. And, um... I just..." She wraps her arms around her stomach. "I don't want to look at it. Okay?"

"Victoria's Secret it is then." I'm not about to ask her to wear lingerie meant for her ex-fiancé. Not that the asshole would have appreciated the effort.

Probably wanted her to dress up sexy for him and blow him while he stared off into space.

I don't blame him for wanting Jules's soft lips around his cock—

Or wanting that sheer white lace draping over her tits—

Fuck, I'm getting distracted. I don't need to dive into this level of detail. Sexy dress. Heels. Lipstick.

That's all it takes to appeal to men.

Hell, only takes one of the three. Especially on someone as gorgeous as Jules.

Shit. I swallow another sip of my iced latte, but it does nothing to cool my blood. This is fucking weird. I don't think about her this way.

Yeah, I have eyes. I can see she's attractive. But I don't want her.

I don't want to see her in that white lace.

Don't want to feel her thighs against my cheeks.

Don't want to hear my name roll off her lips.

"I require one matcha latte for every purchase we make at Victoria's Secret." She paws through her suitcase, pressing the wrinkled t-shirts to one side, leaving the rolled denim on the other.

"You want me to buy your lingerie and your lattes?"

"No. I'll buy the lingerie. You'll buy the lattes."

"You know what, Jules? Drinks are on me. The whole trip."

"All drinks?"

I nod. "All the disgusting, tequila and iced teas you want."

"Okay." She moves to her closet. Which is nearly empty. All her clothes are on the floor. "What am I doing to your place?"

"You're staying with me when we get back."

"I am?"

"You'd rather stay here?"

"No, but your place only has the one bedroom."

"You can stay in my bed."

She stares at me like I'm crazy. "On the sheets stained with sex from eight thousand one-night stands? No thanks."

"I bought new sheets."

"You did not."

I nod. "Wanted you to feel at home." I pull out my cell and show off my recently made bed. The corners are tucked. The Dodgers sheets match the Harry Potter bedspread perfectly.

She laughs. "For the record, Harry Potter is middle grade, not YA."

"You want *The Hunger Games* instead?"

"You did not get *The Hunger Games* sheets."

"You're right." I can't help but smile. "But I did get *Twilight* sheets."

"You're disturbed."

"You're the one who loves sparkly vampires."

"You know I hated those books."

"So much you read them twice."

"Hate read them."

I nod *sure*.

She nods *yeah* and turns back to the closet. She scans her selection of dresses. I recognize all of them. Homecoming, prom, high school graduation, interviews, first date with Jackson, college interviews.

There's this short white sundress in the corner of the closet. It's tight. Sheer. Like something for a cocktail party on the roof. One where you're going to sneak off and fuck on the balcony.

It's short enough and low cut enough to make that very fucking fun.

"That's perfect." I push aside mental images of Jules in that dress. Of her sitting on a patio couch, leaning over, letting her tits spill from the soft fabric.

It's a good move. It's good she'll be able to entice her paramour.

Fuck, I'm no fan of Haley Williams's screech, but I have to give it to her—that name is brilliant. And her orange hair is pretty fucking fierce too.

Not that I have a thing for girls with bright hair. Punk rock goddess is an incredibly appealing—

I'm not going to say flavor again. Women aren't ice cream. Even if I enjoy—

Fuck, now I really sound like my dad.

"Griff—"

Shit, where is my head? We only have an hour and a half to finish this and we're making slow progress. "Yeah?"

"That was going to be my rehearsal dinner dress."

"So?"

"So, you don't think that's bad luck?"

"No, it's good revenge. You can wear that dress when you have the best sex of your life. What better way to celebrate the end of your engagement?"

"Should I bring my wedding dress for round two?"

She's joking, but it's not a bad idea. "Yeah, but that would scare most guys."

She flips me off.

I laugh. "Then again, your wedding dress is pretty hot."

"Is it?"

Yeah, it's this simple silk thing that hangs off her body perfectly. It was custom made at some obscenely expensive place in Santa Monica. But it was worth it, because it was the only thing she and her mom could agree on. "Bring it. In case the moment strikes you."

"If you can fit it in the car, you can bring it."

"You need another dress."

She groans.

"And a bikini."

"Why?"

"It's gonna be a hundred and four. Don't you want to cool off?"

"Fine." She pulls the dress from her closet and lays it on the bed. "Are you bringing a swimsuit?"

"You want to see me in my speedo?" I wink.

Her entire face scrunches in distaste. "How disturbing."

"Brought board shorts too."

"Thank God."

"If you're nice to me, I might wear them."

"That's unusual blackmail."

"If you'd rather I wear nothing…"

"Eww." She shrieks a little louder than she should. Catches herself. Places her hand over her mouth. Then a single finger. A *shhh*.

It's too late though.

A door opens. Footsteps move down the hall.

"Juliette?" Her mom calls. "Are you all right?"

"Yeah, Mom, just packing."

"I see Griffin's car out front," her mom says.

She mouths *shit*.

"Hey, Mrs. King," I say. "How are you?"

Mrs. King pulls the door open. She looks at both of us. Frowns as she takes in Jules's pajamas. "Sweetie, aren't you leaving soon?"

"Yeah, um, Griff is just helping me pack," Jules says.

"Sure." Mrs. King smiles. "It's good to see you, Griffin. Take care of her this weekend."

"Yeah, sure." I return her smile until she disappears into the hallway.

Mrs. King wants me hanging out in Jules's room? Taking care of her? Showing her a good time?

Hell must be frozen right now.

If Mrs. King thinks this is a good idea—

I'm going to have to reconsider some shit.

Chapter Eight

GRIFFIN

"Damn, Juliette, you're dressed to kill." Dean winks and shakes her hand.

Her brow furrows the way it does when she isn't sure how to take something. "Uh, thanks." She smooths her tiny tank top.

He nods *sure thing*. It's about as earnest as Dean gets. The tattoo artist is technically my boss, but you wouldn't know it from his attitude.

He adopts a laid back *I don't give a shit about anything but starting shit* persona. It works for him. He's good at his job, and especially at teaching his apprentice slash girlfriend Chloe.

Said girlfriend smiles and greets Jules with a hug. "You look good."

Jules releases the hug. Her eyes flit to mine. *What the hell are they talking about?*

I know Dean. He's talking about her tits. He plays it cooler, but he's on Wes's side. The *you're obviously into Juliette. I better push you two together* side.

The six foot two former water polo player looks like a

Hollister model (well, one covered in ink), but he acts like—

Well, for all I know, Hollister models are always giving people shit, same as Dean.

Chloe is Dean's physical opposite. She's a full foot shorter. Her dark hair is cropped at her chin. She dresses exclusively in black and always wears combat boots. She's half Korean, half Italian, all punk badass.

He's, well, again, the Hollister thing. They're adorable together. And often hot as fuck.

Like right now. They're already all over each other, making out like there's no tomorrow. And who fucking knows? Maybe there isn't a tomorrow.

There are worse ways to spend your time.

Jules shoots me a look of disgust. It's played up, but the roots are real. She likes Dean and Chloe just fine—she knows all my friends and everyone at the shop—so it must be the show of love.

Really, they don't have to be so obvious about having their shit together when it comes to relationships.

They know Jules just ended her engagement.

I clear my throat.

Chloe jumps backward and shoots us an apologetic look. Then it clicks. Her eyes light up. Her expression fills with sympathy. "Oh, I, uh… I'll be good, promise."

"I don't promise." Dean winks at me. Then at Jules. "But I'll make sure it's more dirty than sweet."

Chloe rises to her tiptoes to whisper something in his ear. He has to lean down to meet her. Which is adorable.

Maybe this is why women are into tall guys. The foot between them just works. She's still every bit the badass, but she looks especially pint-sized.

Dean motions to the minivan sitting in the driveway.

It's a friend of a friend's, but it's still weird seeing him here. Like he's practicing for his future as a soccer dad.

Despite his *I don't give a fuck* attitude, Dean would be a good dad. And Chloe would be a good mom. Tough, but fair. She never puts up with shit from her boyfriend slash boss.

Not that I'd ever tell either of them that.

I don't usually think about that stuff. My family has been nothing but bad news. The second I could, I got the fuck out of that house, and I've never looked back.

The last thing I want to do is fuck up some poor innocent kid.

Maybe if I had my head on straight, I'd consider it. But the odds of that are even lower than the odds of me falling in love.

Multiplying those together?

It's not gonna happen.

We put our suitcases in the trunk and climb into the van.

Wes and Quinn are in the middle seats. They're cozy. Happy.

"You look good, Juliette." He smiles.

Jules's brow knits *what the fuck does that mean*, but she doesn't mention it. "Thanks. It's been a while, Quinn." She nods hello and takes her seat. "Is school good?"

"Uh… I'm glad it's summer." Quinn presses her red lips into a smile. She's nervous, which is normal for her. And, well, it's hard to blame her.

A month ago, she asked Wes to pop her cherry. They've been working on her sexual education since. He insists it's casual, but that's total bullshit.

It's been four or five weeks now and they still haven't done the deed. He says he's savoring it, but, really, he wants the excuse to hang out with her.

It's sweet. Not like him. He's usually manwhore of the year.

Puts me to shame sometimes.

"Me too." Jules smiles back. "Though... I'm not sure Vegas in August is the best idea."

"Whose fault is that?" I take the seat on the far right. She's on the left. The middle seat is between us. Which is how we usually sit. But it feels weird. Loaded.

"Can I blame he who will not be named?" she asks.

"Fuck, you're Voldemorting him?" I ask.

"Yeah, I am." A laugh spills from her lips. "I can't believe you referred to a book."

"There are movies," Wes says.

"They're good," Quinn adds.

I nod *guilty as charged*. I have not read those books, but I watched the movies with Jules a million years ago. She decided I needed to advance my pop culture education. Practically forced me to watch them.

All right, I put up a fight (I always do), but it was all show. Watching movies with my best friend every night for a week straight—

What's better than that?

"They are good." Her green eyes meet mine. For a second, they're full of this perfect, pure joy. Then she blinks and the awkwardness of the trip spills over her expression.

It's understandable, but I'm not taking it sitting down.

I'm getting that joy back.

Whatever it takes.

After another coffee stop (At Peet's, of course.

Jules wouldn't be caught dead drinking matcha from that other establishment), we head out.

For a while, Jules eases into the conversation. She teases back when Dean insults her taste in music. Moves to the middle seat so she can whisper gossipy questions in my ear. Manages to win a game of ten fingers.

That leads to more gossipy questions.

And me whispering answers in her ear. And her resting her head on my shoulder. And me wrapping my arm around her.

So she won't bang into the seat in front of her.

Not because I want my arm around her. Or because she smells good. Or because my body buzzes when my fingertips graze her neck.

She rouses when we stop for lunch. We pull off the freeway at Baker. Drive straight to the World's Tallest Thermometer Park.

Chloe bursts into laughter. "Really?"

Dean nods *hell yeah*.

"Of course, you want to hang out in front of this massive phallic symbol." She looks up at him with a dreamy smile. Catches herself. Tones it down. Motions to the restaurant behind the giant temperature gauge. "This place has the best veggie options. If you want something else, we can drop you there."

"This is fine," Jules says.

"Speaking for everyone?" I tease.

She stretches her arms over her head as she yawns. Her tiny tank top pulls up her stomach, showing off inches of taut skin.

What the fuck is wrong with Jackson? The asshole doesn't realize what he gave up.

Fuck, I'm not going there. He's not an idiot because

Jules is hot. He's an idiot because she's the best friend in the history of the world.

If she's half the girlfriend, she's the best girlfriend anywhere.

She nudges me and motions to the door. "Are you trying to kill me with heat exhaustion?"

"What if I am?"

"You'll die too."

"We'll die together."

"Changing your name to Romeo?" She laughs as she climbs over me. Her ass brushes my crotch. Then my hip. She waits for Quinn and Wes to exit, then she climbs out of the car.

Fuck, she really does have a nice ass.

Not that I care.

I follow her out of the car. Let out my own yawn.

"Why?" She holds her hand over her eyes as she takes in the thermometer.

"Why not?"

"Why do men feel the need to put their dicks everywhere?"

"You saying you never feel the need to put a dick anywhere?"

"That doesn't even make sense." A laugh spills from her lips. "Is this really the quality of your dirty talk?"

"Oh." I raise a brow. "You want to hear something?"

"No." Her nose scrunches in distaste. "God no."

"Sounds like you're asking."

"Sounds like you're holding up the air-conditioning." She points to the fast food restaurant to our right. The one our friends aren't visiting. "Let's eat, yeah?"

I nod, sure, and follow her to the fast food place. I don't mention her preference for the place where our friends are dining.

Two hours in a car with anyone is a lot. With Dean, Chloe, Wes, and Quinn? That's a fuckton. And we have two more to go. If we're lucky.

Jules pulls the door open. Sighs as she walks into the air-conditioning. "Oh my God." She closes her eyes. Thrusts her chest into the air. "That's perfect."

It really fucking is. The AC. Not the way her tank top hugs her tits. Or the way they rise and fall with her breath. I barely notice that. "Get me the first combo with iced tea."

"You don't like iced tea."

"Yeah, but you're gonna drink all of it."

"I will not," she says.

I shoot her a *really* look.

She presses her lips together. "It doesn't make sense to get two drinks when the refills are free."

"Yeah, the two dollars are gonna burn." I pull out my wallet. Grab a twenty. "Order as many cokes as you want."

"Uh-huh." She pushes my hand away. "This one is on me."

"You're so fucking generous."

"Thank you, I was thinking that." She flips me off. "Not all of us are gainfully employed you know."

"Not all of us have parents who pay our bills."

Her brow furrows. Not the faux rage I know well. Actual frustration. She sucks a breath through her teeth. Swallows hard. "Number one, yeah."

"Jules, you know what I mean."

"Go do your business." She turns and moves into line without a word.

I shrug my shoulders, but it doesn't break up the tension in my chest. This isn't a big deal. I'm used to putting my foot in my mouth.

Usually, it doesn't bother me. I certainly don't wince over my wording.

I tell it like it is. Even if it hurts. Even with Jules.

Right now—

It's different. I can't explain how. It just is.

Her pain hits me somewhere deep. Like it's mine.

No, it's worse than mine. It's always been worse than mine. I'd gladly take any hurt headed her way.

Out of pure selfishness. Because I can't bear to watch her hurt. Because I'm fucking terrible at making it better.

She looks back to me and raises a brow. When I don't respond, she picks up her cell and texts me.

Jules: Hurry up and pee. I'm going after you.

Griff: You go first. I'll get in line.

Jules: You won't get the veggies right.

Griff: I've seen you order this a million times.

Jules: I'd rather do it myself.

Griff: Suit yourself.

Jules: You're being stupid.

Griff: How?

Jules: I'm used to you saying stupid things. I know what you mean.

Griff: Do you?

Jules: Yeah, it's normal you're a little resentful of my semi-functional family. I wish I could give you that.

Griff: You know I can't take this kind of shit.

Jules: And I can?

Griff: Didn't you have a boyfriend for five years?

Jules: I thought we had a rule.

Griff: About abstract discussions of your relationship history?

"Miss?" The sandwich artist asks. "Are you ready?"

Jules slides her cell into her pocket and motions to the bathroom. Then she turns back to the counter and starts to order her turkey club, piling it with exactly the right amount of tomatoes, peppers, onions, peppercorns.

She really does have disturbing taste.

I head to the bathroom before she can shoot me another *what the hell is wrong with you?* look.

My bladder is screaming. Which doesn't make this place any more palatable. Why are fast food bathrooms so disgusting?

Honestly, I hate these restaurants. The burger joints especially. The food is fine, but it's also a million bad memories of dinners with my dad. We had plenty of money, but he never wanted to spend it on me. He certainly didn't put effort into cooking.

I scrub my hands until they're raw, but they don't clean what I need gone. There are too many memories. Thank fuck we never went here.

It hits me like a brick to the face—that's why she dragged me here. Not because she's sick of our friends. She hates sandwiches and loves tacos, even shitty fast food ones.

I move into the main room. Join her at a booth in the corner.

She offers me the plastic cup of soda. Iced tea, of course. Then she nods to our sandwiches.

And there are two sandwiches. My twelve-inch meatball. Her six-inch veggie filled turkey club.

"Not even gonna joke about my footlong." I slide into the seat across from her.

"Ew, gross." She tears into her sandwich. Chews. Swallows. "And too much."

"How do you know until you try?"

"You are not."

No, that would be too much. But I'm enough. "Wouldn't you like to know?"

"God no." She shakes her head in a show of disgust, but her gaze still darts to my crotch.

"I'll buy you a dildo if you want."

"Why would I want?"

"Let's call it a backup plan."

"Oh, if I can't get laid, you'll buy me a sex toy?"

I nod *yeah*.

"Because I can't masturbate properly with this?" She holds up her right hand. "You think I'm that bad at sex, that I can't even fuck myself properly?"

No, but I am thinking some incredibly vivid shit. *Jules unzipping her shorts, pushing them off her hips, rubbing herself over her panties.*

Her eyelids flutter closed. A groan falls off her lips. Like the groan she makes over her matchas but a million times better.

Jules bent over my lap. Moaning as I peel her panties to her knees and tease her mercilessly.

Fuck, there's something seriously wrong with me today. My brain is demented. It's trying to run from my memories to something that makes sense.

Sex makes sense.

Just not with her.

That's ridiculous.

"Griff? Are you okay?" she asks.

"Just thinking about what sex toy I should buy you."

"I can pick out my own sex toy."

"It's a deal." I offer her my hand. "Whatever you want."

She shakes. "Twenty bucks says you fail to make it happen."

"What's the deadline?"

"Before we get back to LA."

"To your place?" I ask.

"I thought I was staying with you."

"Really?" My lips curl into a smile. I want her as a roommate. I always have. But with Jackson so jealous, it was never a possibility.

"It won't cramp your style?"

"No, I'll make sure to bring home women who like being watched," I tease.

"Oh my God."

"You'll learn a lot of shit watching me."

She shakes her head. "You're deranged."

"Yeah, but you love it."

"I'll love my twenty dollars." She pulls her hand to her side. "You have to buy it before we get back to our place."

My chest warms. "Our place?"

"It's temporary."

"So's life."

She laughs. "When did you get morbid?"

"Must be the My Chemical Romance you played."

She flips me off.

I steer the conversation back to her taste in music, but my head refuses to get in gear.

It stays fixed on that beautiful mental image.

Jules writhing in pleasure as she groans my name.

Chapter Nine

JULIETTE

After lunch, we head to the second biggest site in Baker: The Alien Fresh Jerky store.

The store beckons patrons with an *X-Files* style green alien head, surrounded by a red logo. The desert parking lot abounds with sedans, minivans, and a silver spaceship.

Inside, the bliss of air-conditioning greets me. This whole Las Vegas in August thing is such a bad idea. But I can't say I regret anything.

I need to be away from home. I need to be somewhere completely different. I need to be with people who don't automatically take Jackson's side.

"You need more iced tea?" Griffin motions to the soda case in the back of the store.

"I'm fine." I'm already buzzing from the caffeine. At least, I think it's the caffeine.

"The next Starbucks is more than an hour away."

"I would never."

Griffin chuckles. His lips curl into a smile that lights up

his eyes. His expression screams *of course, I know. I know everything about you.*

Ahem. "Why are we here?"

Griffin nods to Wes, who is currently showing his girlfriend (fuck buddy? Student?) the samples. They look cute together. He's all inked and carefree, like a poster boy for California, whereas she's prim and proper and pale as the moon.

Like a proper picture of Chicago.

I think.

I mean, I don't really know anything about Chicago. Except for the whole midwestern emo scene. And I so can't mention that to Griff if I want to hear anything but mockery all vacation.

Griff moves toward the drink fridge in the back.

I wrap my fingers around his wrist. Pull him closer. So I can whisper. Not because I want him closer. "Did she really ask him to pop her cherry?"

He chuckles. "You think the answer is going to change the tenth time you ask?"

I nod.

He shakes his head *you're ridiculous*. "You don't think he's up for the job?"

"Why is everything you say about sex?"

"You're the one asking about virginity," he says much too loudly.

The patrons on our right, an older couple sampling dried fruit, turn to us. They readjust their cowboy hats, shake their heads, move deeper into the store.

"Do you not understand whispering?" I ask.

"Why keep your interests a secret? If you ask Wes, I bet he'll offer details."

"Oh my God. You're disturbed. You really are."

"You don't think there's anything sexy about a virgin?"

My nose scrunches. It's not that I have an issue with virgins of any gender. If people want to wait to have sex, more power to them.

It's more the awkward memory of my first time. The fumbling, the messy kisses, the complete lack of lube—

Ick.

"All right. Nothing sexy about a guy who doesn't know what he's doing," Griffin says.

I nod *true* and move to the wall of dried fruit. There's a cornucopia. Pineapple, mango, plums, apricots, cantaloupe. I grab an orange papaya slice and toss it into my mouth.

Griff takes a mango and bites it in half. "Fuck, that's all sugar."

I nod *yeah.*

"You can eat this?"

"Why couldn't I?" I sample the cantaloupe this time. It's equally sugary. More sugar than fruit really.

"You won't drink a matcha latte if I forget to order it unsweetened."

"This is different."

"How?"

"It's just a sample. I couldn't eat the entire bag—that would be disgustingly sweet—but I can have a taste."

He looks at me like I'm crazy, but he still grabs another slice of fruit. "Your first time sucked?"

"You know enough of the details."

"Had to buy a bottle of lube for you."

"Oh my God, Griff."

"Then teach you how to teach Jackson to go down on you properly."

My cheeks flush. Then my chest. This is just… oh my

God. So not going there. Not with him. Not now. And not ever. "You have a point?"

"Imagine you fucked someone who knew what he was doing."

"Who am I imagining?"

"Is Thor still getting you off?"

I flip him off.

"That a yes?"

"Oh my God." I steal his dried plum. Prune, I guess. It's not sweetened like the fruits. Which makes it tart and intense, more flavor than sugar.

"Imagine Chris Hemsworth came to your bedroom, poured you a glass of champagne, pressed his lips to your neck."

"Okay…"

"You're not imagining." Griff slides his arm around my waist. Moves me down the row of dried fruit. Past apples, pears, kiwi. All the way to the corner.

The beverage fridge.

I ignore his request. Rifle through the fridge for something with lots of caffeine and no sugar. There aren't many options, but there is an iced green tea.

Victory.

I press the glass bottle to my chest.

He wraps his arm around my waist. Pulls my body into his. "You're supposed to imagine."

My eyelids press together. He's pulling me closer so he can whisper. Not for any other reason. But, fuck—

My stomach flutters.

My heart thuds against my chest.

My limbs get light.

Thank God he's holding me. I'm about to float to the ceiling.

I press the frigid glass to my neck, but it fails to cool me down.

"Close your eyes," Griff whispers in my ear. "Imagine him."

Chris Hemsworth. Right. I try to conjure his long blond hair, piercing eyes, built chest.

Instead, my head goes right to Griff. To his soft waves, his dark eyes, his tattooed arms.

"Imagine you were completely relaxed, the way you are when you fuck yourself. That he was that good," Griff says.

"Sure." I swallow hard. Relaxed about sex with Griff? Not possible. But I try to push my thoughts in the right direction. Hot celebrity. Alcohol. Hands. Lips. Limbs.

"He strips you out of your clothes slowly. The t-shirt. Then the shorts. Then he unhooks your bra gently, stares like you're the best thing he's ever seen, whispers *you have perfect tits*."

Fuck. I step forward, breaking our touch. "I get your point." My iced green tea is good. Crisp, clear, utterly unable to lower my temperature.

"I'm not sure you do."

"I've had sex."

"You don't wish your first time was better?"

"What use is wishing?" I swallow another sip.

"I do."

"What?" I press the cold glass to my wrist. The one bearing his tattoo design. God, when Jackson found out Griff was the one who designed my ode to… mental health… Thank God that's over. (And please, someone, stop me from consuming tequila while trying to keep secrets).

"I wish my first time was better."

"You do not." I clear my throat, but it doesn't clear my head. This is too much.

Griff and I never talk about his introduction to sex. We fought about it so much at the time. He was stupid—he didn't use protection with a girl he barely knew—and I was pissed at him for being irresponsible. For being with some girl he barely knew. For jumping headfirst into sex and leaving me behind.

His fingers curl into my upper arm. "I wish it mattered to me."

I shake my head. That's not true. It can't be. But then Griffin doesn't lie. Ever.

"I barely remember that night. I was too fucking drunk. It was sloppy and fast."

"Thirty seconds?" I try to joke, but there's a heaviness to it.

"Less." His chuckle has that same heaviness. "Intense, yeah, but not memorable. And the shit it did to us." He pulls me closer. "I remember our fight a lot more than I remember her."

"You see me all the time."

"And you matter to me."

"You're never with people who matter to you."

"Never." His arm brushes mine as he reaches into the fridge. He grabs an iced coffee, one with milk and sugar.

"That, um, that bothers you?"

"Sometimes."

"Usually?"

He shakes his head. Turns so he's facing me. "I have you."

"You don't have sex with me."

"Yeah, and maybe that's why I have you."

I swallow hard. I've thought that too. I mean, I don't think about having sex with Griff. I don't want to have sex with Griff.

It's just other people refuse to believe the platonic nature of our relationship.

They see Griff with his soulful dark eyes, and his strong shoulders, and all that ink on his built arms, and they think *it must be impossible to resist someone that hot.*

It…

Um…

"Hey." Wes's bouncy voice fills the space. "You two trading secrets?"

"Always." Griff shoots Wes a wink.

"Anything about me?" Wes asks.

Griff nods. "Jules thinks you're loaded."

"Oh my God." I play swat Griff. It helps push the heaviness away. It helps keep the mood light. "I do not."

Wes raises a brow *don't you*?

"Sorry, Wes, but I don't think about your cock," I say.

Wes just chuckles. "You can't have it anyway." He nods to Quinn, who's waiting in line with a bottle of black iced tea and a bag of mixed dried fruit. "Exclusively for Quinn."

"That's too much information," I say.

"You're not invited to watch." Wes winks, turns, joins his girlfriend. Um, student.

My nose scrunches. "Why would I want to watch?"

"Be honest. You would." Griff nudges me.

I shake my head *no way*.

"Two hot people going at it—why wouldn't you?"

"They're my friends." I clear my throat. "Thinking about your friends having sex is uncomfortable. I certainly don't want to know anything about your sex life."

"Oh yeah?"

I nod *hell yeah*.

"Twenty bucks says you'll be begging for details by the end of the night."

"Details on?"

"Everything."

"You really like losing money to me." I offer my hand.

He shakes. "I was gonna say the same thing."

Chapter Ten

JULIETTE

All the discussion of sex hangs in the air. Even as we climb into the car, head back to the freeway, cruise at eighty miles an hour.

My head keeps thinking up mental images of Griff in, um, compromising positions.

Or us in compromising positions.

I try to distract myself with my Kindle, but by sentence three, I'm carsick.

I pull out my cell. Switch to the audio of our latest YA book. Offer Griff one of my earbuds.

He moves closer.

I rest my head on his shoulder.

For a while, everything is normal. We share my headphones as we listen to a bouncy teenage girl introduce her life. Her best friend. The male best friend she doesn't want.

Even though she's clearly in love with him.

And totally oblivious to it.

Sometimes people can miss such obvious things.

Just as the teenagers fumble their way through an awkward make-out session, the city comes into view.

A gold skyscraper, a giant black pyramid, a fake castle, the New York City skyline, and a dozen giant casinos beyond that.

Las Vegas is bright in the desert sun.

It's not neon colors and debauchery, but it's gorgeous all the same. Like an actual oasis surrounded by miles and miles of dust.

I squeeze Griff's hand.

He squeezes back.

"We're really here," I whisper.

"In thirty minutes," he says.

"You ruin everything."

"I know."

Chapter Eleven

JULIETTE

"Where do you want it?" Griffin wraps his fingers around the handle of my suitcase. Lifts it over his head like it's weightless.

I shoot him a *get real* look.

He returns it. *This is real.* "Should I unzip it and dump it on the floor so it matches your bedroom?"

"Haha." I roll my eyes. "Why did I come here again?"

"It was your idea, actually."

"Maybe I got hit on the head."

"Maybe you drank too much tequila."

My lips curl into a smile.

Which he totally notices.

Ahem. "Don't you have your own room?"

"Yeah." He taps his crotch. I mean the front pocket of his jeans. The one with his room key. "Can't share a room with you this trip."

"If you say one more thing about how you're going to make sure I get laid—"

He motions *my lips are sealed.*

"Right."

He nods *definitely* then he takes my suitcase and sets it on the bed.

Which is totally where I want it.

But I'm not admitting that.

It's my room. I can leave it messy if I want. If it turns off Mr. One-Night Stand—

This is ridiculous. I don't need a one-night stand. I need a break from that *aww, poor thing, called off your engagement days before the wedding* look of pity.

"I've got it under control." I motion to the door. "I can take it from here."

He nods *sure* but he stays put.

Okay…

Subtlety doesn't always work with Griff. "Go to your room."

He shakes his head *no*.

"We're not getting dinner for an hour. Are you going to stand there the whole time?"

"Your fun is my responsibility."

"And?"

"Can't let you out of my sight."

"And when I find Mr. Right Now and take him back here?"

"I'm sworn not to discuss that."

A laugh spills from my lips. He's ridiculous. He's completely and totally ridiculous.

Logic and conversation aren't going to help.

But this might.

I grab a pillow from the bed and hurl it in his direction.

"Looks comfy. Thanks." He winks.

"Yeah." I point to the armchair. "Get comfy. Close your eyes—"

"You trying to take advantage of me, Miss King?"

"If I am?"

"You have my full consent." He winks. "If you record everything."

"You have not—"

He nods *have too.*

"What is that even?" No. I don't want to know. But… he… why?

"You want to watch the video?" He pulls his cell from his jeans. "It's on my cloud somewhere—"

"You keep sex tapes on your cloud?"

He looks at me like I'm crazy. "Where else would I keep them?"

"But… aren't you… someone could…"

"Need to access them at any moment."

Uh… What?

I just…

No.

Not going there.

"You watch your sex tapes because…" I bite my tongue. I don't want to know. I don't want to see one. I certainly don't want to imagine my best friend fucking some random woman.

"It's hot."

"Isn't that—"

"Really fucking hot?"

"Narcissistic?"

He chuckles. "You've never made one?"

Oh my God. I can't even.

His laugh gets louder. "Fuck, Jules, you look like a ghost."

"Why would I—"

"'Cause it's fun, knowing someone could watch later. Watching later. Watching while it's happening."

"You watch the tape while you're—"

"No." He nods to the mirror across from the bed. It's a

huge thing that takes up the entire wall.

Oh. "I, um…"

"You're missing out."

No comment.

"Try it with—well, I'm not mentioning that."

"Uh-huh."

"Until after dinner."

"You're deranged." I grab another purple pillow from the bed and hurl it in his direction.

This time, it brushes his shoulder.

He smiles. Steps backward. Rubs his skin like he can't stand the pain. "Guess I'll have to take you out."

"I'd like to see you try."

"Oh yeah?"

I nod. Hell yeah.

He stares at me for a long moment.

Then he lunges forward.

His hands go to my hips. My waist. My tank top. The skin of my stomach.

He lifts me and holds my body against his. It's a split second, but it's enough to make my heart race.

With one swift move, he pins me to the bed.

His hand goes to my wrist. He pushes me just hard enough I feel it.

His hips sink into mine.

He stares down at me. For a second, his eyes fill with something I don't recognize. Then he blinks, and he's back to the pushy friend I know so well. "You want to beg for mercy?"

"Are you into that now?"

He shrugs *maybe I am, maybe I'm not.*

"Too much information."

"Don't ask if you don't want to know."

"Are you really?"

"If you keep asking—" He pins my wrist to the bed.

I buck my hips. To push his body off mine.

But it doesn't feel like an aggressive move. More like—

He shifts backward, releasing me. "If you keep asking, I'm going to tell."

I press my lips together. Try to ignore the warmth building below my belly.

My body is confused. It's tired. And lacking sex.

With Jackson.

Not Griff.

I don't want to have sex with Griff.

It's just…

I…

Uh…

Ahem.

I push myself up. Smooth my tank top. It's still riding up my torso, showing off my stomach. Which doesn't usually bother me. There's only one part of my body I want to hide—

Not going there.

Griffin moves around the bed, unzips my suitcase, pulls it open.

"What do you think you're doing?" I ask.

"Speeding up the unpacking."

"I can do it myself."

"Yeah, but the sooner you do it, the sooner we can get caffeine."

"Matcha lattes?"

He nods. "If Yelp is correct."

"Why didn't you just say that?"

He shrugs *where's the fun in that?*

I stand. "I, uh, where is this place?"

"Walkway to the next casino over."

Which means I can wear something warmer. Although—"And after that?"

"Dinner."

"And finding a fuck?"

"Got a whole night planned for your Jules." His lips curl into a smile. A sincere smile. "You'll have a good time. I promise."

My heart thuds against my chest. I want to have a good time with him. I will have a good time with him.

No entanglements.

No strange thoughts of his body on top of mine.

Just two friends hitting the town.

Two friends who are just friends.

Same as always.

APPARENTLY, SHORTS AND A TANK TOP ARE NOT appropriate for dinner.

I drag my suitcase into the bathroom. Compare the two nice dresses—the one I bought for the rehearsal dinner and the one I wore to Jackson's graduation party.

Both are sexy and form fitting.

Both highlight my tits and ass enough to appeal to drunk strangers.

I guess I have to trust Griff. If he thinks a tight dress and heels (well, wedges) are what it takes to appeal to guys in Vegas—

Well, I don't actually want to have a one-night stand.

But I want the possibility.

I want to feel wanted.

I don my white dress, step into my silver sandals, clasp the necklace Mom bought me.

After a coat of lipstick and a little mascara, I look presentable. Pretty even.

Not like me—I don't do dress up—but maybe that's what I need.

I try to tell myself this is the right move, but it does nothing to calm my nerves.

My stomach flutters. My heart thuds. My veins buzz with energy.

If Griff says something stupid—

I just… He… I…

Ahem.

I step into the main room.

Griffin's eyes go wide. "Fuck, Jules."

"What?" I pull my arm over my chest. This is too much. I knew it. "It's… shut up."

"It's good."

My cheeks flush. "Really?"

"Yeah." He gives me a long, slow once over. "You look hot."

I swallow hard. "Thank you."

"You're definitely gonna find someone hot to fuck in that."

"Oh my God." My blush deepens. I… He… Uh… "You owe me twenty bucks."

He chuckles. "I'll buy your first round of chips."

I nod *fair*.

He sets his suitcase on the bed, unzips it, finds his suit.

Then he does away with his t-shirt.

Right in front of me.

Like I'm not even here.

"What are you doing?" I bite my tongue. He's… I… Uh…

"Getting dressed." He unbuttons his jeans and pushes them off his hips.

"Here?"

"Can't let you out of my sight."

"There's a bathroom right there."

"No one told you to look." He kicks off his shoes. Then the socks. So he's only in boxers.

And I…

Uh…

Right. I'm not looking. I turn around. Put my hands over my eyes. "You're disturbed."

"I have to ask you something, Jules."

"Is it why you have no standards of decency?"

"No." His chuckle bounces around the room. "When's the last time you came so hard you couldn't see straight?"

"Oh my God."

He pulls on something. Zips something else. "Look me in the eyes and tell me Jackson fucked you properly."

"You're still half-naked."

"Only half." He chuckles.

My stomach flutters.

"Jules?"

"What?"

"Is that a never?" he asks.

"It's a no comment."

"All right." Clothes brush his skin. "Still making sure you get laid."

"Are you going to remind me of that every ten minutes?"

"Probably, yeah."

"You're seriously disturbed."

"Yeah, but that's why you like me."

Chapter Twelve

GRIFFIN

"Damn, you clean up nice." Dean flashes his trademarked cocky smile.

"Speak for yourself." I pull out Jules's chair.

She shoots me a *you're ridiculous* look, but she still takes a seat. "I don't think Dean has any trouble with that."

He smiles. "Go on."

"You realize they're mocking you?" Chloe asks.

"Yeah, but they're still talking about me," he says. "That's a win."

She laughs in that *I love how ridiculous you are* way of hers.

"Sunshine, you keep doing that, and I'm going to get hard." He pulls her onto his lap.

She squeals as she wraps her arm around his shoulders. "Here?"

He nods *hell yeah.*

She shoots Jules an apologetic look. "I can't take him anywhere."

"Damn straight." Dean sets her back in her seat—their side of the table is a booth—and blows her a kiss. "Juliette, you look good too. Not as good as my man, Griff, but you clean up pretty nice yourself."

"Oh, thanks." She unravels her napkin and lays it in her lap.

"You may have shit taste in music, but you have good taste in friends," Dean says.

Which is his idea of a compliment.

"Are you talking about yourself?" Chloe's nose scrunches in confusion. "Even for you—"

"Talking about Mister Aloof over here." He motions to me. "Doesn't he look extra mysterious in his suit?"

Chloe nods *true*.

"Thanks, I think." Jules crosses one leg over the other. "But I'd really rather not talk about me."

"Luckily for you, Dean loves talking about himself," Chloe teases.

"Love talking about interesting subjects." Dean motions to me and Jules. "How long have you been friends?"

"Since third grade," I say.

"Fourth," she says. "You didn't talk to me in third grade."

"I did. You just didn't talk back," I say.

She shakes her head *no way*.

Dean smiles. "You met in school?"

"Yeah, on a group project," Jules says. "I did the written part. He did the drawing. It was worse than you'd expect, considering." Her fingers brush the tattoo on the inside of my wrist. The one I got for her. The one that mirrors hers. *This too will pass*.

Cheesy shit.

But perfect.

She had a secret, one that was a weight around her neck. I figured it out. God, I was so fucking angry that she was hurting like that. That I hadn't seen it. That I didn't help.

I was an asshole. Made it all about my pain and my failure. About how I didn't see it. About how she betrayed me by lying to me. About how I couldn't handle it.

She was the one who was drowning.

She needed help, acceptance, support, not my stupid ego insisting I had the right to every one of her secrets.

Once I got over myself, I drew up the design for her. It was the only way I could explain how I felt about her.

I could never say *I love you like a sister, Jules. I hate that you felt like you had to hide this from me. I hate that you shouldered this alone. I hate that I hate it, that I'm making this harder for you.*

You're my favorite person in the world. I'd die if something happened to you. I'd die for you. Not because I'm selfless. Because I'm selfish. Because I can't imagine living in a world without you.

Fuck, even thinking that sentimental shit—

My stomach turns. It's too much. There's no way I could say that to her.

So I show her.

I still show her.

All three of her tattoos are my designs. My work.

When she saw them and said yes and let me mark her body forever—that was her saying that she loved me too, that I was her favorite person in the world, that she'd do anything for me.

We don't need to verbalize it.

Fuck, even thinking of the l-word—

I need a drink. "We're pretty sober."

"What's the rush?" Jules asks.

"We need to toast to your freedom," I say.

She nods *true*.

So do Chloe and Dean.

I hail a server. Everyone orders. That disturbing iced

tea and tequila drink for Jules. Rum and Cokes for Chloe and Dean. Straight vodka for me.

It goes with everything. Especially with dissolving thoughts about the l-word.

"Where is Wes?" Chloe asks.

Jules giggles. "We stopped by to tell him about dinner."

"He was indisposed," I say.

"That's surprisingly tactful for you," she says.

"I could just say 'he's finally ready to fuck his virgin,'" I say.

Chloe's eyes go wide. "Is that really what they're doing?"

I nod.

She and Dean exchange a glance that's loaded with history.

I don't know all the gossip, only that Dean took her virginity back in high school. They didn't speak for years, but they're together now. The memory can't be too bad.

"Jules doesn't get the virgin thing," I say.

"Oh my God." Jules shakes her head. "Why do I talk to you?"

"He's pretty hot," Dean says. "And the tattoos."

"Not all girls like that," Chloe says. "Besides, they're only friends."

He leans down to whisper something in her ear.

She shakes her head *no way*. "So, um, what are we talking about?"

"Juliette wants to know why they're making a big deal of the first time," Dean says.

"It's a big deal," Chloe says. "When it's with someone who pushes your buttons and you trust them." She clears her throat. "It's like your first tattoo. It's always going to be scary, but the right person can make you forget your fear. So you're buzzing with anticipation the entire time."

Jules nods with understanding.

It's a good metaphor.

Even if it sends my head to ridiculous places.

Jules looks so fucking gorgeous in that dress.

Thankfully, the server drags me from my dirty thoughts.

She drops off drinks.

We order appetizers. Chloe is a vegetarian, so we get everything meat free. She doesn't make a fuss about it, but Dean always moves heaven and Earth to make sure she's well fed.

"You think Wes will make a good first?" Jules asks.

"He has plenty of experience," I tease.

"Right?" Jules takes a long sip of her drink. Lets out a soft sigh. "Isn't that weird, that she's been with no one and he's been with—"

"A million women?" I offer.

"No, I don't think so." Chloe's gaze shifts to Dean then to me. "It only matters how he treats her."

"That's mature." Jules takes another sip. "I don't know if I'm that mature."

"Your ex wasn't a manwhore?" Chloe asks.

"No. We were each other's firsts." Jules's cheeks flush. "I, um, excuse me." She stands and motions to the bathroom.

I try to place the change in her expression. It's about her ex, yeah, but I can't figure out what.

She won't say shit about why it ended.

It doesn't matter to me.

But it must be weighing on her.

Chloe clears her throat. "She's really great." She swallows a sip of her rum and Coke. "It's sweet you're showing her a good time."

I'm trying.

"What do you have planned?" she asks.

I mention a few items on the itinerary.

She laughs. "Why are men so obsessed with sex?"

"Men huh?" Dean asks.

She nods *of course*.

"Not you?" he asks.

"I'm interested, sure." Chloe brushes her short hair behind her ear, showing off her *I'm a punk rock goddess* earrings.

"So if I wanted to take a vow of celibacy, that would be okay with you?" Dean slides his arm around her.

"Well… um… no, but that doesn't mean I'm obsessed." She clears her throat, but it does nothing to hide her blush.

"Yeah? Then why'd we stop at our room?" He raises a brow.

She clears her throat again. "I can't enjoy making love to my boyfriend?"

"Is that what we call it now?" Dean chuckles.

"No. But… uh… So, Griff, you and Jules, huh?" Chloe fumbles over a change in subject.

"What about it?" I ask.

"You guys are…" Her dark eyes bore into mine. "You like her, right?"

My brow scrunches. Huh?

"Sorry, none of my business." Chloe clears her throat. "But you're clearly into her. And she's clearly into you." She motions to Dean. "He thinks so too, but he doesn't think I should say anything."

"That cat's out of the bag, sunshine." Dean laughs.

She does too. "It's just… well… she is single now. So…" Her gaze shifts to something behind me. "Just think about it."

I follow her gaze to Jules.

Light bounces off her hair and dress. She looks like an angel. Or a goddess.

Like a sex goddess I need in my bed.

But that's just my cock getting greedy.

Tonight isn't about me.

It's about making sure Jules goes to bed satisfied.

Chapter Thirteen

GRIFFIN

"Too short." Jules brings her drink to her lips. Sucks a teagarita (this bar's disgusting combination of iced tea, tequila, triple sec, and lemon juice, "no simple syrup, and I mean no simple syrup—not even a drop") through her straw.

"Maybe you're too tall," I say.

Chloe shakes her head. "No, he's short."

"How can you tell?" I fold one leg over the other. Press my palm into my slacks.

"I'm not that short," Chloe insists.

Dean nods *yeah, you are.*

The happy couple is helping Jules pick out a stranger. Though 'help' and 'pick out' are strong words.

Jules isn't working with me.

This is candidate thirteen. He's as unacceptable as one through twelve. Too tall or too short or too thin or too buff or too redheaded or too douchey.

I scan the bar—we're in the lounge, at a crimson couch halfway between the bar and the dance floor—for hotties.

There are a lot of people here. Men in suits, women in cocktail dresses, bachelorette parties in matching t-shirts.

And some clean cut dudes at the bar.

"How about his friend?" I point to the guy standing next to the shorty. He's a head taller and he's wearing a perfectly normal black suit.

Jules scrunches her nose in distaste.

"What's wrong with him?" I ask.

"He's just not it." Her dress hikes up her thigh as she leans forward. It shows off inches of smooth, soft skin.

Fuck, have her legs always been that long?

I try to pry my gaze from her, but it won't go. Her white dress flows over her lush hips. It hugs her chest and waist, showing off her chest.

"I gotta be honest," Dean says. "I'm about to give up on you two."

Chloe whispers something in his ear.

He shakes his head. "Even with that."

"Ten more minutes." Chloe offers him her hand. "That's it."

"Am I supposed to shake?" he asks.

"You can go." Jules crosses one leg over the other. Which brings her dress another inch up her thigh. "I don't need help."

"You do," I say.

Dean and Chloe nod *you do*.

"Maybe you just don't understand standards." She sucks her drink through her straw.

"You're just asking him to dance." I'm making sure she comes tonight, but one thing at a time.

"Oh my God, Griff, you insisted I fuck someone a million times, and now I'm supposed to believe you'll be happy if I ask a guy to dance and leave it at that?" she asks.

Chloe shakes her head *you're so into her*.

Dean whispers something in her ear.

She laughs.

No doubt it's something about how me and Jules are madly in love.

They can think that all they want.

Jules and I know the truth. That's what matters.

"He's got a douche face." Jules motions to the taller guy. Who has a perfectly normal face. At least as far as we can tell from here.

"Dance with your back to him," I say.

She looks at me like I'm crazy.

"Then his face doesn't matter," I say.

She nods *I guess so*, but she stays put.

"All right." I stand. "We're doing this."

"What are we doing?" Her green eyes fix on me.

"Making shit happen." I take her hand.

She lets me pull her up.

I wrap my arm around her waist. It's an instinct. The place my hand wants to go.

Fuck, she feels good against my arm. Better than she has any right to.

For a split second, she looks back to me. Looks at me like she wants my arm around her. Like she wants my everything around her.

Then she blinks and it's gone.

"Drinks first." Her hips sway as she walks.

My gaze travels up her body. The curve of her back. Those strong shoulders. That long dark hair.

What would it feel like in my hands? Against my chest? My stomach?

Fuck.

I finish my last sip of vodka. Swallow an ice cube. It doesn't cool me down. Or direct my thoughts to a more appropriate subject.

That mental image—Jules stripping out of her dress, showing off her lacy white bra and panties, lying on the bed, beckoning me—stays glued to my head.

It's ridiculous.

Biology.

Alcohol making me horny.

After I find her a proper partner, I'll head to my room and take the edge off. That will straighten my thoughts. Bring them back to something that makes sense.

"Griff?" Her lips curl into a smile. An *I'm going to get my way* smile.

Fuck, she looks gorgeous bathed in that red-purple light. Like a fallen angel.

And I'm tossing that thought right now. "Another Belvedere." The price is a crime. But what good is money if you can't use it to cheer up your best friend?

She nods. Turns back to the bar. Leans over the counter to hail the bartender.

Her back arches. Her hips shift. Her ass lifts into the air.

Her dress—

It's short. And sheer. And hot as hell.

The guy standing next to me stares. He turns to me and nods. *Check it out, buddy*.

My fingers curl into fists. What the fuck does this asshole think he's doing objectifying Jules?

I should punch his lights out.

I should make sure he hurts.

I should get ahold of myself.

He's an idiot who doesn't deserve a second of my thoughts.

Besides, she's here to get laid. It's good guys are looking. It means she has options.

"Griff." She turns. Locks eyes with me. Motions to my cock.

No, my slacks. Fuck, I'm supposed to pay for these. I'm getting way too distracted.

I cut through a group of friends. Hand my credit card to the bartender. "Close it out."

"Already?" she asks.

"We're not staying here all night."

"We're club hopping?"

I nod.

She looks up at me. "You're club hopping?"

"Don't look so surprised."

"You hate clubs."

"You do too," I say.

"So it's fun because we're suffering together?"

"Exactly."

Her laugh lights up her eyes.

Fuck, her green eyes are extra gorgeous today. I want to stare into them forever. I want to do whatever it takes to fill them with joy.

We take our drinks. Toast.

Her lips curl into a smile as she takes a sip.

She stares at me. That *you're ridiculous, how do I even talk to you* stare of hers.

My heart pounds like a war drum. I love that stare. I really do.

"How do you know this stranger is going to be skilled?" She swallows another sip.

"I thought it was just dancing."

"At dancing?"

"At dancing?" I raise a brow.

She nods. "And, well… I'm not completely writing off the possibility of more."

My stomach twists. I hate the idea of someone like douche face taking her home and failing to satisfy her.

But that's ridiculous. I don't have any claim to her.

I don't want to be the one satisfying her.

I just want her to have a good time.

With someone who doesn't have a douche face.

I force my gaze to the dance floor. "Uh-huh."

"It's possible."

"So you want to know if these guys are good fucks?"

She nods.

"I can tell."

She shoots me a *really?*

I nod *really*.

"Okay. Find a guy who's a good lay." She motions to the bar. *Pick anyone.*

Usually, I'm not guessing the sexual ability of dudes. I have nothing against the male body. It's like a water color tattoo. I appreciate a good one, but I don't want anything to do with it.

I don't ask myself if a guy would be a good lay.

It's harder to go by my usual standards.

Not that it's an analytical thing. It's not like I assign three points for hair, two for outfit, ten for smile.

I look at a woman. Talk to her. Watch her move.

I'm not always right, but I always have fun figuring it out.

I knock out all the guys in jeans. They might be laid-back, but Jules deserves someone willing to put in the effort.

"The guy in the corner has potential." Broad shoulders. Slight smile. Expensive suit.

She purses her lips. "Really?"

"What's wrong with him?"

"Nothing, he's just…" She takes another sip. Swallows hard. "What are you basing this judgment on?"

"Instinct."

"That's it?" she asks.

"What else is there?" I ask.

"You're not the one who might suffer two minutes of torturous jack hammering."

"Was that Jackson's move?"

"Haha, so original." She rolls her eyes. "He looks like him."

"He does not."

She nods *he does too*.

Suit guy vaguely resembles Jackson. But only in that he's also wearing a suit.

Jules can insist she's open to anyone if she wants, but I know her too well to fall for that. She likes straitlaced guys who score straight As.

This guy is her type.

And I'm not letting her get away with this *no one is right* thing.

Even if no one here is good enough for her.

"Follow my lead," I say.

"Which will be…"

"It's better if you don't know."

She looks at me like I'm crazy. But she still nods *okay*.

I take her hand. Lead her to the corner of the bar.

Suit Guy's gaze shifts to us. Then to her. Then to her tits.

"Hey." I let go of her hand. "My friend and I made a bet."

"Yeah?" Suit Guy raises a brow.

"She thinks you're straight." I bat my eyelashes. Well, I try. It's not my usual move. If we looked more similar, I'd claim to be her brother. But that isn't gonna fly. So I'm trying this. "I think you've been staring at me."

He does stare at me. Like I'm out of my fucking mind.

Yeah, it's risky accusing a dude of checking me out. Guys are uptight about this shit.

But they're also uptight about straight male wingmen.

Better to let him believe I'm into him.

"No." His gaze shifts to Jules. Her eyes. Lips. Tits. "I'm Rheese."

"Juliette," I say. "She'd love to dance."

"Yeah?" He looks to me like he needs my permission. Which is most guy's move when they see me with Jules. Asshole probably thinks I own her.

Maybe he didn't buy the flirtation.

Or maybe he's just a dickhead.

"Yeah." Her eyes fill with apprehension. "I just called off my engagement."

Fuck. What is she doing?

"Oh?" He takes a long swig of his beer. "What happened?"

"It was time." She folds her arms over her chest. "And, well, I'm supposed to get married tomorrow. Or I was."

"Congrats," he says.

Her brow furrows.

"On dodging that bullet." He holds up his bare left hand. "Got divorced last year."

She nods.

"Cost a fortune. Divorce always does. You know why that is?" he asks.

"No, why?" She looks to me. *What the hell is with him?*

"Because it's worth it," he says.

She tries to force a smile, but it's not happening. "What, um—"

"Excuse me." I nod goodbye to the guy. "We have to go."

"Huh?" he asks.

"My boyfriend called. We're going to have a threesome. We like sharing Jules. She likes watching me come in his mouth," I say.

Disgust spreads over his face. He turns back to the bar, shaking his head *what is wrong with them*?

I wrap my arm around Jules. Pull her into the crowded dance floor. Pull her close enough to whisper.

"What the hell was that?" she asks.

"Worked, didn't it?"

"Where did you come up with that story?"

"You really want to know?" I ask.

"No." She pulls back enough to look me in the eyes. Her teeth sink into her lip. Her cheeks flush.

Or maybe that's the red-purple light.

She looks so fucking beautiful in it.

"Did you really have a threesome with another guy?" she asks.

"I have before."

"And you, ahem, with him?"

"No. Swapped the genders for that story."

"Oh. So you were with a girl and another girl and one of them wanted to watch you—"

"Yeah."

Her nose scrunches in distaste. "Why?"

"Why not?"

"You know, it's impossible to argue with that."

"Good thing you ruled out law school."

Her nose scrunches more. Which is fucking adorable. And incredibly irresistible. "God, Griff, maybe you're right."

"Yeah?"

"Maybe we should ditch the clubs and I should get off on your depraved stories."

"You want to go?" I brush her hair from her neck. Bring my lips to her ear.

Fuck, she smells good.

I want to touch her. Kiss her. Taste her.

Which is ridiculous.

And not happening.

"We can go to my hotel room. Let your shitty music be our soundtrack." My fingers curl into the space between her shoulder blades. It's her bare skin. Fuck, it feels good against my hand.

She arches her back, curling her body into mine. "Can we really?"

"This trip is for you."

"I know."

"If that's what will make you happy, yeah."

"Can we read instead of discussing your sexual dalliances?"

I shake my head.

"What if I say please?"

Say please, Griffin, fuck me hard. Split me in half. Make me come. I pull her closer. So I can whisper in her ear. Not because I want her closer. Or because I want to fuck her. "Give it another hour."

"Do I have to?"

"No. But I'll feel better if you dance with someone."

"You're someone."

"Someone you want to fuck."

Her green eyes meet mine. They scream *what a stupid thing to say. I have someone I want to fuck right here.*

But that's my cock being an idiot again.

Chapter Fourteen

JULIETTE

"He's cute." Griffin motions to a group of guys in jeans. One is wearing a *Soon to Be Property of Cynthia* sash. The others are wearing matching *Groom Support Squad* t-shirts.

I guess Vegas is bachelor party central, but, seriously, what's with all the reminders of weddings?

It's bad enough imagining Jackson thrusting into his coworker without actually seeing it.

I didn't see it. Not in the flesh. That would have been better, honestly. There's no way it's as awful as my mental images.

My eyelids flutter closed and I see it. The mysterious lingerie in my drawer. The sheer red one piece.

At first I was confused—I thought one of my friends left it in my apartment. Or that it was something from my shower I'd forgotten. Or that it was from Jackson.

That he was hiding a gift, a surprise.

That he was finally going to the effort to bring life back into our sex life.

That we were going to talk about the day everything changed.

For a while, I was happy. Hopeful.

Then I showed it to him and he burst into tears. *I'm so sorry, Jules. I didn't plan it this way. We were working together. You know I've had all those long nights. She's so smart. But she's funny too. And tender.*

She doesn't flinch when I touch her.

She wants me.

I thought I could end it, but I'm in love with her.

I'm sorry.

I didn't mean for this to happen.

He didn't even have the courtesy to declare our relationship over. I had to do the dirty work.

"Jules?" Griff hip checks me. "Where are you going?"

"Nowhere." I'm here. At this club. Our third club. It's quieter. More low key. Filled with guys in jeans, not guys in suits.

The music is better.

A little better.

All that house music sounds the same to me.

I force my gaze to the bachelor party guys. Are they celebrating or commiserating? Hard to say. I'm not sure which is more accurate. Not anymore.

"Somewhere," Griff says.

I shake my head.

"Jules, if you lie to me, I'll torture you."

"I'm not dancing with some guy who's already regretting his wedding."

Griff nods. "What about the tall friend?"

"I don't care about height."

"Uh-huh." He nods to the blond guy in the corner. He is tall. And handsome. Like some kind of Nordic king. "He's hot."

"He's not un-hot."

"Ask him to dance."

"You sure you don't want to join? Maybe tell a story about your favorite role play?" I tease.

"I'm always partial to teacher-student."

"Oh my God."

"I know it's a cliché, but those school girl skirts are fucking hot. And one of those white blouses, tied at her chest, nothing under it."

"Like our school uniform?" I ask.

"Yeah." His smile spreads over his cheeks. "Probably explains it."

"Nothing can explain your depravity."

"It's perfectly natural."

"How?" God, why am I asking him this?

"You remember middle school."

"Of course."

"That's when I stopped worrying about cooties. I wanted to kiss girls. And touch them. And see them naked. All of them were wearing green plaid skirts. And fuck, the way girls would hike them up their thighs—fucked myself to it every day."

"This is way too much information."

"You asked."

I shake my head. This is really too much information. And... well... I was one of those girls. I rolled my skirt waistband to show off my legs.

I was full of hormones and insecurity and desire to make out with cute boys.

"I don't fuck myself to that anymore," he says.

"I'd hope so."

"But if a woman wants to put on a plaid skirt and beg me to punish her..." He shrugs *I'm not about to stop her.*

"Oh my God."

"Or just the skirt." He laughs. "That's plenty."

"Is there anything you're not into?"

"Yeah." His expression gets dead serious.

I stare up at him, but it doesn't help me figure out his intentions.

"Liars."

What?

"And unprotected sex."

Oh my God. What? "But the first time—"

"You made me promise."

"You were thirteen."

"I'd never break a promise to you."

I swallow hard. "Even if you had a girlfriend?"

"Promised I'd be safe. If I had a girlfriend, and I was sure she wouldn't step out on me, that would be different." His eyes bore into mine. It's accusatory. Like he knows why I ended things with Jackson.

But he doesn't know.

No one knows.

Ahem.

"You're not proposing to him." Griff presses his palm into my back. Turns me toward the Nordic King. "You're dancing."

"And if he invites me back to his hotel room?"

"If you want to go, go."

My stomach twists. "What if he's an ax murderer?"

He chuckles. "Sneak into the bathroom and fuck him here."

Oh my God, no. So much no.

Griff's chuckle gets louder. "Tell him you're texting a friend his room number. So he knows there will be evidence."

"So he won't get away with it if he murders me?"

"If you think he's an ax murderer, don't go."

That's actually reasonable.

He leans in to whisper. "If you go, text me the location."

"You won't come?"

"To his hotel room?"

Yeah, that's a good point. I can't exactly bring Griffin to watch my one-night stand. I mean, I could. If I asked, he'd say yes. But I wouldn't ask.

"Go. Dance."

"But—"

"Now." He pushes me forward.

Okay. I can do this. I can ask a man to dance.

I mean, it's been five years since I've shown interest in another man. I haven't flirted or dated or danced.

But it's a simple question. *Would you like to dance*? That's doable. That's totally doable.

I suck a breath between my teeth. Exhale slowly. Smooth my dress. Strut.

Okay, it's more of a tipsy sway, but it's something.

Nordic King's gaze shifts to me. My chest. But, hey, I'm not auditioning boyfriends here.

I'm not in this for his personality.

"Hi." I try to find the words *would you like to dance*, but my mouth refuses to open. He's so tall. And handsome. He checks all the boxes—cute, tall, suit, nice smile—but he does nothing to make my stomach flutter.

"Hi." He flashes me a million-dollar smile. Seriously, it's a huge smile.

But it doesn't make my heart race.

It's just dancing. It's not a marriage proposal. It's not even a kiss. It's no big deal.

Deep breath. Steady exhale.

He cuts me off. "Would you like to dance?"

I nod—talking is still not happening—and he offers

his hand.

Together, we move into the fray.

One of his friends yells something, but it dissolves in the pounding music.

He wraps his arm around my waist. Pulls me close. Sways in time with the music.

The beat is fast. I'm not sure how to move. I try to follow his lead, but I don't quite get there. He's not hitting the rhythm of the song.

We're not connecting.

Even so, he looks down at me with a smile (he really is tall). "I'm Adrian."

"Juliette."

"Where's Romeo?" He flashes me that same smile. "Kidding. I get a lot of people screaming *Adrienne*."

What?

"*Rocky?* The boxing movie."

"I'm not familiar."

"There's a scene where Rocky Balboa screams *Adrienne*. His girlfriend's name. I'm not sure people realize the spelling is different." His fingers curl into my lower back. "I understand the pain."

Right. I mean, people do ask me stupid questions about my name. It was annoying in middle school. Not as annoying as the *where are you from, really* or the *why don't you look like your mom* or *why are you so bad at Spanish* questions. (I barely made As all the way through Spanish Four, and I still can't say anything without an atrocious American accent). But it was annoying. "Honors British Lit was especially tough."

"What?" He turns his head to hear.

I rise to my tiptoes so I can whisper in his ear. "Honors British Lit was especially tough." God, what a lame thing to whisper.

Adrian likes it. He laughs. Then pulls me closer. "I bet." His cheek brushes mine as he leans in to whisper. "What brings you to Vegas?"

"I guess you could call it a bachelorette party."

"Oh." He slides his hands down my back. "Who's the victim?"

"Me."

"You have my condolences."

"Thanks." A laugh spills from my lips. Sure, I'm not actually getting married. But that is a good thing. As much as this hurts, I'm really fucking glad I'm not getting married tomorrow. "Your friend is getting married?"

He taps his t-shirt. "What gave me away?"

"Is he happy?"

"I think so."

"Are you happy for him?"

"Damn, Juliette. You're asking the tough questions tonight."

"Sorry. I'm not really… It's been a while since I dated."

"I can imagine." His fingers curl into my lower back.

"You don't care that I'm engaged?"

He pulls back enough to look me in the eyes. "Are we doing anything your fiancé wouldn't like?"

Right. We're just dancing. But something tells me Adrian wouldn't let a little thing like an engagement stop him from having fun. "He isn't the boss of me."

"Smart." His finger drift down my lower back. "You're smart to come here."

"Am I?"

"Yeah." His fingers skim the top of my ass. "You need to have fun before you settle down."

Fuck, this is weird. I pull back.

"You want to have some fun with us?"

My gaze shifts around the room, but I can't find Griffin. Just a throng of people dancing, laughing, making out.

It's nice, normal fun.

Okay, it's not *nice*, but it is normal fun.

I should go with him.

I should tell him I want one last fling before I get married.

I should kiss him. Right now.

"Adrian?" I stare up into his eyes. Try to find the desire to kiss him. He's handsome and tall and funny. Yeah, he's overly willing to bang an engaged woman, but he's not the one who's engaged.

He's not the keeper of my chastity.

If I fuck him, it's my decision. My mistake. My betrayal.

I mean, there's no betrayal. It's all fiction. I don't blame the coworker who fucked Jackson.

I don't even know her name.

Okay, that's a lie. I stalked his Facebook after he told me. I stared at her pictures, their pictures, for hours, wondering how I could be so stupid not to see it.

But I don't blame Patricia.

It was his decision. His betrayal. His inability to keep his dick in his pants.

"Yeah?" He brushes my hair behind my ear. The way Griff did. But it feels different. Awkward.

Even so, I close my eyes. Rise to my tiptoes. Press my lips to his.

I'm kissing this guy.

God, it's so weird. He tastes like stale beer. And he smells like smoke.

This is just—

"Hey." Fingers curl around my upper arm. "Was

looking everywhere for you." Griffin pulls me away from Adrian.

Adrian's expression flashes with fear. "Are you the—"

Griffin looks at me *huh*?

"He's the… um, maid of honor," I say. "He's in charge of my bachelorette party. You know. How my wedding date is tomorrow?"

Griffin nods *yeah*. "And you are—"

"Adrian." He shakes Griff's hand. "I was about to invite your friend somewhere."

"Oh?" Griffin smiles like he doesn't care, but there's something in his eyes.

Jealousy.

Adrian smiles. "We're headed to another club downtown."

"Oh?" Griffin's grip tightens on my arm.

"Yeah." Adrian smiles, completely oblivious. "A strip club. You two want to join?"

Griffin turns my body toward his. He stares into my eyes, looking for something.

I don't know what it is.

Only that I want him staring.

His hand feels so fucking good around my arm.

I have no idea where this jealous, possessive side of him came from.

But I really fucking like it.

"Yeah." I nod. "We want to join."

Chapter Fifteen

JULIETTE

Adrian and his incredibly drunk friends pour into a party bus. An actual party bus.

It's basically a mini club. Purple lighting. Burgundy couches. Mirrored walls. Open roof. Champagne.

Adrian spreads his legs wide. Cops that *blow me* gesture guys love.

As if.

I don't care how big his cock is or how nicely he asks.

I spent five years putting my needs second. I'm not doing it anymore.

Not that I don't enjoy—

I mean if it was someone I wanted—

Like Griff. I mean, not like Griff. But someone who cared about my needs the way Griff does.

Ahem.

Griff takes the spot across from me. He stares like I'm about to step off our perfect plan.

Which is ridiculous. This is the plan. Fun with a strange man.

That's why I'm here.

Not because I want to make Griff jealous.

That would be stupid.

"Champagne?" The future groom picks up the bottle. He looks around the room of drunk guys—they're all cheering, but it's not over anything in particular—and pops the cork.

Foam pours over the glass.

Is that why men like champagne? Because it reminds them of their dicks?

They're obsessed.

Griff chuckles.

"What?" I stare into my best friend's eyes. They're so dark. And intense. And pretty. He really is pretty. He's more handsome than pretty, but he really is pretty.

"You thinking what I'm thinking?" He motions to the drunk groom, who's trying and failing to pour bubbly into flutes.

"That is why men like champagne," Griff says. "'Cause they want to show how powerful they are when they come."

"I wasn't thinking that." I'm still thinking that.

"Uh-huh."

"It is an obvious thing to think." I clear my throat. "But I wasn't thinking it."

"It's all right. You like thinking about cum." Griffin's smile lights up his eyes. "Nothing wrong with that."

"You're disgusting." I shake my head.

"You never think about it?" he asks.

"Of course not." I mean, not the substance. The action, sure. But not the actual substance.

"Really?" He raises a brow.

I nod *really*.

Adrian turns to me. "You're obsessed with semen?"

Oh my God. "No." My cheeks flush. Which is ridiculous, because I'm not obsessed. Or even interested. It's not like I ever craved Jackson's… Oh my God, I can't even think it. "I'm interested in phallic imagery."

He nods *okay*. "Are you an English student?"

"Why do you ask?" Am I really that obvious?

"You seem like one," he says.

Griffin shoots me a *really* look.

I find my cell in my pocket. Shoot him a text.

Jules: This was your idea.

Griffin: Dancing. Not watching some groom cheat on his fiancée.

Jules: We're visiting a strip club, not a brothel.

Griffin: Haven't you seen that movie where the groom fucks a stripper and accidentally kills her and the guys have to hide the body?

Jules: WHY WOULD I WATCH A MOVIE LIKE THAT?

Griffin: You watch a lot of stuff.

Jules: Not like that. What the hell are you watching in your free time?

Griffin: What free time?

Jules: When I was with Jackson?

Griffin: It's not what I was doing. It's who.

Jules: Gross.

Griffin: You're jealous.

Jules: Of some girl whose name you don't remember?

Griffin: Of the fact I've had good sex in the last five years.

Jules: Last five days, probably.

Griffin: Well…

Jules: Really?

Griffin: It's been a few weeks.

Jules: That's shocking.

Griffin: I had a sext thing going. It was all teasing. And it was fucking hot.

Jules: Do I want to know?

Griffin: Depends? You into begging a guy to come in your mouth?

Jules: She did not.

Griffin: She did.

Jules: But it was virtual?

Griffin: She's away for the summer.

Jules: So you fucked her before?

Griffin: Not fucked, no.

Jules: Who are you? Bill Clinton.

Griffin: I'd never come on a dress without permission.

Jules: OH MY GOD

Griffin: It's pretty hot coming on a nice pair of tits. But not on fabric.

Jules: GROSS. SO GROSS. THE MOST DISGUSTING THING I'VE EVER HEARD.

"Should I give you a moment?" Adrian asks.

I clear my throat. "No, just, um—"

"Questions from the best man," Griff covers.

Adrian nods *sure*. He leans in to whisper in my ear. "My dad gave me and my brother a piece of advice."

"That's your brother?" I motion to the groom.

He nods *yeah, isn't the resemblance obvious*? (It is not). "He said that once you're wearing that ring it's over. If you need one last fling to help you embrace your wife, do it."

"It doesn't count?" I ask.

He nods.

It takes the utmost concentration to maintain my poker face. Is this dude really so shady that he's trying to talk me into cheating on my fictional fiancé?

It's one thing if I'm going for it. He's actually encouraging it.

My phone buzzes in my lap.

Griffin: What did he say?

Jules: That it's good to have a one-night stand before your wedding. Get it out of your system.

Griffin: You're still talking to this asshole?

Jules: You don't want to go to a strip club?

Griffin: We can go by ourselves.

Jules: We can go now.

Griffin: All right, but I'm going to show you a good time here.

Jules: What does that mean?

Griffin: You'll see.

Griffin slides his cell into his slacks. His eyes meet mine. His lips curl into a smile.

Not a friend smile.

A something else smile.

A something confusing smile.

MUCH LIKE THE LIMO, THE STRIP CLUB GLOWS WITH RED light. It's named after Beelzebub himself and the imagery is, well, obvious.

Devil horns sit atop the cocktail waitresses' heads. Or wigs, as the case may be. Most of the women are wearing extensions, but some must be faking that hair completely.

They're in red lingerie, Devil tails affixed to the backs of their bustiers.

Of course, their shoes—a mix of platform boots, platform heels, and platform mules—are red.

Their shoes are tall. How the hell are they walking in those?

The women on stage—well, the stages—are even more ornately adorned (or undressed, depending).

To the right, a woman in a schoolgirl outfit skips around a pole.

To the left, a woman slides off her black thong. She

hooks her leg around the pole, turns herself upside down, and spins.

Naked and upside down.

God, it's weird. Amazing—how is she doing that—but strange. What with her complete lack of clothing.

The bachelor party heads to a booth on the right. Once again, Adrian motions for me to sit next to him.

Griff's fingers curl into my wrist. His thumb brushes the ink covering my skin.

Then the scars.

It's like he's screaming *listen to me Jules. I know you. I love you. I'm not letting anything bad happen to you.*

Not that he's ever used that word.

Or that I want him to.

It's just—

"I need a drink." That's it. That's all it is.

"I'll get it for you, sweetie," Adrian says. "What are you drinking?"

"Tequila and iced tea," I say.

His expression fills with distaste, but he still turns toward the bar.

"Vodka straight, for me," Griff says. He chuckles as Adrian moves toward the bar.

"Are you really letting him buy your drink?" I ask.

He nods. "If that's the price he wants to pay to seduce an engaged woman."

"I'm not actually engaged," I say.

"He doesn't know that." Griffin slides his arm around my waist. Pulls me closer.

There's no reason for it.

No explanation.

But I don't want an explanation.

I want to sink into his body. I want to stare into his

eyes. I want to kiss him like the goddamned ship is going down.

"Hi." A chipper woman interrupts my train of thought. With her bright pink bra and panty set, matching nails, bleach blond hair, and massive fake boobs, she looks like a cheerleader in a teen movie.

She's pretty.

And, God, her boobs are enormous.

But Griff doesn't check out her cleavage.

His eyes stay glued to me.

"You really want to stay here?" he asks.

I nod *hell yeah*. I mean, I'm not sure how I feel about strip clubs. But the women here seem happy enough. And they're making money. So more power to them.

"My friend wants a dance," Griff says.

"What?" I blink twice, but it does nothing to wake me from this nightmare. A lap dance. No. I… Uh…

The dancer smiles. "Your friend is cute." Her eyes fix on me. "I love dancing for couples."

She loves—

Oh my God.

I stare at my best friend. "Is this—"

"On me." He pulls out his wallet. "How much is a dance?"

She leans in to whisper in his ear.

He pulls out a wad of cash and presses it into her palm. "Shall we?"

"But… I… Huh…" My gaze shifts to Adrian on his way back from the bar with my drink.

Adrian's gaze shifts to the dancer. To her ass.

It's nice. I can't blame him for looking. But isn't he trying to get into my pants?

He could at least pretend I'm the only person who interests him.

Are all men scum or just most of them?

I take my drink from Adrian and flash him a fake smile. Griff is right. He's a loser. He's not worth my time or effort. "I'm getting a dance."

"A few, actually." Griffin's fingers curl into my side. "We'll see you later." He winks at Adrian.

Adrian's face screws with confusion. Then that look I know well. *Oh, so she's your girl, you lying asshole.* "Fucking slut." He shakes his head. "You gonna fuck him too?"

"Oh, that's where you draw the line?" I ask. "Not me cheating on my fiancé?"

"I don't do threesomes. Not like that." Adrian's gaze shifts to the dancer.

Her expression stays serene. "Shall we?"

"We shall." I wave goodbye to the asshole philanderer. I mean, I guess he's not technically the one philandering. And it didn't happen. But the intent is there.

Griff pulls me closer.

I stay closer.

It feels good. He feels good. Or maybe I'm drunk and lonely.

But, God, he's so much better than Adrian or Jackson or all the other assholes who think fidelity is optional.

I follow him, and the dancer, past the tables. Through a red velvet curtain (of course). Into a room with red couches.

And half-naked women.

And naked women.

It's the lap dance room.

It's not crowded, exactly. There are four lap dances in progress.

And, God, I can't stop gawking.

It's weird seeing naked women grinding against fully dressed men.

But it's kind of hot too.

Griff turns to me and raises a brow. "You ready for this?"

I think I'm going insane, because I nod *yes*.

I am.

I really am.

Chapter Sixteen

JULIETTE

"So," the dancer purrs, "what brings you to Vegas?"

"I… Uh… We… What's your name?" I try to wipe my palms on my dress, but the fabric is too slick.

"I go by Barbie." She smiles. "Like Barbara. Not the doll."

Right. Like Barbara. Not the doll.

There's a slight accent to her voice, something southern. Maybe her name really is Barbara. Maybe she was named after her grandmother. Or her mom. Or both.

I'm sure she has a full life, a history, likes and dislikes.

She's more than tits and ass. Even if she's incredibly well-endowed in both departments.

"Care to take a seat?" She motions to the crimson couch in front of us.

Right. We're doing this.

I sit. Cross my legs. Uncross them.

This is a lap dance. She needs access to my lap.

I'm okay with that.

I am.

My gaze shifts around the room. The mirror across from us. The "couple" in the corner, too far away for proper detail. The dancer to our right.

She's dressed in a black corset and a matching thong, with shiny boots that go way up her thighs.

Her customer is in a suit and he's staring at her like she's the center of the universe.

The way I always wanted Jackson to look at me.

Like he's desperate to get his hands on her.

She runs her fingers along his chin. Tilts his head so he's staring into her eyes. Leans down to thrust her chest into his face.

She climbs into his lap. Takes his hands. Brings them to the lacing of her corset.

He licks his lips like an eager puppy as he undoes the lacing.

"What's your name, sweetie?" Barbie asks.

"Oh, uh—" I pry my gaze from the goth stripper right as her boobs pop out of the corset. Hers are real. Smaller. Almost as small as mine.

"Juliette," Griff says. "I'm Griffin."

"I'm going to wait for the next song if that's all right." Barbie's smile is serene.

The next song. Sure. We pay by the song. And Griffin offered her a fat stack of cash. So we must have more than one song.

"Are you celebrating something?" she asks.

"Yeah." Griff scoots closer. So his thigh is pressed against mine. "Jules called off her engagement."

"Oh?" Interests perks in Barbie's eyes. I think. With the fake lashes and the bright blue eyeshadow, it's hard to tell. Plus it's her job to pretend she likes us.

I guess there's no harm in believing it. "Yeah." I nod. "We're celebrating my freedom."

"No better place," Barbie says.

"This is for her." Griff stares into Barbie's eyes. "I want you to show her all your attention."

"Not all." I clear my throat. "I mean, Griff needs attention too." Not too much. I can't handle watching him touch her. What if he groans like the guy to our right. If he starts feeling her up?

Oh my God, the pair to our right are seriously going at it.

He's actually touching her.

Groaning like he's going to come.

Maybe he is. That is a lot of friction.

This is going to—

Griff is going to—

Fuck.

The song fades into the next.

Barbie's nails scrape my chin. She turns my head, so I'm facing her. So I'm staring at her tits.

"You're so cute." She wraps her fingers around my wrist. "I want to play with you all night."

"Thank you." My stomach flutters.

"Can I?" She brings my hand to her chest. Rests it on her collarbone.

"Huh?" I look to Griff for a clue.

"She wants to touch you, Jules," he says.

"What?" My eyes go wide. I… He… Huh…

He chuckles as he turns to Barbie. "She's shy."

"I know." She presses her chest into my hand. "I love the shy ones." Her eyes meet mine. "Can you help me with this, darling?" The southern accent drips into her voice.

I nod. Sure. I can help the dancer take off her bra. No problem.

It's a simple clasp. I undo it in a single gesture.

"Thank you." She smiles as she pushes her bra off one shoulder. Then the other.

Her boobs are right there.

They're huge. Round. Unnaturally round. But still appealing in a certain way.

I'm not uptight. Not *that* uptight. I appreciate nice boobs as much as anyone.

Okay, not anyone. But anyone who isn't attracted to women.

Barbie rests her hands on my shoulders and slides into my lap.

The weight of her body sinks into me. It's different than it was with Jackson.

Than it is with Griff.

My gaze shifts to him.

He's not staring at her enormous boobs. Or adoring her plump ass.

He's watching me.

His dark eyes are wide.

His cheeks are flushed.

His chest is heaving with his inhale.

He tries to make eye contact, but I look away. To Barbie. Then to the mirror behind us.

I don't watch her straddle me.

I watch him watch me.

Barbie shifts her hips in time with the music.

She stares into my eyes like she's desperate to touch me.

Then she touches me.

Her fingers brush my neck, collarbones, chest.

She traces the neckline of my dress.

Griff's pupils dilate.

It's illicit, watching desire spread over his expression.

Him watching this—whatever I want to call this.

But it's not because of me. It's the buxom blonde in my lap.

Her fingers curl into the straps of my dress. "You mind, darling?"

Griff's tongue slides over his lips.

He wants her undressing me.

Because she's a certified ten.

Because he has some fantasy of two girls going at it.

Not because he wants me.

There's no way he wants me.

That's…

I…

Uh…

I nod.

She peels my dress down my shoulders. Chest. Stomach.

Her fingers trace the outline of my bra.

My cheeks flush.

My heart pounds.

My veins buzz with nervous energy.

He's right there. If I close my eyes, it's like he's the one touching me.

Not that I want that.

I mean, I don't not want that.

It's just—

It's confusing.

Barbie slides off my lap. She stands. Stares down at me. And at Griff.

Through the mirror, my eyes find his. God, his dark eyes are so wide. He's transfixed.

I love that he's transfixed. Even if it's by another woman.

I mean—

I—

He—

Fuck. I don't know what I mean. Only that the desire in his expression is making me hot all over.

Barbie spins on her heels. She bends at her waist. Rolls down one vertebra at a time. Until her fingers are on the ground and her ass is on display.

It's a nice ass. The kind of ass that graces magazine covers.

But Griffin isn't looking at her.

He's watching me.

He raises a brow *you okay*?

Okay is the wrong word. I'm buzzing with a mix of nerves and desire.

The dancer is pretty and skilled, yes, but I don't want her.

I—

No, I can't say it. Not yet.

I nod a *yes*.

Barbie hinges at her hips. She rises as slowly as she went down. Then she shifts onto my lap.

She flips her hair as she turns to Griff. She studies his expression. Gauging what he wants, I guess.

She must decide he's plenty happy with this, because she stays in my lap.

She grinds against me slowly.

She reaches back for my hands. Brings them to her hips.

The song changes to the next. Barbie turns. Shifts her weight on Griffin's lap.

"How many?" I ask.

"Three," she purrs. "But you can always buy more." She leans over as she grinds her ass against him.

God, she's right there.

In his lap.

My cheeks burn. But it's not desire. It's something else.

Why is she touching him? She shouldn't be touching him.

I should—

No, I shouldn't.

This is crazy.

She shifts out of his lap. Turns to me. "I think your girl is lonely like this."

My exhale is shaky.

Griff's is steady. He has a nearly naked woman in his lap, but his attention is on me. "I think she is." He whispers something in her ear.

She nods, turns, climbs back into my lap.

She doesn't writhe or grind. Just sinks into my thighs as she runs her fingers along my jaw. Neck. Chest.

This time, she doesn't stop at the outline of my bra.

She dips her hand into my cup.

Her fingers brush my nipple.

It's under my bra. Griff can't see. But it feels like he's watching me come. Like he's seeing everything.

"Help me out here, darling." Her fingers skim my sides. My ribs. The back of my bra.

I don't know why, but I arch my back to help her.

She unhooks my bra and peels it off my skin.

The nude fabric lands on my thighs.

Fuck.

I don't care that I'm topless in front of strangers. Only that I'm in front of Griff.

His eyes stay glued to me.

Not to her.

To me.

He watches as she toys with my boobs.

I close my eyes. Let the music pour through my ears.

Let the smell of his shampoo fill my nostrils. Let myself believe it's him.

The song shifts to the next.

She climbs out of my lap. Pushes her panties off her hips. Kicks them from her ankles.

She bends again, putting *everything* on display.

Griff still isn't looking at her.

He's watching me.

His gaze travels down my body, stopping at my chest. He stares like it's the best thing he's ever seen. Like I'm the best thing he's ever seen. Like he's desperate to be the one toying with my nipples.

Fuck, I bet he's good at that.

I bet he can make me purr with a few flicks of his thumb.

My sex clenches.

My fingers curl into my thighs.

I watch as Barbie climbs into his lap and grinds against him, but I'm not watching her.

I'm watching him.

And he's watching me.

We stay like that until the song ends.

Instantly, Barbie slides out of Griff's lap. She slips into her bra and panties. "You know, I'm really rooting for you two." Her smile is sincere. Like she wants us to come together as badly as I—

No.

I can't want this with Griff.

I can't want his lips on my lips and his hands on my chest and his cock inside me.

But I do.

I really fucking do.

Chapter Seventeen

GRIFFIN

I try not to gawk as Jules pulls her dress over her tits, but it's hard.

No. Hard is an understatement.

I'm pretty sure I can cut diamonds at the moment.

My best friend's cheeks flush. "Thank you." She nods a goodbye to the dancer.

The smile Barbie returns is somewhere between *I'm madly in love with you* and *I'm so happy to help and I'd love to help more, in exchange for more cash.*

It's her job to pretend she's interested. To convince horny men she desperately wants to feel their cocks against her ass.

Fuck.

Now that image is in my head.

Not the dancer. She's pretty, yeah, but she doesn't interest me.

Jules—

Her chest heaves with her inhale.

Her hips sway with her step.

Her lips part with a sigh.

God dammit, I want to roll that dress fabric to her waist, pull her body against mine, grind my cock against her flesh.

Which is out of the question.

I can't want Jules.

This trip is for her. So she can find someone to fuck. So she can get over her ex by getting under someone.

That someone can't be me.

It needs to be a stranger she'll forget the next morning.

It needs to be hot, sweaty, dirty sex. And nothing else.

One great lay, a night of sleep, a little sightseeing, bam—she's over that asshole Jackson.

She's mine again.

Fuck.

All right, I want to hear my name on her lips. I want to taste her cunt. I want to pin her to the bed, tear off her dress, and split her in half.

Fuck, this train of thought isn't doing shit to cool me down.

I turn away from her, but it does nothing to hide my hard-on. The entire room is mirrors.

"Griff." Her gaze stops on my crotch. "We're not supposed to hang out here unless we're getting a dance."

Fuck, I know that. I've been to strip clubs plenty of times. I know the etiquette.

I nod *yeah* and follow her through the velvet curtains.

The room is still glowing red, like hell itself. Or like a bondage club. The latter is probably more accurate. Especially if the dancer to our left is any indication.

She's wearing strappy black leather. Contorting herself around the pole like she's tied to it.

It's hot, but my gaze still shifts to the mirror behind her. To Jules's reflection.

My best friend watches with rapt attention.

"You sure you're into guys?" I nudge her shoulder with mine. I need to get back to teasing. To whatever it takes to convince my cock to cool it.

Jules makes a show of rolling her eyes. "You really figured me out, Griff. One dance was all it took for me to realize I lust for pussy."

"Three dances."

She rolls her eyes the other way.

"You're showing off."

"You're... Uh..." Her gaze shifts to my chest. Stomach. Crotch. "You really liked her?"

No. I like you. I want you. I want to fuck you until you're screaming.

Or are you quieter when you come? Like you're so lost in bliss you can't even get a word out?

I have to know.

I don't have to touch you or taste you or bury myself inside you, but I do have to know.

No, that's bullshit.

I need all of it. Now.

I swallow hard. I don't lie. I don't tell half-truths. I don't sugar coat.

If I start doing it now—

"Griff?" Her green eyes fix on mine. For a second. Then they're on the ground and her cheeks are bright red.

She's nervous about my response.

She's adorable nervous.

And hot.

And her tits—

I need to see her tits again. Need to feel them against my palm. Around my cock.

"That's why we're here, right?" She clears her throat. "You're supposed to get *ahem*." She motions to my crotch.

"We're here for you."

"Yeah, but—"

"Are you wet?" I ask.

"Oh my God." Her blush spreads to her chest. "That's so—"

"If you're horny as hell, you might actually fuck someone." Someone else. Someone who won't change things.

"So you want me to lower my standards?"

I want you against that wall. Take off your dress. And the panties. You're coming on my face. Now. "I want you to go to bed satisfied."

She shakes her head, but it's not with her usual *you're an idiot*. It's different. Loaded.

Like she's also thinking about coming on my face.

But that's not what's happening.

That would never happen.

All this evidence of her desire—

It's because of the skilled dancer.

That's the only logical possibility.

"Hey!" A loud guy slides his arms around our shoulders. "Good to see you. I knew Adrian was kinky, but he'd never admit it."

Huh?

Oh. It's the groom from the wedding party. The one ready to cheat on his fiancé.

At least, according to his dickhead brother.

"How you doing?" My voice drips with disdain.

He doesn't notice. "Good. It's sweet all these guys threw me a bash." He holds up his drink—green liquid in a martini glass—to toast someone on the other side of the room. Said liquid spills over the sides of his glass. On his hand. And my shirt. "They're trying to buy me a lap dance."

"You don't want a dance?" Jules asks.

He shakes his head. "No. I just want Amanda." His

smile is serene. "I can't tell the guys. They'll make fun of me. But, honestly, I'd rather watch TV with her all night than be here."

"That's sweet." Her voice is soft. "When are you—"

"Next week." He smiles. "At the beach in Malibu."

Jules's lips curl into a frown. Her wedding was supposed to be at the beach in Malibu.

Fuck, it would have been beautiful.

She would have been beautiful.

And sexy as hell.

This deranged mental image flashes through my head: me, tearing off her wedding dress. Pinning her to the bed. Fucking her senseless.

"Adrian isn't like that. He sleeps with anything that moves." He pulls us a little closer. "He always wanted to have a threesome with a couple, but he could never admit it." He tries to whisper but fails completely. "But honestly, he wanted to touch your dick, didn't he?"

Jules shoots me a *what the fuck* look.

This is good. This drunk idiot is steering the conversation to things that don't turn me on.

Things besides my best friend's soft lips.

And lush thighs.

And perfect tits.

"Mostly, he wanted to watch." I pull my hand free. Pat his shoulder. "In fact, we're gonna go for round two in our hotel room."

"Yeah!" He holds up his drink. Spills even more green liquid. "Go for it." With his other hand, he pulls a card from his pocket. "Take the party bus. Just make sure to send it back here."

I look to Jules and raise a brow *should we*?

She nods *yeah*.

I take the card. "Thanks." I go to shake his hand.

He pulls me into a hug and pats my back. "Adrian is gonna say this isn't a big deal, but it is. He's always wanted this. Make sure he enjoys it."

"Sure." I pull back.

He hugs Jules. "You're really good people."

"Um… thanks." She steps backward. Looks to me for guidance.

I shrug. It's almost sweet how much he cares about his brother's threesome. "Congrats."

He holds up his drink again. This time, without spilling. "To you too."

I slide my arm around Jules's waist and lead her toward the exit. We need to get out of here before that asshole Adrian sees us.

He's the type who wants to start a fight.

I can knock him out if it comes to that—and it will if he tries to touch Jules—but I'd rather not break my hand.

Not before Jules comes on it.

All right. I'm officially drunk. That's the only reasonable explanation for this train of thought.

Or maybe the alcohol is wearing down the walls in my brain. The ones that keep me from seeing her like this.

Maybe I'm finally seeing things as they are.

Maybe, this is exactly how I feel sober.

Jules giggles as she stretches out on the vinyl bench. "I can't believe we have this to ourselves."

"Until Mr. Monogamy realizes we're not having a threesome with his brother," I say.

She laughs. "How long does that give us?"

"He was pretty sloshed."

"Two hours?"

"If we're lucky."

She nods *got it*, moves to the icebox, grabs a bottle of champagne. "I've never done this before." She sets the bottle between her legs. "You think that's enough?"

I arch a brow.

"To symbolize my massive cock." She nestles the bottle between her thighs. "Or closer?"

"It's gonna spill all over your dress."

Her brow scrunches as she assesses the booze. She pushes the bottle forward. Grabs the cork. Twists.

Bam—

The cork hits the ceiling.

Foam spills over the bottle.

Over her thighs.

My cock stirs. I need to spread her legs and lick every drop of champagne.

Then every drop of her.

Jules laughs. "Oh my God." She brings the bottle to her lips. Sucks the spilling foam from the glass.

Fuck the places my head is going.

"It's such a mess," she says.

"Always is."

Her cheeks flush. "Not in my experience."

"In all your experience having a cock?"

"No. Um… utilizing a cock."

"Is that what you call it?"

She nods *uh-huh*. Smiles her usual *I can tease you forever* smile. Then something dirtier. "What do you call it?"

"I prefer being specific."

"Oh?"

I nod.

"In my experience making men come." Her voice drops to something low and dirty. "Is that specific enough for you?"

"Men?"

"A man." Her eyes flit to mine as she licks foam from the bottle. It spills over her lips. Dribbles down her chin. Hits her chest.

I swallow hard.

"You want some?" She finds a clean champagne flute behind the ice box. Pours messily.

I move closer, which is a bad idea. I already want to touch her, taste her, kiss her.

I really want to fuck her.

Right now.

My fingers brush hers as I take the glass.

The fruity bubbles burst on my tongue. They dissolve what's left of my inhibitions.

I finish my glass.

She pours me another. Drinks straight from the bottle. "A lot less classy this way."

But a lot more interesting. Fuck, her lips look good wrapped around that bottle. It's filling me with ideas. Way too many ideas.

"We're not going to Adrian's hotel room." She wipes her lip with her thumb.

"Unless you swiped the key."

"No." She giggles. "I wasn't interested in anything in his pants."

"You seemed like it."

"That's how I wanted to seem."

"Why?"

Her eyes meet mine. "Where are we going?"

"You need Paramore and YA yet?"

"We can make music requests, can't we?" She motions to the intercom.

I press the button. "Hey. This is Griffin."

"James," the driver says.

"Can we request music?" I ask.
"Sure. What do you want?" he asks.
I name her favorite album.
He chuckles. "Where am I taking you?"
"You're good to stay out?" I ask.
She nods *hell yeah*.
I know just the place.

Chapter Eighteen

GRIFFIN

Jules's eyes go wide. "No."

"Yeah." My fingers brush her side. I'm not sure what the fuck I'm doing. Only that I need to keep doing it.

"We're not…" Her tongue slides over her lips. Her gaze shifts to the shop in front of us. "You are not buying me a sex toy."

"You owe me twenty bucks."

"It didn't happen yet."

"It will." I press my palm into the small of her back.

For a second, her eyelids flutter closed. Her expression shifts to something serene. Then she blinks and she's back to wide-eyed innocent.

Is she really that innocent?

I need to corrupt her.

I need to teach her everything.

No. I need to get ahold of myself. Even if that's a lost cause.

Without a word, I lead her into the shop.

It's a bright space the size of her hotel room and it's

packed with merchandise. Lingerie, wrapped DVDs, vibrators, dildos, pillows, whips, platform heels.

"Oh my God." Jules presses her palms into her thighs. "It's so…" Her gaze shifts to the back wall.

There's a sex toy on display. A vibrator.

No, it's more of a thruster. It's attached to a swing and it's thrusting forward and backward.

It's a toy that will actually fuck her.

Fuck, I want to see that.

I want to watch her eyes roll back in her head, hear a groan roll off her lips, feel her limbs shake.

I can't.

But I have to. We have to.

"That's… But… ow." She turns to me, her green eyes wide with wonder. "Don't even—"

"At least I'd know you've been fucked properly."

"Is that your line?" She moves forward, breaking our touch. "Do you slide up to women at bars and whisper, *baby, have you ever been fucked properly? 'Cause I'd like to prove you haven't.*"

"Am I that much of a tool?"

She holds up her thumb and forefinger *a little.*

I arch a brow *really?*

She tries to hold her poker face, but it cracks fast. She bursts into laughter. Pulls her hand over her stomach as she leans forward.

Her tits spill into her dress.

The white fabric slides down her chest. Shows off the top of her lacy beige bra.

Fuck, I've seen that bra on her floor a million times. It was a fact of nature, not the sexiest thing in the world.

Now—

I can't unsee it.

I can't unwant her.

I certainly can't stop imagining my name rolling off her lips.

This night is all about her coming hard and fast.

If this is what it takes—

If dragging her to the limo, pinning her to the seat, and—

No. This isn't some altruistic act.

It's not being a good friend.

It's my cock making very dirty demands.

"I don't need help masturbating, you know." She stops at the lingerie display. Eyes a scrap of black lace. "I, um, have a lot of practice."

"Me too."

Her eyes meet mine. Her cheeks flush. "Really?"

I hold her gaze. Try to figure out if she's asking me to speed up or slow down. I'm not sure, so I go with my gut. Not that is has much of a say at the moment. My cock is steering the show. "Yeah."

"But you're a slut."

"So?"

"Where do you find the… stamina?" Her blush spreads to her chest.

My balls tighten. I need to fuck her. I really do. But that's going to change everything. It could ruin everything. She could wake up tomorrow, realize she can't stay friends with me, disappear.

I can't lose her.

Whatever happens, I can't lose her.

"Griff?" She moves closer. Until she's close enough to whisper. "How often do you come?"

"On average?" My fingers brush her hip.

"Yeah." She shudders from my touch.

"A few times a day if I'm with someone. Once if I'm not."

"Every day?"

"Don't have time to fuck someone every day," I say.

"Only most days?"

I nod.

"And when you do… you go all night?" Her breath is heavy. Needy.

"Yeah." I brush her hair behind her ear.

"Oh." Her chest heaves with her inhale. "And you do? With the same woman?"

"Don't really want to talk about other women right now."

"Oh."

"Come on." I swallow the declaration that rises up in my throat. *I want to talk about you. About you coming on my face.* "Let's find you something."

"I'm looking at things."

"I owe you lingerie."

"From Victoria's Secret." She motions to the wall of porn behind us. "Not from a place with a wall of barely legal videos."

I can't help but chuckle. "If you want Victoria's Secret, we'll go to Victoria's Secret."

"I'm the one buying it."

My cock stirs. "So I'm there to observe?"

"Um… well… I mean… Um." She presses her lips together. "Do you like that?"

"Like what?"

"Lingerie?"

"Yeah." My fingers skim her hips. She's so warm and soft. That dress is paper thin, but I still need it gone. "But I prefer naked."

She nods.

"I want to feel every inch of my skin against someone's."

"With your one-night stands?"

"No." With her. Only with her.

"Oh. Are we—"

"I don't know."

"Okay. I… um… You are right. I need to be fucked." She sucks a breath through her teeth. "But that's a little much." She motions to the thrusting sex toy.

"I'm sure it has other speeds."

"It's more the power." Her blush deepens. "It's been a while. And, um, I think I'll need easing in."

Whatever you want, Jules. I don't care if it's soft, slow, hard, fast. So long as you're coming for me. "How do you normally like it?"

"Uh—"

"Hard?"

Her tongue slides over her lips.

"Or softer?"

"I don't know." She looks up at me, equal parts needy and nervous. "We… Um…" Her eyes bore into mine. They scream *what the fuck are we doing here*?

I don't have a good answer.

I want her. In every fucking way it's possible to want someone.

But not if she's going to regret it in the morning. Not if it's going to fuck everything up.

"How do you like it?" Her ass brushes my crotch as she moves past me. She rises to her tiptoes. Reaches for a sleek, modern vibrator sitting on the glass.

I try to stay present. To focus on the hitch of her breath, the flush of her cheeks, the arch of her back.

My cock steers my thoughts to dirtier places.

She grabs a toy. A bullet vibe the size of an egg.

"You ever use one?" I ask.

"No."

"You never wanted to?"

"I thought… I guess I always thought I should be able to do it."

I shake my head.

"Or that he—"

"I know you fucked your ex."

She stares at me, her green eyes on fire. "I don't want to talk about other guys."

My balls tighten.

I need to buy this now.

I need to drag her back to the limo.

I need to fuck her senseless.

"It's a tool, same as any other." I place my body behind hers. "Try it."

She turns the toy over. Pushes the *on* button. Gasps as the device buzzes against her palm. "Are they all this strong?"

"Like this." I take her fingertip and press it to the silicone.

Her eyelids flutter closed. Her brow furrows and relaxes. Her expression gets far away. Dreamy.

She's imagining it against her clit.

It pushes my thoughts straight to the gutter.

"That's… Fuck." Her eyes blink open. She hands the toy to me.

I test it the way she did. Try a higher speed. A lower one. Different pulsing.

I need to use this on her.

Now.

"You like this one?" I breathe.

She nods. "I, um…" She tries to find the words to explain this, but she doesn't.

I don't have them either.

I wrap my arms around her waist.

Her heart beats against my chest. Her breath warms my ear. Her fingers curl into my stomach.

The fabric of my shirt.

Then beneath it.

"I…" She looks up at me like she's going to kiss me. But she doesn't. "How soon can I try it?"

As soon as you take off your panties. "I need to rinse it off. Charge it."

She nods *sure.* Follows me to the line. Blushes through the checkout.

I lead her back to the limo.

The sky glows with every shade of neon. It's beautiful, in a weird way.

A perfect way.

The driver smiles as he opens the door. "I'll give you some privacy." He helps Jules into the car. "Just press the intercom when you know where you'd like to go."

I slide into the car.

She scoots to the corner. Wraps her fingers around the bottle of champagne. "Shit, I think I've lost my power."

"Yeah?"

She nods. Pours a glass of flat wine. "Tragic."

"Is it?" I take the seat next to hers.

"Yeah."

"You need something powerful between your legs?"

Her eyes find mine. "Exactly."

My fingers go to her hips.

Slowly, I pull her onto my lap.

She gasps as my hard on brushes her cunt. There's all this fabric in the way—her dress and panties, my slacks and boxers—but I can still feel her heat.

"Griff." Her hand knots in my hair. "Are we… Are you…"

"Yeah."

"For how long?"

"I don't know."

"Me either." Her palm cups my cheek. "I… You… We…"

"Come here." I bring my hand to the back of her head.

Her eyelids flutter closed.

Mine follow.

I pull her into a kiss.

It's soft. Slow. Sweet.

It's fucking magic.

Chapter Nineteen

GRIFFIN

Jules groans against my mouth.

She tugs at my hair. Digs her fingers into my shirt. Grinds her crotch against mine.

Fuck, she feels good.

I scrape my teeth against her bottom lip.

She groans a little louder.

It races through my head. *I'm kissing Jules. I'm kissing my best friend. I'm kissing the girl who thought I had cooties in fourth grade.*

She tastes so fucking good. Like champagne and like Jules.

My fingers dig into her hips. I pull her closer. Guide her pelvis over mine.

She pulls back to groan. "Fuck, Griff."

Those gorgeous green eyes are even prettier with heavy lids.

At the moment, it's so fucking obvious.

I need Jules.

I need her every way I can have her.

She groans as her clit grinds against my cock. That stupid fabric is in the way, but it's still bliss.

"Are we—" She tugs at my tie. "Are we doing this?"

"Take off your dress."

Her throat quivers as she swallows. "You first."

"This first." I peel her strap down her shoulder. The right. Then the left.

I trace the outline of her bra as slowly as I can manage. Over her breasts, her ribs, her back.

There.

I undo the clasp.

She does away with her bra.

She's topless in my lap.

She's exactly where she belongs.

The limo is like the club. Every surface is either red or reflective, or both.

I can see her back in the mirror. The soft curve. The lush ass. The heels falling off her feet.

And here she is, in front of me.

Dark curls falling over her green eyes. Pink lips parting with a sigh. Chest heaving with her inhale.

"Fuck." I cup her breast with my palm. "You're perfect."

Her eyes bore into mine. "Griff—"

"You are."

She shudders as I drag my thumb over her nipple.

"Your tits are gorgeous."

Her cheeks flush. Part arousal. Part honest embarrassment. "They're not too small?"

"Fuck no."

"I always thought—"

I take her nipple between my lips.

"Fuck." She tugs at my hair. "That's—"

"Perfect." I mumble into her skin. God dammit, she tastes good. And this is barely the beginning.

I need every inch of her skin.

I need her coming on my face.

But one thing at a time.

I flick my tongue against her nipple. Softly. Then harder.

Up and down.

Left and right.

Slow circles.

Zigzags.

Her groans bounce off the mirrored walls. Land in my ears.

"Fuck." She rocks her hips, rubbing her clit against my cock. "Griff."

"Yeah, baby?"

"Say that again?"

"Yeah, baby?"

"Fuck." She rocks harder. "You… I… I can't be quiet."

"Good."

"But." She motions to the screen behind us.

"He's heard it before."

"Still." Her gaze shifts to the intercom. She sighs as she climbs out of my lap, but she still moves to the button. "Could you play that music from before?"

"Of course, miss." The intercom turns off.

Jules's favorite album fills the car.

She climbs back into my lap. Stares down at me with that perfect mix of need and affection. "I know you hate—"

"No." I bring my hand to the back of her head. Pull her into a slow, deep kiss. "I fucking love it."

"Always?"

"Now." I wrap my lips around her bottom lip. Suck softly. Then harder.

She groans as I scrape my teeth against her flesh.

Her groans mix with the peppy melody, the singer's screech, the throbbing bass.

Fuck, this is my new favorite song.

My new favorite album.

My new favorite band.

I'm listening to it every day, all day, for the rest of my fucking life.

Jules rocks her hips, grinding against me.

My cock whines. It wants her soft skin. Her lush lips. Her sweet cunt.

It's a greedy motherfucker.

But then so am I.

I want her coming on my hand, my face, my cock. One right after the other. All fucking night.

Every night.

Forever.

For a second, my brain attempts to reason with me. This might change everything. It might ruin us. I might lose her.

But I have to take that risk.

I have to have her.

I drag my lips over her chin, down her neck, along her collarbone.

Jules groans as I take her nipple into my mouth. I suck softly. Then harder. Then hard enough she tugs at my hair.

"Griff." She grinds against me. "Don't stop."

Like hell.

I use that same speed, same pressure.

She rocks against me, moaning my name like it's a curse.

I tease her until I can't take her begging anymore, then I move to her other nipple, tease it just as mercilessly.

Her eyes close.

Her lips part with a sigh.

Her hips rock against mine.

Again and again—

Fuck.

That feels too fucking good.

I try to think of cold showers and Arctic temperatures and Angels players, but it doesn't work.

She's too fucking sexy.

I need her coming too fucking badly.

I need her coming now.

I release her nipple. "Take off your panties."

She nods as she lifts her ass. She reaches under her dress. Slides her nude bikinis down her hips. Below her knees.

"On your back." My fingers skim her hip. Her ass. "You need to come on my face."

Her eyes go wide. With desire. Then something else. "I... Um... I need to tell you something."

"Now?"

"I... Um..." Her hair falls over her eyes as she turns her head to her side. "Griff." The apprehension drops from her voice. "I need you inside me."

"You need to tell me that you need me inside you?"

"Yes." Her chest heaves with her inhale, but I can't tell if it's desire or something else. "I need you, Griff."

"Are you—"

"Please." Her fingers dig into my neck. "Fuck me. Please. I need to be fucked so fucking badly." Her hair swings to the other side as she turns her head.

Her eyes bore into mine.

They beg for something.

For everything.

She wants more than my cock inside her.

This is so much more than a fuck.

This is fucking everything.

"Griff," she breathes. "Please."

Fuck, the need in her voice—

"Come here." I pull a condom from my back pocket.

She rests her ass on my thighs. Fumbles over my belt. My button. My zipper. My boxers.

Her eyes go wide. "You—"

"Yeah."

She wraps her fingers around my cock.

My last conscious thought flies away.

Her hand feels so fucking good.

She drags her thumb over my tip. Then she wraps it around me. Strokes me up and down.

Fuck.

"God, Griff." Her breath is needy. Heavy. "You're that hard? For me?"

"Yeah."

"Have you—" She slides her hand over my cock. "Have you thought about me?"

"I try not to."

Her eyes meet mine for a moment. Then her gaze shifts downward. She watches herself work me. "What do you think about?"

"Everything."

"Me too." She shifts off my legs. Onto her knees. Her lips brush my chest. Stomach. Cock.

Fuck.

The pressure is feather soft, but that only makes it more intense.

She drags her lips around my tip. Slowly. Then faster. Harder.

Her lips close around me.

Jules takes me into her mouth.

Fuck, she looks good between my legs.

For a moment, my gaze shifts to the mirrors reflecting us.

I watch her take me deeper.

My cock disappears in her pretty mouth.

Her hair falls over her cheeks.

Her chest heaves with her inhale.

I reach down. Bring my hand to her chest. Toy with her nipple.

My touch is too hard, too aggressive.

But it only makes her groan.

And, fuck, that groan—

"I want to come inside you, baby." I tear the condom wrapper with my teeth. Tug at her hair. Pull her back up my body.

She climbs into my lap. "I want you everywhere."

Fuck. How is she so fucking good at this? It defies reason.

My sweet, innocent, bookworm best friend is a sex goddess. And she's about to fuck me senseless.

I roll the condom over my cock.

She wraps her hand around me. Holds me in place as she lowers her body onto mine.

My tip strains against her.

Then she envelopes me.

"Fuck." Her fingers dig into my shirt. "You're—"

"Yeah."

"I… fuck."

It's the only thing in my head. She feels so fucking good. Soft. Warm. Tight.

She's nervous.

I am too.

I'm inside my best friend. Jules. The woman who's been by my side since fourth grade.

Who's seen me through every ugly moment and every triumph.

Who wears my art like it's a badge of honor.

Who—

Fuck.

She groans as she takes me deeper. It's equal parts agony and ecstasy.

Then I take her nipple into my mouth, and the ecstasy takes over.

My fingers curl into her hips. Press the fabric of her dress into her skin.

I guide her body over mine. So she takes every inch slowly.

Then I do it again.

And again.

She rocks her hips forward, rubbing her clit against my pubic bone.

I groan against her chest. "I want to touch you, baby." I offer her my hand. "Show me."

Her nod is heavy. Her expression is bliss. Her groan is music.

She keeps one hand on my shoulder. Wraps the other around my wrist.

She takes my hand. Places it at her pelvis, my thumb against her clit.

Fuck, she feels good against my digit.

My gaze shifts to the mirror.

I watch as she takes me again and again.

As she grinds against my thumb.

She stares down at me for a moment, then she follows my gaze. Her cheeks flush as she catches her reflection.

Her breath quickens. Her gaze shifts. Her hair falls over her eyes.

I brush stray strands behind her ears. Watch as her eyelids press together. As pleasure spreads over her expression.

Her groans run together.

Her legs shake.

Her fingers dig into my skin.

Jules groans my name as she comes.

Her cunt pulses around me.

It pushes me right over the edge.

I groan her name into her chest.

She rocks me through my orgasm. Then she slows. Wraps her arms around me. Presses her lips to my ear. "That was really fucking—"

"Yeah."

"Can we do it again?"

"Yeah." I kiss her hard. "After our next stop."

Chapter Twenty

JULIETTE

Hayley Williams praises her husband (now ex-husband) as the limo slides to a stop.

My head doesn't go to the melody or the symbolism or the irony.

It goes to Griff's dark eyes.

They're no longer wracked with pleasure, but they're every bit as enticing.

Deep brown. Full of life. Wicked.

His expression screams *I'm going to fuck you until you beg me to stop*.

God, I want that.

I want him.

He's so handsome. And demanding. And surprising.

I mean, I always figured he'd be good in bed—he certainly has enough practice—but actually experiencing his talents?

My body is still buzzing. My heart is still singing. My head is still—

Well, it's making all these ridiculous suggestions. But I can't go there yet. I can't tell him yet.

I want to explain everything. About Jackson. And why I called it off. Why it was so fucked the last year. Why I broke my promise to Griff then hid it from him for way too long.

I will.

But not yet.

Right now, I believe in magic. In fairy tales. In perfect.

Tonight is magic. We must have a fairy godmother somewhere. Or a genie. I don't know. But I do know how this one goes.

When the clock strikes midnight, the magic fades. The coach turns into a pumpkin. The gorgeous gown disappears.

Sure, we're not literally living Cinderella. We have until sunup. But the idea is the same.

One perfect, magical night.

Then everything goes back to normal.

Or maybe it falls apart. I might lose him tomorrow. He might wake up and realize he made the biggest mistake of his life.

I can't worry about that now.

Right now—

Right now is really fucking good.

"Where you going, baby?" His voice drops to a low command.

It makes my sex clench. I need our bodies intertwined again. I need to soak up all the magic.

We're best friends. We can't keep doing this. We only have until the spell ends.

"Jules?" His fingers brush my forearm. My wrist. The scars covered with his design. "You okay?"

I stare into his dark eyes. They're filled with this perfect mix of enthusiasm and affection. He wants to show me the world. But he'll stop if that's what I need. He'll hold me if I want to cry. (And God knows I will want to cry if I keep downing tequila). "I am." Maybe I won't be okay tomorrow, but right now, I'm basking in the afterglow. The actual glow. Whatever I call it.

"You need something to drink?"

"Only if it comes in an oversized container shaped like—"

"A dick?" His eyes light up.

"Ideally. But anything phallic works."

His smile spreads over his cheeks. It screams *I love you. I know you. I need you. And most of all, I really, really want to fuck you*. "I'm about to make your dreams come true."

"Are you?"

He nods *hell yes* and motions to the door.

The driver—what the hell is his name?—pulls the door open and offers his hand. "You've arrived."

I slide out of the car on my own. "Thank you."

Griff follows. "We'll call when we're ready."

The driver nods *of course*, shuts the door, slips into the auto. He says nothing about our activities. I guess he is used to it.

"This phallic enough for you?" Griff motions to the sky.

We're at the base of an enormous tower. The Stratosphere Hotel. Its white legs crisscross the entrance. They build to a high base then jut into the sky.

The tower bulges at the head, umm, observation deck.

From here, it's hard to see the needle, but I know it's there. And, God, it's perfect.

"You're obsessed," I say.

"I'm obsessed?" His fingers brush my quads. Then higher. Higher—

I step backward, reflexively.

His expression gets dead serious. His eyes fix on me. They study me, looking for cracks.

No, it's not adversarial. He's concerned. He's caring. He's really fucking good at reading me.

I press my lips into a smile. "Not here."

He nods, accepting my answer. Mostly. His brow stays furrowed. "Come on." He wraps his arm around my waist. "Let's get to the air-conditioning."

"Yes." It is a million degrees out here, but that's not why I'm flushed.

I need to tell him.

Soon.

Really soon.

I try to find the words, but they're so bare, so honest. I can't strip myself naked. Not yet.

Griffin, I still remember that night in eleventh grade. You fell asleep in my bed. When I came back from the shower, I changed into my tank top, and my hoodie, fell asleep next to you. But I got too hot. Tossed the sweater aside.

When you woke up, you saw the scars.

You were scared. And angry. Your eyes filled with something I'd never seen before. Disappointment.

That felt worse than anything. It hurt more than anything.

I never told you, but it drove me right back to my razor.

It wasn't about you. It wasn't about your need to know my secrets or my ability to trust you. I did trust you. I still do.

That's not why I keep this to myself. It's about me, Griff. It's mine.

It's hard to explain, the way shame grips my core. I don't have a good reason for cutting. It's not like I'm suffering from an abusive family or even one that expects perfection. My parents love me. You love me. You can't say it, but I know you do.

It's just, my head is a mess. And sometimes it's so overwhelming. I feel like I'm going to burst. And that's the only way I can fix it.

I guess I should have told you that. But you seemed so scared, so wounded, so judgmental. I couldn't take that.

I know you figured it out. Realized it wasn't about you. Apologized.

That night when you came to me, arms open, design in hand, and you whispered, "I'm sorry, Jules. I'm such a fucking idiot. Forgive me?" And you promised you'd always be there. It was perfect.

Until you asked me to promise I'd never cut again.

I tried, I did. But I couldn't.

It's still the only thing that helps calm the storm inside me.

God, that sounds lame. And cliché. It's just, I don't have a good explanation. I do it because it's the only thing that helps.

Every time I pick up a blade or catch a glimpse of a scar, I think about that promise.

And that shame sinks deeper into my bones.

I know you didn't mean for that to happen. I know you were only trying to help. You did… until you didn't.

That's why I started dating Jackson. Because he didn't know. Because he didn't expect anything of me. Because he didn't care when he saw my scars. He believed my excuses. And never pried deeper.

I wanted it to be you.

Deep down, I wanted it to be you.

I didn't realize it then. Didn't put two and two together to make four. But it's obvious now. Even in my drunken haze. Or maybe because of my drunken haze.

I tried to stop so many times, but I couldn't.

And that's why I couldn't have you.

That's why I can't have you. Because once I tell you, the magic fades, and we go back to normal.

I can't lose that magic. Not yet.

"You sure you're okay?" He leads me into the casino.

I nod. "Just, um, thirsty."

"You want water or a drink?"

"Water."

He nods *sure*, heads to the bar on our right, buys two bottles of water.

The moment with my thoughts is too much. I try to divert my attention away from my head. To my surroundings.

The casino glows with yellow light and flashing slot machines. There's no music, certainly nothing as awesome as Paramore, certainly nothing as sexy as Griffin's groan—

Uh, what am I talking about again?

Right. The casino. It's buzzing with laughter, conversation, clinking drinks, and the *beep-boop* of slot machines.

Griff returns. Hands a water bottle to me.

I push my thoughts to dirty places. "We're here because of the phallic implications of the tower?"

He nods *hell yeah*.

"Does that mean we're heading to the top?"

"Something you'd rather do?"

No. Nothing. But then I don't care what I do so long as I can do him. Fuck, that's cheesy. But it's true.

Tonight is ours. For laughing, kissing, touching, fucking.

Reality crashes into us tomorrow.

I tell him tomorrow.

I face the consequences tomorrow.

Right now—

"Kiss me." I turn to him. Wrap my arms around his waist. Rise to my tiptoes.

He sucks on my bottom lip with just the right pressure. Then it's the soft scrape of his teeth. Something harder. Something that demands every ounce of my attention.

His fingers dig into my ass.

He pulls me closer. Until I can feel his hard-on against my stomach.

Fuck, he feels good. And that—

I don't care what anyone says. There's nothing better

than a hard cock. Feeling the evidence of a partner's desire—

It's so fucking hot.

I want him in my mouth again.

I want him coming on my lips, my back, my tits.

I don't care, as long as it's mine.

Some pervert took over my brain. But then I don't care about that either. Not when it feels this good.

"You want to do that?" He scrapes his teeth against my ear.

I nod.

He takes my hand. Brings it to his crotch. No, to his pocket.

There's something hard.

Oh. The bullet vibrator.

He looks down at me with a wicked smile. "I have plans for you, Jules."

My sex clenches.

"And?"

"You want to go to the top first or you want it in your mouth?"

My tongue slides over my lips. Hell yes. I want him in my mouth. He tastes so fucking good. And there's something about knowing it's Griff in my mouth. About knowing I'm the reason he's rock hard.

It's not like it was with Jackson.

It's awesome.

God, I must be drunk. I'm usually more articulate. I have an English degree. And a computer full of unpublished short stories. And one half of a very shitty novel I started in high school.

It's about a girl falling in love with her best friend. She doesn't cut, but she has her own secret, and he's just as determined to save her.

I stopped writing it when I started dating Jackson.

At the time, I didn't think anything of it, but now—

God, I must be the most oblivious person on the planet.

"Baby, if you keep drifting off I'm going to have to punish you."

Yes. Hell yes. His voice is so fucking hot like this.

His smile is devious. It screams *I'm going to tease you until you can't take it anymore.*

His fingers curl into my ass as he pulls me closer.

His hard-on digs into my stomach.

There are only three layers of fabric in the way.

He brings his lips to my ear. "Where do you want it, baby?" He brings his thumb to my lips. "In that gorgeous mouth?"

I nod against his hand.

"Or in that sweet cunt?" He drags his fingers over the flesh of my ass, pressing my dress into my skin. "Or maybe in that lush ass?"

My sex clenches. "I've never."

"You want to?"

"Yeah. But not tonight." My brain tries to step in, to remind myself that tonight is it, but my body pushes those concerns aside.

"You're good with that pretty mouth." He sucks on my earlobe.

My cheeks flush. "Thank you." It's weird, taking that compliment. No one's ever told me I was skilled in that way. I mean, it's only been Jackson, and he certainly requested that act a lot, but he never made me feel skilled.

"But I'm not letting you put those lips around my cock yet."

My sigh is a whine. God, how can he make that so hot?

"Not until I get this against your clit." He presses my palm against the toy. "Understand?"

My nod is heavy. Needy.

I'm impossibly turned on.

I'm about to burst. Or at least demand we check into a hotel room here and fuck until dawn.

But I don't.

I follow him to the elevator for the observation tower.

One way or another, we're doing this at the top.

Chapter Twenty-One

JULIETTE

I press my palms into the railing and peer over the edge. The bottom floor of the deck is below us. And beneath that—fuck, that's a sharp drop.

"Careful." Griffin slides his arms around my waist.

"Careful?" It's good advice, but I can't follow it. Caution will serve me well tomorrow. Tonight—

I need every ounce of tonight.

"Yeah." He holds my body against his. "You can't die before I've had my way with you."

"What do you call what happened in the limo?"

He brings his lips to my ear. "Pretty sure you had your way with me."

My cheeks flush.

"You always that demanding?"

I shake my head. I have no idea where this sexy, dirty Jules came from, but I really fucking like her. "If you want me to watch my step, you probably shouldn't press your cock into my ass."

"You want me to stop?"

"No." I want him to go. I want him to fuck me here.

He pulls me backward. Wraps his arm around me. Leads me around the deck.

Las Vegas Boulevard glows against the dark sky. Neon, glass, steel. Everything shines in the moonlight.

Sin City is beautiful. It's a fantastical place where anything is possible.

"Let me guess." Griffin nips at my ear. "The Paris is your favorite hotel."

"Is it?"

"Yeah." He bites a little harder. Hard enough it hurts in the best possible way. "It's the tallest."

"Isn't this one the tallest?"

"So it's all size with you?"

"I don't know." I arch my back, to rub my ass against his crotch. He's still hard, and it still feels so fucking good. "I'll have to give the equipment another test drive."

His chuckle is low and hearty.

"Unless you'd rather not."

"Unless I'd rather not fuck you?"

I nod.

He wraps his lips around my earlobe. Sucks softly. "You're out of your fucking mind."

Yeah, I am.

I really am.

But it feels good.

I close my eyes. Arch my back to rub my ass against him.

He holds me close. Toys with my ear, neck, shoulders. He winds me so fucking tight, then he steps back, takes my hand, and leads me around the observation deck.

The big, silver moon casts a soft glow over the sprawling suburbs and the desert beyond it. It's serene beauty. The opposite of busy, bright Las Vegas Boulevard.

"Which do you like better?" He brushes my hair behind my ear. "The city or the desert?"

"Why do I have to choose?"

"'Cause you want to go to that MFA program in Iowa."

"I missed the deadline."

"Next year." His teeth scrape my neck.

Next year is way past tomorrow. Which means it's not a subject of conversation. Not tonight. "UCLA has a good program."

"But it's not a great program."

"Griff—"

"Yeah?"

"Can we not? Please?" I turn so we're face-to-face. God, he has such gorgeous eyes. They're so dark and full of life. "Not tonight."

He cups the back of my head with his palm. "Why not?"

"It's magic. Tomorrow… I don't know what happens tomorrow. Fuck, Griff, three days ago, I thought I was getting married tomorrow."

"You thought that up until the moment it ended?"

"I don't know." I press my forehead to his chin. "I just… I need tonight to stay magic. I need to kiss you and touch you and fuck you and not worry about the consequences."

"What if I want a tomorrow?"

"Then we discuss it tomorrow." I tilt my head upward, so I can make eye contact. "Can we do that?"

"Live tonight like there's no tomorrow?"

"Exactly."

He presses his lips to mine. Softly, then harder. His lips close around my bottom lip. Then it's the gentle scrape of his teeth.

Fuck, he's a good kisser.

He pulls back with a sigh. "Okay, but you need to know something, Jules—"

"Yeah?"

"I want every fucking tomorrow."

My chest warms. It's not quite a blush and not quite affection. Both. Or maybe something in between. "I—"

"You want the very best of this tower, right?"

A laugh spills from my lips. "Right."

"This way." He leads me to the stairs. The small, curving flight that takes us to the very peak of the tower.

No, that isn't accurate.

The slingshot ride in the middle of the platform is the peak.

It shoots half a dozen thrill seekers up its tracks. They scream as they reach the top, glide back to the bottom, shoot up to the top again and again.

Fuck, that's really high. And really terrifying.

It's been a long, long time since I've been on a roller coaster.

Griffin squeezes my palm. "You can say no."

Yeah, but I don't want to. Tonight is a new Jules. A brave, sexy, dirty Jules who says yes to possibilities.

Okay, maybe that's an overreach, but I still want to do this with him.

My heart thuds against my chest. My stomach flutters. My limbs get airy. I'm light enough to float off the tower. To float all the way into the stratosphere.

Oh, that's why it's called The Stratosphere.

Duh.

I squeeze his hand.

Nerves rush through my veins as we watch the thrill seekers depart the ride. The attendant turns to us. Motions to the empty line.

"You two ready?" His voice is flat, unaffected. "We're closing in twenty minutes. It's now or never."

Now or never.

Like tonight.

I can do now.

I can.

I suck a breath through my teeth. Push an exhale through my nose. Sure, the ride shoots me another hundred feet in the air.

In theory, it's possible for the car to go right off the track. To shoot into space and crash into the ground.

But it's been here for years.

It's safe.

It's a lot safer than handing Griffin my heart.

I open my mouth to say yes, but the words don't get out.

Griff leans in to whisper. "Are you ready?"

I just barely manage a nod.

He smiles and those butterflies in my stomach crash together. I'm not sure which makes me more nervous—the thought of this being forever or the slingshot ride.

They're terrifying in different ways.

They're really fucking scary.

He interlocks his fingers with mine as he leads me to the gate.

The attendant pulls it back. Motions *after you.*

We cross the concrete to the ride.

Griff helps me into a seat. Takes the one next to me.

The attendant shrugs. "Guess we're good to go with you two." He pulls the harness style bar over my chest and clicks the belt. "You feel secure?"

Not even close. "Yeah."

He does the same with Griff. "And you, sir?"

"Yeah. I do." Griff offers me his hand.

I take it. Squeeze.

The guy nods sure. He recites a safety speech, then moves back to his control panel, and hits the button.

Whoosh.

We shoot up, up, up.

The city comes into view. Every inch of neon, glass, steel, concrete.

Griff squeezes my hand.

I scream.

Then he screams.

We hit the top, glide to the bottom, hurl toward the top again.

Nervous energy races through my veins. Every part of my body is buzzing. The third climb sends me into overdrive.

Nothing—not screaming or holding Griff's hands or getting my feet on the ground—brings me back to Earth.

"Not too bad, huh?" The attendant helps me out of my seat.

I think I nod, but, honestly I'm not sure.

He unhooks Griff. "The last elevator down is in twenty minutes." He surveys the patio beneath us. "Looks like you're the last guests."

Griff whispers something in his ear.

The attendant nods. "Yeah, you should have a little privacy on the observation deck." He smiles. "But you only have fifteen minutes to get the job done."

Griff shoots me a devious smile. "I can work with that."

Chapter Twenty-Two

JULIETTE

Griff slides his arm around my waist. Brings his lips to my ear. "You want to do this here or inside?"

Inside makes more sense—it's a million degrees—but there's something about being this close to the city. It feels like I can reach out and touch every casino on The Strip.

Of course, I'd have to start with The Paris. For obvious reasons.

I'm not sure where the joke ends and the truth beings.

Only that I want to touch Griff.

That I want him to touch me.

But that…

It's way too loaded. It's not something that belongs in a perfect, easy night. There's nothing perfect or easy about the scars on my thighs.

They're out of the way enough he might not notice. I was smart enough to focus on my quads and hips. To cut high enough I can still wear stylish shorts.

That I can still…

Fuck an oblivious guy, I guess.

He might not notice.

But if he does…

I can't stomach that.

"Jules." His fingers skim my chin. "You okay?"

"Yeah." I press my lips together. I can be okay. I just need to stop thinking about this. I need to stop drinking. Or drink more. One of the two.

"What are you thinking?"

"I want you to touch me." *But I'm terrified you'll feel my scars. That you'll run away like you did that day in eleventh grade. That you'll hate me for breaking our promise.*

"You're tense 'cause you want me to touch you?"

"We're a thousand feet in the air, surrounded by a dozen employees, with a fifteen minute clock."

His chuckle is low and hearty. "That's not a turn on?"

"It is. It's just also…"

"We don't have to do this here."

"But…"

"We can go back to the limo."

It's darker in the limo. But there are also mirrors everywhere. And Griff likes to watch. Which is incredibly hot. Fuck, the thought of watching his cock drive into me again and again—

My sex clenches.

"Jules?" He drags his fingertips down my neck. "You want to stay here or you want to go?"

Both. Neither. Everything. I want to be normal. For one night. I want to forget Jackson and the years of avoiding sex and the general disrepair of my life.

"Need to do this now if we're going to do it." His fingers skim my collarbone. "Or we can leave. Do it somewhere else."

No, that isn't normal. I mean, it's not exactly normal getting off at a Las Vegas attraction. But it's certainly not normal avoiding sex because of cutting scars. "I can't wait."

He presses his lips into my neck. "You sure?"

"Yes." I want this. Really badly. I just have to… I have to guide his hands. Which is hot anyway. And I… Maybe he won't notice. He didn't notice before.

"Then take off your panties." His voice drops to something low and demanding.

My knees knock together. He's so fucking sexy like this. He makes it easy to forget.

That's what I want.

One night of freedom.

One night without all the shit weighing me down.

Is that really too much to ask?

I arch my back, pushing my ass into his crotch.

He lets out a low, deep groan.

I reach under my dress. Push my panties to my thighs. They stick on my legs, binding them. Which is really fucking hot.

But also drawing more attention to my thighs.

And I…

No.

I'm not thinking about this.

I'm fucking my best friend in view of the entire city.

That's the risk here.

Not the scars on my skin.

This is… It's really fucking hot.

"Fuck, Jules." He pulls something from his pocket. "You're gonna kill me."

"Yeah?"

He nods into my shoulder. "You're too fucking sexy."

The compliment makes me blush. I close my eyes. Let the praise spread to my chest, stomach, limbs.

I'm here. In this moment. Not worrying about yesterday or tomorrow or anything except coming.

And making Griff come.

I really need to make him come again.

"Speak for yourself." I rub my ass against his hard-on. Fuck, that feels good. It's primal. I need his desire. His need. His passion.

All right, I need his cock.

It's not poetic, but it's true.

"Fuck me." I rub my flesh against him.

He groans into my ear. "Not until you come."

I swallow hard. I can do this. I can forget.

He shifts his hips backward. Pulls the toy from his pocket. Turns it on.

The steady buzz fills my ears.

"Have you ever?" He shifts his hips, pressing his crotch into my ass.

"No." I arch my back to meet him. Fuck, his cock feels so good against my flesh. There's all this fabric in the way, but I can still soak up his warmth and hardness.

"Let me know if it's too much." He brings the toy to my inner thigh. Presses it against my skin.

The buzz is intense.

And his hand is so, so close to my scars.

But his fingertips aren't brushing my skin.

The toy is.

I can forget.

I swear I can.

"Keep going." I rub my ass against him.

He wraps his arm around my waist. Holds my body against his.

Slowly, he drags the device up my inner thigh. Closer and closer and—

Fuck.

That's intense.

My eyelids press together.

My fingers dig into the railing.

My teeth sink into my lip.

"Too much?" He nips at my ear.

I shake my head.

"You want more?"

"No. Just…" My breath hitches in my throat. The vibration is intense. Almost too much to take. "Higher."

"Show me." His voice is a command.

Which is so fucking hot.

And so fucking perfect.

Jackson wanted to figure everything out himself. If I tried to give him feedback, he got mad. Or moody. Or passive aggressive.

Griff wants to make me come.

And he's not shy about demanding I show him how to do it.

If I guide his hand—

No, I'm not thinking about this. Tonight is easy. Fun. Free.

No more worrying about my scars. Or tomorrow. Or anything.

Griffin is making me come.

That's what matters.

Not anything else.

I place my hand over his. Guide the toy a little higher. To the right. There—

"Fuck." I press my palm into the railing. It just barely steadies me. This is so fucking intense. And I still want more.

I want his cock inside me.

I want him groaning my name.

I want everything.

Griff scrapes his teeth against my ear. "I love the way you moan." He rocks his hips, pressing his hard-on against my ass. "It's so fucking sexy."

My response is a groan.

"You're driving me out of my fucking mind," he murmurs into my neck.

I rub my ass against him. Guide his hand into place.

The vibration is intense. A lot more intense than my hand. It's not better, exactly, but it's stronger.

He drags his hand up my stomach, between my breasts, over the neckline of my dress.

He pushes the dress aside. Then my bra cup.

My breast spills from the lingerie.

I'm on display for the entire city.

It's so fucking hot.

He's so fucking hot.

I close my eyes. Press my neck into his lips. Push my chest against his hand.

He draws circles around my nipple with his thumb. Lightly. Then harder and harder and—

"Don't stop." I grind my ass against his cock.

He groans into my neck.

I guide his hand into place.

He winds me tighter and tighter.

It's intense. Almost too much to take. But I still need more. I need everything.

He sucks on my skin as he winds me tighter.

Bit by bit, my thoughts slip away. I forget about tomorrow and Jackson and my scarred thighs and all those nights when I considered telling Griff.

I surrender to the bliss overtaking my body.

To his deep groans and his soft lips and his skilled hands.

He plays with my breasts.

He holds the toy against my clit.

I rock against it.

Fuck, it's intense.

"Griff." I squeeze the railing.

He scrapes his teeth against my neck.

He winds me tighter and tighter.

Almost.

"Come for me, baby," he breathes. The tension in my sex winds tighter and tighter. So tight I can't take it.

Then tighter.

Almost—

There.

My world goes white as I come.

It's perfect, pure, blinding pleasure.

His body and mine and every bit of trust and need in the world.

My sex pulses, sending bliss through my pelvis, stomach, limbs.

I groan his name as I come.

He works me through my orgasm. Then he turns the toy off and slips it in his pocket. "That's the best thing I've ever heard."

My response is a messy collection of vowels.

"We have to go." He helps me into my dress. Then my panties. "But I'm not even close to done with you."

Chapter Twenty-Three

JULIETTE

"Perfect." I wrap my hand around the massive plastic container. It's over a foot tall and shaped like a… like The Stratosphere Hotel.

"Not till you get your lips around it." Griff takes his credit card from the bartender.

Said bartender shoots us a curious look, but he doesn't say anything.

Maybe it's weird ordering a gallon of alcohol this late at night.

But this is Vegas.

Drunk fools are par for the course.

"Does he have an attitude?" I whisper to Griff.

Griff's eyes flit to the bartender. "Yeah."

"I knew it."

"He wants to be that souvenir cup." His fingers brush mine.

I am holding the cup like it's a dick. But that's the only way to hold a cup with this girth. "He's not looking at me like that."

"Maybe I'm mixing things up." He leans in close

enough to whisper. "Maybe I'm the one that wants to be that cup."

My cheeks flush.

"Or that straw."

Fuck, it's impossible to wrap my lips around said straw. It's a thick plastic thing. Not nearly as thick as, ahem… It's really more like a finger. As thick as a finger. I mean… fuck.

"I love it when you blush."

My blush deepens.

"I always have."

"I know."

"Remember that day in elementary school where I pulled you hair?"

I nod.

"I wanted a reaction from you. Any reaction." His eyes bore into mine. "I wanted all your attention."

"You had it."

"Do I still?"

"You've had it for a long time."

He nips at my ear. "I still want to pull you hair."

Fuck.

"You like that?"

My nod is heavy. Needy. I came twenty minutes ago, but I still need to come again.

I need him.

I need him so fucking badly.

His fingers brush my neck. "You gonna drink that, baby?"

"You want some?"

"I'd rather watch you drink it."

"'Cause it's—"

"Yeah."

I swallow hard. Okay, I can sip my slush of—I'm not

sure what the hell this is, actually. Does it matter when it's mostly ice and sugar?

My eyes find Griff's.

I wrap my lips around the straw. Suck a sip into my mouth. Swallow hard.

My blush spreads to my chest.

God, the desire in his eyes. It makes me nervous and fluttery. I want to watch him watch all night.

"This is it." His fingers brush mine. "The most dick you can get."

I motion to his crotch. "And that?"

"Hmm… Might be able to help you out."

"You might?"

He nods. "If you ask nicely."

"What if I beg?"

His pupils dilate.

"What if I get on my knees"—I lean closer, so he has a perfect view of my boobs, and I rest my hand on his thigh—"and beg you to come on my chest?"

He swallows hard.

Fuck, it feels good having him under my thumb.

"Where did you learn to talk like this?" His fingertips skim my collarbone.

My sex clenches. "I don't know." I take another sip of my slush. Lime. Tequila. Sugar. More sugar. "Maybe all those stories."

"You never want to hear them."

"You still tell me," I say.

"'Cause I want to make you blush."

"You do."

"I think"—He leans down to press his lips to my collarbone—"I always wanted to turn you on."

"Yeah?" I lean into his kiss. It feels good. Too good. I'm ready to strip right here in the hotel lounge.

"Didn't realize it. Not consciously. But, fuck, I think I've wanted you for a long time."

"Me too." I take another sip then offer him the straw.

He takes a long sip. Swallows hard.

"I, um, Jackson said that was part of why he… why we…" God, I don't want to face this. I want it to disappear. But it won't. I know what happens when I run from my feelings. I have the scars to prove it.

But knowing it doesn't work doesn't make it any easier.

There has to be a reason why this didn't happen sooner.

He always knows what he wants.

He always tells me what he wants.

If he really wanted me all this time—

"He cheated on me." I push the words from my lips. They're messy. And ugly. But I need to tell someone. "I didn't know. I didn't have any idea. Until I found this extra lingerie in my dresser. When I asked him about it, he confessed. He wanted to tell me. He wanted out."

"You didn't?"

"I don't know. I was thinking about that, honestly. It didn't occur to me that we were supposed to get married. I mean, it did. But I didn't go wanting to call it off. I just wanted to know the truth."

"Do you?"

"Kind of. I mean, he told me what happened. But I… I don't know why it happened." I swallow another sip of lime slush. "He blamed you."

"He's the one who stuck his dick in someone else."

"No. I… I think he was right. He thought I was in love with you. I mean, I don't know if it's that… I—"

"I know what you mean."

"He said there was always something missing." My cheeks flame, but it's not desire. It's the shame I know so well. "That he could tell I was never all in. But he didn't realize it until he found someone who was."

Griff nods with understanding.

"And I… he was right, Griff. I wasn't all in. The only reason I stayed with him… it was because I didn't have to be all in. I mean, seriously, who gets married at twenty-two? In Southern California?"

He chuckles. "Figured you were pregnant."

"Really?"

He nods *yeah*.

"You don't think I'd tell you?"

"What else could it be?"

That's a good point. "I… He thought it would be better for his career."

Griff nods. Jackson is older. He was in college when we started dating. Now, he's done with his MBA and ready for the working world. He's supposed to have a wife.

But… I guess it will be someone else.

I didn't want to be married at twenty-two.

But when he asked… it felt inevitable. I wasn't going to do better. I needed to say yes. To get it over with. To numb the part of me that cared about romance and magic and fairy tales.

Right now, I believe. I want to believe. I really do.

It's just…

Tequila and confessions never mix well.

I reach for a change of subject. "We never had good sex. He tried. But he would get frustrated. And I'd feel awkward. I wasn't always present. I guess we didn't connect that way." It was good at first. Not great, but satisfactory. "Honestly, when I first found the lingerie, I was happy. I thought it was for me. That he finally wanted to fix what was… not broken, I guess. But not whole either."

"He didn't make you come?"

"Sometimes." When we first started dating, he didn't care about the scars. But the first time he found a fresh one, he went limp on the spot. He looked at me like I was broken. Said he wasn't in the mood anymore. I was so embarrassed and hurt… I didn't try again.

He didn't try again.

We had sex a dozen times over the last two years.

Less even.

And only from positions where he wouldn't see.

He certainly never put his hands or his face between my legs. Not after that.

"I didn't… it's hard to explain to someone who's never been in a relationship." I try to find all the honesty I can. "I did love him. And we were building this life together. We had all this history. I… I really did love him."

"I know."

"I thought I was all in. Well, as in as I could be. I was the same as him. I didn't realize it could be more." I hug my drink to my chest. "I didn't think… I could never talk to him the way I talk to you."

His eyes bore into mine. "You gave him everything you could."

No, I didn't. I can see that now. See how much my heart has been with Griff. But I can't say that. Not yet. "I thought I did."

"What else can you do?"

"I…"

"He's the one who fucked someone else." He squeezes my hand. "You can't take the blame for that."

"But—"

"No, Jules. I know you. I know how you handle everyone else's mistakes. They're not your fault."

"But—"

"Maybe you made mistakes. But he's the one who couldn't keep his pants zipped."

"But—"

"Did you fuck someone else?" he asks.

"No." But isn't this worse? If I really have been in love with Griffin all this time? That's worse than sex.

Not that I'm in love with him.

I mean, maybe I am.

It's confusing.

And the tequila isn't helping.

"Maybe you could have asked for more," Griff says. "But he could have offered too. He could have climbed between your legs and licked you until you were screaming his name."

"Well…"

"Fuck, I need you coming on my face."

My blush deepens.

"I know this isn't the fucking conversation, but I do." He stares into my eyes. "You're so fucking sexy. And knowing it's you—I want to make you come all day, forever."

"Thank you." It's all I can think to say.

"He's a fucking idiot. He didn't deserve you. He really didn't."

"I was going to marry him."

"Even after you found out?"

"I don't know. Maybe. Probably." My gaze shifts to the elevator. Two newlyweds stumble onto the carpet. They're drunk on love. And maybe a little on champagne too.

He wraps his arms around her and spins her.

Her dress twirls.

It's beautiful, but it makes me want to throw up.

"I thought… I thought I couldn't do better." My gaze

stays on the happy couple. "I just… I didn't think anyone would accept me."

"Jules?" Concern drips into his voice. He has no idea what I'm talking about. Or maybe he does.

He knows.

He and Jackson are the only people who know.

Neither handled it well, not at first.

Griff tries. He does. But he doesn't know.

If he freaks again…

"You're the smartest person I know, Jules, but you can be a fucking idiot," Griff says.

"What?"

He follows my gaze to the happy couple. "Yeah, you're messy. You have terrible taste in music. And you wear way too much royal blue. But you're also passionate, and sweet, and caring, and honest, and beautiful. You're so fucking beautiful. I know that's not what matters, but it has to be said." He brings his hand to my chin. Turns my head so we're eye to eye.

God, he has such pretty eyes.

"You throw yourself into what you love. And when you find something, you get this look in your eyes. You laugh with your entire body. You love with your soul. Even when it's some shitty YA series."

"I don't read shitty series."

"You can admit you liked *Twilight*."

"I didn't love it." I clear my throat. "I only love excellent stuff."

He chuckles. "All right. You love excellent YA series with your soul."

"Thank you."

Griff smiles that *you're ridiculous* smile. "Any guy in his right mind would be lucky to marry you."

"Griff—"

"This is our night, right?"

"Yeah."

"One perfect night in Vegas?"

Exactly. I nod.

He reaches into his back pocket. Pulls out something. "We're missing one part of the Vegas experience."

"What?"

He unfurls his palm to reveal an engagement ring.

"Griff—"

"Marry me, Jules." He drops onto one knee. "I don't want this to end when we wake up. I want you forever."

"But—" Fuck, that ring is massive. And familiar.

Oh.

It's his mom's engagement ring.

The one she left when she bailed on his family.

The one that fucked up his head.

I…

Fuck.

"We're drunk." It seems like a salient point.

"Yeah, but I know how I feel."

"How do you know?"

"I just do."

"I was engaged three days ago."

"Yeah."

"Did you know then?"

He shakes his head.

"In three days, you've figured out you want to spend the rest of your life with me?"

"Always wanted to spend my life with you. Just didn't picture it like this."

"Griff—"

"If you change your mind tomorrow, we can get an annulment."

"That…" Seems like a bad starting point for a

marriage. Kind of like looking up tattoo removal before you commit to the needle.

"I want to do this tonight." His dark eyes bore into mine. "I want to marry you."

"Uh…" What the fuck? "What if you change your mind?"

He holds up the ring. "I won't."

"But—"

"You were right. Tonight is magic. Let's make the most of it."

"But we—"

"No, buts, baby. It's a simple question. Yes or no." He takes my hand with his. "Do you want to marry me?"

Chapter Twenty-Four

GRIFFIN

"Okay." Jules's green eyes fill with joy. "Let's do it."

"Yeah?"

She nods. "Yeah." Her lips curl into a shy smile. "I, uh… this is insane."

"I know." I hold up the ring.

She offers me her left hand.

I slide the massive rock onto her ring finger.

It's weird, seeing it on her hand. For years, that ring has been a symbol of everything wrong with my family.

With love.

Hell, I brought it here as a visual aide. To help me explain that marriage is bullshit. So I could say *look at this ring. It single-handedly ruined my mom's life. You think she would have stayed with my dad after his first affair if this wasn't on her finger?*

Fuck no. She would have left, found someone else, enjoyed her life.

Instead, she committed to him, let him treat her like shit and sleep with every woman who crossed his path. She took it until she couldn't take it anymore, then she bailed, and left this on my desk.

Probably to warn me not to get married.

Marriage is bullshit.

I still believe that. Mostly.

But I also want to marry Jules.

I can't explain it. I certainly can't reconcile the beliefs. Marriage is a bullshit trap and I'm desperate to marry my best friend.

Right now.

"Where are we doing this?" She stares at the ring. "Has it always been this huge?"

"Only if you play with it."

Her smile spreads a little wider. "Is that how you want to remember this moment?"

I nod to her half-full souvenir cup. "The two of us, surrounded by phallic imagery."

"Unable to discuss anything else."

"Have plenty I'd like to discuss."

"Yeah?" Her eyes meet mine. They fill with earnest vulnerability.

Fuck, I love this side of her. I don't get to see it much. Jules always has her guard up. Even with me.

But when she lets it down—

It's beautiful.

Not because her green eyes are gorgeous. Or because those curls frame her face perfectly. Or because her ass is—

Shit, I'm getting distracted.

I want to fuck her, yeah, but that's not what I appreciate.

It's the way she looks at me like I'm worth her trust.

She doesn't give out trust easily.

Knowing she's giving it to me?

That's everything.

"Griff?" Her fingers skim my chin. My neck. My shirt. "You there?"

"Thinking about you coming on my face."

Her eyes fill with fear.

But that doesn't make any sense.

Jules swallows hard. "I, um… it's getting late. We probably need to do this now."

"You don't like it?"

"What?"

"Oral?"

"No, I, do… I just… remember that thing about today being magic?" she asks.

"Yeah."

"That conversation isn't magic. Can we have it tomorrow?"

"Is it important?" I ask.

She chews on her bottom lip. "Yeah. But it can wait."

"You promise?"

She offers me her hand. "I do."

I take it. "Good practice."

A laugh falls from her lips. "That's cheesy."

"You liked it."

"Maybe."

"Definitely."

She shakes her head, but it's written all over her face. She loves it.

Jules fishes her cell from her purse. She unlocks it. Taps the screen a few times. "Is it tacky getting married in a drive-through?"

"Yeah, but the bigger issue is our lack of a car."

"The party bus?"

"Doubt it's still ours."

"It might be." Her eyes fix on mine. "But I have something better than a drive-through."

"Yeah?"

"Yeah." She nods. "I do need a car. So we better hope

those assholes are too sloshed to notice their limo is missing."

"You feeling lucky?"

"Yeah. I am. I really am."

Chapter Twenty-Five

GRIFFIN

Thankfully, the assholes are completely unaware they're missing their limo.

Jules refuses to tell me where we're going. She directs James to our hotel and instructs him to wait. (We can't wear the same outfits we wore for a lap dance for our wedding, apparently).

We grab our clothes, pick up paperwork at city hall (minutes before closing), head straight to a tiny chapel way down the strip.

It's surprisingly classy. Like an actual church where Elvis gives sermons.

The King marries a couple in matching Joy Division t-shirts.

I nudge Jules. "That could have been our outfit."

She smiles that *I hate you* smile. "So original. How do you do it?"

"I think of what would get the biggest reaction."

"Oh yeah?"

I nod *hell yeah*.

"That's been our entire relationship, huh?"

"Yeah."

"You're always trying to make me blush."

I nod. It feels good teasing her, but there's so much more I want to say. Ever since that day in elementary school I saw that bitch Sandra mocking Jules for reading at recess, I've wanted to help her.

I want to protect her.

To hold her.

To love her.

I want to show her all my ugly broken parts and find acceptance in return.

It's hard, even thinking it. All my life, I've been sure love was what my parents had.

That it was hurled insults and harsh words and knives in backs.

Dad never hurt Mom. Not physically. But the shit he said, the shit he did behind her back, was as bad as any beating.

He convinced her she was worthless and unloveable until she believed it.

He pushed her until she left. Then he blamed me for it. Turned his insults to me.

He'd hit me when I stepped out of line.

Jules is the only person who knows. The only person who's ever known.

"I now pronounce you, husband and wife," Elvis croons. "Show me some sugar, baby."

The happy couple squeals. They jump into each other's arms and make out like there's no tomorrow.

There's not.

That's what Jules wants. Only tonight.

But then I want—

Fuck, I can't think about this shit anymore.

"Hello." A woman in a pastel pink suit steps out of the

back door. She waves hello. "Are you the King Prince wedding?"

"Yes." Jules offers her hand. "Nice to meet you."

"Just don't go by The King." She laughs. "Elvis doesn't like that."

"Right." Jules nods with complete sincerity. She hugs her suit bag to her chest. "How long do we have?"

"Ten minutes in the dressing room." She motions to the back door. "This way."

Jules looks to me *you okay*?

I nod and take her hand. Fuck, I'm drowning in all the things I want to say. How the hell can I explain this to her?

She's showing me that love doesn't have to be ugly.

That it's possible for me.

That it's possible the world is a beautiful place.

I try to find the words, but they get stuck in my throat. I'm not good with words. Pictures have always been more my speed.

Fuck, if only my vows could take the form of a tattoo.

That's it. That's perfect.

I follow Jules and the wedding planner through a hallway. "I have a stop after this."

"Yeah?" She looks up at me. "Because I was thinking we'd go back to my hotel room and fuck like rabbits."

My smile spreads over my cheeks. "We will. After my stop."

"You're a tease." Her cheeks flush.

"I know." I lean down to kiss her.

The wedding planner laughs. "Save it for the ceremony, kids." She pulls a clipboard from the door. Hands one paper to me and one to Jules. "We have some paperwork for you. Leave it in your suite." She motions to the door to our left. "The bride's room." Then to the one on the right. "And the groom's."

"Thank you." Jules folds the paper.

"There's champagne and mirrors." She turns her head to one side. "Do you need anything else?"

"No, um… I don't think so." Jules's eyes find mine. "Is my hair okay?"

"Perfect," I say.

"My makeup running?" she asks.

"You look perfect." I swallow the lump in my throat. Fuck, I can't handle this kind of honest emotion. How the hell does anyone do it?

I always thought I was good at experiencing everything. At telling it like it is. And seeing things as they are.

But I'm not.

I've been holding back my entire life.

Except with her.

And now—

Fuck. I take a deep breath. Exhale slowly. "I guess I'll see you in ten minutes."

Jules smiles. "Yeah."

The wedding planner escorts her into the suite.

I move into the groom's room. It's a tiny office with a mirror and a single chair.

I ditch my clothes. Change into fresh ones. I'm not sure what inspired me to bring two suits to Vegas but thank fuck for that.

My body buzzes with nervous energy. I'm not used to it. I'm not used to putting my heart on the line.

Jules is the best thing that ever happened to me.

I can't lose her.

Whatever happens, I won't lose her.

There isn't champagne in the groom's room (if I can be so charitable as to call it a room). Only bottles of water.

I uncap one. Drink it in three gulps. Try to find a trash can.

A knock interrupts me. "Mr. Prince, we're ready for you."

I open the door.

Th perky wedding planner smiles. She offers her arm, escorts me through the hallway, down the aisle, all the way to the altar.

The King winks. He mumbles words of advice. Something about taking care of my wife and taking care of business.

Music drowns him out.

The wedding march.

Fuck.

My heart pounds like a war drum.

This is really happening. I'm really marrying my best friend.

Holy fucking shit.

Jules steps onto the aisle in her wedding dress.

She's every bit the angel in that ivory silk. It clings to her chest, waist, hips.

Her eyes meet mine.

Time stops.

I stare at her.

She stares at me.

The music fills the room.

I swear to God, she floats to the altar.

I take her hands.

Elvis mumbles something about how we need to love and cherish each other.

Then Jules stares into my eyes and promises to give me everything she has.

She slides a silver band—included with our three-hundred-dollar package, of course—onto my ring finger.

Elvis tries to feed me vows, but I take over. "I promise,

no matter what happens tomorrow, you'll always be my best friend."

I slide the ring onto her finger.

I don't wait for instruction.

I kiss her like she's everything I want.

Because she is.

That's what I get now.

She's everything.

Chapter Twenty-Six

JULIETTE

As promised, we make one stop after the ceremony. It's perfect. Better than perfect.

After, we climb into a limo, pop a bottle of champagne, drink like fishes.

By the time I step into the hotel, I'm giddy and drunk and completely exhausted.

I trip over my dress. Really, who came up with the idea of a train? It's incredibly impractical. As is a dress that skims the floor.

Griff wraps his arms around me before I can dive face-first into the tile. "Come here, baby." He slides one arm under my ass. Slings the other under my armpits.

In one swift move, he lifts me and holds me to his chest.

I giggle as I wrap my arms around his neck.

He's so strong and comfortable.

And mine.

I know it's not forever. It's only tonight. The magic ends tomorrow.

The ring and the dress and the promises—

It's all part of the spell.

When the spell wears off…

Griff carries me into the elevator. "Can you do me a favor?"

"Mhmm?" My eyelids get heavy. It must be late. There are no clocks anywhere. It's some sort of Vegas conspiracy. No clocks, no natural light, no way to tell the time.

"Reach into my back pocket."

I slide my hand into his slacks. Mmm. He's so hard and warm. His body feels good. There are more poetic ways to describe it, but, God, he really does feel good.

I pull the key from his pants. Turn enough to slide it into the reader. Tap the button for our floor. "My room or yours?"

"Which has a bigger bed?"

"They're identical."

"Which is closer?" he asks.

"Yours."

"There you go." His entire body shakes with his laugh.

My fingers curl into his neck.

He holds me closer. "I've got you, baby. Don't worry." He presses his lips to my ear. "No matter what happens, you're safe with me."

Chapter Twenty-Seven

GRIFFIN

Somewhere between the elevator and the door, Jules falls asleep in my arms.

I carry her into the room and lay her on the bed.

She looks fucking gorgeous in her wedding dress, but it can't be the most comfortable sleepwear.

I push it off her shoulders.

She rolls onto her side. "Ten more minutes."

"Jules."

"Ten more minutes." Her eyelids flutter open for a second. She looks up at me like she loves me more than anything. Then she closes her eyes and rolls onto her stomach.

I find a t-shirt and boxers in my suitcase. Lay them on the bed for her.

After a shower, two bottles of water, and my own change of clothes, I climb into bed with her.

She's in the t-shirt and shorts.

Fuck, I have no idea how she did that in her sleep.

But it's really fucking adorable.
As good as fucking her senseless.
No, nothing is as good as that.
But sleeping next to my wife is pretty fucking great.

Chapter Twenty-Eight

JULIETTE

Bright light streams over my face and chest.

I try to open my eyes, but it hurts too much. Everything hurts. My head is throbbing. My mouth is bone dry. My bladder—

I really have to pee.

I throw off the covers.

They hit the person lying next to me.

Griff.

Fuck.

Memories of last night flit through my head. His suit hugging his shoulders. His *find someone to fuck* dare. His *hell yes, I'm buying you a lap dance* smile.

A busty blonde in my lap.

My dress at my waist.

Mirrored walls reflecting us.

At the strip club. Then in a limo. A limo we stole from some drunk assholes.

And we—

Fuck.

That happened. The vibrator in his palm. That giant souvenir cup. The whole Jackson cheated confession.

The—

I must have dreamed some of this. There's no way I, no way we…

There's no way.

I table my thoughts as I move into the bathroom. Pee. Wash my hands.

My fingers hit something hard. Then something smooth and round and metal.

No.

I press my eyelids together. *Please tell me that didn't happen. Please tell me I didn't fuck my best friend. Please tell me that isn't what I think it is.*

But it is.

It's right there, on my left ring finger: a massive rock.

I married Griff last night.

I married my best friend.

I married the boy who pulled my pigtails in the fourth grade.

The only person in my life who really cares about me.

And now—

Shit. I was supposed to marry Jackson today. I was… I…

Fuck.

I wash my face a few times, but it does nothing to offer clarity. It does away with the stuck mascara, but it's completely useless on the clarity front.

It's impossible to think with my head pounding like this.

I just…

We…

He…

Fuck.

I step into the main room.

Griff stretches his arms over his head. His eyes meet mine. His lips curl into a smile. "Hey."

"Hey." My gaze goes right to the ring. "I… uh… I have to go."

"Jules?"

"To change. And, uh, shower. And… uh… let's talk later, yeah?"

"Jules."

"I'll just… um… I'll see you soon."

He stares at me like I'm crazy, but he doesn't try to stop me.

Chapter Twenty-Nine

GRIFFIN

All through my shower, my head throbs. Two bottles of water and a dose of ibuprofen do little to help.

When I pick up my cell, I give up on headache relief.

Turns out, we posted our wedding pics on social media.

The entire world—or at least all our "friends" and followers—know we stumbled into a wedding chapel.

Not that I stumbled.

I—

She—

Fuck.

I made her a promise last night. A promise I'm honoring. I want Jules in my life forever. But I want her happiness more than I want mine.

If this isn't what she wants—

If I'm clipping her wings—

No, I can't think about that. Not now.

The glow of the screen is making my stomach turn.

I shoot Jules a quick text.

Griffin: Are you okay? I have ibuprofen and that pink stuff that settles your stomach.

Jules: Does it always hurt this much?

Griffin: Hangovers?

The chat is quiet for a moment. She means something else. Something besides the throbbing skull and churning stomach that come with excess drinking.

But she sticks with her story.

Jules: Yeah. I don't usually drink this much.

Griffin: I'll drop off the meds.

Jules: No, I think I need to sleep a little more. I'll text you when I'm up.

Griffin: If you changed your mind, we can talk.

Jules: I can't think, much less talk. Later, okay?

Griffin: Okay.

I dress in jeans a t-shirt, check my other texts, then go in search of my second best friend.

I like Wes, I do, but I really hope I don't have to promote him to best friend.

If I lose Jules over this—

That's a fate worse than anything.

I FIND WES AT THE POOL.

He's hanging with his girl, staring into her eyes like she's the center of the universe.

Maybe she is.

A few days ago, I didn't believe Wes was capable of falling in love.

Last night, something changed.

A lot changed.

My friend looks at me like I'm crazy—I am wearing

jeans in hundred degree weather—then he spots the ring on my left hand and the fresh ink on my forearm.

His look shifts from the fun *you're crazy* to *you might actually be insane.*

He bids his girl goodbye, climbs onto the concrete, leads me to the hotel.

People shoot us weird looks as we cross the casino to the elevators—he's only wearing his swimsuit—but I don't mind.

There are only a few people whose opinions matter to me.

My clients'.

My friends'.

And Jules's.

Judgmental strangers can go fuck themselves.

And all the near strangers liking my nuptials on social media—they can put their thumbs somewhere else.

Fuck, the headache is making me pissy. I don't want people intruding on this. It's ours.

I can handle the opinions.

But Jules?

She's probably staring at her cell with horror right now.

I'm tempted to go straight to her room. To bust down the door, drop to my knees, and plead *stay with me, baby. Give me a chance. Give us a chance.*

Whatever it takes to get through to her.

But I know better.

That kind of shit will only put more pressure on her.

And, besides, I'm not capable.

I can barely think *I need you, baby, please don't go*. I certainly can't say it.

"Which should we discuss first?" Wes steps into the elevator. "The ring or the tattoo?"

I follow him into the metal box. "We are tattoo artists."

His laugh is bouncy. Typical Wes. "Is there something notable about the design?"

"You tell me."

The shiny silver doors press together.

Wes wraps his fingers around my arm. Leans close enough to examine my fresh ink. Juliette in thick, black letters. "You know what that means?"

I shake my head.

"You can't hit the pool today."

I can't help but chuckle. It's the perfect thing to say. The Wes thing to say. "There go my plans." I slide the key into the reader. Hit the button for his floor.

He arches a brow.

"Figured you'd want to put on pants."

"Not sure I do." His laugh bounces around the space. "The heat is almost tolerable in this getup."

"Makes sense."

He rests his back against the metal railing. "Does she have one too?"

"Yeah."

"Where?"

"None of your fucking business."

"Oh?" He raises a brow. Shoots me that *you better expand on the dirty shit* expression.

But it's not dirty. It's sweet. Well, bittersweet. I love that Jules tattooed my name on her skin. But I hate that a stranger did it. Even if it's my name. And my design. And my—

Fuck, I don't want to call this.

"Give me a hint." Wes unwraps his towel. Brings it to his head. "Somewhere I can see in her usual getup?"

"What's her usual getup?"

"Like you don't notice her ass in those tight shorts."

"I'm not blind," I say.

"Three days ago you insisted you didn't see her that way?"

"That I wasn't in love with her. Not that I didn't realize she's hot."

He towel dries his hair. "Uh-huh."

I nod *uh-huh*.

"You really claiming you didn't look at her ass?"

"No."

"What about those tits? Fuck, those tight tank tops she's always wearing—" He makes a show of fanning himself.

"You're objectifying my wife."

He laughs. "You're fucking serious with this?"

"Yeah."

He shakes his head *you really are crazy*. "Your wife has fantastic tits."

"Aren't you crazy in love with your virgin?"

His smile gets dirty.

"You fucked her?"

"Don't talk about my girl like that."

"Don't talk about my wife like that."

His laugh gets louder. "Fuck, that's a good one-up."

"Makes your relationship look pathetic."

"Tact, Griff. Tact."

I shake my head. "Not familiar."

We both laugh. It eases the tension in my chest. Settles the twisting of my stomach.

The elevator doors slide open.

We move down the hallway then into Wes's hotel room.

It's nicer than mine. A suite with a perfect view of Las Vegas Boulevard.

The city is gorgeous in the desert sun, but it's too fucking bright.

I pull the curtains.

Wes chuckles. "How much did you drink?"

"Enough."

"Enough?"

I nod.

He shakes his head *you're insane*, moves to the Keurig, brews a pod of coffee. "You want one?"

"If you're polite enough to offer."

"What do you call this?"

"Dunno yet."

"I have more manners than you."

Probably. After Mom bailed, I ran away from that shit. "Manners are just a fancy way of bullshitting people."

"The bullshit is what makes the world go round." He peels the top off a pod of half-and-half. "You ever tell a client their idea is stupid?"

I shoot him a *really* look.

He laughs. "Almost forgot who I was talking to."

"What happened with Quinn?"

He motions to the unmade bed behind me.

"Don't tell me there's dried cum in those sheets."

"Didn't ask you to sit." His smile lights up his blue eyes. "I don't know, Griff. Doesn't feel right offering details."

"Really?"

"It's personal with her."

"You in love with her?" I ask.

He rests his back against the wall. "That's the million-dollar question, isn't it?"

I study my friend's expression, trying to figure him out. He is in love with Quinn. Can he not see that? Or does he want to keep it to himself?

Usually, I'd berate him for either. But I can't really talk.

Besides, I get why Wes is hesitant. His family history is as fucked as mine.

It's hard to see love as something beautiful when it's caused you so much ugliness.

"She's supposed to fly back to Chicago tomorrow," he says. "Unless I ask her to stay."

"That's a lot."

He nods *yeah*. "I can't ask her to give up her dreams."

"I know what you mean."

"But I can... If I don't do something, it's over." His expression gets pensive.

"You can't do long distance?"

"There's something about this summer." He turns back to the Keurig. Fixes a cup of coffee with two packets of cream. Then starts brewing another. "If she leaves... I think it's over."

"You have a plan?"

"I'm working on it," he says.

"You gonna tell me?"

He shakes his head *no*. Picks up the fixed coffee. Hands it to me. "I'm not ready to say it out loud."

"That's perceptive, for you."

"I'm smarter than I look."

"That's my line." I take a sip of java. It's not great—hotel coffee never is—but it's comforting. Familiar. Like this is a normal morning.

"You need something for the hangover?" He motions to the closed curtain. *If you can't handle light, it must be bad.*

It is. But it's nothing compared to the emptiness in my gut.

If Jules really wants out of this—

"It was amazing," Wes says. "I can't give you details. But, fuck, I really have taught her well."

"Go on."

"The way she groaned my name. It was like I was everything she's ever wanted."

"It's been like that before," I say.

"Yeah, but not like this."

"You never cared like this?"

He runs his hand through his hair. "Something like that."

"You're in love with her."

His cheeks flush. He turns to the coffee maker. Picks up his cup. Drinks it black. "Fuck, this really is shit coffee."

"You're a snob."

"I'm drinking it, aren't I?" He pushes himself onto the dresser.

I scan the room for a place to sit. Not the bed—no way am I sitting on his used sheets. Not the floor. The armchair in the corner.

I can work with that.

"Give me a minute." Wes moves into the bathroom. He returns in shorts and a tank top and tosses me a bottle of water. "Probably want that."

I nod. "Thanks."

He returns to his seat on the dresser. "You married your best friend."

"Yeah."

"And you're sticking with that choice?"

"Yeah." I look into his eyes. "If she'll have me."

"You're that sure?"

"It's Jules."

His laugh bounces around the room. "Fuck, Griff. Either you're blessed with a gift for clarity or you're out of your fucking mind."

"Maybe both."

His laugh gets louder. "Maybe both."

Maybe I am crazy.

Maybe this is stupid.

But I know what I want.

I just don't know what the hell my best friend needs.

Chapter Thirty

GRIFFIN

"Hey." Jules greets me with a sleepy smile. Her eyes fix on mine for a moment. Then they shift to the tattoo on my forearm and her smile disappears.

"I brought you something." I offer her the takeout coffee cup in my left hand.

Her fingers brush mine as she takes it.

My body buzzes from her touch.

Right now, it's obvious. I need her. I need this.

If she needs something else—

There's an easy way to figure this out.

I have to ask her.

To have the painful conversation.

To open myself up to a bitch-slap from the truth.

Usually, I'm good at that.

Or maybe I'm all wrong about myself. Maybe I'm only capable of taking hard truths because I'm not invested enough to care.

With Jules, it's different. I'm all in.

There's no easy way to do this. I have to talk to her. Figure out what she needs. Even if it's not what I want.

"Thank you." She takes a long sip. Lets out a low, deep moan.

My balls tighten.

My wife is moaning over her matcha latte.

My wife is standing in her hotel room.

My wife is fucking beautiful.

Those words feel too good. I want to swim in them. I want to whisper them in her ears. Hear them in mine.

But I made a promise.

I have to honor it.

"Can I come in?" I slide my hand into my front pocket, but the gesture doesn't feel casual.

"Sure." She steps backward. Motions *after you.*

I move into the room. It's the same room—same bed, same blue suitcase, same pile of clothes on the floor—but it's completely different.

This is my wife's hotel room.

"That really is good." She stifles her moan. "I, um… I guess everyone knows, huh?"

"You saw that?"

She nods. "I don't remember posting anything."

"Me either."

"Oh." Her brow relaxes. "I thought…"

"You were the only one who got too drunk to remember shit?"

She nods. "Yeah." Her laugh is awkward, but it still warms the room. "I, um… what do I say here?"

"How you feel."

"My specialty."

I can't help but chuckle. She's the same Jules. I'm the same Griff. A lot has changed, but that hasn't. "You think I'm happy about that?"

"It was your idea." She takes a seat on her bed. Presses her legs together. She's back in her street clothes—a cropped top and high waisted shorts.

"You look gorgeous today." I press my feet into the ground. I want to sit next to her. I want to wrap my arms around her. Hell, I want to pin her to that bed, push her shorts to her ankles, and dive between her legs.

But, right now, I need to give her space.

"Thank you." Her fingers curl into her thighs. "You do too." She takes a long sip. For a second, her eyelids flutter closed. Her brow relaxes. Her chest heaves. She groans a perfect, needy groan. Then she catches herself and clears her throat. "You, um… that's a really big tattoo."

"Yeah."

"Did you mean to get it so big?"

I nod.

Her gaze stays fixed on my fresh ink. "I, um, I didn't remember that when I woke up. Not until the shower. And the, uh… it looks good. Did you—"

"Designed it, yeah, but I didn't do it."

"Oh." Her lip corners turn down. "I was hoping… I don't know. It's stupid. I… I don't even know if I…"

"I'm going to honor my promise."

"Huh?" She presses her palm into the sheets.

"If you want to annul this, we can."

"Oh." Her gaze travels up my body. Stomach. Chest. Shoulders. Chin. Lips. Eyes. "Do you?" Her green eyes bore into mine. They beg for something.

"Do I?"

"Want that?" Her voice is soft. Vulnerable.

I'm not sure if she wants a yes or a no. Either way, I owe her the truth.

"No." My heels sink into the carpet. "Do you?"

"This is crazy." Her gaze shifts to the windows. Her

curtains are open wide. The Strip shines in the morning light.

Well, afternoon light at this point.

It's beautiful.

And really fucking bright.

"You want me to close the curtains?" I offer.

She shakes her head. "No. I think—"

"Is your head killing you?"

"Yeah." Her laugh is awkward. "It feels like someone bashed it with a baseball bat."

I can't help but chuckle.

"What?" Her gaze flits to me. She shoots me that *why are you teasing me, what is it you're getting at* look.

"Of course it's baseball."

She nods *of course.*

I try to place what's in her expression, but I can't. "Is that a yes or a no?"

"Huh?"

"I agree. This is crazy. But that doesn't mean we need to erase it."

"What if…" Her gaze shifts to the floor. "You're my best friend, Griff."

"You're mine."

"The only person I trust." She sucks a breath through her teeth. "I… I don't want to lose that."

"Me either."

"Maybe it's better if we…" She taps her toes together. "If we forget it ever happened."

"Jules…"

Her eyes stay on the floor. "I can't lose you."

"I can't."

She presses her knees together.

"If you want to call this off, I will. But there's no way I can forget last night."

"I…"

"I'm never going to forget the taste of your lips. Or the feel of your hands on my skin. Or that sound you make when you come." My eyes meet hers. "It's the best thing I've ever heard."

"I…"

"I don't want to lose you, Jules, but I can't pretend I don't want you."

"I… um… okay."

"Okay?"

"Yeah. Okay." Her eyes meet mine. "I was engaged three days ago. I thought I was going to marry someone else. I saw the rest of my life. It wasn't perfect. It wasn't even good. But it was stable and secure and understandable. Now… It's just… it's kinda confusing."

"I was your best friend three days ago?"

"Of course."

"Did you think I was going to stop being your friend?"

"No, but… it was different. With Jackson."

Yeah, it was.

"I just… I think about this. About last night, and I get all fluttery. It was… I've never felt like that before. But then I think about today. And tomorrow. And next month. And what happens when the magic fades."

"It doesn't have to."

"I want to believe that." Her eyes meet mine. "Do you?"

"Yeah."

"You believe in fairy tales?"

"Yeah."

She arches a brow *really*?

"Your YA has brainwashed me."

Her laugh lights up her eyes. "I want to believe it. I do. I just…"

"So believe it." I close the distance between us. "I meant what I said last night. Everything I said."

"I..."

"You don't remember everything because you were drunk?"

"Yeah." Her laugh is awkward. "I, um... this is really weird."

"I know."

"Can we... be normal?"

"What would be normal?"

"I can play some Paramore and you can complain about it."

I shake my head. "It's my new favorite band."

Her eyes go wide. "Oh." Her cheeks flush. "Then, um, a different band. Give me a second." She grabs her cell from the counter. Glares at the screen full of notifications. "You have these too?"

"Yeah."

"People have a lot to say."

"They always do."

"I..." Her eyes fix on the screen. Her brow knits. Her lips turn down.

This isn't helping her relax.

I need to drag her away from other people's expectations.

"The music," I say.

"Right." She pulls her Bluetooth speaker from the dresser.

I can't help but chuckle.

"What?"

"You packed your speaker?"

"I thought we had emo and YA afternoons planned."

"Yeah."

"So... how were we going to listen?"

"We could share your earbuds."

Her blush spreads to her chest. "We could… but I get confused when you're that close."

"Confused how?"

"I want to touch you."

"You're my wife. You can touch me."

Her brow knits with confusion.

Fuck, I'm too excited about this. I can't reel it in. I don't want to.

I understand why she's mixed up, but I can't pretend I feel the same.

Still.

If I want this to last, I need to be a good husband.

It's just…

How the fuck do I do that?

I've never seen a functional marriage before. Not up close. Not even from afar.

A peppy guitar riff flows from the speakers.

Her second favorite band.

My lips curl into a smile.

Her cheeks flush. "Why do you keep looking at me like that?"

"'Cause you're Jules."

"If you want to say something about how this song is anything less than great, you can keep it to yourself."

My smile widens.

Her teeth sink into her bottom lip. "I… uh…"

"We can do normal. If that's what you want. We can head to Coke World and you can mix your diet with some disgusting flavor."

She nods. "I only do that at movies."

"Uh-huh."

"Then we can wander through the fake Paris streets

and the fake Venice canals and make fun of the people paying thirty bucks to ride in a gondola."

"We can."

"We can do all that sightseeing shit you like."

"Okay."

"As friends."

Her eyes meet mine. "Can we?"

"Or—" I hold up my left hand.

"I…"

"We can do it as husband and wife."

"What does that mean?"

"I'm not sure." I bring my hand to her waist. "But I'm pretty sure friends don't get to do this." I pull her closer.

She nods. "They don't."

"Or this." I bring my hand to the back of her head.

She looks up at me.

I stare down at her.

Her eyelids press together. Her lips brush mine.

Fuck, she's a good kisser and she tastes like matcha and honey. It's her signature.

I pull back with a sigh. "We can stay friends if that's what you want. But it's not what I want."

She stares back at me.

"Give me a few days." I take her hand. "Please." My throat quivers. It's hard to get the words out, but I manage. "Give me a chance. Give us a chance."

Chapter Thirty-One

JULIETTE

"Okay." I press my lips together. "Okay."

"Yeah?" Griff's eyes light up.

I want a better answer. I want to feel as sure as he does. To scream from the mountaintops.

I really do want to believe in magic.

But this is crazy. Impulsive. Foolish.

Can something this ridiculous really last forever?

If I fuck it up and lose Griff—

That can't happen.

I need to do something to hold onto him. "While we're in Vegas." I swallow hard. "Then we go back to LA."

"As friends?"

Yes. We need to stay friends after the magic ends. "We give it the trip. Then we decide."

He nods *okay*.

"And if either one of us decides 'no,' we go back to how it was. Like this never happened."

"Jules—"

"We don't have to pretend. We'll just… we'll only be friends."

His eyes bore into mine. "I'll always be your best friend."

"You promise?"

"Yeah." His voice is earnest.

But it doesn't convince my heart.

Chapter Thirty-Two

JULIETTE

The Coca-Cola store is a shrine to branding. The bottom floor shows off Coca-Cola shirts from every decade and country, in every color of the rainbow.

Griff picks up an old timey gumball machine. "What do you think?"

"It's a knickknack."

"Would look good next to our TV."

"Would it?"

He shakes his head, sending his wavy hair in every direction. "But this." He holds up a snow globe—two polar bears drinking soda. "This really captures the Christmas spirit."

"In August?"

"It's never too early," he says.

"You hate Christmas."

His smile is bittersweet. "Yeah. But I have some good memories."

God, there are a lot of memories.

We sneak away every Christmas. For a short hangout

session if we're in the same place. Or a long phone call if we're not.

We have all these traditions.

We have a life together. It's not a normal, married life, but it's something and it's ours.

I can't lose that.

I can't lose him.

Griffin presses the snow globe to his chest. Moves closer. Close enough to touch me. "Where you going?"

"I just…"

His fingers skim my hips.

I jump backward. Out of habit. There's no way he can feel with my jeans in the way—he couldn't with my dress. But it's too close.

"I scare you?"

"Yeah." Not the way he means, but he did.

"I want to get something."

"Here?"

"Anywhere." He slides his arm around my waist. Looks down at me. "A memento." He holds out the snow globe for me. "If this isn't for you, lead me to something that is."

"What happened to the dick cup?"

"I think you left it in the party bus."

"Oh yeah." My memory is fuzzy, but that sounds familiar. "I… uh… God, this is so weird."

"It's still us."

"Yeah?"

He nods. "You don't have to turn into your parents because you're married."

God, what a horrible thought. I mean, I love my mom and my stepdad, but they're so… normal. It's bizarre how normal they are. They're functional and boring and happy. I always feel like a freak when I watch their easy interactions.

Nothing is easy for me. I don't know why. It's just not.

"Did you think…" His gaze shifts to the escalator. He motions *shall we?*

I nod. Yes. Artificial sugar and caffeine should help with the headache.

Okay, that's bullshit.

But they're delicious and comforting and familiar.

And I'm so fucking confused.

My heart is screaming *hell yes, stay with Griffin forever.*

My body is whining *drag him to the spare room and fuck him senseless.*

My head…

UGH.

"You must have imagined married life." He presses his palm into my lower back to lead me to the escalator.

I step onto the metal stair. "Yeah. But it was more an inevitability."

His eyes bore into mine. Not in that cross-examination kind of way. In an *I understand* kind of way.

"Everyone thought me and Jackson were good together. I'm not like you, Griff. I can't stand disappointing people."

He packs a dozen years of history into his nod.

"I… I just… I thought it was better, being with someone who only checked some of my boxes."

"Better?"

"Than being alone."

"You have me."

"I know. I just thought… I mean, you're not a subtle guy."

He chuckles. "What gave me away?"

"I always thought… if you wanted me, you'd take me. That's who you are. So I figured you didn't."

"I didn't realize it."

"Me either."

"I was stupid." His fingers slip beneath the hem of my crop top.

His touch makes my body buzz.

It calms the flutter of my stomach.

Eases the tension in my shoulders.

This makes sense. When it's me and Griff and the moment.

I want that.

We have two days left in Vegas. One and a half, really. I need to soak up every moment.

I step off the escalator.

He pulls me closer. "You don't have to worry about me."

"Hmm?" I move into the line. Scan the menu. There are exotic sodas from around the world—a dozen drinks only available in this store—but I know exactly what I want.

Diet with sugar free vanilla and cherry.

Why can't I have that kind of clarity with Griff?

"You don't have to worry about disappointing me." His lips brush my neck.

"I have before."

"No. I failed you that night. Not the other way around."

God, why is this always on the tip of my tongue? I have to tell him. Before he commits.

It might scare him away.

It did that night.

And I… "Maybe. But I saw the look in your eyes."

He pulls me closer. "Yeah. I was hurt. And I might be hurt if you decide you don't want to do this. Or if you decide to go to school in Iowa. Or if you get your next tattoo from Wes."

"I'd never."

His chuckle breaks up the tension in his jaw. "Fuck, it's really hard talking like this."

"I know."

"How do people do it?"

"Alcohol."

His laugh gets louder. "I know a place where we can get more."

I shake my head. "Never again." My lips curl into a smile. "I… I, um, I want that too. I mean, you hurt me sometimes. You can be a complete asshole."

"I know."

"But I'd rather you tell me the truth."

"Not just that." He brushes my hair behind my ear. "I don't ever want to hold you back."

My heart thuds against my chest. It's too fast. Too hard. Too heavy.

"Any choice you have, don't weigh that. Don't worry about disappointing me. Okay?"

"Only if you promise to stop this conversation."

He chuckles. "I'm gonna keep asking about Jackson."

"You're a terrible person."

"I know." He leans down to press his lips to mine.

Fuck, he tastes good. Like mint and sugar and Griff.

He pulls my body into his. Scrapes his teeth against my bottom lip. Groans against my mouth.

I slip my hand under his t-shirt. He's so warm and hard and mine.

For two days, he's mine.

The magic is still here.

Maybe it can last forever.

Maybe that's possible.

He pulls back with a sigh. "You're going to get me arrested."

"*I'm* going to get *you* arrested?"

He nods *hell yeah*.

"You kissed me."

"After you looked at me like you wanted to tear off my clothes."

My cheeks flush.

"I ever tell you how much I like your hair?"

I shake my head.

He runs his fingers through my curls. "I want it in my hands the next time I come."

My sex clenches. It's weird, jumping to sex so quickly. But it's exactly what I need. "Yeah?"

He nods *yeah*.

"You're gonna have to wait awhile for that."

He presses his palm into my ass. Pulls my body into his.

His hard-on brushes my stomach.

It's completely inappropriate, but I don't care.

"What would you like?" The cashier asks.

"Diet with sugar free vanilla and cherry." He winks at me.

My flush spreads to my chest. I'm not sure which makes me more fluttery—how well he knows me, or how well he dirty talks. "Two, please."

"Would you like a small, medium, or large?" she asks.

"Uh… which is the small?" I ask.

She picks up a massive cup.

"Large," Griff says.

"That's too much," I say.

"Twenty bucks says you drink the whole thing," he says.

"Don't you owe me forty bucks?"

"Double or nothing then."

I can't help but laugh. "Okay, double or nothing." I offer my hand.

He shakes.

The cashier looks at us like we're crazy, but she still trades our cash for sodas.

We take seats on red vinyl stools. This place is trying way too hard to look like an old timey soda fountain, but there's something charming about the effort.

I take my first sip. Mmm. Vanilla. Cherry. Cola. Artificial sweetness.

"You love it," he says.

"No comment."

"You do." He rests his hand on my knee.

I press my legs together reflexively.

He looks at me funny. Like he's picking up on my, um, avoidance.

No, he is.

He knows something is wrong.

He's too fucking perceptive.

"Not here." I cross my legs. Swallow another sup of soda. "This is amazing."

"I know." He smiles.

"You love it too."

"Yeah." His eyes fix on mine. "I do."

He's not talking about the soda.

He's talking about me. About us.

I want to believe it. But I can't face that whole *I broke the promise I made five years ago* thing.

I will. Soon.

Tonight.

Right now, I need something that makes sense.

I pull out my Kindle. Read our current YA book aloud. Tease him about his inability to appreciate quality literature.

We finish our sodas (okay, he was right about that), then head to the fake streets inside the casino next door.

It's quaint, like an actual small-town main street. The

store fronts look like something out of an episode of *Gilmore Girls*.

The floor is fake tile. The ceiling is bright blue with puffy white clouds. The lighting is dim. Gentle. Like a beach morning.

And there's the store I promised to visit with him. Complete with private dressing rooms and floor to ceiling doors.

I motion to the shop at the corner. "You still want to pull my hair when you come?"

His breath catches in his throat. "Fuck yes."

Chapter Thirty-Three

JULIETTE

"Welcome," a saleswoman chirps. "Can I help you with anything?" Her gaze shifts to me and Griff.

To his shoulders, lips, eyes.

She smiles.

Then she spots his left hand, and her lips curl into a frown.

She's a pro—much better than I was the summers I worked at Forever 21. She turns her frown upside down in three seconds flat.

"Yeah." Griff pulls me closer. "My wife is looking for something to wear tonight."

"Do you have something in mind?" she asks.

He nods. "Something nice. We're celebrating."

"Oh?" she asks.

"Yeah, we got married last night." He beams the way he did when I made varsity softball.

More even.

And there's no *oh God, Jules, are you going to do anything but practice, read, and listen to that horrible music? You're never going to find a boyfriend like this.*

She crosses the room to us, motions *follow me*, leads us through a dozen displays of panties, mannequins adorned in pastel bras, rows and rows of satin thongs.

Straight to the fancy lingerie. Teddies, one-pieces, baby dolls, stuff with names I've never heard before.

All in white.

This is the bridal section.

"It might be a little late, but it should do the trick." She smiles *enjoy* and takes her leave.

I pick up a sheer one-piece casually. Like I'm not thinking about how quickly I can get to the dressing room to suck off my husband.

Fuck, is this really so expensive? I thought this store was more in my price range.

My gaze shifts to the saleswoman at the counter. A man perusing black lingerie. Two friends comparing cotton panties.

They're so casual.

We're so obvious.

Can I really do this?

Can I really meet my husband in an empty dressing room and suck him off?

My sex clenches. I want to. I really do. But without the liquid courage, an illicit rendezvous is as scary as it is exciting.

Griff's fingers curl into my side. My crop top. Then my stomach. "She's so into us."

"You think everyone is into you."

"Me, yeah." His lip brushes my ear. "But she's into us."

"What does that mean?"

"She wants to watch."

"You think everyone wants to watch." I try to make my

voice even, but I'm not there. My body is buzzing. My heart is pounding. My stomach is fluttering.

The risk is a thrill.

But it's terrifying.

I press my eyelids together. Soak in the warmth of his body. The soft brush of his lips. The rough scrape of his teeth.

I want *this*.

His body and mine and nothing else.

That makes sense.

With Jackson, it never made sense.

But with Griff?

I want to drag him to my bedroom and have my way with him. All day. All night. Forever.

But that means—

Okay, I'm not going there. Not now.

I'm going all in tonight. Telling him while he has a chance to fold.

Or, um… I should have paid more attention during Inked Hearts poker games. The rules are fuzzy. And it's so damn appropriate using gambling metaphors, what with our current location.

"Baby, you're going off somewhere." He presses a long, hard kiss to my neck then he steps backward. "You keep doing that."

"I always do that," I say.

He chuckles. "Not this much."

I nod *I do too*.

He shakes his head *you do not*.

"Maybe I'm thinking about you naked."

He intertwines his fingers with mine. "You don't have to imagine it." His smile gets wicked. "You can make it happen."

Right. I can make it happen.

I can tear off his clothes, wrap my hands around his cock, stroke him until he's groaning my name.

I can get him under my thumb.

I really, really want him under my thumb.

"Should we go separately?" I motion to the dressing room.

He nods. "Smart."

"I should, um—" I find a cream bra. "And maybe something that matches?"

"Here." He grabs a matching pair of panties. Hands it to me.

"Thanks." My cheeks flush. I can't stop staring into his eyes. He's so handsome. And dirty. "And this." I grab a stack of red lingerie in my size. "I'll leave the door open."

He nods *sure*.

I hug the clothes to my chest.

Slowly, I move through the store. Past the saleswoman and the chatty customer. Past two girlfriends comparing black slips. Past a woman perusing the bras.

There. The dressing room is open. Empty. No sign of saleswomen anywhere.

I take a deep breath. Exhale slowly.

One step at a time, I cross the room. Open the door. Move into the stall on the far right. Click the lock.

Shit, I need it unlocked.

I turn the handle. Take a seat. Rest my back against the wall.

Okay, carefree sex maniac Jules is more *nervous yet horny Jules* in the sober light of day.

But there's that saying about fear and bravery.

You have to be afraid to be brave.

Okay, making my husband come in a dressing stall isn't exactly the definition of courage. It's certainly not what people mean when they throw around the word hero.

But it's really fucking hot.

My sex clenches at the thought of Griff's low, deep groan.

I can't stay quiet. But he…

Well, he has practice with this kind of thing.

And I'm the one in control. I'm the one leading. I'm the one driving him out of his mind.

Fuck, that's really fucking hot.

I pull my crop top over my head. Do away with my bra. Cross my legs.

I'm topless in a dressing room waiting for my husband.

God, it still sounds so strange—*Griffin is my husband* —but it's appealing too. It's scary how appealing it is.

I want to believe this is possible.

It's batshit crazy.

But, God, I want it to be possible.

My gaze shifts to my reflection—the walls are covered in long mirrors. The sight of my flushed cheeks and bare chest make my body buzz.

There's something so hot about watching.

I really fucking like it.

The door creeks open.

Griff steps inside and clicks the lock.

His eyes travel down my body slowly, like he's savoring every inch. "Fuck, Jules."

The need in his voice makes my sex clench.

He closes the distance between us.

His hands brush my skin. My lips meet his.

I kiss him hard.

He groans against my mouth.

He works me expertly. Draws slow circles around my nipple with his thumb. Then the index finger, middle, ring, pinkie, and back again.

Fuck.

I dig my hand into his hair, but it's not enough to contain my bliss.

I stifle a groan. Rock my hips against his.

Mmm. He's already hard. Fuck, that feels good. He feels good. The way he groans against my lips, and toys with my chest, and grinds his cock against my flesh—

My sex clenches.

My body buzzes.

My heart—

I can't even begin to consider my heart. Not right now.

Right now, I'm listening to my body. And it's screaming *more Griff now*.

I slip my hand under his t-shirt.

He groans as I drag my fingertips up his torso.

Hard muscles. Soft skin. Raised lines of ink.

I want to explore every inch, but I don't have time to linger. I need to do this fast. Before the saleswoman notices we're missing.

I break our kiss to pull his t-shirt over his head.

He presses his palm into my lower back. Pulls me into a slow, deep kiss.

God, he tastes good. Like vanilla. Like Griffin.

My tongue dances with his. Then he pulls back. Drags his lips over my chin, neck, collarbone.

He leans down to take my breast into his mouth.

He sucks softly. Then harder. Then so hard I—

Fuck.

I press my hand to my mouth to stifle my groan. I'm too loud. It feels too good.

But then I don't care.

I want to soak this in forever.

I want—

No, I need to make him come.

I really fucking do.

I cup him over his jeans. Even with the denim in the way, I can feel his warmth. His hardness.

I dig my hand into his hair. Tug his head up my body.

He straightens. His eyes meet mine. He stares like I'm everything he needs, then he closes his eyes, and presses his lips to mine.

He claims my mouth with his tongue.

I pull back with a sigh. "I want to suck you off." My cheeks flush. Then my chest. It's a lot harder issuing dirty demands sober. But it's a hell of a lot more thrilling too.

He takes a half step backward. Motions to the mirror. "Watch."

I nod.

"Watch while I come on those pretty tits."

Holy fuck. I… He… We…

"Get on your knees, baby."

My nod is impossibly needy. He's too hot. It's unfair. It's criminal. It's perfect.

Slowly, I lower myself to my knees.

He slides his hand into my hair. Presses his palm to the back of my head. "How do you like it?"

"Huh?" I stare up at him, trying to comprehend the question. I… He… oh my God.

"You like it rough, baby?"

"Oh. Um… I don't know."

"You don't know?"

"Yeah. I… um… I was never into it with Jackson."

"You don't have to—"

"I want to." My tongue slides over my lips. I want it, but how the hell do I want it? "Rough. But not too rough."

He nods. "I want you to watch."

I press my palm into his hip.

"Watch as I fuck that pretty mouth."

Holy shit. My sex clenches. I barely manage to unhook his belt.

He stares down at me like I'm the only thing he wants.

I undo his button. Then the zipper.

Griff pushes his jeans to his knees. Then the boxers.

Mmm. He's as big as I remember. And even more inviting.

I wrap my hand around his cock.

His fingers curl into the back of my head.

I stare into his eyes as I brush my lips against his tip. He tastes good. And there's something about feeling him against my mouth—

I really fucking like it.

I tease him with another soft brush.

Then another.

His eyelids press together.

His fingers curl into my hair.

He groans as I take him into my mouth.

I watch our reflection. Watch my lips strain against him. Watch his cock slide into my mouth.

I flick my tongue against his tip. The top. Then the bottom.

His hand knots in my hair.

Mmm. He feels too fucking good. He really does.

I try a harder flick. Then higher. Lower. There—

He tugs at my hair.

Griff looks down at me with heavy lids. "I'm gonna take over, baby."

My response is a groan.

"Give me your hand."

I do.

He brings it to his ass. "Let me know if it's too much."

My fingers curl into his skin.

He presses his palm into the back of his head. "I'm gonna fuck that pretty mouth."

My sex clenches.

I wrap my lips around my teeth.

He shifts his hips, driving his cock into my mouth.

A short, slow thrust.

Then deeper.

Harder.

Fuck. I swallow to relax my throat.

He drives into my mouth again.

I dig my fingers into his ass.

He slides his hand down my torso. Takes my nipple between his first two fingers.

It's harder than before.

So hard it aches.

In the best possible way.

My gaze shifts to the mirror.

I watch him work.

He rocks his hips, pushing deeper and deeper.

Again and again.

I groan against his cock.

He tugs at my hair.

He fills my mouth with long, deep thrusts.

I'm not in control anymore. I'm the one under his thumb. But I really fucking like being under his thumb.

His eyelids press together. "Fuck." He rocks his hips, driving his cock into my mouth.

I press my tongue against the bottom of his shaft.

Suck on him as he fills me with those same steady thrusts.

His fingers knot in my hair.

My nails scrape his skin.

His lids get heavy.

I watch pleasure spread over his face. Then my gaze shifts to the mirror.

I watch Griff drive into my mouth again and again.

"Fuck, Jules." He tugs at my hair.

With his next thrust, he pulls back.

His cock pulses as he spills onto my chest.

He groans my name as he comes.

His gaze stays heavy. Even as he dresses, cleans me up, helps me into my clothes.

He stares at me like I'm everything he wants.

It occurs to me for the first time.

Maybe I am.

Maybe this can happen.

Maybe he will accept my secrets.

Chapter Thirty-Four

JULIETTE

Outside, it's a beautiful day—bright blue sky, big yellow sun, steel and glass and neon everywhere, temperature a million degrees.

Griff hails a cab. Helps me inside. Whispers, "I'll take it from here, baby," in my ear.

My sex clenches. God, I already need him again. "Okay."

He leads us to a matcha shop in Chinatown. Then it's lunch at a noodle house, a museum devoted to the atomic testing (way more interesting than it sounds), another tea shop (just as good as the first), then back to the strip for the Shoppes at the Grand Canal.

It's more fake, Vegas perfection.

And when he leads me to the gelato stand and points to the matcha gelato—

I know he's mocking me.

But I love it anyway.

"WHY ARE YOU STARING?" I SWALLOW ANOTHER BITE OF gelato. Mmm. Creamy milk. Rich matcha. Just enough sugar.

"Am I staring?" Griff sets his cup—one scoop of chocolate, one of coffee—on the table. He wraps his arms around me. Repositions my body so I'm facing him.

It gives me a perfect view, not that I'm looking at our surroundings. The Grand Canal Shoppes are nice. The fake canal is quaint—who doesn't like men in striped shirts singing Italian loves songs? The storefronts are cute.

But they're nothing compared to Griffin's smile.

God, that smile… It makes me warm everywhere. It really does.

A gondola glides along the canal. The operator's love songs drift into our ears.

It's fake as hell, but the intentions are real. The happy couple on the ride are here to fall in love.

And they are.

I…

I'm not going there yet.

I tell Griff tonight.

Sometime before midnight, I confess the secret I've been keeping for half a dozen years.

He might take it well. He might freak out. Either way, things change.

This might be the end of the spell.

If these are the last few hours of magic…

Well, I'm not about to spend them wallowing.

"Baby, if you keep drifting off, I'm going to have to punish you," Griff mumbles into my neck.

The mom sitting next to us scowls. She shakes her head *these kids have no manners* then hurries her children to the line at the ice cream shop.

Griff's chuckle is deep. "You can't take me anywhere."

"I know."

"How do you deal?"

"It's been a tough—"

"Lifetime?" he teases.

"It has been." I take another bite of my gelato. Let the green ice cream melt on my tongue. It's perfection. It really is.

Or maybe that's because I'm sitting in Griff's lap.

Because he's looking at me like he loves me.

Right now, I don't want to question it.

"Why do you put up with it?" He brings a scoop of ice cream to his lips. Sucks it from his spoon.

"Why do I put up with your inability to keep your mouth shut?" I ask.

His nod is earnest. "This might be news, but a lot of people find me annoying."

"I find you annoying."

"You always have," he says.

"But in a way I like."

He arches a brow.

"I don't know, Griff. You've been a lot of things, but you've always been there."

He nods. "You too."

"I try." I take another lick of ice cream. Mmm. It's distracting how good this is. "I'm not sure I can have an emotional conversation with something this good in my mouth.

"Go on."

My cheeks flush. "See. That. Everything is always sex with you."

"With me?"

I nod.

"I'm the one that dragged you into a clothing store?"

"You enticed me."

"Did I?"

"Yeah." My fingers skim his temple. "You were too beautiful."

"Damn. Can't deny that." He smiles.

"Yeah. Don't do the crime if you can't do the time."

His voice drops to something low and demanding. "Tell me more about this crime."

A laugh spills from my lips. "Mmm… how about, instead, you tell me why you think about sex all the time."

"Why wouldn't I?"

It's an awfully compelling argument.

His eyes fix on me. "You're trying to kill me with this, right?"

"With what?" I take another bite of ice cream.

"With what?" He shakes his head *you're ridiculous*. "You're practically deep throating that thing."

"And I'm obsessed?"

"You're the one going down on your cone."

"This is how everyone eats ice cream."

He shakes his head. "No. The way you do it makes me hard."

"You're not—"

He shifts my hips, so my ass brushes his crotch.

Fuck. He is hard.

My blush deepens. "You just—"

"I know."

"Are you always so fast?"

"No."

"So that's because—"

He brings his lips to my ear. "Because you're the sexiest woman in the universe."

Heat spreads to my fingers and toes. I want to have him here. I really do. But I can't.

We're out in the open.

And, well… I have to tell him first.

Ahem. "I can get out of your lap if it's a problem."

"Fuck no." He brings his hand to my cheek. Pulls me into a slow, deep kiss.

Mmm. Griff. Coffee. Chocolate. Sugar.

I sigh as he releases me. "You're good at that."

"You too."

"You have more practice."

He shakes his head. "Don't do a lot of kissing."

"No?"

"It feels—"

"Too personal?"

"Yeah," he says.

"So, you, um…" God, I have no idea how to broach this. It's not like I can talk. I was with Jackson for the last five years. I was sure I was in love with him. But Griff—"You've been with a lot of women."

"Accurate."

"We, um, we've talked about Jackson a lot."

He nods. "He's not really my type."

"Oh?" I take another bite. Fight a groan.

"I prefer more tattoos."

"All three of mine?"

His fingers tap my ribs, over my crop top. "Four."

Right. I have his name tattooed on my ribs. He's on my skin for the rest of my life. Which is amazing. But also terrifying.

"And green eyes." He takes another bite of ice cream. Lets out his own moan. "I need gorgeous green eyes."

"Jackson had green eyes."

"Not gorgeous ones."

My blush spreads to my chest. "Did you always—"

"Want to fuck you?"

"Jesus, Griff." I motion to the family two tables away. "I really can't take you anywhere."

He chuckles. "I'll keep it PG-13."

"I'm not sure you can."

"I can try." He slides his arm around my waist. "No. Not always."

"I was going to say: did you always think my eyes were beautiful?"

"Always."

"But not in a romantic way?"

"It was a fact of life. You had pretty eyes. Then, one day, I noticed you had a pretty face. Then the tits and ass showed up, and, I noticed that."

I'm sure he's trying to make this less dirty, but holy fuck. My entire body is buzzing.

"I've always thought you were beautiful, Jules. It just never occurred to me that you could be mine," he says.

"Me either." I take another bite of ice cream. Let the cold dessert melt on my tongue.

I should say something about Jackson and how obvious it is now that I was running away from us.

But I don't.

"You sleep with a lot of women." I crack a chunk of cone. Casually. Like I haven't been dying to have this conversation forever.

"I did, yeah." He rubs his wedding band with his thumb.

"Why?"

"You know why."

I have guesses why. But I've never asked point blank. "No… I… You know I don't like hearing about it."

"You were jealous?" His eyes fill with curiosity. And something else. Something I can't place.

"Yeah." I take another bite, but it doesn't buy me

enough time. My words are still messy. "But not because they were with you. I was jealous of you."

"If you're about to tell me you were into Barbie, I'm gonna… not sure what I'm gonna do, but it's going to involve making you come."

My fingers dig into my thighs. I clear my throat. Direct my attention to my cone. But licking the ice cream only fills my head with more ideas.

"It was more…" I chew. Swallow. "The experience."

"Yeah?"

"You're so free about sex."

"That's tactful." He chuckles.

"Okay, you're a slut. But you're also free."

"Sorta."

"You don't… enjoy that?"

He wraps his fingers around mine. Brings the cone to his lips. Sucks matcha gelato into his mouth. "I love the taste of matcha."

"Since when?"

"For a while."

"How long?" I ask.

"Since you got into it." His eyes meet mine. "It feels like home. And nothing… nothing has ever felt like that."

I don't know what to say, so I steal the ice cream back.

"I fucked a lot of women. It was fun. It felt good. I came and made a lot of women come. But it never felt like that. Like— okay, don't let me use this flavor metaphor again."

"Okay."

"I sound like my fucking dad."

"You don't."

He shakes his head *I do*. "I tried a lot of shit. Different types of women. Different positions. Different styles of sex."

"Like what?"

"Name it."

"Have you had an orgy?" I ask.

"What counts as an orgy?" His lips curl into a half-smile.

"You have not."

"I haven't. But I've had a few threesomes."

"How few?" I ask.

"Lost track."

That's not a few. But I keep that to myself. I know Griffin is a slut. That doesn't matter. That's never mattered. "I… uh… how many women do you think?"

"I don't keep notches on my bed post."

"I… um… that's just—"

"Don't do that," he says.

"What?" Ice cream melts onto my hands.

"Compare yourself."

"I'm not." Fuck, I am. With three bites, I finish my cone.

Griffin wraps his fingers around my wrist. He brings my hand to his lips. Licks melting ice cream from my palm. "I'm not going to sell you some story about how I was fucking my way through some deep emptiness."

"Well, you could, there is an emptiness."

He chuckles. "That's terrible."

"I know."

"Now, you sound like my dad."

"Really?"

He nods.

"Then I take it back." I press my lips together. "I hate him."

"Me too."

"I know you don't want to talk about him. I just had to say that."

He takes my pinkie into his mouth. Sucks the melting ice cream from it.

"Do you still think about him?"

He shakes his head. Moves to my ring finger. Runs his thumb over my wedding band.

The intimacy of the gesture makes my stomach flutter.

I…

I really, really like him.

More.

But I can't say that yet.

Soon.

But not yet.

"That's good. I mean, it's okay if you do. Or if you want to talk about him. Or something else. I can listen." I swallow hard.

He releases my finger. "I know."

I nod.

"I'm not good at it either," he says.

"We're pretty bad at talking for two people who have been best friends most their lives."

"Mommy issues."

"Just like Wes," I say.

He chuckles. "Don't tell him I said that."

"Have I ever spilled one of your secrets?"

He shakes his head. "Not that I know about." He moves to my middle finger. Sucks it clean. Flicks his tongue against the pad of my fingertip.

It's impossibly hot.

I… Uh… We…

Ahem.

"You were saying something about how you weren't filling a deep loneliness." I clear my throat.

"I wasn't. I did it because I liked it. Because it was fun. Because I didn't have anything better to do."

"Right."

"But then… remember last time we tried a new matcha shop. The one in Little Tokyo?"

"The terrible one?"

He chuckles. "It was fine."

I stick my tongue out. Sure, it was fine, but only fine.

"You drank your latte faster."

"Of course," I say. "When it's great, you have to savor it."

"And when it's just okay, you need more to satisfy."

"Right. You, um, you're using food as a metaphor for sex again."

"Shit." He laughs as he picks up his cup of ice cream. "I'm a pig."

"Yeah." I steal his spoon. Bring a scoop of chocolate to my tongue. Mmm. There's a tiny hint of coffee mixed in. It's just enough bitterness to bring out the flavor of the cocoa.

"But you do know what I mean?" he asks.

"Sorta."

His brow scrunches with concentration. He steals the spoon back. But instead of bringing a scoop to his lips, he brings it to mine. "You ever go on a date with someone you really like?"

"I broke up with my fiancé four days ago."

He chuckles. "I remember your first date with Jackson. You were freaking out."

"Well, yeah, I was seventeen and I'd never had a real boyfriend. Just a lot of sloppy make out sessions."

"Oh, I remember that party."

"Can we not—"

He laughs. "Okay. We can not. But you need to stop distracting me."

"What now?"

"You keep groaning over your ice cream." His lips brush my neck.

I lean into the gesture. "You keep feeding it to me."

Right on cue, he offers me another bite.

Mmm. It really is good.

He kisses me harder. "I like your groan too much to stop."

"How do you get anything done?"

"Don't usually have you in my lap," he says.

"So with other women—"

"That's what I'm trying to say, Jules. It's not like this with other women. It's fun, yeah. I come, yeah. But I don't get invested. It's easy because I'm not invested."

"I get that." Sorta.

He sucks ice cream from his spoon. Then he scoops another bite—the last bite—and offers it to me.

I take it. "I, um, I always thought you were invested. The way you talk about sex—"

"I was. But not in the sex. In causing a reaction." He takes the spoon, and the cup, and sets them aside. Then he rearranges my limbs so I'm straddling him. "Your reaction."

"You slept with half of Los Angeles for me?"

His chuckle is easy. "Kinda, yeah. I didn't realize it, but I compared everyone to you."

"The last girl you dated?"

"Dated?" He arches a brow.

"Okay, that you *enjoyed*—"

"Enjoyed?"

"That you engaged in sexual relations with." I bring my hand to his shoulder. "Is that acceptable?"

He nods *yeah*.

"She was gorgeous. And smart. And her boobs were

seriously huge. She jumped into the pool topless at Dean's party."

He laughs. "I forgot about that."

"Oh my God, the look Jackson gave me. It was like *are you sure you want this guy as your friend? Look at the company he keeps*."

"She was a PhD candidate," he says.

"I think the giant boobs distracted him." My teeth sink into my lip. "And, well, I… How could she not compare to me?"

"How could she?"

My brow furrows.

His fingers brush my lips. "You don't need giant tits to be perfect."

"But—"

"Your tits are perfect, for the record. But that isn't what makes you incomparable."

I stare into his eyes.

"It's the sound of your laugh. That look you get when you're listening to Paramore. That royal blue suitcase you carry everywhere. The way you text me after every Dodgers and Angels game to brag you support the better team."

"That stuff—"

"I should probably say something romantic here."

"Maybe that we're puzzle pieces that fit together," I suggest.

"Is that supposed to be romantic?"

I nod.

"Sounds more dirty to me."

"How?"

"Do I really need to explain it?" he asks.

Oh. Obviously. But, come on. He is obsessed.

I like that he's obsessed. But he really is obsessed.

"So, um, you think the reason why you've never made it past a third date is that you've compared every woman you've been with to me?" I ask.

He doesn't blink. "Yeah." He runs his thumb over my temple. "You've always been here." He takes my hand and rests it on his chest.

"That's cheesy."

"I know."

"You're lucky you're hot, or you couldn't get away with that kinda thing."

His lips curl into a smile. "I'm lucky that you like cheesy."

"I like no such thing."

He nods *you do.*

I shake my head *I do not.*

Again, he nods. "You do." He intertwines his fingers with mine. "I do too."

"I do not."

"Yeah?" His lips brush mine. "That's why you're smiling?"

"I just…"

"Yeah?"

"This is really perfect." I want it to last forever. I want him to keep looking at me like that.

Will he keep looking at me like that after I tell him?

Chapter Thirty-Five

JULIETTE

It echoes through my head.

I need to tell him.

We walk around the fake Venice, lose a hundred dollars at the Blackjack table, grab dinner at a Mexican chain on The Strip, alternate between melting in the desert heat and freezing in the hotel AC on the way to our casino.

I need to tell him.

There are plenty of ways to extend tonight. Shows, bars, arcades, tattoo shops, slot machines.

But all those roads lead to the same place.

I need to tell him.

He intertwines his fingers with mine. Steps into the elevator. Hits the button for our floor.

I press my back against the mirrored wall, but it doesn't give me any space to think.

There are three strangers in here—two drunk guys escorting a completely plastered friend.

The taller guy gives me a long, slow once over. His eyes stop on my chest. My lips. My thighs.

It's not like I hide my scars. Not all of them. Not the faded ones Griff knows about.

The others—

I got smarter about where I did it.

As long as I wear shorts with a few extra inches and avoid walking around in skimpy bikini bottoms, I keep these secret.

Even from Jackson.

He's seen the old ones too. But these—

They're mine.

I needed them to be mine.

It's not a logical thing. It's not like I woke up one day and thought *you know what would really be fun: if I started dragging a blade against my skin? I better hold that close to the vest, because the secret is half the thrill.*

The first time I tried it, I didn't know what I was doing. I was hurt and overwhelmed and confused and I didn't know how to make sense of everything.

My family is supportive. Yeah, they don't get my taste in music or my inability to articulate my emotions or my feelings of displacement—it's weird walking around, looking like a father I've never met, a father who wants nothing to do with me, who has this entire culture I know nothing about.

I can't talk about that with them. They get defensive. Insist there's nothing to say, no reason to wonder. And maybe they're right. Mom and Dad love and support me. It shouldn't matter that my stepdad isn't my biological father. He's been there most of my life.

It's not like I have some horrible, traumatic event I'm trying to suppress. My life is normal. I lose friends, I get hurt, I study hard. Sometimes, I make the grade, sometimes I don't.

Like anyone.

I just… I don't know how to process all the stuff going through my head.

I'm not sure where I got the idea. I had friends who cut. I'd heard songs that made it seem like beautiful damage. I'd watched TV shows treat it like a dilemma for a very special episode. Something that could be solved in forty-five minutes flat.

If I wasn't so scared of sex and drugs, I might have tried that. But I knew I couldn't ask Griff for either. And I knew I couldn't find either without tipping him off.

No, it was more than that.

I didn't want anyone else involved.

I was so tired of other people's expectations.

I was always the model daughter, the perfect student, the excellent athlete.

It was too much fucking pressure.

Cutting was my only outlet.

For the first time in forever, I was in control.

There was something sublime about channeling every ugly thing inside me into a quick burst of pain.

Sometimes, it was the only way I could get through the day.

Sometimes, it was the only thing I had.

I knew I needed to stop. That I should have been journaling or jogging or drawing. But it was the only time I ever let go.

And that felt too fucking good.

It still does.

The elevator dings. The tall guy turns back to his drunk friend. He and the shorter guy help Drunkie into the hallway.

The shiny silver doors slide together.

Griff presses his palm into mine.

I suck a breath through my teeth.

I have to tell you something, Griff. I don't want you to be scared. Because it's not scary. It's not a big deal.

No. That's more bullshit. It's only going to make him mad.

If there's one thing Griffin hates, it's lies.

This…

Maybe he'll understand.

We're older. Wiser. More equipped to handle difficult situations.

We did get married on a drunk whim, but, uh…

Fuck.

The elevator stops on our floor.

I squeeze Griff's hand. Move into the hallway. Around the corner.

Straight to my room.

Beep-beep.

I open the unlocked door. Motion *after you.*

He steps inside.

The door slams shut behind me.

Griff's hands go to my waist. He pulls me into his arms. Lifts me. Pins me to the wall.

"Fuck, I need to be inside you." His lips press into my neck. "Are you safe?"

"Huh?"

"Jackson was cheating."

"Oh. Yeah. We, um, we hadn't in a while. And I got tested at my last checkup. And—"

"You complain about your IUD every month." His lips curl into a knowing smile. An *I love your quirks* smile.

Because he does.

And I love that he loves them.

And I love his too.

And I'm pretty sure I love him in a way I've never loved anyone. A way that goes beyond Griffin my best friend.

That goes to, well, to the way I'm supposed to love my husband.

As if I need more pressure.

I'm not confessing to my best friend.

Or my fuck buddy.

Or my boyfriend.

I'm telling my husband I'm a disappointment.

Awesome.

So awesome.

I…

He…

"Jules?" He cups my cheek with his palm.

"Yeah."

"You sure you're okay?"

I try to hold his gaze, but I can't.

This isn't okay. I'm not sure what it is, but it's definitely not okay.

I'm sorry I'm distracted, Griff. It's just that I've been lying to you for the last five years. I went back on my promise. I failed you and I couldn't face that. I can't face your reaction. Because this isn't yours. It doesn't get to be yours.

Maybe that's enough.

It doesn't have to be perfect.

It has to be true.

It has to be something.

My gaze shifts to the clock on the bedside table.

There are three hours until midnight. Three hours of magic. Three hours until I have to do this.

"Jules?" He brings his hand back to my ass. Shifts his hips backward. Sets me on the ground.

"Yeah?"

"You gonna talk to me about this?"

I reach for a distraction. "Are you safe?"

"Yeah. I got tested a few weeks ago."

"You hadn't—"

He nods. "It was just the text thing with Lee Ann."

I bite my lip. I hate hearing the name of some woman he fucked. But I can't pretend that's the problem. Even if it's unfair.

She gets to fuck him without all this baggage.

She doesn't have to worry about him finding her scars, deciding she's a lying disappointment, running away.

I...

He...

Fuck.

"Jules?" he asks.

"Yeah?"

"You upset about Lee Ann?"

"No." I wish that was it. That would be so much easier.

"Are you gonna tell me why you're upset?"

"What if I don't?"

His dark eyes bore into mine. They fill with hurt. Confusion. Betrayal.

A hint and he's already so hurt.

I can't do this.

I really can't do this.

I suck a breath through my teeth. Let out a steady exhale.

His eyes stay glued to me.

Mine go to the floor. "I, um... I think I should..."

"What the fuck?"

"I should—"

His fingers curl around my wrist. "Talk to me."

"No, I..." I try to keep my eyes on the floor, but I can't. His dark eyes are too compelling. And they're still brimming with confusion. "Please let go."

He stares at his hand like he's not sure how it got around my wrist. "I..." He shakes his head. Releases me.

Deep breath. Steady exhale.

Fast. Like a Band-Aid.

I'm sorry for being oblique, Griff. I'm not trying. It's just hard to say this. The truth is, I didn't keep my promise. I tried, I did. But I couldn't do it.

I still cut.

I cut three days ago. After I got to my mom's house.

It was the only way I could process calling off my engagement.

I know I promised I'd call you first but come on. Did you really believe in that fairy tale?

We both know fairy tales are bullshit.

"You keep going off." He takes another step backward, putting more distance between us.

"Yeah."

"Where?"

"I…"

"You wanted to tell me something."

I fold my arms over my chest. "I should."

His eyes bore into mine. "You can tell me anything."

"I know."

"So…" *Why is this so hard? What are you waiting for? Why have you been hiding this for so long?*

I don't have an answer. Not a good one. This is mine. Maybe that's wrong, maybe it's unfair, maybe it's stupid. But it's still mine. He doesn't get to make it about him. He doesn't get to claim it as his.

"Does Jackson know?"

"What does that matter?" I press my back into the wall. It's not enough space. And it's too much.

I want to pull him closer, whisper this in his ear, dissolve in his arms.

And I want to run to my room, hide under the covers, cry myself to sleep.

But there's nowhere to run.

There's no home.

My parents' place isn't home.

Jackson's place isn't home.

Griffin's place—

I always thought that could be home. But only if I—

"What do you need?" He presses his palms against his thighs. "Tell me what you need."

"I…"

"I want to help. Whatever it is." His voice softens. "I'm not good at this shit. I can't help unless you talk to me."

I try to find the words—*Griff, I still cut*—but they refuse to make it to my lips.

"Do you want to talk?"

No. Yes. Maybe.

"Jules."

"I want to… but I… I can't."

Hurt streaks his expression.

"I'm sorry, Griff. I just… I can't. Not yet."

"You can't what?"

"I can't." I try to find a better explanation. Something that will comfort him. That will promise we're still best friends. That we're still married. That we still have a fucking chance.

But there's nothing else to say.

"I'm sorry," I whisper. "I can't."

He stares back at me, confusion in his dark eyes.

But he doesn't fight me. Or ask me to stay. Or beg for an explanation.

"No," he whispers. "I can't do this."

He turns and walks out the door.

I stare at the thing, waiting for him to come back, to knock, to somehow understand.

But he doesn't.

Chapter Thirty-Six

GRIFFIN

An hour in the hotel gym and a hot shower do nothing to clear my head.

There's only one person I want when my head is this fucked up and she—

I don't know what she's doing. Or not doing.

Only that she can't tell me what she's feeling.

I pick up my cell. Tap out a text to Wes. Delete it.

He's taking Quinn to the airport tomorrow. Flying to Chicago with her, or asking her to stay, or saying goodbye forever.

I know what he's planning, but a night is a long time. His plans might change. If this is going to be his last night with her—

I can't intrude.

I don't want to intrude.

I want Jules.

The bed is comfortable enough. The layers of blankets provide plenty of warmth, but my body stays cold.

Sleep eludes me. My head keeps going back to Jules and all the hurt on her face.

She doesn't trust me.

She doesn't believe I'm worth trusting.

I don't blame her.

I don't trust myself either.

Not with things that matter.

Not with her heart.

I thought maybe, this could be different, that we could be different.

But we're not.

We're—

I don't know what the fuck we are.

Eventually, I give up on sleep. I find my cell. Stare at days of texts. And dozens of pictures. And the single photo on her social media account—the two of us post-wedding, smiling into the camera, drunk and happy.

That was twenty-four hours ago.

She was mine twenty-four hours ago.

Now…

I want to be what she needs.

But I have no fucking idea how to do that.

Chapter Thirty-Seven

GRIFFIN

After way too little sleep, I head to the shop Jules likes. Coffee and hardboiled eggs settle my stomach, but they fail to ease my headache.

My head throbs. It screams *you're not enough for the only person you've ever loved.*

Not that I'm capable of that word.

Or explaining this to her.

Or understanding her.

But I am capable of this—

I buy her a matcha latte and a blueberry muffin. Head back to her hotel room. Knock on the door.

"Hello?" Her footsteps move closer. Then stop. She pulls the door open. Stares at me dumbstruck. "Griff, I…"

"Check out is in an hour."

"I know."

"Dean was thinking we'd leave after lunch. He has an early appointment tomorrow."

"Do you…" She bites her lip.

I swallow a sip of my cold brew. It wets my parched

throat, but it doesn't make conversation any easier. "I'm working all day tomorrow."

"Right. Good. You're good at your job. So that's good."

"Yeah." My fingers brush hers as I hand over the take out cup and the paper bag. "We're gonna eat at the restaurant downstairs."

"Oh."

"You're welcome to join."

She shakes her head. "No, I…" She takes a long sip of matcha. Lets out a soft sigh. Catches herself. "Sorry."

"Don't apologize." I still love her groan. And not just because I love watching her come. Because I love her bliss. Every kind of bliss. I always will.

"But—"

"I'll see you later."

"Griff, I—" Her gaze shifts to her engagement ring. "Thank you."

I don't know what to say, so I settle on—"you're welcome."

THERE ISN'T MUCH TO PACK, BUT IT STILL TAKES forever.

I don't want to leave this room. It's the place where Jules and I spent our wedding night.

Sure, she was so exhausted she fell asleep.

And it's entirely possible she no longer wants anything to do with me.

It's still the bed I shared with her.

Fuck, it's been so long since I've slept in her bed. Or invited her into mine. I missed the warmth of her body. The softness. The way she murmurs in her sleep.

At ten minutes to checkout, I do a final sweep, roll my suitcase to the elevator, pay my bill in the lobby.

Fuck, my head hurts. The shitty fluorescent lighting in the restaurant doesn't help. Nor does Dean and Chloe's giggling.

It's great they're happy and in love.

That it's easy for them to communicate and express their emotions.

They don't have to make it so obvious.

I shrug my shoulders. Cross my legs. Order a cup of coffee.

Dean takes a long look at me and shakes his head. "Day two of married life harder than day one?"

I flip him off.

He chuckles his usual good-natured chuckle.

Chloe whispers something in his ear.

He shakes his head *no way*.

"Is everything okay?" She takes a long sip of her tea.

Usually, I keep everyone out of my business. I keep everyone as far away from my business as possible.

It's safer.

But it's lonely too.

I need help. I hate to admit it, but I do. "No."

"You want to talk about it?" she asks.

"You're a woman." I bring my eyes to hers.

"What tipped you off?" Dean teases.

I ignore him. "You ever want space?"

"Sure. Who doesn't?" She turns to Dean. Half-smiles. "Well... Most people do."

He wraps his arm around her.

"How do you tell him?" I ask.

"Bluntly," Dean says.

She nods. "I'm not the most tactful."

"And I am?" I arch a brow.

She laughs. "It's always hard. Even when you love someone. Things get lost in translation."

"Yeah." My gaze shifts around the diner. It's as nondescript as it gets. Beige walls. Red booths. Grey tables. Like it's trying to be forgettable.

"It's not really my place, Griff, but have you considered not staying married?" Chloe's voice is soft. Caring. "That's a lot of extra pressure on a relationship."

"He's never gonna do better," Dean says.

She nods *probably*. Or maybe *I understand*. "I know you care about her. But maybe… Maybe this is one of those times where you have to let her go."

"Maybe." My stomach turns at the thought.

"Sunshine, you're bringing down the mood." Dean offers me a slice of his toast—they're eating a late breakfast.

I take it. Spread strawberry jam over the top. Eat it in two bites.

"How about we talk about something we can all enjoy?" Dean asks.

Her expression gets apprehensive. "What would that be?"

"How many times Mr. Aloof made his wife come." Dean raises a brow. "With as much detail as possible, preferably."

She rolls her eyes.

"Hey, if you'd rather we talk about my cock piercing, I'm game for that," he says.

She shoots him that *you're so ridiculous, I can't help but love you* look of hers.

He motions *come here*.

She wraps her arms around his shoulders.

He leans down. Presses his lips to hers.

Their kiss is soft. Slow. Sweet.

Sickening.

I steal another slice of Dean's toast. Wash it down with more coffee.

I don't blame them either.

If it was that easy for me…

Fuck, I wish it was that easy for me.

Chapter Thirty-Eight

GRIFFIN

Jules meets us at the valet.

She climbs into the back seat. Dons her headphones. Closes her eyes.

I volunteer to take the first shift.

Even though Jules is listening to an audiobook—she gets this look on her face when she's wrapped up in a story—I play her favorite band.

It's still my favorite band.

Even if it tugs at the confusion in my gut.

And it does.

I try to distract myself with the desert scenery, but the album pours into my soul.

With every song, I want to understand her more.

I miss her more.

I need her more.

After an hour and a half of driving, I hand over

the reins. Take the spot in the middle. Watch the desert whip past the windows.

My head gets heavy.

My eyes get tired.

I lean against the window…

Wake to a buzz in my jeans.

Jules: I want to talk to you. I do. I just don't know how. I'm sorry. But please be patient.

I shift out of my seat, look to her.

She mouths *I'm sorry*.

I pick up my cell. Tap a reply.

Griffin: Don't be sorry.

Jules: I completely locked you out.

Griffin: You were honest about it.

Jules: I'm not sure that's true.

Griffin: Have you lied to me?

Jules: Is that supposed to be an accusation or a comfort?

Griffin: A question.

Jules: I don't know. I don't think so.

Griffin: You come on some other guy's face?

Jules: You're obsessed with that.

Griffin: I know what I like.

Jules: Obsessed.

Griffin: That makes sense to me.

Jules: Cunnilingus?

Griffin: Sex.

Jules: Well, yeah, it's been your coping mechanism forever.

Griffin: That's not it.

Jules: It's not?

Griffin: Yeah, I've used sex as a way to kill time. Or drown out my thoughts. But it's mostly been something to do. With you, it's different. It's like every molecule in my body understands every molecule in yours.

With sex, I understand her. I know what she wants,

what she needs, how to give it to her.

Right now?

I have no fucking clue how to be what she needs.

Jules: We've only done it once.

Griffin: I want to fix that.

Jules: You're not mad?

Griffin: When do I get mad?

Jules: When someone hurts me.

Griffin: Has someone?

Jules: Not like that.

Griffin: Like what?

Jules: You know I called off my engagement four days ago.

Griffin: Five now.

Jules: Damn, you got me. That fifth day makes it so much easier to process.

Griffin: You still love him?

Jules: I don't know. You can't turn off loving someone. Even when they did something to poison your love.

Griffin: It's okay if you do.

Jules: You won't be jealous?

Griffin: He's slept next to you for the last four years. Of course I'm jealous.

Jules: I've never seen you jealous before.

Griffin: You still can't.

Jules: I have the back of your head. It's cute jealous.

Griffin: How can you tell?

Jules: The way the hair curls.

Griffin: That's a load.

Jules: Maybe it's like… there's this storytelling principle. If you show a blank expression, then a hamburger, then the same blank expression, people will assume a character is hungry.

Griffin: And you skipped lunch?

Jules: Yes, but that's not my point.

Griffin: You didn't eat?

Jules: I'm not hungry.

Griffin: Fuck that.

I unbuckle my seatbelt. Grab my backpack. Sling it over my shoulder.

Jules squeals as I climb over the middle seat. "We're going eighty miles an hour."

"If you two have sex back there, I'm gonna crash," Dean says.

Chloe chuckles. "Are you suggesting they do it or not?"

"Just informing them of probabilities." He laughs.

She laughs louder. Then she turns the music up until it drowns out her laugh.

It's grunge, of course.

I motion to the speakers and shake my head.

Jules nods. She pulls out her cell. Taps a text.

Jules: How can these guys be so miserable? Aren't they high on heroin?

Griffin: Aren't your emo musicians high on misogyny?

Jules: How do you get high on misogyny?

Griffin: I don't know. But that one guy really likes to moan about how his ex needs to drive off a bridge.

Jules: He doesn't even write the lyrics.

Griffin: Maybe he just identifies.

Jules: He's actually married to his high school sweetheart.

Griffin: Not that you care.

My backpack isn't exactly a stash of snacks, but I have enough. I pull out the jerky I bought at the weird alien themed attraction.

Jules shakes her head. She says something that disappears in the music.

I motion to my ear *I can't hear you.*

She scoots closer. "I'm not hungry."

"Then hold onto it." My lips brush her ear.

Her eyelids press together. "Griff…"

"That a keep going or a stop?"

"Not here." She turns to me. Stares into my eyes. "I…"

Her words dissolve in the music.

I tap a response on my cell.

Griffin: I will.

Jules: Huh?

Griffin: Be patient.

Jules: Oh. Thanks.

Griffin: We are married.

Jules: It's completely insane.

Griffin: Yeah. You're stuck with me now.

Jules: I was going to say the same thing.

Griffin: You got the worse end of this deal.

Jules: Are you kidding? You have a job. I'm about to start an MFA program.

Griffin: You'll figure it out.

Jules: Or I'll work at Starbucks my entire life.

Griffin: You'd never work at Starbucks.

Jules: Okay, I'll beg for a job at that matcha shop on Abbot Kinney.

Griffin: With how much you'd save, your salary would be worth double.

Jules: True. But it's not a career.

Griffin: You're smart. You will figure it out.

Jules: I want to believe that.

Griffin: It's okay you're scared.

Jules: I'm doing it. And I don't want your input on how I'm supposed to feel about it. Even if your input is "whatever you feel is okay."

Griffin: Is that your way of saying "fuck off, Griff."

Jules: Maybe.

Griffin: I love when you bitch-slap me.

Jules: Is that a kink of yours?

Griffin: No, but if you're into it, I'm game.

Jules: Uh… no. Not at all.

Her lips curl into a half-smile. It's easy. Normal.

That's what I want.

Everything I want.

Griffin: Make me a promise?

Jules: Okay.

Griffin: Be patient with me too.

Jules: I promise.

Chapter Thirty-Nine

GRIFFIN

By the time we arrive at my place, I'm dead tired.

I get our suitcases out of the trunk. Wish Dean and Chloe goodbye.

They wish me good luck, get in their borrowed car, and drive away.

Jules hugs her purse to her chest. "Griff, I—"

"You don't want to stay anymore?"

"I do."

"So what's the question?"

"Oh, I just thought you—"

"Don't want to share an apartment with my wife?"

Her eyes go wide. "It doesn't feel real."

"I know."

"Do you think it will?"

"We have until Monday."

She nods *right*, even though that's not quite accurate.

Yeah, she agreed to give me the weekend, but it's not like there's some curse compelling her to stay past Monday.

If she wakes up Tuesday and decides she wants a divorce—

Fuck, I'm not considering that possibility. Not yet.

"You hungry?" I roll my suitcase to the apartment door.

She follows. "The better question is: where can I get a matcha right away?"

"It's—" I motion to the dark sky. There isn't a single hint of light. Just the blue sky, the silver moon, the distant stars. "Late."

She nods *true*. "What about matcha soft serve?"

Fuck, that fills my head with ideas. I need to taste her lips again. I need to taste every inch of her skin.

Tonight.

I need her coming on my face tonight.

No, I need to listen. To wait. To give her space.

My cock doesn't give a fuck about space. Only about her soft lips, her perfect tits, her sweet cunt.

Shit, there I go again.

"You're distracting." I fish my key from my pocket. Unlock the door. Motion *after you*.

She smooths her tight white tank top. "I'm distracting?"

My gaze goes straight to her ass. Fuck, those jeans hug her skin like they were made for her.

Her hips sway as she steps into the house.

"What do you call this?" Her fingers brush my bare shoulders. "Since when do you even own muscle tees?"

"Since I realized I liked women staring at me."

"So… third grade?"

I chuckle. "Pretty much."

"How come I never see them?"

"You weren't paying attention." I follow her inside. Pull the door closed. Click the lock.

Jules looks around the apartment with wide eyes.

It's mine. I love it just for that.

It's a nice place, considering the rent and the proximity to the beach, but it's not exactly spacious.

She deserves better.

She's used to better.

I motion to the couch. "If you want the bed, it's yours."

"You don't want—"

"I do."

"Oh." Her lips press together.

"I want to peel you out of those clothes—"

"Griff."

"Let me finish, baby."

She nods *okay*.

I try to make my voice steady, but it still drops to something dirty and demanding. "I want to strip out of these clothes, tear off yours, and press every inch of my skin against yours."

Her lips press together.

"I don't want any space between us."

"I…"

"But I want to give you what you need more."

Her eyes meet mine.

"Tell me what you need."

"Besides matcha?"

"You know where it is." I move to the fridge. Find her favorite jar of matcha. "You want one now?"

She shakes her head. "Dinner is good."

"Yeah?"

"Yeah."

"You want to sleep in my bed?" I ask.

"Okay."

"With me?"

"Yeah." Her gaze shifts to her wedding ring. "With clothes."

"I like my way better."

Her smile is bittersweet. "I know."

I try not to read into it.

I hate that she's hurting. I hate inviting distance between us. I hate how much I hate it.

But I'm gonna get the fuck over it.

I'm going to be the husband she needs.

"Not sure I have any food." I check the cabinets. It's mostly frozen burritos and canned soup, but there's enough to throw together dinner. "What do you think about shrimp and broccoli?"

"Mmm. Food?"

I chuckle. "Go. Put your suitcase away. Then come back."

"Away where?"

"In my room."

"It's yours?" she asks.

"Ours."

She looks at me funny. "We, uh…"

I shouldn't press the whole *we're married* thing, no matter how much I want to. "Until Monday at least."

Her shoulders relax. "Okay. Until Monday." She carts her suitcase into my bedroom. Our bedroom.

I fill the rice cooker, bring a pot of water to boil, add frozen shrimp, then frozen broccoli.

It's not the finest meal in the world, but it's enough.

"Jackson didn't like it when you cooked for me." She wraps her arms around my waist. Her lips brush my neck. Her chest sinks into my back.

Fuck, she feels good.

I need her this close.

I need her to always be this close.

I don't understand much, but I do understand that.

"He was too jealous." I offer her the spoon.

She stirs the boiling shrimp and veggies. "Yeah, but

then… well, it's kinda hard to say he was wrong. Considering."

I shake my head. "Wouldn't have happened if he'd kept his pants zipped."

"You think so?"

"Yeah."

She takes a spot next to me. Warms a pan and coats it with olive oil. "You really didn't realize?"

"That I was in… that I wanted you?"

"Yeah."

"I didn't," I say.

"You were going to let me marry this guy you hate?"

"He's not good enough for you."

"You were still going to let it happen."

"Since when can I stop you from doing anything?"

Her lips curl into a soft smile. "You have your ways."

"Manipulation and bribery, yeah. But they're not my preferred ways." I place the colander in the sink. "That morning, did you want to go through with it?"

"I don't know. It felt so… inevitable. There was all this pressure. It didn't feel like I was driving. More like I was on a train, being led to a destination."

"You can get off a train."

"At a stop, yeah, but that felt like the next stop."

"Less embarrassing to get divorced after six months than to call off the wedding?"

"Kinda, yeah." She pulls her arm over her chest. "I… I did love him. I don't want to play that down. Because I really did."

"I know."

"I wanted to dance with him at prom. I wanted to walk on the beach. To make love—"

"You did not say make love."

"I did. And I wanted to make love on his bed, the weekend his parents were out of town."

"It was terrible."

"Not the point." She pulls fish sauce and sesame oil from the pantry.

I drain the shrimp and veggies. Turn off the burner.

"It was good. We were good. For a while. But then, we weren't. And I didn't love him anymore. I didn't realize it, but I didn't. I wasn't sure what happened. Or why. Or how I could stop it. And I..." She presses her lips together. "I didn't do anything about it."

I pass her the colander.

Her fingers brush mine as she takes it. "I knew. That Valentine's Day junior year when I called you crying. I knew we'd broken in some way. That I didn't understand the person he was then. That he didn't understand me. That there was some fatal flaw. But I was too scared to leave."

"Did he—"

"No, not like that. It was more... I was scared of what it would mean. About me. And about us, too."

"You and Jackson?"

"You and me." The pan sizzles as she stirs ingredients together. "I didn't think about it, consciously, but I think I knew, deep down. As long as I was with Jackson, things between us couldn't change."

"I know what you mean."

"Is that stupid?"

"No."

"I, um... we weren't having good sex. That's true. But it was me as much as him." She passes me the spoon. Steps backward. Moves to the couch.

"I don't believe that."

She presses her ass against the armrest. "You don't believe me?"

"I've fucked you, Jules. I know what it's like."

Her cheeks flush. "It's... God, I wish I could explain."

"You can."

"I... uh... hold on. I have to pee." She rushes to the bathroom and slams the door shut.

I try not to read into it.

My attention shifts to the stir fry. It's nearly done, but it will be another half an hour until the rice is ready.

My stomach growls from the scent of sesame and orange.

I put the burner on low. Pour a glass of water. Take a seat on the couch.

Jules joins me. She places her Bluetooth speaker on the coffee table, connects her phone, plays her favorite Paramore album.

"We listened to this in the car," I say.

"And?" Her lips curl into a half smile, but there's something off about it. Something missing.

"Fair point."

She turns the volume up. Leans back. Closes her eyes.

There's something about the way she soaks in a song. It's just so fucking Jules.

The chorus fades into the outro.

Into an intro.

"Griff?" she asks.

"Yeah." It takes all the restraint I have not to add *what do you want, baby? You want to come on my hands? Cock? Face? Against that toy again?*

"I, um... hold on." She looks to her phone. Taps something.

Jules: I want to tell you. But I don't think I can say it out loud.

"You can write it."

She shakes her head and motions to the screen.

Okay. If this is what she needs, I can do it.

Griffin: You can write it here.

Jules: That's the thing. I'm not sure I can. I'm not sure I've ever written it before.

Griffin: Have you said it out loud?

Jules: No, but I think that will be harder.

Griffin: You don't have to do it now.

Jules: This weekend is for you too, right?

Griffin: Yeah.

But there's no way I'm going to decide I don't want to stay married to her.

She's Jules.

She's fucking everything.

Griffin: Are you pregnant?

Jules: God no.

Griffin: Related to a cousin?

Jules: Of course I'm related to a cousin. That's what makes them a cousin.

Griffin: Didn't think that one through.

Jules: You don't need to guess.

Griffin: One more guess.

Jules: Okay.

Griffin: You secretly a cam girl?

Jules: Hell no.

Griffin: Porn star?

Jules: If I was?

Griffin: I'd look you up right away.

Jules: Watch me fuck other guys?

Griffin: I'm hoping you stuck to solo videos, but, yeah, I'd watch.

Jules: Why do you want to watch me fuck other guys?

Griffin: I want to watch you fuck.

Jules: You are seriously depraved.

Griffin: Because I want to make love to my wife?

Jules: You have never thought "make love" in your entire life.

Griffin: I just did.

She shakes her head *you did not.*

Jules: I still don't know why I put up with you.

Griffin: It's the face.

Jules: It is nice.

Griffin: It's a gift. And a curse.

Jules: When has it ever been a curse?

Griffin: Sometimes, I'm too beautiful. People don't take me seriously.

Jules: Uh-huh. The people who pay you ungodly hourly rates to permanently mark their bodies don't take you seriously?

Griffin: Sometimes.

Jules: Or do the girls so desperately want to fuck you that they leave enormous tips?

Griffin: That's the part where it's a gift.

Jules: Or maybe it's all a gift.

Griffin: Maybe the gift is when you come on my face.

Jules: Griff.

Griffin: Yeah?

Jules: There's a reason why I haven't let you.

Griffin: It's really hard not guessing.

Jules: I know.

Griffin: You could help me out. Tell me.

Jules: I'm working up to it.

Her gaze shifts to me. She sucks in a shaky breath. Stands. Moves into the hallway.

Then the bedroom.

She presses the door closed.

My phone buzzes.

Jules: You think I'm insane, don't you?

Griffin: You have a unique charm.

Jules: You do too.

Griffin: Don't tell me you don't like it anymore.

Jules: I do. I just. I know how you feel about honesty.

Griffin: How is that?

Jules: You have a violent hatred of anything less than the complete truth.

Griffin: What are you saying, Jules?

Jules: I'm trying to tell you something.

Griffin: You can tell me anything.

Jules: Promise you won't be mad.

My chest gets heavy.

It's impossible to breathe.

There's only one thing that comes to mind.

I don't want it to be that.

But what the fuck else could it be?

Griffin: I'm not going to make a promise I can't keep.

Jules: Promise you'll try.

Griffin: Try how?

Jules: Promise you'll stop and think before you say anything.

Griffin: You hiding for my benefit or yours?

Jules: Both.

Griffin: I promise.

The screen is blank for a long moment.

Finally, it flashes with her text.

Jules: I still cut.

Chapter Forty

JULIETTE

My heart rises in my throat.

I press my back against the door. Attempt to find some steadiness.

There's not enough.

My grip slips.

My cell tumbles onto the carpet.

My ass slides down the wood.

I sit, pull my knees into my chest, bury my head between my legs.

This is what people do in the movies when they're going to throw up.

It's not working.

I'm still shaking.

My heartbeat is loud enough to drown out the music.

I know where the song goes. My head can fill in the blanks. But it's not the same.

It's the broad strokes, not the specifics of every single note.

And this—

My cell buzzes.

I jerk backward. Slam against the door. Back. Shoulders. Head.

Fuck. That hurts.

Not enough to center me.

Only enough to hurt.

Dammit. Even in the middle of a teary confession, I crave my bad habit.

Shit.

A tear catches on my lashes.

Then I blink and my vision blurs.

I push off the wall. Reach for the cell. It's slippery against my palms. It takes three tries, but I manage to unlock it.

Griffin: Are you okay?

I'm telling my best friend I'm a disappointment.

No, I'm telling my husband I'm a disappointment.

I'm not okay.

But that isn't what he's asking.

It's the bigger, uglier question. The one people dance around (not that I give them a chance). The other implication of taking a razor to my skin.

"Jules." His footsteps move closer.

The music moves with them.

He's carrying the speaker to my room.

It's teasing and silly and perfect.

Maybe this will be okay.

Maybe he won't run.

Maybe he'll accept it.

"Jules." His fingers brush the door.

I try to reply, but the words get stuck in my throat. My thoughts are a mess. I can't explain it. I don't even understand it. How can I make him understand it?

Jules: Don't open the door.

Griffin: I won't.

Jules: Thanks for the tunes.

Griffin: Have to admit something to you.

I'm a disappointment.

He's mad.

He hates me.

Griffin: This song makes me hard now.

Jules: OMG.

Griffin: It does.

Jules: Is this the time?

Griffin: Are you smiling?

Yeah, I am. It helps. It really does.

Jules: Maybe.

"I fucked this up last time." His voice is earnest. Caring.

"A little." My words are a squeak.

"I'm not good at this stuff."

"I know."

"But I want to be. I want to give you what you need."

I nod. Of course, that isn't helpful. He's on the other side of the door.

Jules: I don't know what I need.

Griffin: You told me for a reason.

Jules: You should know the truth. Before you decide if you want to stay married.

"Jules…"

I can't place his tone. It's not a good tone, but it's not bad either.

Jules: Are you mad?

Griffin: Does it matter?

Jules: To me.

Griffin: I'm not seventeen anymore. I'm not making it about me this time.

Jules: I want to know.

He taps the door. "This will be easier if you open the door."

I shake my head. It won't. It's easier if I don't have to look him in the eyes.

If I don't have to bring the words to my lips.

If I don't have to face his reaction.

I type it out again.

Jules: Are you mad?

"I'm not answering that." His voice is low. Frustrated.

I don't know what it means.

I'm not sure I want to know.

"Please." I press my cell to my chest. "Are you?"

"Yeah."

I swallow hard.

"You promised." Hurt seeps into his voice.

I try to find the words, but there's nothing I can say.

Jules: I'm sorry.

"What for?" he asks.

Too much.

"That night, I thought you meant it. That you really would stop." His fingers brush the door.

"I did. I… I tried."

"At some point, I realized you couldn't promise that. It was like when Hunter promised he'd stop drinking. He meant it. But he couldn't do it on his own."

"I did. I did mean it."

"I know." The handle shakes. "Can I come in?"

"Not yet." I suck a breath through my teeth. Let out a steady exhale. "You think I'm that bad?"

"Huh?"

"As Hunter?" I ask.

"I have no fucking idea."

Oh.

"I didn't know you were still cutting." His voice softens.

"I've seen marks. But I figured they were old scars. Fuck, I really believed you'd tell me if it happened again."

"I'm sorry."

"Don't apologize."

"But… I lied."

"Yeah. And that fucking hurts. It kills me that you didn't trust me enough to tell me."

My heart sinks.

"But that's not what matters."

"Griff—"

"I hate that you went through this alone."

"Well…"

"Oh." His sigh is heavy. "He knows?"

Is he jealous?

I want to slap him for the imposition—who the fuck does he think he is, being jealous of my goddamn fiancé, ex-fiancé, whatever?

How can he be jealous of this?

How can he make it about him, again?

But he isn't.

I mean, I don't think he is.

I'm reading into things.

Griffin is allowed to be hurt or pissed or disappointed.

I just…

I can't take that. Or help him with it. Or absolve him of it.

"Jules?" he asks.

My exhale is sharp. "Jackson figured it out."

"What does that mean?"

My inhale is shallow. "I told him when we started dating. I mean, it was sort of unavoidable."

"Yeah."

I trace the design on my wrist. Griffin's design. The lush flowers. The curving words. *This too will pass.* We laughed over how overwrought it was. Over how cheesy it was. Really *this too will pass*? It belongs on one of those motivational posters. It's something my mom would hang on the wall.

When my mom saw it, she gushed about how beautiful it was. (She's insecure about the whole *you don't even know your father's name* thing. She tries, hard, to be as accepting as possible about any of my "eccentricities." I think she blames them on my "daddy issues").

She loved the message. And she didn't notice the scars. She might have noticed that I suddenly started wearing short sleeves again, but she never mentioned it.

Jackson… he wasn't the most observant guy. He wouldn't have noticed the scars under my cover-up. But the ones on my hips and thighs? The ones Griffin didn't know about?

There was no hiding those. "He didn't really think much of it. I told him I'd stopped, that it was an old phase, and he believed me. For a long time. Or maybe he just wanted to believe me."

"I get that."

"Did you?" I ask.

"Did I what?"

"Want to believe me?"

"Yeah." His voice gets louder. "I hate when you hurt."

"It helps."

"Maybe. But it's not like you're slicing your skin because you're doing well."

"I… I'm careful."

"Is that supposed to make me feel better?"

Yes. Of course. But how can I blame him for worrying? If it was Griffin taking a razor to his skin—

I couldn't handle that. I really couldn't.

His finger brushes the knob again. "I… I should check the rice."

"Griff."

"Yeah?"

This is going to be okay. This can be okay. It needs to be okay. "I just…"

"You need something to drink?"

"Water. Thanks."

"Sure." His footsteps move away from the door.

The speaker stays here. I try to melt into the chorus the way I usually do, but it's impossible.

It's so *here*.

It's everywhere.

I lean against the door. Try to find support. The surface is too hard, too unyielding.

I slip my cell into my pocket, climb onto the bed, slip under the covers.

The *Twilight* covers.

That wasn't a joke. He really did find a comforter with Robert Pattinson's face on it.

Where the fuck did he find this?

A laugh spills from my lips. It breaks up the tension in my jaw. It's not enough to relax me, but it's something.

"Hey." Griff knocks on the door. "You want me to leave this or—"

"Come in." I pull the comforter over my head.

He turns the handle.

The door creeks open.

A chuckle spills from his lips. "I take it you like the decor?"

"Yeah." I roll onto my side, so my back is to him, so there's no possibility I'll have to look him in the eyes. "How's the rice?"

"Almost finished."

"Good. I'm… well I'm not really hungry anymore."

He moves closer. Sets the water on the bedside table.

Then he climbs into bed next to me.

He leaves the comforter between us as he places his body behind mine.

I want to soak up all that intimacy.

But I can't.

Not yet.

"I know you're disappointed," I say. "Just don't… don't look at me like I've failed you."

His sigh is heavy. "Jules, no."

I swallow hard.

"I don't want to get wrapped up in that shit."

"But—"

"It hurts you didn't tell me. That you lied. That you could tell him and not me. But that pales in comparison to knowing you went through this."

"Oh."

"I don't know what to say either." He rests his head in the crook of my neck. "But I want to be here. To listen."

"Okay."

"If you need to lie here by yourself—"

"No." I pull the blanket tighter. "Stay."

"When was the last time?"

"Do I have to answer that?"

He tries to keep his voice steady, but he doesn't get there. "Yeah."

My heart thuds against my chest. "After I called it off."

"That was five days ago."

"I know."

"Fuck." Fear drips into his voice. "Where?"

"I can't show you yet."

"Why not?"

"I just… I'm not there yet."

"Okay." His fingers skim the top of the blanket. "Can I get under here?"

"If you don't look me in the eyes."

His voice is soft. "I'm not gonna look at you like you failed me."

"I did."

"Doesn't do any good assigning blame."

"You sound like my therapist."

"You still go?"

I shake my head. Not anymore. Not for a long time.

Griffin pulls the blanket up.

He slips under it. Presses his chest to my back, his crotch to my ass, his quads to my hamstrings. "What happened with Jackson?"

"Oh, right." It's easier talking about him. It doesn't matter anymore. "I was drunk one night. Forgot to turn off the lights and direct his attention… elsewhere. He saw them. Went soft. Started blaming me for disturbing his precious erection."

"Fuck."

"I stopped trying after that."

"Trying?" He pushes my hair behind my ear.

"With him. With sex. With everything, I guess. The last two years… we were going through the motions. I knew it. He knew it. You probably knew it."

"I knew you weren't happy."

I swallow hard.

"Are you happy?"

"I'm too everything to be anything."

His fingers brush my temple. "That was two years ago?"

"About that."

"So you've—"

"I stopped for a few months. I tried, Griff, I did. But it

was too much. After a week, I felt like everything was spilling out of me. I didn't have anywhere to go. I'd convinced Jackson it didn't matter. I'd promised you I wouldn't. I… maybe you would have listened when I said I wanted to, but after the way you looked at me… I couldn't tell you."

His fingers skim my chin. "I'm sorry."

"You don't—"

"I know. But I am. I… It means the fucking world to me, that you're telling me this."

My stomach flutters. "But… I lied. I broke my promise."

"I know."

"Aren't you—"

"You gonna ask if I'm mad again?"

"Yeah."

"Stop asking about shit that doesn't matter."

"It does—"

"It doesn't." He drags his fingertips down my neck. "I'm not asking to berate you."

My inhale is shallow.

"Or guilt you."

My exhale is shaky.

"I'm asking because I'm terrified of something happening to you."

"I'm—"

"Don't say you're careful. That's only gonna scare me more."

"You don't get to take this," I say.

"I know."

"You don't get to make it about you being scared or worried or hurt."

"I don't want to." He draws a line over my shoulder, down my arm, all the way to the tip of my index finger. "But I'm not gonna let you shoulder this alone, baby."

"I..."

"I know you can handle it. You've been handling it for the last five years."

"I..."

"I'm not gonna let you do that anymore. If I'm over-stepping, you can tell me to go fuck myself," he says.

"And you will."

He chuckles. "Yeah. It will be fucking painful not touching you while I do it, but I'll come like that"—he snaps his fingers—"with you watching."

My laugh breaks up the tension in my chest. "How can you still go back to sex?"

"You telling me this isn't about sex?"

"No..." Okay, that isn't true. Not exactly. "It's complicated."

"I'm sorry I failed you the first time. I really am. But I'm not that stupid kid anymore. I'm stupid, yeah. But I'm better at this."

"What if I'm not?"

"You're telling me, aren't you?" he asks.

"Barely."

"You are." He turns my arm over. Traces the scars on my wrist with his thumb. "I can't promise perfection. I can't promise I'll be cool. Fuck, when things hurt you I see red. I can't think. I want to destroy whatever it is that's causing you pain."

"But I'm... it's not like that."

"I know. And I'm gonna try to be better. But I'm gonna fuck it up sometimes."

"Me too."

"You have to stop."

"I know."

"No, baby. I'm not Jackson." He traces the design from my wrist to the crook of my elbow. "I'm not gonna shrug this off and assume you know best."

"I... it's my body."

"Yeah, and this is *our* relationship. I'm not gonna watch while you hurt yourself."

"So this is..." I suck a deep breath through my nose. Push the exhale through my mouth. I have to look at him. To face him. To face this.

There's no anger in his dark eyes. There's fear and frustration and affection, but there isn't a single hint of disappointment.

"Is this an ultimatum?" I ask.

"More like—" He cups my cheek with his palm. "I can't stand by and watch you hurt."

"So if I don't stop—"

"If you don't try—"

"That's it?"

"Yeah," he says.

"And, what, I need to decide by Monday?"

"Don't you want to stop?"

"Yeah, but..." It's mine.

"But what?"

"I..." I can't explain this. It's not that I don't want to stop. I do. I just don't know how to function without it.

"It's not supposed to be adversarial." He rubs my temple with his thumb. "We want the same thing."

I'm not sure about that.

"We want you to be okay."

I lean into his touch. I do want that. It's just... This is the way I've been okay. For such a long time. What the hell am I without it?

"I don't want to make it an ultimatum. But it is. I'm not sure what the fuck I'm supposed to say here, so I'm gonna tell you what I need." His eyes bore into mine. "I need you to try. I'll do whatever I can to find you help. But we both know it won't do shit unless you're willing to try."

"Yeah."

"Will you?" He traces the scars on my wrist. "Will you try?"

Chapter Forty-One

GRIFFIN

Jules's green eyes fill with frustration.

Her chest heaves with her inhale. "I can't think about that yet." Her voice is soft. Apologetic. "I… I do want to stop. I hate that I'm not strong enough to stop. But I'm not—"

"You're the strongest person I know."

"But—"

"Feel whatever you feel, baby. But don't expect me to agree." I wrap my arm around her. Pull her closer.

She shakes under my touch. "Griff, I… I don't know what to say."

"Me either." There's so much going through my head. She's right about everything. I'm mad. I'm hurt. I'm disappointed.

My best friend's been lying to me for years.

She didn't trust me.

I didn't see it.

Her idiotic boyfriend saw it and I didn't see it.

It hurts like hell.

But that doesn't compare to the fear gripping my stomach.

Maybe that's my baggage.

Maybe I'm asking too much of her.

But I can't stand here and watch her hurt herself.

"Can we talk about this later?" Her fingers dig into my chest, over my t-shirt.

"If that's what you need."

She nods *yeah*.

"Okay." I want to forget this as much as she does. But I can't. I can't pretend like shit is normal.

I can give her time and space.

I can be the guy she needs.

We're gonna have to finish this conversation, no matter how ugly and painful it gets. But we can do that later.

Right now—

I pull her closer.

She slips her hand under my t-shirt.

Fuck, her touch feels good. It erases all the shit running through my head.

Quiets that voice asking if I'm doing the right thing.

It makes sense.

And this—

"You know what this means, baby?" I ask.

She shakes her head.

"I can taste your cunt."

"Oh my God."

"Yeah?"

"Why is it always sex?" Lightness drips into her voice.

"Why is it always sex when you're tugging at my t-shirt?"

She laughs. "Not tugging…"

"You don't want me to take it off?"

"I wouldn't turn it down."

I do away with my t-shirt.

Her eyes meet mine. They beg for love, affection, forgiveness.

I wish I could explain this to her. That I could make her understand how I feel about her.

But the words are jumbled.

I'm not good with words.

I'll have to show her.

I cup the back of her head with my palm.

She closes her eyes.

I press my lips to hers. Softly. Then harder.

She sucks on my bottom lip. Tugs at my hair. Rocks her hips against mine.

She wants to erase this confusion.

She wants to connect.

She wants to come.

Fuck, how I want to make her come.

I bring my hand to her chest. Cup her over her tank top. Then under it.

She groans as I drag my thumb over her nipple.

I do it again. Again. I tease her until she breaks our kiss. Rolls onto her back. Closes her eyes.

She's so fucking beautiful wracked with pleasure.

I want to toy with her forever. To keep her in this place where I understand everything she wants. Where I can give her everything she wants.

This is the only time I can give her everything she wants.

I draw circles around her nipple.

Her head falls to one side.

I keep those same slow, steady circles.

"Griff." Her nails scrape my chest. "Don't stop."

Like hell.

This is everything I want.

No, I want more. I want everything with Jules. I want every thought in her head. Every bit of trust. Every promise of forever.

But that's a confusing mess.

No more thinking about tomorrow.

Only this.

All of this.

I draw circles around her nipple until she's writhing, then I switch to my index finger and I do it again.

Again.

Middle.

Ring.

Pinkie.

And back again.

Her palm goes flat against my chest.

I kiss her hard.

She parts her lips to make way for my tongue.

Fuck, she tastes good. And this—kissing her, touching her, claiming her—is everything.

We're a perfect circle of need.

I toy with her.

She groans into my mouth.

I drag my lips down her neck.

She writhes under me.

I suck on her nipple.

She scrapes her nails against my chest.

The hint of pain sends blood rushing south. Not because I get off on pain—though I'm game to try that.

Because she's so lost in bliss she's claiming me.

Fuck, I want to be hers. To know I'm hers forever.

"Griffin." Her nails scrape my shoulders.

My balls tighten. I need her saying my name like that. I need it more than I've ever needed anything.

I flick my tongue against her tender bud.

"Mmmm."

"Say my name, baby." I tease her again.

"Griffin." She rakes her nails over my chest. "Please."

Goddamn, that sounds good on her lips. I want to tease her forever.

But I want to make her come more.

I release her nipple. Press my lips to the spot between her breasts.

Her stomach.

Her bellybutton.

"Griff, I…" She arches her back. Unhooks her bra. Flings it aside. "I want you to. But they're bad." Her eyelids flutter open. "Don't freak out, okay?"

I can't promise that. But I can promise this. "I need to make you come, Jules."

"I know. I just…"

"Take off your pants."

"Don't freak out."

"Now." I nip at her soft skin.

Her eyes fill with apprehension.

This is a big deal. For both of us. But I'm not treating it like that.

I'm not letting that ruin this.

I'm not letting anything ruin this.

"Don't make me ask twice." I drop my voice to something low and demanding.

Jules's pupils dilate. She nods *yes*, unbuttons her jeans, slides them off her hips.

Her eyelids press together.

Her brow furrows.

Still, she pushes her jeans to her knees.

I peel them off her feet. Toss them aside. Climb between her legs.

I'm eating out my wife.

It doesn't have to be more than that.

But it is.

It's *there*.

I drag my fingers up her thigh. Over her smooth skin. Over the scars that crisscross her legs and hips.

They cover her skin. Of course they do. She's been hiding it for years.

She's been doing it for years.

My chest gets heavy.

Words claw at my throat. *What the fuck, Jules? How could you hide this for so long? How could you pretend everything is okay?*

I swallow them. It's not the time. Or the place. It's not my place.

Yeah, I'm terrified.

But I'm thrilled too.

She's dropping the walls around her heart.

"Griff." Her voice is an apprehensive squeak. "Is it… it's okay if you want to stop."

"Fuck no." I press my lips to her inner thigh.

"Is it ugly?"

"No." I trace her scars with my thumb. There's nothing beautiful about Jules hurting herself. But this, her letting me in—

Fuck, it's everything.

"Every part of you is beautiful." I drag my lips higher. Higher. Higher.

She groans as I press my mouth to her clit. Her panties are in the way, but I can still feel her warmth.

I blow hot air over her cunt.

Then I move to her other leg. Plant a row of kisses over her thighs.

Over the scars.

Then the smooth skin.

Then back again.

"You're not..." She sucks a breath through her teeth. "Fuck."

I reach up. Wrap my fingers around her wrist. Bring her hand to my crotch.

She groans as her palm brushes my hard-on. "Griff."

"Yeah, baby?"

"You're still hard?"

"Of course."

"You're not—"

I want to reassure her, I do. But I can't wait another fucking second. "You need to come on my face now."

Her last hint of apprehension slips away. She nods *hell yes* and pushes her panties off her hips.

Slowly, I roll them to her ankles.

I place myself between her legs and I pin her to the bed.

Jules groans as I bring my mouth to her.

I lick her up and down, taking my sweet, sweet time tasting every inch of her. Studying the way she groans or writhes as I tease her.

She tastes so fucking good.

And knowing it's Jules—

Fuck. My cock whines for satisfaction. It wants to be inside her. It wants every inch of her warmth.

Soon.

This first.

Now that I know—

Always this first.

I explore her. I suck on her lips. Scrape my teeth against her tender flesh. Softly. Then hard enough to make her yelp.

She tugs at my hair. "Griff."

I toy with one side. Then the other.

"Fuck." She writhes against me.

I plunge my tongue inside her.

Slowly. Then faster.

Softly, then harder.

Once I've explored every inch, I bring my tongue to her clit. Take my sweet, sweet time figuring out what she likes.

I try softer, harder, slower, faster, higher, lower, right, left—

There.

Her breath hitches.

Her thighs fight my hands.

Her fingers curl into my hair.

I press my palms against her inner thighs. Not hard enough to hurt. Hard enough to remind her she's mine.

"Fuck, Griff." She tugs at my hair. "Don't stop."

For a moment, I look up at her. Watch her brow soften, her cheeks flush, her lips part.

She isn't thinking about our fight. Or her scars. Or our drunk wedding ceremony.

She's right here. In this moment. Under my control.

Mine.

I want that so fucking badly.

I bring my mouth to her clit.

Lick her just how she needs me.

Again and again and again.

Until she's panting and writhing and shaking.

Then harder.

Harder.

There—

"Fuck." She rakes her nails over my stomach. "Griff." Her breath hitches. "Fuck."

I keep that same steady pace.

I bring her right to the edge.

Almost.

Almost.

There.

Jules pulses against my lips.

She groans my name as she comes. Her voice hits a fever pitch, then it gets lower. Softer. Like she's slipping into a world of pure, blinding bliss.

It's the best thing I've ever heard.

But I still need more.

I give her a second to catch her breath, then I bring my lips to her clit.

I push her right back to the edge.

Then over it.

My name is a curse on her lips.

Her nails are steel against my chest.

My cock—

Fuck, I need to be inside her.

I pull back. Bring my eyes to hers.

Those gorgeous greens are filled with pure satisfaction.

She reaches for my jeans. "Fuck me."

"Fuck yeah."

She undoes the button. Unzips the zipper.

There's no patience in her touch. Only pure, unbridled need.

She cups me over my boxers. Rubs me softly. Then harder. "No condom."

"You're sure?" I push my jeans and boxers off my hips.

She nods. "I want to feel you." Her eyes bore into mine. "Please, Griff." She wraps her hand around my cock. "Come inside me."

Fuck. Conscious thought flees my body at an alarming rate.

I kick off my jeans and boxers.

Jules wraps her legs around me.

I lower my body onto hers.

Fuck.

There's nothing between us.

I can feel every soft, wet inch of her.

The trust of that—

The intimacy—

It overwhelms my senses.

I have to close my eyes.

It's still there. It's in every molecule of air, every shift of my hips, every scrape of her nails.

We're connected.

We're one.

We're every cheesy metaphor in the world.

And I don't give a fuck that I'm a sappy romantic. Only that she's mine. And I'm hers. And it's fucking everything.

With one steady thrust, I drive into her.

She pulls back to groan. "Fuck, Griff." Her eyes fix on mine. Then they close.

Her lips crash into mine.

Her kiss is hard and hungry.

I kiss back with the same need. Then I drive into her again and again.

She arches her hips to meet me.

We fall into a perfect rhythm, moving together, groaning together, breathing together.

I fill her with steady thrusts.

She rocks her hips to push me deeper.

We stay locked together until she's there.

Her groans vibrate down my throat as she comes. She claws at my back. Tugs at my hair. Rocks her hips harder and faster.

Her cunt pulses around me.

It pushes me over the edge.

She holds me close as I come inside her.

Pleasure spreads through my pelvis, stomach, arms, legs, fingers, toes.

And there's something else too. This satisfaction that goes all the way to my bones.

She's mine.

No matter what happens, I need to hold onto that.

I need to hold onto her.

Chapter Forty-Two

GRIFFIN

Eventually, we drag ourselves to the kitchen, eat dinner with our current YA book on the speakers, listen as the couple falls madly in love, fucks everything up (it's hard to blame teenagers for being unable to communicate, but come on), cries through the loss, then comes back together.

The guy makes a big gesture, shows up at prom dressed as a character from the fictional cartoon they watch together.

It's sweet, but it's so over the top.

Wouldn't it be better to show up at her house with an apology and an honest promise to try harder?

Anyone can be the perfect boyfriend for a night.

Showing up and trying every fucking day—that's what counts.

We debate the book—Jules thinks the gesture is sweet—through dessert (matcha ice cream, of course).

Then we take a long, slow shower together.

Her scars are more obvious in the bright room.

They terrify me. They do.

Not because she's a damaged freak.

Because she's out of her depth.

We both are.

I've always loved Jules as a friend. But this—I can't say those words yet. I can't think them. But I feel a lot more than like for her.

The woman I lo—

The woman I need—

Neither one of us knows how to fix this.

I try to push the thought away as I help her soap and shampoo. It stays in the back of my head. Even as I rinse her hair. Kiss her neck. Run my fingers over her chest.

Even as I pin her to the wall and bury myself inside her.

She is mine.

I need her to be mine.

But I need her to be okay more.

If those two things are in opposition—

Fuck, I really hope they aren't.

"Is this what married couples do?" Jules slides into the booth and pats the spot next to her.

"I would know?" I sit.

She smiles as her knee brushes mine. "And I would?"

"Yeah." I intertwine my fingers with hers. "Your parents are still married."

"My parents were never married." She unfolds her napkin. "But, yeah, my mom is still married to my stepdad."

"He's your dad."

"Yeah, but he's not… you know what I mean."

"You think you'd be better off if you knew your biological father?"

"I don't know. I used to. But I see your family—"

"And you realize you'd rather get away from that kind of fucked-up shit?"

Her smile is slight. "Maybe my mom was right. Maybe it's better I don't know. Even if… I guess knowing him wouldn't really help me learn Spanish."

I can't help but chuckle. She is terrible at Spanish. She tries so fucking hard, but she can't get it. It's rare to see Jules struggle at anything academic.

"Oh my God. You shouldn't mock my inability to connect with my heritage."

"We can take classes together."

"The four years in high school didn't help." She bites her lip. "Or, you know—"

"The two in college, where you repeated the four years of high school?"

"Why do I talk to you?" She shakes her head with mock disdain.

"Beautiful face."

"No…"

"Massive cock?"

Her cheeks flush. "Well, um, I… That is true."

"Go on…"

"We're talking about uh… what are we talking about?"

"Your parents."

"Right. They, uh—"

"They're happy. Your mom and your stepdad."

She nods. "He's just kinda of…"

"Old?"

"Away a lot." She breaks eye contact to look around the restaurant. The Venice Beach cafe is tucked into a residential neighborhood, away from the tourist traps downtown. Or the hipster mecca of Abbot Kinney (which she loves. It has her favorite matcha shop).

We found the spot when I first moved here. It's a few blocks away, like an oasis in... God, it's hard to describe my neighborhood. It's not suburban or urban. It's somewhere in between.

I love Venice Beach, but it's a weird city. It tries, desperately, to hold onto its gritty parts, even as developers push to turn old houses into three-thousand-dollar-a-month lofts.

This place is a mix of both. The decor is pure 1950s—cherry red vinyl, bright white booths, jukebox in the corner. The food is hipster paradise.

Right on cue, a waitress drops off menus. "Can I get you something to drink?"

"Water," Jules says. "And a matcha latte. No sweetener."

The waitress turns to me.

"Coffee." I squeeze Jules's hand. "And water. Drained all my fluids fucking my wife."

Jules turns bright red.

"Uh... sure." The waitress clears her throat. "Did you want the regular coffee or a latte?"

"Cold brew," Jules answers for me. "With two percent milk."

The waitress nods with indifference. "You ready to order?"

"Yeah." I order for Jules.

She orders for me.

We know each other too well. We always get the same things.

Matcha pancakes with blueberries on top for her.

The veggie omelet with a side of bacon and an English muffin. Strawberry jam and butter for me.

Jules beams as she hands over the menu. It's like last night never happened. No, it's more like last night happened better.

Like we both know how to handle this.

I don't. But I'll figure it out. Fast. She only promised the weekend. I can't count on more time.

"If my parents are any indication, then this is pretty married." She turns her body toward mine. "Same restaurant. Same drinks. Same breakfast."

"Same outfit." My fingers brush her pink tank top.

"I have limited clothes in my suitcase." Her lips curl into a smile.

"Limited options that show off your tits?"

Her blush deepens. "Well…" She clears her throat. "It's not that… Exactly."

"Uh-huh."

Her expression gets playful. "It's more that I like the way you stare."

"I have more where that came from."

She laughs. "I, um, I like that one idea too. Doing it again, I mean."

I arch a brow.

"About you. Ahem. On my. Ahem." She nods to her chest. "It was hot."

Hell yes. I have to bite my tongue to keep my thoughts in line. I know exactly what she's saying. I can make this easy. But I'd rather make her blush. "What do you mean, baby?"

"You know what I mean."

I shrug like I don't have a clue.

"Okay, well, if you don't get it, we can just not do that. I mean, I was thinking about dropping under the table—"

"You were not," I say.

"Okay, not here. But maybe tonight. If we go out to some bar. I think… that could be hot, yeah?"

Fuck yeah. "I need to see it."

"Huh?"

"To see you."

"To see me as you come on my chest?" Her hand goes to her mouth. Her entire face turns red. "Oh my God. You… I… I knew you knew."

"Maybe."

"You did too." She play swats me. "You're impossible."

"Thanks."

"And a total pervert." She shakes her head with mock horror. "It's always sex with you."

"I brought this up?"

She nods *uh-huh*.

I shake my head *nuh-uh*.

Her lips curl into a smile. "I like it."

"Sex? Fuck, I hope so."

"How obsessed you are."

"Yeah?" I am obsessed. With her. And making her come. And being one with her. And all that cheesy stuff. "Married couples have sex."

"Do they?" Her nose scrunches. "I mean, my mom makes an effort. Which is too much information. But I guess they both have expectations."

Yeah. Her mom makes great effort to maintain a "bikini body" year-round (don't get me started on the ridiculous idea that women need to look a certain way to wear a bikini). Her dad—I don't have the details, but there's something kinky going on there. It's weird, but it works for them. "Maybe that's a good thing."

"Probably. They both know what they want. And they're happy as long as they get it."

"They love each other."

She presses her lips together. "Yeah. But…"

"You only think there's too much distance because you don't see their sexting."

Her nose scrunches with distaste. "Oh my God."

"Can you imagine the pics your mom takes?"

"Oh my God."

"She's probably setting her timer while she does one of those yoga poses nude."

"Do you want to have sex with my mom?" Disgust spreads over her face. "Oh my God, Griff, you know I couldn't invite guys over all of high school."

"You got me," I pretend to confess. "I fucked myself to your mom every day."

She stares in horror.

I try to hold my poker face, but it only lasts for a few seconds.

"Thank God." She swats me again, a little harder. "Wait. Did you?"

"Did I fuck myself to your mom?"

"Yeah? Ever? Even once?"

I can't recall any specific fantasy from middle school or high school. Back then, the thought of tits was enough to make me hard. And, well, Jules's mom is hot. Really hot. But—"No. She felt too much like family."

"Really?"

"Yeah. The way she looked at me like I wasn't good enough to hang out with you."

"Griff." Jules presses her lips to my cheek. "Fuck, I'm sorry."

"Don't be."

"I am. I'm sorry you went through that. I'm sorry you don't have anyone."

"I have you." I rub her wedding ring with my thumb. "You're my family."

"But, if we… we're not sure this is happening."

"You'll still be my family."

"If we break up and you meet someone else?" She traces the tattoo of her name. "How are you going to explain this?"

"My love of Shakespeare."

She laughs. "That will only work until she meets me."

"I'll have to find a woman who can't put those pieces together."

"Uh-huh."

My lips brush hers. Fuck, she tastes good, like mint toothpaste and Jules. "No." I pull back with a sigh. I have to tell her the truth. Every ounce of it. "You're it for me."

Her eyes bore into mine.

"You've always been it."

"Griff—"

"I know you don't like pressure, but I can't lie to you, Jules. You've ruined me for other women."

She swallows hard. "You really think so?"

"I know so."

"So, um, is this what married people do? Make big, romantic declarations?"

"That's what your parents do."

She nods *true*. "They, um, they do stay in touch when he's away."

I raise a brow.

She cringes. "I guess, well, I guess we get to say what our married life is like."

"Yeah."

The waitress interrupts with our drinks.

Jules thanks her, then she brings her matcha latte to her lips and lets out a low, deep sigh.

"You trying to torture me, baby?"

She takes another sip. Lets out another sigh. "Mmm."

"That's a yes."

"The world doesn't revolve around you."

"You sure?" I wrap my fingers around my mug. "I think it might."

Jules makes a show of rolling her eyes.

"Married couples do this."

"Think the universe revolves around them?"

"Tease each other."

Her lips curl into a smile.

I bring my hand to the back of her head. Pull her into a slow, deep kiss.

Fuck, she tastes good. And the way she groans against my mouth—

I'm already hard.

This isn't the place or the time, but I can't help it. I need more of her. I need all of her.

She pulls back with a sigh. "Griff."

"Yeah?"

"I... Uh... I forgot what I was going to say."

"Good." I rest my hand on her inner thigh.

She pulls back. When she catches herself, she shakes her head. "Sorry. Habit."

"It's okay."

"I... um... it's our marriage. We set the terms, right?"

"Yeah."

"We're not going to linger on *that*. Okay?" Her green eyes plead for mercy.

I offer her what I can. "Not today."

"And, we, uh, we'll have breakfast together."

"Every day?"

"Every day."

"And dinner?"

"Well." Her gaze shifts to her cup. She takes another sip. Lets out another sigh. "I can't promise every day. Not when school starts. But we should have a night. That's ours."

"Saturdays."

"Today is Saturday."

"That's a funny coincidence."

She shakes her head. "So coincidental."

"You want another day?"

"No… Saturdays are good. I just… People know."

"You posted it on Facebook."

"It was your idea," she says.

I vaguely remember that.

"So, um… I woke up to like five messages from my mom."

"Oh."

"And one from Jackson."

"Fuck him."

Her eyes turn down. "I didn't listen yet."

"Don't."

"Griff."

I'm getting jealous and possessive, but I don't care. "He doesn't deserve your time."

"It's my time."

"Don't. Please." My heart rises in my throat. I shouldn't be jealous of that asshole. It doesn't matter that he got five years with her. That he got her secrets. That he had her a hundred times.

I'm not that guy.

I won't be that guy.

Jules's eyes turn down. She turns her attention to her matcha. Pretends like we're talking about whether we're getting Thai or Indian for dinner. "I'll think about it."

I swallow a sip of my coffee. Try to convince myself I'm not jealous of her ex.

What's it matter if she returns Jackson's call?

It's not like he has some claim to her.

It's not like she wants him.

It's not like I can't stand she was his five days ago.

"What are you gonna do today?" I try to find a neutral subject.

"Besides avoid my mom's calls?"

"Yeah."

"Read. Drink more matcha. Fuck myself with my new toy."

What?

"Kidding." Her lips curl into a smile. Her eyes light up. But the hint of tension remains in her brow.

"Take a video."

"Oh my God."

"Pretty please."

Her face goes ghost white. "I can't… I… Um…"

"I'll send you one."

"Where?"

"To your email," I say.

"How?" She clears her throat as the waitress approaches.

The server drops off our breakfasts. Shoots us that same *tsk, tsk, you realize you're in public*? look then leaves.

Jules takes her knife and fork. Cuts her pancakes into even rectangular slices. "You have work all day."

"Yeah."

"Where are you going to take this video?"

"In the bathroom."

She pours syrup over her pancakes. "In the bathroom at your place of employment?"

"Or the office."

"But… It's your work."

"It won't be the first time someone came there."

"Still." Her brow furrows. "That's your job."

"Won't be the first time someone came there this week."

"Oh… Well…" She stabs a stack of squares, brings them to her mouth, moans through a bite. "Matcha really is the greatest thing in the world."

"You're a parody of yourself."

"I'm a parody of myself?"

I nod *hell yeah*.

"I'm not the one so obsessed with sex I want to record a masturbation session at work."

"You saying you don't want to see that?" I ask.

"Well… Um…"

"'Cause I can keep the recording to myself."

"No, I… Uh…" Her cheeks flush.

"Or you could drop by at lunch with my digital camera. And we could take a video together."

Her cheeks flame red.

"Or at home."

"Not, um, not on the *Twilight* sheets."

"If we get new bedding?" I ask.

"That, um… that sounds like good married life."

"Sex tapes?"

"Bedding."

I chuckle. "Then sex tapes?"

"Well, um… I guess… if you feel inspired. I wouldn't turn it down."

"You know how to inspire me."

Her blush spreads to her chest. "I'll keep that in mind."

My cock begs me to drag her to the bathroom, slide her jeans to her knees, fuck her senseless.

It takes every ounce of restraint to stay put.

Chapter Forty-Three

GRIFFIN

Despite the August weather, Inked Hearts is freezing cold.

The shop is the same as always. Bright, light, airy, humming with shitty music.

Chase's favorite band flows through the speakers. It's Jules's second favorite band. And after our fuck in the limo—

I don't hate it the way I normally do.

I want to hear more.

I want to play it on repeat.

It's not the same band, just a similar sound, but I still want it in my ears forever.

The music fades. The shop goes silent.

Hunter rises from his suite. "Wes isn't here." My friend shoots me a wide smile, one beaming with pride. "So it's my job to do this."

He brandishes a bottle of sparking apple cider—he got out of rehab last year—and peels off the foil.

"Yes!" Someone exclaims from the counter. Emma,

Hunter's girlfriend and the shop manager. She taps something on the computer. Switches the song to *White Wedding*.

Em and Jules have exactly the same taste in music. If she's willing to change something this "obviously amazing," she must be happy for me.

"Cups!" She pushes herself over the counter. Skips to the office.

Hunter's smile spreads over his lips. "It won't foam when we open it."

My head goes right back to the limo. To champagne spilling over Jules's thighs. And my intense need to taste her.

"Defeats the purpose, doesn't it?" I tease.

He nods *yeah*. "Hate to be the guy who ruins the fun."

"Don't do that." I take the bottle. "Nobody wants to drink at eleven a.m."

"Speak for yourself. A year ago..." *I'd already be drunk.* His chuckle is knowing. "Fuck, can you believe it?"

"Which part?"

"All of it?" He motions to his girlfriend, Emma, as she skips back into the room with a stack of plastic cups (okay, she's not skipping, so much as bouncing. She's always bouncy when he's around).

"You're good to her," I say.

"I try." His eyes get dreamy. "Fuck, sorry. This is supposed to be about you."

"Wes tell you?" I ask.

He nods. "Em was first. It's all over social media."

"So I hear." I'm not really a social media person. My feeds are all tattoos, all the time.

"Wes was next. Then Dean. And Chloe. She's rooting for you the most of anyone." He laughs. "Not that she'll admit it."

Emma joins us. Passes out the plastic cups. Throws her

arms around me. "Congratulations." She squeezes hard. "You and Juliette belong together." Her hand goes to her chest. Her lips part with a sigh. "Tell me it's perfect."

"Is anything?" I unscrew the cap. Fill her glass with sparkling cider.

Her lips curl into a frown. "God dammit, Griffin. If you give me some bullshit about how you need to sow your wild oats." She cringes. "You're better than that."

"Am I?" I fill Hunter's glass with cider.

"You better be." Emma's expression gets fiery. "Or I'll kick your ass."

"I'll kick it first," Hunter says. "Though, if Chloe gets to you… there won't be any ass left to kick."

I chuckle. Chloe is a badass, the aikido equivalent of a blackbelt. If she wants this enough to hurt me—

It's comforting. Sweet. My friends want me and Jules together so badly they're threatening my life. "If I lose her, I deserve that."

Emma nods *good*.

Hunter takes the bottle. Fills my cup. "Baby, it's none of our business."

"When has Griffin ever minded his own business?" she asks.

He nods *true*. "Is there any bullshit about you needing to fuck the rest of Los Angeles?"

"If there are any available women left." She sticks her tongue out *come on*.

Hunter laughs and wraps his arm around her.

She rests her head on his shoulder. It's cute. In her wedges, Em is taller than Hunter.

Neither of them mind.

There's something about being eye to eye with the woman you love—

Not that I—

Fuck, I still can't think that word.

Not the best way to start my married life. But she has to know what a mindfuck it is.

It's not like she's said it.

I do. I feel that way about her. I have for a long time.

But after the way my dad threw *I love you* around like a weapon—

My stomach twists.

"You all right?" The teasing drops from Hunter's expression.

I nod *yeah*. "You two taking bets on when it ends?"

Emma's nose scrunches with distaste. "Do you really think we're that—"

"Yeah." I scan the room. Emma's older brother Brendon is in his suite, working on a short woman's wrist. The guy isn't the *make bets mocking friends* type. But some of the tattoo artists—"I've worked here a long time now."

"It wasn't that different at Blacklist," Hunter says.

He, Wes, Chase, and I used to work at another shop in Culver City. When Hunter lied about getting sober, Chase kicked him out of the shop.

Hunter got a gig here. It was a favor from Brendon, I guess. Of course, Hunter repaid Brendon by fucking his baby sister (Em is nearly nine years younger than Hunter).

I guess they got through it, because they're friendly now. And Hunter was close enough with Brendon to get us jobs here.

It took forever to get Chase to accept the gig—the guy wears his unforgiving attitude like it's the season's latest and greatest—but he did.

We're here. Together. Friends.

Family even.

I don't think about it like that often, but it's true. The guys here are my family.

Jules doesn't have that.

She should have that.

"Wes doesn't think it will last." Hunter chuckles. "I'm sure he told you."

"In his way," I say.

"There are arguments," Emma says. "That any decision made after that much alcohol won't last." She pulls her cell from her denim skirt. Taps the screen a few times. Turns it to me to show off a picture from Jules's feed. It's us, just after the ceremony, smiling as we toast champagne.

We're happy.

And drunk as hell.

"You could even say it's not a legal marriage," Emma says. "That you can and should get an annulment." She clears her throat. "There are cautious people." She nods to her brother. Just stops herself from rolling her eyes. "Who are concerned about your impulsive decision."

"But you're impulsive enough you want to believe?" I ask.

Hunter chuckles. "You always word things in the best way."

I shrug *what?* "Impulsive isn't an insult."

Emma shakes her hand *sorta*. "Some people just don't understand romance." She turns to Hunter with a smile. Wraps her arm around him. Brings her lips to his.

He kisses her hard.

It doesn't make my stomach turn the way it usually does.

I'm not jealous of their easy rapport.

Or his ability to touch the woman he wants.

But the whole *they know where their relationship is going*?

Yeah, I could go for some of that.

The bell rings as Chase steps inside. His gaze goes right

to us. "We toasting?" He nods a curt hello to Hunter. A more polite *hey* to Emma. A warm *congrats* to me.

I think.

It's hard to tell with Chase. His warm is most people's cold.

Chase's lips curl into a frown as he spots the bottle. Then he reads the label and his brow relaxes. "You happy?"

"Yeah." I take a cup from Emma. Pour Chase a glass.

He nods *thanks* as he takes it. "You love her?"

My stomach twists.

He shakes his head *that's not good.* "Wasn't she engaged recently?"

"A week ago." Emma coughs. "Not that I keep tabs. I just… uh… we're friends."

"Facebook friends," I say.

"It was on Facebook," Emma says.

Hunter's gaze flits from me to Chase. "I should get back to work." He offers me his hand. "Really, Griff. Congratulations. Don't let anyone tell you this isn't a great thing."

I shake his hand.

He pulls me into a hug. Pats my back.

It's reassuring. The way I always imagined a hug from a parent or mentor.

I guess Hunter is a mentor. He's a fantastic artist and a smart guy. He turned his fucked-up life into something happy and healthy.

Maybe I should take more advice from him.

Chase waits until Hunter and Em are out of earshot. He leans in to whisper, "She's a good kid."

"Yeah."

"You are too." His voice is steady, even, impossible to read. "I hope you two figure it out."

"Not dedicated to destroying love?" I ask.

He shakes his head. "It's good for some people." He doesn't say it, but the implication is clear. It's not for him. Not after the way his ex-girlfriend ripped his heart out. "I never thought it was for you."

"Me either."

"Don't fuck it up."

I chuckle. "That's what I would say."

"That's how you know it's good advice."

He's right. As much as I want to shrug and pretend like I don't care, I can't.

This is the most important thing in my life.

Jules is the most important person in my life.

I can't fuck it up.

Whatever it takes, I won't fuck this up.

Chapter Forty-Four

JULIETTE

After an entire YA book, a long run, and a hot shower, I face my voicemail inbox.

My mom's tone shifts from concerned business woman to worried mother to excited romantic as her message count increases. By the time she hits message seven, she's gushing.

"Juliette King, embarking on a new marriage is a beautiful thing. I've already called the airline and the hotel. We've rescheduled your honeymoon for next week. You and Griffin need to go. You need to celebrate a new marriage." The concerned business woman takes over. "I saw your pictures. Everyone saw your pictures. You looked so beautiful and so drunk. Sweetie, if this was a mistake, that's okay. If it's what you want, that's okay. But you need to talk to a lawyer, so you know your options. Your dad suggested someone at his firm. You have an appointment with Mr. Kim at nine a.m. on Monday morning. I won't take no for an answer." She pauses. "I love you. Call me."

I don't call her. But I do reply with a text.

Jules: Thanks, Mom, I'll be there. I'm good. Griffin is too. I'll let you know if I need anything. I'm staying at his place for a few days.

I don't get into the whole *is it his place or our place* thing. There's enough on my mind.

She's right. We should talk to an attorney. We should know our options. Even if we decide to stay married.

The timing is good. We're giving it until Monday. The appointment is Monday.

It's smart. Logical. Sensible.

So why does it make my stomach turn?

Why do I want to throw up?

Why does it seem like the stupidest thing I've ever done?

Chapter Forty-Five

GRIFFIN

Everyone stops to offer their congratulations—Brendon, Ryan, Walker, the guy's girlfriends (the ones I barely know, and the ones I know well), old clients.

Current clients.

It feels good—like I'm a part of something—but it steals my ability to concentrate.

By the time I break for lunch, I'm out of mental energy.

I let my thoughts go. Sketch the piece I'm doing this afternoon.

It's amazing. A traditional pinup modeled after my client's wife. She's been so sweet through the entire process. She insists I thicken the thighs or nip the breasts or crop the hair. She wants the tattoo to look like her wife, not some cartoon version of the perfect woman.

(Or, as she'd say "the perfect woman, according to straight, horny men who don't understand organs take up space").

It's perfect.

Exactly what I want with Jules.

I don't want some doll like version of her. I want the real person, with the messy hair, and the oversized Dodgers t-shirt, and the scars.

I don't know how to tell her that.

It would be easier to show her. To tattoo her image to my chest. Or steal a soliloquy from Shakespeare or write her name on my skin.

No, I've already done that.

It's not enough. She needs to hear the words. I need to find a way to say them.

I send the final image to my client. Find a quiet spot at the sandwich shop. Check my texts.

Jules: I have this idea.

Griffin: Go on…

Jules: Not that kind of idea. Well, maybe that kind of idea. But this one doesn't involve discussion.

Griffin: Yeah?

Jules: I kinda already started.

Griffin: Baby, you're gonna make me hard.

Jules: Are you attached to the Twilight sheets?

Griffin: We came on them, didn't we?

Jules: OH MY GOD.

Griffin: I can come on new sheets.

Jules: You. Are. Obsessed.

Griffin: Obsessed with making my wife come, yeah.

Jules: Hmm… when you put it that way…

Griffin: What are you doing?

Jules: Lying in bed, naked, waiting for you to get home.

Griffin: I'm already hard.

Jules: You think I wait around for you all day?

Griffin: Think? I'm not thinking anything right now.

Jules: You are not.

Griffin: Exactly. I'm not.

Jules: You're not hard.

Griffin: Like hell.

I can't take a proper photo here, but I still snap a shot of my crotch. My jeans are a fucking tent. It's not exactly poetry, but it's still hot.

There. I send it.

Jules: Oh my God. You're not…

Griffin: I am.

Jules: Are you gonna send more?

Griffin: Only have fifteen minutes until my next appointment.

Jules: Is that a no?

Griffin: Are you asking for more?

Jules: Not yet.

Griffin: You have to ask.

Jules: I'm not waiting for you.

Griffin: Does that mean you're already fucking yourself?

Jules: No. I mean, I'm not the kind of wife who waits.

My chest warms. Fuck, I love when she says that. I love everything about it.

Jules: I do like that idea.

Griffin: Am I supposed to be following this conversation?

Jules: Yeah.

Griffin: Not sure there's any blood left in my brain.

Jules: That doesn't sound safe.

Griffin: Who needs safe?

Jules: It doesn't sound very stimulating either.

Griffin: Stimulating?

Jules: For conversation.

Griffin: Is that what you're after?

Jules: Well, I'm not lying in bed, naked.

Griffin: Lying on the couch, naked?

Jules: Not lying.

Griffin: Masturbating furiously?

Jules: Why furiously?

Griffin: You really need to come.

Jules: You got me. I'm at Bed, Bath, and Beyond, with a blanket over my lap, masturbating furiously.

I know she's joking, but, fuck, that's a beautiful mental image.

Griffin: Can't talk. Need to come.

Jules: Really?

Griffin: Yeah.

Jules: That's all it takes?

Griffin: Thinking about my wife coming makes me hard, yeah.

Jules: I like it too.

Griffin: Thinking about yourself coming?

Jules: No. When you… you know what I mean.

Griffin: You could make it happen.

Jules: The video?

Griffin: You send me one. I send you one.

Jules: Why don't you send me one?

Griffin: Is that a dare?

Jules: Maybe.

Griffin: You know I'll take it.

Jules: Take it if you want to take it.

I do. But I want to have this conversation too.

Griffin: What are you doing at Bed, Bath, and Beyond?

Jules: Buying things for the bed, the bath, and beyond.

Griffin: One of those sponges shaped like a smiley face?

Jules: It's pink and has a bow.

Griffin: I love it.

It's hard, using that word, even when it's about a sponge. But I have to start somewhere. I have to get there.

Jules: You sure you're okay with me decorating your place?

Griffin: It's our place.

Jules: Right. That's why I'm here, actually. So it feels more like our place.

Griffin: Help yourself.

Jules: What if I adorn the living room in wall-to-wall Paramore posters?

Griffin: What if you didn't?

Jules: I wouldn't.

Griffin: You should.

Jules: I'll consider that.

Griffin: Consider that video.

Jules: You first.

Griffin: I will.

Jules: I'll believe it when it happens.

Chapter Forty-Six

JULIETTE

The top left corner of the poster falls forward, threatening a permanent indent. I peel the sticker off a poster mount and reach for the paper.

No good.

I'm too short. I need Griff here. Yeah, he only has two inches on me, but, right now, I need those inches.

All his inches. Not just the height. Also the *ahem*.

My body buzzes at the thought of his thick cock. I want to touch him, taste him, fuck him. Tonight is our night. My night with my husband. My night to fuck my husband in our apartment.

My heart pounds so loud it drowns out the Paramore song. I know, it's a bit much playing a band while hanging said band's posters. Even I feel ridiculous. But then Griff was right about newfound associations.

This album drags my mind straight to the gutter.

When I close my eyes, and listen to the song, I see bliss streak Griff's expression. I feel his strong hands on my chest. I taste the champagne on his lips.

Fuck, it tastes good.

And this last poster is still threatening to buckle.

I drag a dining chair over. Press it against the wall. Hop on.

There. I stick the mount to the paper, press the poster to the wall, count to fifteen.

Hayley Williams belts the chorus.

I get why Griffin criticizes. She doesn't whine, but she does pack eight tons of emotion into every note. She's tiny, but her voice is huge. It fills the entire stadium.

I wish I could do that.

Not the singing itself, though I wouldn't mind her vocal skills.

I wish I could stand on a stage in front of ten thousand people and sing my heart out.

Hell, I wish I could stand on this fucking chair, stare into Griff's eyes, and explain every messy thing in my heart.

I wish I was that good at expressing myself. I'm okay at pouring my thoughts onto paper. But only okay.

The MFA program that starts in two weeks—

It's terrifying.

Yes, I love books. I love reading. I love writing ten page term papers on symbolism in British literature.

But the program is as much creative writing as anything else. I have to spill my guts. I have to read my writing to classmates. To share the ugly stuff in my heart.

Sure, I don't *have* to dig deep or reveal myself. I can get through the program and stay on the surface. But I know how that goes—I took creative writing in high school. This isn't math or science. There isn't a simple formula.

I get out what I put in.

It's the same as it was with Jackson. I didn't put enough into our relationship, so I didn't get enough out of our relationship.

It's the same with Griff.

If I don't reveal myself, let my guard down, offer him my heart—

I have to put myself on the chopping block.

I have to risk everything.

That's the only way. It's always the only way.

I find a spare notebook in the bedroom. Try to channel my thoughts onto paper. I used to journal all the time. It's just like relationships.

It's scary and painful, sorting through my messy thoughts. So scary and painful I neglect the task. But there's too much at stake.

Griffin is my best friend.

And I…

Do I love him? I think I do. No, I know I do. But am I in love with him? How can I know? I thought I was in love with Jackson, but he didn't know me. I didn't know him. I had no idea he was fucking his coworker.

It doesn't even bother me. Sure, I hate that I was oblivious. I hate that my judgment was so compromised.

But that sting of betrayal? It's not in my gut. I'm relieved. I'm glad Jackson was fucking someone else.

That he gets some of the blame.

I'm glad it's over. Because God knows I wasn't going to end it.

I loved Jackson, yeah, but I wasn't in love with him. He wasn't the one.

It's always been Griff.

If I screw this up…

I can't lose him.

I can't.

I scribble messy thoughts until the room goes silent.

We're good. This is good. But it's scary and overwhelming and I'm not good at overwhelming.

I play the next album. Set the mood—dim lights, candles, rose petals on the bed.

I do away with my jeans and tank top. Don my lingerie. The white lingerie, the sheer robe I bought for my honeymoon.

This is my honeymoon. It's not the one I imagined. It's better. It's so much better.

But it's scarier too.

It's like Griff said. It's easy when you aren't invested. But when you are?

It's terrifying. It really is.

Keys jangle. The handle turns. Griffin's voice booms. "You home, baby?"

"Yeah." I pull my robe tighter, though it does nothing to cover me. The white chiffon is completely see-through. Which is insanely hot. And insanely revealing.

I mean, the point is that it's revealing. That I'm practically naked.

But I *feel* naked. Like my scars are on display. The physical ones and the more metaphorical ones.

The new decorations are completely and totally me. They're a lot. Too much even.

"Why do you have the lights—" The orange glow of sunset fills the room as he opens the door. "Fuck."

"You like it?" I pull my arm over my chest.

"Yeah." His gaze shifts around the room. The Dodgers blanket hanging over the couch. The matching royal blue pillows. And the bright red ones that highlight his Angels blanket.

The posters taped to the wall. I had to drive to three music stores to find all those band posters, but I managed to cover most of the living room.

His lips curl into a smile as he takes in the posters. His

gaze shifts to me. His tongue slides over his lips. "Fuck, Jules."

"You like it?" I try to make my voice seductive, but it's more stilted. My stomach is too full of nervous energy. I want him to like the decorations. To like the outfit. To like me.

I want him to love me.

I want to stand up in front of the world and scream *I love you, Griffin Prince.*

But I'm not there yet. I can barely write it on a piece of paper. I'm not sure what possessed me to apply for an MFA program—some masochistic streak, I guess.

I'm going to spend the next two years learning how to communicate in writing. Maybe I can offer him that. *I know I suck at talking now, Griff, but in two years I'll be halfway decent. At writing. We can always text, right?*

"Do I like it?" His voice gets low. Breathy.

My nod is shy.

"Fuck." He closes the distance between us. Brings his hands to my hips. Runs his fingers over the sheer fabric. "You look gorgeous."

"That's not a yes."

"Fuck yes." He leans down. Presses his lips to mine.

I part my lips to make way for his tongue. His kiss is hard, hungry, intense.

Mmm, he tastes so good. Familiar. Like home.

It's been twenty-four hours, but this does feel like home. Maybe it's the posters or the blanket or the rose decals I put up in the bathroom.

Or maybe it's him.

He's my home too.

I…

I love him.

My heart thuds against my chest. It's fast. Hard. It drowns out the song. And the whisper falling from his lips.

I love you. Not like a friend or a brother or a roommate. Like a wife loves a husband.

I'm madly in love with you.

"Baby, where are you going?" He brings his palm to my cheek.

"I just… you promise you like it?"

"You really asking if I like your scrap of white fabric?"

I shake my head. "The apartment."

His expression softens. "Yeah. What I can see of it." He nods to the light. "But I can look after if you're trying to set a mood."

"After?" I play dumb.

He doesn't. "After I make you come until you beg me to stop."

"Fuck." My sex clenches. He's too good at this. He really is.

"If you'd rather show me the decorations first, we can do that."

"Maybe just… a little." I press my lips together. I want to fuck him. Badly. But I want this too. I want to exist in the same space as him. For it to be ours.

Jackson's place never felt like ours. I had my desk, sure, but that was it. The rest was his.

Griff nods. He flips the switch. The light flickers on. It's a soft, white thing, but it's still harsh compared to the candles.

Griff's gaze travels over my body slowly. It stops at my lips, chest, hips, thighs.

He stares at my scars. Not like he's disgusted or scared or confused. Like he's savoring the sight of me. Like he loves them as much as he loves every part of my body.

My heartbeat quickens.

My breath catches.

My knees knock together.

This is too much. But I still want more. I always want more. "You like it?"

"Baby, I gotta be honest with you."

"Yeah?"

His breath is low. Needy. "I have no fucking idea how you've decorated."

"I—"

"Not gonna be able to look at anything else while you're wearing that."

"Oh." My cheeks flush. "I… Uh…"

"Should probably tell you something before I fuck you senseless."

"You don't have to."

He wraps his arms around my waist. "I made you a video."

"What?" My sex clenches. God, that's so hot. How did I miss it? I need to see it. Now. "Where is it?"

"In your inbox."

Oh. "I've been—" I motion to the posters. "I haven't looked at my phone."

"Did it at the office."

"Yeah?"

"Dean almost walked in on me."

My blush deepens. "Really?"

He nods *yeah.*

"That didn't kill the mood?"

He shakes his head. "Not when I knew you were waiting."

"I wasn't—"

"You dared me, baby."

I shake my head.

He nods *hell yeah, you did*. "I'm not complaining." He lifts my body. Holds it against his. "I'm glad."

"When can I watch this video?"

"After you come on my face."

"Griff—"

"Baby, I know you like it." He carries me to the bedroom, kicks the door open, moves inside. "If you have an objection it better not have anything to do with these —" He sets me on the bed. Kneels between my legs. Brings his fingertips to my hips.

His fingers skim a scar. They press the chiffon against my skin. It's a different texture. Rough and soft at the same time.

"Fuck." He nudges my legs apart. "Jules..."

"Is that a... please tell me it's not about..." I can't even say it.

"I can do a cover up if you want."

"Can you?" There are a lot. A serious fuckton. I'd need a tattoo on each thigh. Both would be huge. Ridiculously huge.

"Yeah." He pushes my robe up my hip. Presses his lips to my skin. "You don't need one. But if you want one."

"You don't think they're—"

"Every part of you is beautiful."

"But you—"

"I'm terrified." He moves to my other hip. Peels the robe aside. Traces a fresh cut. It's new. A scab, not a scar. "I'm gonna stay terrified until you stop."

"Griff—"

"We don't have to talk about it now. But we... I want to stay married to you, Jules. But you have to try. That's my term. I only have two fucking terms. You have to be honest with me. And you have to try."

"I..." I don't know what to say. I want to. I do. A lot.

But what if his idea of try is different than mine? Is he going to freak next time he finds a fresh mark? Is he going to accept that I need space? That I won't be able to tell him right away?

Can we…

God, I want to fuck him so badly. It's making it way too hard to think.

"I can't think right now." I reach for him. Get his shoulder. "Not in this position."

He nods and presses his lip to my thigh. "Already lost my train of thought."

"Was it important?"

"Probably." He drags his lips a little higher. "But less than this."

Fuck, his lips are soft and that touch is feather light.

"Should probably tell you—"

"About the video?"

He shakes his head. "We're going to karaoke tonight."

"We are?"

"Yeah. I was a little out of it when I got the invitation."

"What with having just *ahem*—"

"Fucked myself for your future viewing pleasure." He nips at my inner thigh. "We can cancel if you want—"

"Is this really—"

"Yeah." His lips are soft against my skin. "Need to know how much time I have to fuck you."

"If we go?"

"Two hours. Maybe three," he says.

"I can work with that."

"Not sure I can. But I'll do my best."

Chapter Forty-Seven

JULIETTE

Griffin drags his fingertips over my thighs. "I tell you how beautiful you are?"

"Yeah," I breathe. "But you can say it again."

"You are." He peels the robe off my right side. Lays the fabric on the bed.

Then his fingers are on my skin. My waist. My side. My hip.

My scars.

He stares as he traces them down my hip and over my thigh. His eyes stay fixed on me, but they don't cloud with fear or concern or disgust.

They stay still, patient, observing.

Or maybe I'm imagining things.

I should probably talk to him.

Or demand we stop talking and fuck like rabbits.

One of the two.

The latter. Definitely the latter. We can talk about my bad habit later.

It's less important than this.

Everything is less important than this.

Griff traces the last scar on my right leg. He drags his fingertips up, over my hip bone, along my pelvis, all the way to my left leg.

He pushes the lingerie aside. Traces scars along my hip. Over my thigh. Down and up again and again.

My breath hitches.

My sex clenches.

There's something about the way he touches me. It shouldn't be hot as hell. But it is. It really is.

"Griff—" I dig my fingers into his shoulder. "You… Do you think… Do you think anything?" I'm inviting conversation. I'd much rather fuck him. God, I want to fuck him. But if he thinks… I'm not sure what he thinks.

"Yeah." He drags his lips over my inner thigh. "I think you have the prettiest cunt I've ever seen."

"What?" My cheeks flame.

He drags his lips higher. "You can scare me, baby." He places his hand on my hip. Runs his thumb over a scar. "But you can't scare me away."

"I'm not—"

"I'm not good at talking."

"Me either."

"There's a lot I want to say to you. This is how I'm gonna do it."

"Okay."

He drags his thumb over my pelvis bone. "Okay?"

"Yes."

He nips at the skin of my inner thigh. Softly. Then harder. Hard enough to hurt.

"Fuck yes." I rake my nails over his shoulder.

He scrapes his teeth against my skin. "You look like a fucking angel."

"Yeah?"

"Yeah." He drags his lips a little higher. "Fucking gorgeous."

"Thank you."

He nips at my skin. "Say my name when you come."

My yes is a groan.

He drags his lips higher. Higher. Almost—

He moves to my other leg. Places a kiss on the inside of my knee.

Then it's the soft scrape of his teeth.

Then harder.

Harder.

Hard enough it hurts in the best possible way.

He works his way up my leg. Kissing, sucking, biting.

Higher and higher and—

Almost.

His lips brush my clit. It's feather soft. I can barely feel it.

He does it again.

Again.

Again.

I arch my hips to meet him. That feels so fucking good, but I need more. I need everything.

He teases me again and again.

His kiss stays so fucking soft.

He brushes his lips against me again. And again. And—

There.

He brings my clit into his mouth. Sucks softly. Then harder. Harder—

Fuck.

"Griff." I tug at his hair.

He does it again.

Pleasure floods my senses.

God dammit, his soft, wet mouth is intense. It's too much. And not enough. And everything.

It's the only way to describe him.

He's everything.

"Please." I rake my nails over his shoulder until he groans against me. I need that. His reaction. His need. His lust. "Make me come, Griff."

"Fuck." He nips at my inner thigh. His eyes meet mine for a second. They fill with deep, pure need.

Then he brings his mouth to me.

His fingers curl into my thighs. He pins me to the bed as he licks me up and down.

He takes his sweet, sweet time teasing me with the soft brush of his lips or quick flicks of his tongue or the gentle scrape of his teeth.

He teases me until I'm panting.

Then he flicks his tongue against my clit.

He moves higher, higher, there—

"Griff." I tug at his hair. "Don't stop."

His nails scrape my inner thighs. Not hard enough to hurt. Just hard enough to remind me I'm his.

It's too fucking sexy. It's wrong. It's evil. It's everything.

I knot my hand in his hair.

He licks me exactly how I need him. With just the right pressure. Just the right speed. Just the—

Fuck.

"Griff." For a second, I take in the sight of him between my legs. Then the reflection. The way his head moves, the way his fingers curl into my thighs, the way his shoulders tense and relax.

Then my head falls back and my eyelids flutter closed.

It's too intense.

It's too much.

It's not enough.

It's everything.

"Griff." I dig my heel into his back.

He flicks his tongue against me.

Again.

Again.

Again.

He winds me tighter and tighter and tighter.

His nails scrape my thighs.

His palms pin my legs.

His tongue works its magic.

Almost.

Almost.

There—

With the next flick of his tongue, I unwind. My world goes white, nothing but pure, blinding, bliss.

I groan his name as I come.

Then I tug at his hair. Pull him back up my body.

He leans down. Presses his lips to mine.

I kiss him hard and deep. It's strange, tasting myself on his lips. But I like it. I really fucking like it.

I tug at his t-shirt.

He breaks our kiss to toss it aside.

I motion to the mirror. "I want to watch."

"Fuck, baby." He wraps his arm around my waist. Helps me onto my knees. Shifts onto his knees.

My eyelids flutter closed.

His lips find mine.

I part my lips to make way for his tongue.

His kiss is possessive, loving, perfect. It says everything he can't. Everything I can't.

It says *I love you.*

I'm desperate to watch him fuck me and I'm thinking about how I love him.

I've got it so bad.

But that's not a surprise. I've loved Griff for a long time. For as long as I can remember.

I fumble over his button.

He cups my breast. Toys with my nipple as he kisses me hard.

Mmm. He's too good at that. He's way too good at that. I have to pull back. To motion to the mirror. Push him onto his back. Tug his jeans off his hips.

Then the boxers.

Dammit, I love the sight of him. Thick, long, hard.

Ready for me.

Mine.

I climb onto his legs. Press my lips to his chest. His stomach. His pelvis.

I look up at Griffin as I take his cock into my mouth.

He knots his hand in my hair. For a moment, he stares down at me. Then his eyes go to the mirror.

Mine do too.

I watch as I take him deeper. As I wrap my hand around him. As I work him.

My sex aches. I love watching. I love *this*. But God, I'm so empty, and I need him filling me. I need it so fucking badly.

I pull back.

My eyes lock with his as I push my robe off my shoulders.

He nods *hell yeah*. Brings his hands to my hips. Guides my body over his.

I straddle him.

He digs his fingers into my hips. Reaches up. Takes my nipple between his thumb and forefinger.

His eyes lock with mine.

Then they shift to the mirror.

He watches himself play with me. Watches as my chest heaves and my cheeks flush and my nipples redden.

My gaze stays on the mirror as I press my palm into his chest and lower my body onto his.

His cock strains against me. I tease him. And myself.

I tease him until he's panting and I'm aching and neither one of us can stand it.

Then I take every sweet inch.

"Jules." He digs his nails into my hips.

My sigh is pure relief. *This* is where I'm supposed to be. Exactly where I'm supposed to be. Just his body and mine and the greatest view in the world.

Why can't it always be this easy?

It should always be this easy.

It should—

He rolls my nipple.

It pulls me into the moment. Into the view that makes my heart race and my sex clench. Into this beautiful world where the two of us are one and everything makes sense and conscious thought is long, long gone.

He watches as I take him deep.

I watch him watch until I can't take it anymore.

Then I watch.

Bliss spills through my senses. It's not just the tension in my sex. It's every single molecule.

He. Is. So. Fucking. Sexy.

My husband is the sexiest man on the planet.

I love watching my husband fuck me.

I love my husband.

I love every fucking moment of this.

My eyelids flutter together. I dig the heel of my palm into his chest. Use it for leverage to take me higher again and again.

He brings both hands to my hips. Works with me, guiding my body over his.

I pull up until I only have his tip.

Then I glide down, take every delicious inch.

I do it again and again.

"Watch, baby." He drags his nails over my hips. The skin and the scars.

He doesn't wince or pause or look at me funny.

He watches our reflection as I fuck him senseless.

Fuck.

I drive down on him again and again. Until I can't take it anymore.

He brings his thumb to my clit. Holds it against my flesh, so I can rock against him. So I can fuck his digit as I fuck him.

My sex winds tighter and tighter with every shift of my hips.

Almost.

Almost—

There.

My sex pulses as I come. Bliss spills through my pelvis, down my legs and arms, all the way to my fingers and toes.

Every part of me buzzes.

Griffin rocks me through my orgasm. Then he untangles our bodies. Arranges me on my hands and knees in front of him. Holds onto my hips.

He drives into me.

It's not gentle or sweet. It's hard and fast and dirty as hell.

I watch our bodies join. Watch his nails scrape my side. Watch my chest bounce.

I watch as his movements get harder and faster. As his breath catches and his brow knots and his eyes close.

"Fuck, Jules." He groans my name as he comes.

He rocks through his orgasm, digging his fingers into my skin as he fills me.

Once he's spilled every drop, he untangles our bodies. Wraps his arms around me. Presses his lips to my neck.

He holds me like he's never going to let go.

Right now, I believe it. That this is possible. That we might be forever.

WE LINGER IN BED FOR AS LONG AS WE CAN. THEN WE shower, dress, drive to the karaoke joint in Little Osaka.

It's late enough traffic is dead. We get there fast. Stride into the room to meet a booming "Congrats."

Everyone is here.

And I mean everyone.

It's sweet and overbearing and totally perfect.

Until Griffin hands me a mic, summons a Paramore song, and insists I sing.

Chapter Forty-Eight

JULIETTE

"I can't sing." My heart thuds against my chest.

"What do you call what you do in the car?" Griffin slides his arm around my waist. He pulls my body into his. Brings his lips to my ear. "What if I sing with you?"

"You hate this song."

He shakes his head. "My new favorite band."

"It's not from that album."

"Still."

"It's everything you hate about this genre of music."

He points to the screen. A countdown flashes. Four, three, two—"Sing with me or don't." He picks up the other mic. Steps onto the table in the middle of the room. Offers me his hand.

I take it.

Okay, I'm standing on a table in the middle of a crowded room, surrounded by a dozen of our closest friends, and I'm singing my favorite song.

No, he's singing my favorite song.

I'm—

Fuck, I have to do this.

Maybe I can't yell *I love you* in front of the entire room. Maybe I can't tell him I don't trust him to react calmly about my cutting. Or about the appointment with divorce attorneys. Or—

Maybe I suck at communicating.

But I can stand in front of people and sing.

I can.

Deep breath.

On three.

One, two, three—

I jump in at the third line of the verse.

My eyes open. They go straight to the TV screen flashing lyrics. I don't need the reminder—I know this song like the back of my hand—but it helps having a focus.

My cheeks flame. My chest heaves. My stomach flutters.

But, still, I get through the verse.

I launch into the chorus.

Griff squeezes my hand. He looks around the room. Motioning to friends. Gestures something.

He turns to me. Pulls me closer. Sings his heart out.

He's not technically proficient—neither of us is—but he's there, in the moment, pouring emotion into every word.

I try to get there. To meet him.

My heart races. My breath hitches. My legs wobble.

But I do it. I sing with as much feeling as I can muster. Through the next verse and chorus, through the breakdown, through the outro.

I sing my heart out.

Then I step off the stage, hand the mic to someone, take a seat next to Griff.

Sadly, it's not the end of the attention.

Dean is climbing on the table (is this a thing we're doing?), serenading us with *Let's Stay Together*.

One by one, everyone takes a turn. Everyone sings a song about love or marriage or forever.

They belt their heart out, then they come to us, whisper (or scream) their congratulations, hand the mic to the next victim.

It's way too much.

But it's perfect too.

"Is this killing you?" Brendon Kane, the most quiet and responsible of all the shop owners (Brendon, Ryan, Walker, and Dean co-own the shop together), sits next to us.

Griff chuckles. "Must be killing you." He nods to the front of the room. Brendon's sister Emma and his girlfriend Kaylee are singing a truly amazing pop-punk song. One of my favorites. One Griffin hates. Which means Brendon hates it. They're very aligned in their hatred of emo music.

Or they were, until the whole Paramore fuck thing.

My stomach flutters.

Brendon chuckles. He has a deep, low chuckle. He's that kind of guy. Tall. Handsome. Imposing. There's something intimidating about him.

Maybe it's that he's half a dozen years older. Maybe it's the quiet intelligence. The way he stares like he can wait forever for you to answer.

I don't know him well. I know he's hot (so hot). I know he fell madly in love with his sister's best friend while she was staying at their place. I know he treats his girlfriend Kaylee like a queen.

But other than that—

Well, I guess I know about his hatred of emo music.

"I meant the attention." Brendon's smile is slight. "It's a lot."

"Turns out people like talking about weddings," I say. "Especially when they were rash decisions."

"I have a client who did that," Brendon says.

"Oh?" I ask.

"Someone is getting on our turf?" Griffin laughs.

Brendon nods *they are*. "They were strangers. Met that night. But he knew. After a few hours, he knew."

"And now?" I ask.

"They've got a kid," he says. "They're the happiest couple I know."

"Besides you and Kaylee?" I ask.

His smile is sweet. Loving. And a little dirty. "Wasn't counting myself."

"When did you know?" I motion to his girlfriend. She's adorable with her champagne-blond hair and her blue glasses and her pastel cardigan. Adorable and young. She must be nineteen or twenty. Whereas he's in his late twenties.

"I knew for a long time," he says. "But I didn't want to believe it."

"You didn't want to admit you're a dirty perv?" Griffin asks.

I laugh. "Wes is right about tact."

Brendon shrugs *it's okay*. "No, you're right. I didn't want to cross that line. And I didn't think I was good enough for her." His smile gets dreamy. "Kay's an angel. She hates when I say she's perfect, because it's too much to live up to, but she is."

"You're not saying you expect her to be perfect," Griff says. "Only that she's perfect for you."

"Yeah?" I ask.

Griff nods *yeah*. "You're perfect for me."

My cheeks flush.

Griffin pulls me into a slow, deep kiss.

Half the room claps.

My blush deepens. "We're popular."

"Think they'll keep watching if I keep going?" Griffin teases.

Oh God.

Brendon shakes his head. "He will."

"I know." I pull back. Press my knees together. "He's incorrigible."

Griff just smiles. "I take that as a compliment."

"I know." I clear my throat. "I..." *I love you.* "I know you."

He nods *you do*. "I know you too."

"Yeah?" I ask.

He nods *yeah*. "And I know you want to sing another Paramore song." He points to the book. To a song. *The* song.

I shake my head. "I think I'll spontaneously combust."

"How about I serenade you?" he asks.

"I still might," I say.

"Is that a bad thing?" he asks.

I shake my head.

He takes the mic from Emma. Gets up on that table. Skips right to the song.

I swear to God I melt.

I really do.

BY THE TIME WE GET HOME, I'M READY TO POUNCE.

I drag my husband to our bedroom. Tear off his t-shirt.

Unzip his pants.

I fuck him senseless.

Then he flips me onto my stomach, pins me to the bed, fucks me senseless.

After, he pulls me into his arms. Holds me close. Whispers sweet nothings in my ears.

It flits through my head—his request for honestly, our appointment Monday, my inability to communicate properly.

I need to tell him.

I need to tell him about the appointment, that I think it's a good idea, that I'm going.

That I'm still not sure I'm committed to this marriage.

I love him, I do, but I still don't trust him completely. I still don't believe we have the same idea of trying or honesty.

I turn around, stare up into his eyes, try to find the words.

I love you, Griffin, I do. But we need to hash out this whole honesty thing. Because I can't tell you everything I feel, right when I feel it. I need to process sometimes.

I'll try to stop cutting, but I've tried before. And it's not easy. It doesn't happen right away. The more I feel like I have to do it, to make you happy, to be the person you want me to be—

The more I do that, the worse it will be.

The harder it will be.

So, yes, I'll be honest with you. But on my timeline. And I'll try, but that's on my timeline too.

That's why I'm keeping this appointment. Because I don't know if we'll ever be there, if we'll ever see eye to eye about this.

I don't say any of that.

I bring my lips to his chest and whisper *I love you* into his skin.

But I don't say anything else.

Chapter Forty-Nine

JULIETTE

Of course, our friends insist on throwing a party in our honor. We wake up to an invitation to a barbeque at Dean's place. An invitation that is not optional.

Everyone will be there and it will be awesome.

We linger at our apartment all morning. We make tea and fix pancakes and read YA aloud.

Then we grab matcha lattes on the way to the beach, walk along the sand, dart into shops, grab lunch and ice cream and iced drinks.

It's a perfect day, from my last sip of matcha to my long, slow shower with Griff, to his reaction to my dress—my white dress, the rehearsal dinner dress, is the only clean thing I have left.

It's perfect, until I check my phone and see that reminder email.

Appointment at the offices of Agos and Associates at 9 a.m. Monday.

Chapter Fifty

GRIFFIN

The party is packed.

Dean's parents' place is bopping with friends and strangers. People mingle on the couch, pour drinks at the bar outside, dive into the pool.

It's mostly people from Inked Hearts or Blacklist, but I only know half of them.

I guess when you throw a party, you get to pick the guest list.

And this is a hell of a party. I have to hand it to Dean. When he goes for something, he goes for it.

Said host is currently at the grill, flipping sliced bell peppers with a pair of green tongs, his girlfriend by his side.

They spot us and nod hello. Then they turn to each other, whisper something, turn back with a smile.

Jules laughs. "Do they think they're subtle?"

"Pretty sure they do." I wave to them.

Dean nods *hey*. Chloe forces a smile. Nods a more awkward *hi, we totally weren't talking about you. We'd never…*

"You'll have to forgive my brother. He thinks he's charming." Ryan, one of the co-owners of Inked Hearts and Dean's older brother, nods hello. He's donned entirely in black—Converse, jeans, t-shirt, tattoos. "Congratulations."

Jules shakes. "Thanks."

"How's married life treating you?" he asks.

"Good." It really is.

He turns to Jules and raises a brow.

She nods. "It's different. But good."

Ryan offers me his hand.

I shake. I know better than to go for a hug. The guy hates when people touch him. With one exception:

His girlfriend Leighton rushes to meet us. She's Ryan's opposite—loud, outgoing, stylish. He calls her his punk rock princess. Which is adorable and cheesy and totally fitting.

Between her row of ear piercings, her thick eyeliner, and her hot pink skull print bikini, she's dressed the part.

She's hot. I'm human. I can see that. But she's never interested me.

Even before she and Ryan got together, she was his. She was crazy about him. They were best friends, and he was oblivious, and, well, I guess I sympathize with both of them.

She beams. "It's so romantic. The pictures were beautiful." She squeezes her boyfriend. "Tell me you have more pictures."

He chuckles. Just barely blushes. "Not here."

"Of course here." She brushes a purple strand behind her ear—Leighton has been rocking purple hair for ages now—then offers me a hug. "You're being good to her?"

"Fuck, I just got here," I say.

"Are you?" Her green eyes fix on me. They get serious. Intense.

"I don't know. Am I?" I slide my arm around Jules's waist.

Jules presses her lips to one side. Scratches her head like she's thinking hard. "Hmm... well, you did buy me three matchas."

I nod *true*.

"And you, um, *ahem*, during our shower." She blushes.

"Go on..." I run my fingers over her side.

Her blush deepens. "Ryan and Leighton don't want to hear about our sex life."

Ryan nods *please no*.

Leighton nods *please yes*. She nudges her boyfriend. "He does. He's just shy."

"Baby, you know that's not true," he says.

She laughs.

He wraps his arms around her waist. Pulls her body into his. Whispers something in her ear. Something dirty.

Leighton turns to her boyfriend. She kisses him hard.

He kisses back without a hint of shyness.

Seriously, they're moaning and tugging at clothes and rocking their hips like they're about to get naked.

Jules clears her throat.

I shake my head. "They don't stop."

"But he's always so... not like this." Jules laughs. She's seen Ryan a dozen times, but he's always been alone. He's always been the quiet all business guy who hangs out in the corner.

He's different around his girlfriend. Warmer. Brighter. More alive.

I know the feeling.

Jules is—

I wrap my arms around my wife. Pull her into a slow kiss.

She groans against my mouth.

I press my palms into her ass.

She pulls back with a sigh. "Tell me there's someplace private."

"Don't even think about using my bedroom," Ryan says.

"Which one is yours?" I ask.

"It's not *your* bedroom anymore." Leighton's breath is shaky. "You moved out ten years ago."

"No one else has come there and I'd like to keep it that way," he says.

"What about earlier?" she coos.

"You know what I mean, baby," he says.

"You had sex without making your girl come? Shameful." I shake my head.

"Nobody comes without me." He shoots her a knowing look.

Leighton smiles. "Don't give Griffin ideas. He'll invite you to watch."

Not inaccurate. I turn to Jules. "What do you think?"

"Um… that's really flattering, Ryan, but I prefer having my husband all to myself," she says.

Leighton presses her hand to her heart. Sighs like we're the most romantic thing she's ever seen. "When did you know?"

"Know what?" I ask.

"That you were in love with her?" Leighton presses her hands together. "With Ryan… I wanted him right away. Even when he was with his ex. I wasn't going to do anything about it. Hell, I figured I was suffering from the same bad taste that had led me astray for… ever."

"You were gonna wait forever?" he asks.

"I wasn't waiting for anything. I just wanted to be around you." She takes his hand. "Then you and Penny broke up—"

His chuckle is low, deep. "That's a nice euphemism."

Everyone knows Ryan's story. He walked in on his ex balls deep in her khaki wearing coworker. She promptly left him for said coworker. Got engaged. Invited Ryan to the wedding.

That's where Leighton came in. They were already best friends. Coworkers—she used to run the front desk at Inked Hearts.

She volunteered to play his girlfriend, so he wouldn't be that loser who showed up at his ex's wedding single.

I guess pretending only stays pretend for so long. Because they got back from the wedding making out like there's no tomorrow.

They're an adorable couple. And hot too. He always kisses her like he's about to tear off her clothes.

Leighton clears her throat. "It was really stupid, insisting I play his girlfriend. But I couldn't stand the way Penny threw her engagement in his face."

"And you wanted to kiss him?" Jules asks.

Leighton blushes. "Well, that, um… it wasn't a completely selfless decision."

"You're so deceptive, baby." Ryan squeezes her.

Her blush deepens. "I was upfront. It's not like I thought the ruse would lead to this."

"Never?" he asks.

"I hoped…" She turns to us. "I always loved him, but I didn't realize I was *in love* with him until I was really with him."

Jules nods.

"Was it like that for you? When did you realize you were more than friends?" Leighton turns to me. "Have you been watching her and her ex, pining all this time?" Her sigh is dreamy. "It's torture, until it's not."

I run my hand through my hair. It's a good question. It is. But I don't have a good answer. "It was always in front of my face." My gaze meets Jules's. "But I didn't realize it until that night."

"Me either." Her lips curl into a smile. "He was always Griff. My best friend. I never thought it could be more."

Leighton nods attentively.

Ryan whispers something in her ear.

Both of them fade away. All I can see is Jules's smile. Her gorgeous green eyes. Her joy.

This time, I kiss her like everyone is watching. Like my kiss is a declaration. Like I'm screaming *I'm madly in love with Juliette King*.

I am.

But, fuck, the word still makes me queasy.

"There's something about falling for your best friend." Leighton runs her fingers through Ryan's hair. "You know you can trust them to catch you."

He smiles at her.

She smiles back.

They giggle like middle schoolers.

"They invite you to an orgy?" Chase nods hello. He holds up his bottle of beer to toast.

"How'd you know?" I tease. Fuck, it's weird seeing Chase with booze. But it's good. Means he's getting over his brother's betrayal.

"Same shit you always do." He takes a swig. Turns to Jules. "I tell you about the time your husband invited me to a threesome?"

Jules's eyes go wide. "No. He… You… Really?"

Chase chuckles. "He was at a bar with a girl. She was begging for a third, I guess. So he texted me." He raises his voice an octave. "Hey, Chase. You busy tonight? You want to double team this babe with me?"

"He did not." Jules stares in horror.

Chase nods *he did.*

"He said 'double team this babe'?" she asks.

"Yeah." He pulls his cell from his back pocket. "I took a screenshot."

"You…" She looks to me. "When?"

Honestly, I've had a lot of those conversations. It's hard to recall an exact one. But I do remember Chase's reaction. "About two years ago."

"What did you say?" she looks to Chase.

I drop my voice an octave to imitate him. "There's no fucking way I'm taking your sloppy seconds, Prince. I know this is your idea of a compliment, but I'm not interested."

Chase chuckles. Continues imitating me. "You can go first. Come on. The best way to get over someone is to get under someone else."

I laugh too. "He went on for a while after that. A lot of shit about how that's bullshit. And he can hold onto his feelings about his ex for as long as he wants."

"Uh… okay… Did you…" Jules looks to me. "Did you find someone else?"

"Of course." I can't help but laugh. "I aim to please."

"Oh." Her face goes white. She stammers. Tries to find her footing. "So, um… you think you missed out, Chase?"

He shakes his head. "Never got the big deal."

"About threesomes?" She turns her head to one side. "Don't guys usually want two chicks going at it?"

"Casual sex." He takes another swig of beer. "Doesn't appeal to me."

"Really?" Her eyes go wide. "And you… but hasn't it been a long time?"

He nods *yeah*. "Two years, yeah."

"Two years without sex? But… you… how?" She presses her lips together. "I mean, I guess… probably longer, right?"

He shoots me a curious look. *Is she okay?*

I nod *yeah.* I mean, I think she is. I know Jules better than I know anyone, but I can't always read her. She hid so much. For so long.

I don't blame her, exactly.

But how can I be sure I know her now?

How can I be sure she's being honest?

She still hasn't accepted my terms.

She hasn't promised she'll try. She hasn't promised she'll always be honest.

I want to believe it. That we're past secrets. But it's hard.

"Got a lot of stories like that," Chase says.

Her eyes get big. Curious. "Tell me one."

"It was a few weeks after that," Chase says. "He stopped by my place one night. Must have been eleven. I was already in my pajamas. Reading."

She laughs. "Wild nights."

"Who needs wild?" he asks.

She nods *true*. "Probably made him think of me."

I nod. "It did. Made me all over protective and worried."

"Really?" she asks.

"Yeah." I worry about her. Too much. But I can't help it.

Chase looks between us. Smiles an easy smile. He really is happy for us. But he's still torturing me. "Your husband looks at me and shakes his head." He imitates me. "Chase, buddy, you gotta pull your shit together. Reading at eleven on a Friday? You're heartbroken, not dead. Let's go out. Meet some babes."

"Did you?" she asks.

"Oh yeah," I say. "He wouldn't change, so I dragged him to a bar in his pajamas."

"Wouldn't let go of the book either," Chase says.

"He sat there, on his stool, reading, completely oblivious to all the women checking him out," I say. "And there were a lot. Fuck, every other girl came up to him to ask what he was reading."

"You didn't respond?" she asks.

He nods. "Don't want to be with someone who interrupts me when I'm reading."

Jules smiles. "Very true. But some interruptions are worth it." She shoots me a knowing look.

Chase shakes his head *I know what that means*. "Should I give you two a minute?"

"A minute isn't gonna be long enough," I say.

"Don't know. I've heard things about your stamina." He winks at Jules. "Rumors about quick endings."

"You want to watch and find out?" I tease.

He shakes his head *hell no*. "Just want your wife to know the gossip."

Jules laughs. "I appreciate that."

He nods *my pleasure*. "How about I get you a drink, Juliette?"

"Yeah. Tequila and iced tea." Her phone buzzes against her pocket. She pulls it out. Stares at the screen. "Or something citrus. Orange or grapefruit juice. But nothing with sugar." *Incoming call from Jackson Jones*. "Actually, I'll be right back."

"Don't." My voice is desperate, needy, pathetic.

It's not a big deal. It's a phone call from her ex. It's not like he's about to say *I'm sorry, Jules, I love you. I love you more than I've ever loved anything. I made a mistake. I want you back. Please come back.*

Even if he did—

She won't leave.

She doesn't want him.

She wants me.

"I'll just be a minute." She squeezes my hand. "I promise."

"Yeah." I swallow the words that rise up in my throat. *Don't. Stay. Tell me you don't love him. Tell me you love me. Tell me you'll stay. That you'll promise to tell the truth. Promise to try*.

"Save me a few stories, okay?" She nods goodbye to Chase. Shoots me one last look *please, leave it alone*, turns, moves into the house.

Chase looks to me and raises a brow. "Her ex?"

"Is it that obvious?"

He nods *yeah*. "Never seen you pissed before."

"I'm not pissed."

He shakes his head *yeah right.*

This isn't a big deal. He doesn't have any claim to her.

But what if I don't have any claim to her either?

She hasn't promised.

She needs to promise.

Chase's voice stays low. Gentle even. "You think she's over him?"

Mine doesn't. "I thought I was the tactless asshole."

"Would you prefer I beat around the bush?" he asks.

No. I'd prefer this situation not exist.

But it does.

She's talking to her ex.

That's fine.

It's nothing.

She's mine.

She's not his. She's mine.

I just need to distract myself through this bullshit fit of

possessiveness. I pull out my cell. Check my texts. My messages. My email.

From: The Law Offices of Agos and Associates

Subject: Your Appointment with David Kim.

What the fuck?

Chapter Fifty-One

JULIETTE

"Hey." I press my cell to my cheek. "Give me a second." The house is crowded. Mostly with people I've never seen before. Judging from the excess of tattoos, I'm guessing most of these people are friends of Dean's. Or at least friends of the shop.

It's not like there's anyone I wanted Dean to invite. Yeah, I have friends, but half of them moved the week after graduation. And none of them compare to Griffin.

I move through the crowded room, up the stairs, down the hallway.

I step into an open door. The room is all black—curtains, bedspread, desk. It must be Ryan's room.

It's a good place to talk. Quiet. Private. Calm.

I can do this.

I can close the book on my relationship with Jackson.

"Hey." My fingers glide over the cell. "Are you there?"

"Yeah."

I suck a breath between my teeth.

"Are you okay?" he asks.

"At a party."

"Whose party?" That controlling tone drops into his voice. *Who are you seeing? What are you doing? Why aren't you living the life I think is the right life?*

I don't answer. "It's loud. But I have a minute." I take a seat on the black bedspread. Recall Ryan's mention of sex. Jump off it. I'm not squeamish, but I'm not sitting on used sheets either.

"One of your friends? The one with the pool with all the topless women?"

"One woman, one time."

"Your husband's date. I guess he likes women who show off. Is that what you two like?"

"What do you want, Jackson?"

"I miss you." His voice is slurred, but I can't tell if it's from exhaustion or alcohol.

Maybe this is a drunk dial. It doesn't matter. I need this closure as much as he does.

"You don't." It's not as simple as that. He misses the idea of me. The idea of a stable relationship. The attention and praise that comes with a big wedding. The fantasy of a house in the suburbs and two kids and a dog (never mind my allergy to anything with fur and feathers and my lack of desire to have children).

I get it. I felt a shade of that. I loved the fantasy, but I didn't love him.

No, I did. Once. But it was a long time ago. Too long.

"Yeah, I do." His voice drops to something lower. "I love you."

I don't have a response to that. I guess I can tell him he's a controlling asshole, that he only misses being able to whine about how Griffin and I were too close, but I don't have much moral high ground on that particular point. "How is she?"

"Who?"

"Red lingerie."

"We're not… she doesn't want something long term."

"Oh." So he has buyer's remorse. Poor baby. It must be so hard, cheating on your fiancée, expecting your mistress to stay with you. "That's too bad."

"Jules."

"Don't call me that."

"Juliette…"

I bite my tongue. As much as I want to hate Jackson, I don't. I sympathize. It sucks that his whatever-I-should-call-it ditched him. It sucks that his idea of love is more about being right than him being half a team. It sucks that we wasted the last two years believing in something that wasn't there.

"I just wanted to say congratulations," he says.

"Thank you."

"And…"

I take a deep breath. Exhale slowly.

"How long?"

"What?"

"How long have you been in love with him?"

"You slept with someone else."

"How long?" His voice is ragged. Jealous. Petty.

"I don't know." I wish I had a better answer, but I don't. "I've always loved him."

"But how long—"

Too long, considering. "What do you want me to say, Jackson?"

"The truth."

"It doesn't matter."

"It matters to me."

"Yeah, I've been in love with Griffin for a long time. Yeah, I was in love with him while we were together. But I didn't see it. I thought… I guess I thought I was stuck with what we had."

"We had something good."

"At first. But it changed." It changed after he realized I was cutting again. After I locked him out. Which is my fault. But he let me do it. He… the person he was and the person I was were never going to get through that. "I pushed you away. That's on me. But you didn't try either."

"I…"

"It's not your fault. Or mine. We were young and stupid and hopeful. Maybe I'm still stupid and hopeful. I'm trying to do better this time. But I'm still fucking it up."

"Juliette…"

"I'm sorry, I am. Not that I was in love with Griff. I'll never be sorry about that. But I'm sorry I stayed in limbo for so long. I'm sorry we wasted the last two years. If I was stronger or smarter, I would have ended it earlier."

"You think it was that bad?" he asks.

"Don't you?"

He sighs. It's a sigh I know well. *I hate that you're right.*

God, I hate that sigh. It always comes with this look *how could you be right when I'm clearly so much smarter than you are?*

But that doesn't matter now.

I'm done with Jackson. I really am.

I try to think up a proper goodbye, but something stops me. The door.

Griffin pulls it open. He steps inside, his eyes turned down, his shoulders tense.

"We're meeting with a lawyer tomorrow?" His voice is curt, all business.

Fuck. I try to find some way to explain, but my mouth is too sticky. "It's just options."

He shakes his head *that's bullshit.*

"I was going to tell you."

"But you don't trust me?"

"No…" I don't have a better explanation. Yeah, it slipped my mind a few times. But I knew I needed to tell him. I planned to tell him. I just…

"Promise."

"What?"

His eyes bore into mine. "Right now, tell me you want to stay married."

"I…"

"Promise you'll always be honest. Promise you'll try."

"Griff—"

"What the fuck is that? 'Griff, I'm sorry, but I'll never trust you enough'?"

"It's not that."

"Promise, Jules. Promise." His eyes plead. They beg.

God, I want to promise. I do.

But I can't. "It's not that simple."

He shakes his head *it is*. "Do you want to stay married? Yes or no? Can you say, right here, in front of everyone, that you want to stay my wife?"

I do. I just… I can't agree to those terms. Not the way he means. "I…"

His eyes turn down. He takes a step backward. Stares at the floor. "I guess I'll hear from your lawyer." He turns, marches down the stairs, and walks out the door.

I stare, waiting for him to come back.

But he doesn't.

Chapter Fifty-Two

GRIFFIN

By the time I get home, the sky is dark. Los Angeles dark. A deep indigo that blankets the city and the stars.

I've never missed the stars. What good is a twinkling sky? That kind of romantic shit doesn't appeal to me.

Symbols are useless.

Moonlit walks on the beach, soft kisses under starry skies, sweet declarations at sunset—

That stuff is nice in a movie.

But it's not love.

Love is sticking around every day. Being good to someone every day. Putting them first every day.

I don't want to lose Jules.

Yeah, I still can't say those three words out loud, but I don't want to lose her.

It's impossible hanging out in our apartment. She's everywhere—the framed posters on the walls, the royal blue blanket on the couch, the rose decals in the bathroom.

That's Jules.

My best friend.

My wife.
My everything.
Only she's not. She can't be.
I'm not about to clip her wings.
If she wants out, she wants out.

Chapter Fifty-Three

JULIETTE

Chloe gives me a ride home. She doesn't mention Griffin or marriage or relationships. She doesn't talk at all.

She hands me the aux cable and drives.

When she pulls up to my mom's house, she offers me a sad smile. "I really do think he loves you."

I try to force a smile, but I can't. "This is what he wants."

Her black nails tap the steering wheel. "I hope you're wrong."

"Me too."

"Call if you need anything, okay?"

I nod *okay*.

She offers me a hug.

I take it.

It feels good, even though she's so wrong about the situation. Griffin does what he wants, whenever he wants, however he wants.

That's how he's lived his entire life.

If he's ready to go through with the divorce, it's because he wants it. And I…

If I can't stand there and say *yes, I'm ready to be married forever. I'm ready to commit my heart, body, and soul to you. I'm ready to agree to every one of your terms*, what can I do to stop him?

God, I thought I was there. But I thought I was there with Jackson too.

I never thought Griffin would run like that. Maybe I'm wrong about him too.

Maybe I'm meant to be alone.

I grab my purse, nod goodbye, walk the steps to my house.

The lights are on, but maybe no one's home. Maybe I can run to my bedroom, collapse, hide under my blankets, cry my heart out.

No such luck.

Mom is sitting at the kitchen island, sipping a glass of wine, picking at a plate of cheese.

She takes one look at me and shakes her head with sympathy. "Oh, sweetie."

I try to find the words, but they're still stuck in my throat. I can't tell her. I can't even admit it to myself.

I failed at marriage again.

And, worse, I failed Griffin. He failed me. I'm not sure where the blame goes. If it matters.

I'm losing my best friend.

I'm losing my favorite person in the world.

I'm losing everything.

"I… I guess we…" My throat quivers. "We're talking options tomorrow."

Mom's lips curl into a frown. "I'm sorry."

A sob falls off my lips. "Why is it so hard? Why is it so

complicated? It should be easy. We care about each other. That should be all that matters."

"I know." She pulls me into her arms. "It should be all that matters."

But it's not.

She doesn't have to say it. We both know it.

Love isn't enough.

Love has never been enough.

This is it. We can't go back to normal.

Sure, we can go through the motions. Dissolve our marriage. Go to dinner and a movie. Test craft cocktails. Walk on the beach.

But it won't be *us*.

I've loved him my entire life.

I've known him my entire life.

I've needed him my entire life.

This is it. Everything or nothing.

Either my promise to try is enough or it's not.

I want it to be enough, but that look of disappointment in his eyes…

How can I believe it's enough?

Chapter Fifty-Four

GRIFFIN

My phone buzzes with texts from friends. Mostly, people tell me what an idiot I am for letting Jules walk away.

I can't really argue—she's the best thing that ever happened to me—so I do the next best thing.

I turn my cell off. Seek distraction in a cheesy action movie. It's one of Wes's favorites. I've seen it a million times. But the familiarity fails to comfort.

Dinner doesn't help. A drink doesn't help. Staring at the framed posters on the walls doesn't help.

I want her here.

I want her to explain this.

I want every thought in her fucking head.

If she won't give them to me—

I can't make Jules trust me. I can't make her love me. I can't make her want this.

She's been there forever. Been mine forever. But she was mine in a different way.

Yeah, we fought sometimes. We drove each other crazy.

We stopped talking for weeks, or screamed until we got kicked out of IHOP, or cursed each other's names.

But I always knew she'd be back. That we'd get over it. That I'd climb into her room, wrap my arms around her, whisper apologies in her ear.

This is different. This is a forever fight. The kind of thing that ends a relationship.

I can stomach losing her as a wife, as awful as that is. But losing my best friend?

Fuck that.

There's no comfort—or clarity—in my shower, or my sketchbook, or another mindless action movie.

A guy with a gun mumbles something about how he's going to take out the bad guys. He sprays them with bullets, laughing as their blood hits the walls.

Footsteps move closer.

Someone knocks on the door.

Shit. That's my door.

Maybe it's her. Maybe she figured it out. Realized she's madly in love with me. That she wants to stay my wife.

I suck a deep breath through my teeth. Exhale slowly. "Jules?"

"Afraid not." Chase's paternal voice booms. It's his usual tone. *I know best, and it's not this. Quite frankly, I'm not sure how you've managed to live to see twenty-three. You need my help. Thank God I'm here to provide it.* "You gonna open up?"

"Yeah." I let him inside.

His eyes move around the room. "I like what you did with the place."

"Suits me, right?"

His lips curl into a half-smile. "It's like you designed it just for me."

"It must be embarrassing, having the same taste as a twenty-two-year old."

"That's your wife."

I can't help but frown.

"You realize everyone heard that fight?" He moves into the kitchen. Checks the pantry for… something.

"Can I help you?"

"No, but I can help you." He pulls out a bag of coffee beans. Finds the grinder. The French press. The kettle. "Sit down."

"It's late for coffee."

"When's your appointment?"

"Nine a.m."

"You figure out what you're doing?" He arches a brow *we both know you haven't. You're helpless. Honestly, I'm not sure why I try. You're just not there.*

"She wants out."

He shakes his head *God, you're stupid*. "Do you even look at her?"

"Of course, I look at her."

He motions *sit*. "At something besides her tits?"

"That's my wife you're talking about."

"Not with that attitude."

"Fuck off." I do sit. But not because he suggested it. Because the entire world is off its axis.

He shrugs *you're helpless* then he goes right back to fixing coffee, like it's an ordinary day.

"What the hell do you think you're doing giving me advice?"

"You want to tell me how fucked up my love life is?" he asks.

"It is."

He nods *sure*. "Yeah, she broke my heart. It hurt. Maybe I'm not interested in getting hurt again. But I know where I stand. Do you?"

"Yeah."

"Do you?"

"What the fuck does that mean?" I ask.

He shakes his head *seriously, what the hell am I going to do with you?* "You think this has anything to do with her ex?"

I shrug like it doesn't matter, even though it does.

"Seriously, Griff. You're better than this."

"Easy to say when you don't give a fuck about anyone."

"Yeah. It is." The kettle steams. He grabs it. Fills the French press with hot water. "You know that as well as I do."

That's a fair point.

"This is the first time you've given someone the chance to hurt you."

"Maybe." I'm usually game for this level of honesty. But the intimacy? No thanks. I don't need Chase digging into my head. I don't want anyone there except Jules.

But he's right.

I don't have a fucking clue how I'm fixing this. As much as I hate to admit it, I need his help.

"Hell yeah." He turns. Rests his ass against the counter. "It sucks. Like someone ripped your heart out of your chest."

"You felt like that with her?"

"For a long time."

"Did it stop?"

"No, but it got easier. I felt it a little less every day. Until one day, I barely felt it."

"Now?"

"Depends on the day." He turns back to the coffee. "You're not gonna distract me. I grew up with Wes."

"And Hunter."

"Yeah." His shoulders tense. "You can call me an unforgiving asshole. That won't distract me either."

"You know you're an unforgiving asshole."

"If I could get over it, I would."

"Can't you?" I rest my back against the cushion. It's too soft. It gives too much, supports too little. Is that better or worse than a cushion that's too firm, that gives too little?

Am I really looking for clarity in couch cushion metaphors?

Fuck, I am lost.

"There's a difference between forgiving someone and trusting them." Chase grabs two mugs. Fills them with equal amounts of coffee. "Milk, no sugar?"

"Yeah. Thanks."

He grabs the milk from the fridge. Fixes our coffees. Brings both to the couch. "You know something about that."

I take the coffee. "Thanks."

"You don't trust her."

That's ridiculous. "Of course I do."

"No. You don't." He doesn't explain or elaborate. He just lets the words drop.

Fuck, maybe he's right.

That's what it comes down to.

I don't trust her to tell me what she needs. I want to, I do, but I keep thinking about that day back in high school. I keep thinking about the scars on her wrist and the heart-break on her face and the crack in her voice.

She didn't want me to know. She didn't want to share her burden with me. I was pissed. Eventually, I understood it.

But she went back to it. She kept it secret for years. She went to great lengths to hide it from me—

What the hell do I do with that?

"You love her, don't you?" he asks.

I barely manage to nod. "I do." The words don't make me nauseous. They feel good. Right.

"So you have about ten hours to figure out how to win her over."

"About that."

"Fuck. That's a bad situation."

I can't help but laugh. "Thanks for the update."

"You're not that clever either. It will be hard."

I flip him off.

He returns the gesture with a half-smile. It's playful for him.

But that feels good too. "You still can't trust Hunter?"

He nods.

"But you want to?"

"Yeah."

"How the fuck do you explain that to him?"

He arches a brow *really*?

Yeah, it's a dumb question. He doesn't. The frost between the two of them is crystal clear.

"All right. What the hell do I do?" I take a long sip of my coffee. It's good. Strong. Enough to jump start my brain. "How the hell do I convince her to go all in?"

Chapter Fifty-Five

JULIETTE

Eventually, I give up on sleep, pour myself into my Kindle, try to find distraction.

This book is great, but I can't stomach a tender romance right now. Not with the ache in my chest.

I settle into my desk. Stare at the massive rock on my left hand.

Griffin's mom's ring. The one she dropped in his room the night she left. The one that completely fucked his idea of love and commitment.

That's not fair to the ring. Or his mom. His dad was the one who treated her like shit. Who pushed her until she didn't have a choice.

It would have been better if she'd taken him with her, but it wasn't really an option. And now…

I wish he'd forgive her. Not for her sake. For his.

For mine.

Only, as of right now, it's not mine. I have no stake in his life. Or I won't, as of nine a.m.

Eventually, I move into the kitchen. Make breakfast.

And a matcha. Find a thriller to read—one of those books about people treating each other like shit.

It's an effective distraction. I block out the world. Pour myself into the pages.

Even when everything else is shit, books are there.

Books are everything.

They're going to be my only thing if I fuck this up. Someone is going to stand at my funeral (some librarian, I guess) and say *Juliette didn't have a lot of love in her life, but she had her books.*

My second matcha helps. The situation is still complete suckage. But between the book and the latte, life is survivable.

I get a third of the way through the book and halfway through a third matcha when the doorbell rings.

"Jules." Griffin knocks. "I know you're in there."

I pull my sweater over my chest reflexively.

"Can we talk?"

My gaze darts to the clock. Shit. It's eight. I need to be dressed. I need to be on my way.

I'm not going to face my soon to be ex-husband like this.

Not in my pajamas.

"Give me a minute." I down another sip of matcha. It's amazing, it really is, but it's so not the time. "I need to get dressed."

"You look fantastic."

I clear my throat. "Stop looking through the window."

"Don't sit in front of it with the blinds open."

"Okay. I won't." I close the blinds.

He chuckles. "I didn't want to do this."

"Do what?"

He moves. Shuffles something. Taps something.

The door handle jiggles. Turns.

Griffin steps into the foyer. Holds up the spare key. The one under the cacti planter. "Not exactly rocket science."

"You, um, I thought you'd use the ladder."

"Didn't think you'd want me climbing into your bedroom right now."

"We're supposed to be at the lawyer's office in an hour." I zip my hoodie. Slide my hands into my pockets. Which does nothing to hide the fact I'm wearing boxers and fuzzy socks on my bottom half.

He's in a suit. He's *wearing* that suit.

Fuck, he looks yummy all cleaned up. The fabric covers his tattoos, makes him look like the kind of nice boy you take home to Mom.

Not that I can fool my mom.

Just, uh… is it hot in here? Fuck, it's really hot in here.

My knees knock together. "I, uh, I see you're ready."

He nods. "Seemed prudent."

"Right." Prudent. Because we're getting a divorce. Because he's an idiot. And I'm a bigger idiot. And we made a stupid drunk mistake that's going to ruin our friendship. "I should also do that."

"I'd rather you wear your birthday suit."

"That's a good one. Or maybe I'm tired."

His chuckle is soft.

It warms me everywhere. It's hard to believe it's barely been twelve hours since he stormed out of that party.

But I guess that's what happens when you give your marriage a week. Everything feels fast.

"I am." He places the key back under the planter. Closes the door. Clicks the lock. "You need help getting dressed?"

"I can handle it, actually."

"Still like to watch."

"Uh… I mean…" *Are you here to tell me you've found your*

own lawyer? Are we discussing asset allocation? Is this a formal meeting? Or are you going to tell me you love me and want to stay mine forever? "Why are you here?"

"Would you rather we meet at the law firm?"

I don't know. "It would be easier."

"Easier how?"

"Less painful."

His dark eyes bore into mine. "Are you in pain?"

I push my hands into my pockets. "Griff, can we not?"

"Not what?"

"I don't know. Whatever that is. I'm tired. And I… it's not like I'm psyched to sign divorce papers."

"Yeah." He motions to the stairs *shall we*? "We can talk and dress at the same time."

That's true.

"If we don't, we'll be late."

Also true.

Still, I don't want to invite him into my space. Not if he isn't mine. Not if he's here to discuss the details of our divorce. Not if this is the end.

"Give me a minute." I motion to the couch. *Sit.*

He nods *okay*. Watches me move up the stairs.

I press the door closed. Press my back against it. The wood laminate is far from solid, but the weight is still comforting.

Not as comforting as his arms or his chest or the smell of his shampoo.

Fuck, I miss him.

It's been half a day and I'm aching. How am I supposed to survive losing him completely?

I can't. I just can't.

I strip out of my pajamas. Slip into my interview suit. Pencil skirt. Button up shirt. Blazer. Flats.

A deep breath does nothing to steady me. Neither does a coat of lipstick. Or an all business ponytail.

I guess there's no feeling steady when you're tearing apart your marriage. Even if it's an incredibly young marriage.

It should matter, that it was only a few days, that it was a drunken idea, that it was crazy.

But it doesn't. It still hurts. It still feels like this huge mistake.

Not the marriage part.

This part.

I…

I'm running out of time.

"Hey." Griffin knocks on my door. "We, um, we only have a few minutes."

"Right."

"I guess it's a dick move to ask, but could you drive? I haven't slept."

"Sure, yeah." I suck in another deep breath. "You want to go now?"

"Will you let me in?"

I want to. I do. I'm just not good at it. "Sure, yeah." I open the door.

He's standing there in the frame, all tall, dark, and handsome.

I want to collapse in his arms. To kiss him hard. To soak up every ounce of his comfort.

But only if he's mine.

"I… Uh… you look good. For not sleeping." I smooth my blazer. "You clean up nice."

"You too." His fingers brush my hip. My wrist. My ring finger. "It looks good on you."

"Thank you." I swallow hard.

"You should keep it."

"What for?"

"I don't want anyone else to have it." His eyes bore into mine. "Jules, I… I'm sorry about last night." He cups my hip with his palm.

"What about it?"

"Freaking about your call."

"Oh."

"He was part of your life for a long time. I respect that. I just… fuck, I'm not good at this."

"Me either."

"Can I start over?"

"Okay." I bite my tongue so I won't blurt out every thought in my head. "But, um, we're probably gonna be late."

"I know." He moves closer.

I step backward, moving with him.

He presses the door into the frame. So it's just us in my high school bedroom. The place we've been a million times. The place that felt like home.

My world. The one I invited him into. I want to do that again.

I just have to…

I have to say it.

And soon.

His fingers skim my temple. "I love you."

"What?"

"I'm in love with you."

My heart pounds against my chest. "You are?"

"Yeah. I have been. For a long time. But I didn't see it until recently."

I try to come up with some response, but my mouth is too sticky. I barely manage a nod.

"I've seen it for a few days now. But I couldn't face that word. It was too loaded. Too much like my parents. Like everything wrong with the world. I couldn't get over the idea that love was this word grown-ups invented as an excuse to hurt each other."

"Maybe it is."

"Maybe. But it's something else too. It's the only way to explain how I feel about you. When you smile, I get warm all over. Like I'm at the beach on a summer day, coming out of the water. The ocean is cold, too cold, but with the sun on my skin, I'm the perfect temperature."

I stare into his eyes.

"It's like the taste of a really great cup of coffee when I'm dead tired. Or the comfort of my favorite song. Which is still the one that played in the limo."

My cheeks flush. "Me too."

"I want the best for you, no matter what. No matter how badly it hurts me. And I'd gladly die for you, because I'd rather die than live in a world without you."

"Griff—"

"I want you to soar, no matter what. I could never clip your wings. Ever. So if you want to end this marriage, if you want a divorce, I can do that. I won't be happy about it, but I'll do it."

I shake my head. "No, I…" A tear wells up in my eyes. Then I blink and my vision is blurry. "Griff, I… I love you too."

"Yeah?" His voice perks.

"So much."

"We don't have to—"

"I want to." I wrap my arms around his waist. "I love you. And I want you as my husband."

"I want you as my wife."

"We're gonna be late."

"Fuck that appointment."

"But we—"

"We're staying married. Why do we need to see a divorce lawyer?"

A laugh spills from my lips. "You sure?"

"I've never been more sure." He leans down and presses his lips to mine.

He kisses me hard and deep, like he'll never let go.

Because he won't.

Neither one of us will.

Epilogue

GRIFFIN

"Is it going to hurt?" Jules's eyes go wide. She bites her lip. Presses her toes together. "Tell me it won't hurt."

"Baby, you've done this before."

She nods *I know,* but she still squeezes the chair. "More or less than the ribs?"

"You remember those?"

"Not the first part. But the rest." She sucks a breath through her teeth. Exhales slowly. "What do I call it?"

"I like 'the rest.'" My hands go to her side. It's pure instinct. But then it's not like I need the excuse to touch my wife.

Yes, I want to trace the roses I added to her ribs. To my name.

It was our one year anniversary celebration. Her idea. She loved the tattoo but hated that I wasn't the one who did the work.

So we compromised. Fleshed out the design. Thorny vines wrap around the letters, end in lush red roses.

Guarded but beautiful.

Like her.

Like us.

I have to fight to get past her defenses, but when I do—

Fuck, there's nothing better than that.

She sucks another breath through her nose. Pushes out a shallow exhale. "Less or more?"

"Less." Ribs are at the top of the pain threshold. But hips aren't much lower. Not the bony parts. Not when they're covered with scar tissue.

"How much less?"

"It's gonna hurt."

She nods. Presses her lips together. Forces a slow, deep breath. "But it will be fast. Because it's only one word. So it will be fast, right?"

"I'll go as fast as I can."

Her green eyes bore into mine. "But not too fast? I mean, I don't want you to mess it up. You won't mess it up, will you?"

"Well, I am gonna write *I love cock* here." I trace a line over her right hip. Over her smooth skin and her raised scars.

I'm wearing gloves. I can't feel her flesh the way I want to. But I can still feel her warmth. Her shudder. Her—

Fuck, I can't keep thinking like this or I will mess it up.

Yeah, my wife is sitting on my chair in nothing but a tiny tank top and panties.

Yeah, said panties are lacy white things that make my blood rush to my cock.

But, uh…

Shit, what was I talking about?

Paying attention.

I'm focused.

I'm not thinking about dragging those things to her

ankles, pushing her legs apart, bringing my mouth to her cunt.

Not thinking about tasting her. Or touching her. Or burying myself inside her.

"Griff?" Her chest heaves with her inhale. "You were saying?"

I shrug my shoulders. I need to get my head in gear. To get in the game. To tease her just enough to set her at ease. "*I love cock* on one hip. *I love cum* on the other."

Her eyes go wide. "I will kill you in your sleep."

"You're jumping straight to murder?"

She nods *hell yeah*. "I'll have Chloe help."

"She's a vegetarian."

"So?"

"She won't kill a chicken, but she'll kill me?"

Jules nods. "You're pure evil. Whereas a chicken is innocent. And kinda cute too."

"I'm not cute?"

She shakes her head. "I guess you're okay." She shrugs like she doesn't have any fondness for my eyes, nose, mouth. But her gaze goes straight to my lips. Then the shoulders, chest, stomach, hips.

Her tongue slides over her lips.

Her chest heaves.

Her eyes fill with desire.

God, I want to strip her to nothing. I want to tear off my clothes. Feel every inch of my flesh against hers.

It still defies reason.

Juliette King is my wife.

Juliette King and I are celebrating our two year anniversary.

She asked me to mark the occasion with new ink. Her first ink since she tattooed my name to her ribs. Well, since I added to the design three-hundred-sixty-five days ago.

The tattoo was her idea, but the design was mine. She wanted something to go over her scars. Not a cover up, exactly. More a promise to herself. A reminder that she was strong enough to get through anything.

The design is simple. *Beautiful* in a thin script, over the curve of her hip, over the scars that mark her hip and thigh.

It doesn't cover the scars. It certainly doesn't hide them. It doesn't even touch most of them.

Instead, it reclaims them.

It's hard to explain. I can never explain myself with words. But this idea, this design—it's my way of telling her I understand.

I get it.

I'm sorry I put her though so much shit.

I'm sorry it took me so long to understand.

I love her just the way she is.

And even if she went back to cutting, I'd still love her. I'd do whatever I could to help her—

No, to get her help.

This isn't my battle. I'm not her shrink. I can't take the weight of that. *We* can't take the weight of that.

But I can be here. I can stand by her side, offer her comfort when she needs it, give her space when she needs that.

I'll never like giving her space. Hell, I'll always hate it when she locks me out and recedes into herself. But I get it now.

That's her way.

She has to process things on her own. She has to sort out her thoughts before she can share them.

"Well, um…" Her fingers graze my temples. "You're pretty cute."

I arch a brow. "Pretty cute? That's it?"

"Don't push it."

I stare back.

She holds her poker face for half a minute. Then it falters. Her lips curl into a smile. Her eyes brighten. "Very cute. And incredibly handsome."

"Too handsome to kill?"

"Hmm… maybe."

"You could have her tattoo *Douchebag* to my forehead instead."

She nods *maybe*. "That would ruin the handsomeness."

"Then I wouldn't be too cute to kill."

"Ooh, good loophole."

"I'd still be good at making you come." My gaze goes right to her thighs. Fuck, it's distracting having her in this position. In this state of undress. But there's no way I'm letting someone else do this.

"That is true. But, I, uh…" She clears her throat. "I have other means." She holds up her right hand. "Plus the toys. God, the toys." She shakes her head *you're ridiculous*.

It's true. I am ridiculous. I've bought her a lot of toys. But it's not like she's shrugged them off.

We use them together all the time.

She uses them alone all the time.

When I'm lucky, she sends me pictures (or video) of her solo activities.

And I'm already hard.

Fuck, I need to concentrate. I take a deep breath. Recite the Angels line up. Think about the Dodgers World Series win. Could anything more despicable happen?

Jules hasn't stopped bragging.

The boys in blue could go a hundred years without making the play offs, and Jules would still be bragging about their World Series win.

She's adorable when she does it.

God, the way her cheeks flush and her eyes light up. The way she shakes with energy—

Shit, this isn't working. I need to think about something that isn't sexy. Which means I need to think about something besides my wife.

Even when she annoys me or hurts me or frustrates me, I want her. I want my hands on her. I want her lips on mine. I want her skin against mine.

Not just because she's gorgeous. Or because I love the sound of her groan. Or because I love the way she says my name.

Because I need her. All of her.

This is a big deal. She's letting me mark her skin. She's letting me mark her scars.

After we celebrated our marriage properly, we had a long, uncomfortable talk about what it meant for her to try. For both of us to be honest.

She bitch-slapped me with the truth. Made it clear I needed to give her space. Stay out of her healing. Never, ever make it about me and how it hurt when she lied or hid things from me.

It did. It still does. But I don't put that on her anymore.

It wasn't easy. She tried to white knuckle her way through quitting for a while. She'd slip up, hate herself for it, lock me out.

I got mad. Hurt. Angry. I thought I kept it to myself. I thought I dealt with it on my own. But she could tell. She could feel it radiating from my pores.

I guess that's what happens when you love someone with every molecule of your being. You can't hide shit from them.

We went to couples counseling.

I know, I couldn't believe it. I had no interest in spilling my guts to a stranger. But it helped. We built better boundaries. Learned how to process shit before we jumped. Learned how to really communicate with each other.

Then I started seeing someone on my own. I sorted out a lot of shit about my need to protect Jules, my inability to communicate verbally, my parents.

I still ignore my dad's calls, but I finally replied to one of my mom's letters. We're talking now. Well, we're getting there.

Jules started seeing someone too. It helped, but it wasn't a magic bullet. She started talking to her therapist. Finding other coping methods. Jogging or writing in her journal or scribbling lyrics on her skin (I don't know why it works, but it does).

One day, she woke up, and she realized she hadn't cut in a month.

Then it was two.

Three.

Six.

A year.

She came to me that day—it was only a few weeks ago—and told me she wanted to mark the occasion.

She didn't know how to do it or what she wanted, so I came up with this.

The scars aren't beautiful, exactly. But the strength she shows every fucking day—

That is.

She really is beautiful. Her heart, her soul, her—

Well, I can't start listing all the parts of her body I adore or I'm going to be here a very long time. And I'm going to have very little blood left in my brain.

"Griff?" Jules drags her fingertips down my chin.

"Yeah?"

"You there?"

"Thinking about you naked."

"I can tell." She nods to my crotch.

I guess the situation is obvious.

Her cheeks flush. "I'd offer to put on pants, but it's not exactly an option."

"Over my dead body."

Her lips curl into a smile. "I'm going to get some water. You want something?"

"I'll get it." I stand. Lean in enough to press my lips to hers.

The kiss she returns is hard and hungry. Need pours from her to me. From me to her.

This is a big deal. For both of us.

As much as I hate to admit it, this has been a wall between us. Since we were kids. Since she hid it from me back in high school. Since I found out and guilted her for it. Since she fell into old habits.

Since she hid that.

Since the day she told me.

And the day she said she wanted to stay my wife.

It's not easy. I love her more than anything, but that doesn't make it any easier. If anything, it makes it harder. Because my heart stops and my throat closes when I think about her hurting.

I see red and I lose logic.

It's taken a long, long time for us to get here. To this place where we can talk about her self-harm without her hiding or me freaking.

I hope, more than anything, that she never hurts herself again. But I don't expect it of her. If she slips, she slips. I'll be here to catch her, but it will still be her battle.

I can't fight it for her.

School helped. Her MFA program kept her busy. It gave her an outlet. Jules always loved reading and writing, but it was a hobby, not a calling. I'm not sure what kept her from embracing it before—practicalities or insecurity or that controlling asshole Jackson. Maybe all three.

But now, after finishing her program, and writing a gajillion words of fiction and "creative non-fiction"—

She's in love with the written word. She goes there first. Before she goes to me. Before she goes to a blade.

My wife is still figuring out what she's doing with her life. She has a gig at a lifestyle website. It's not a forever job. But it's enough for now.

It pays the bills.

It gives her time and space to work on her own shit.

It makes her happy.

At the end of the day, that's all I want. The only thing I want.

I want Jules happy and healthy.

I'll do whatever it takes to make that happen.

I take another deep breath. Let out another steady exhale.

Yeah, this is a big deal. But it's also my job. I know how to put ink to skin.

I need to focus on that. To get through the practical part of this exercise.

Work first. Then I let it hit me.

I pour her a cup of water. Take a sip. Bring it back to her.

She drinks it in three gulps.

I change my gloves. Take a seat on the stool. Push her into the chair. "Are you ready?"

She looks down at me with all the trust in the world. "Is it going to hurt?"

"Yeah."

She bites her lip. Watches as I clean her skin, apply the stencil, pick up the gun. "Okay. I'm ready."

"You sure?"

"Do it."

I turn on the gun.

She yelps as it hits her skin. But she still makes it through the first tattoo.

Then the second.

She sighs as I turn off the gun. "Thank God."

My lips curl into a smile. She's so fucking perfect, but I need to stay focused. My work isn't done.

I clean her up. Bring her to the mirror. Show Jules her reflection.

Her eyes go wide as she takes it in. Her lips part. Her hand goes to her mouth. "Griff. It's… I…" A tear catches on her lashes.

"Jules."

"I—" A tear rolls down her cheek. Then she blinks, and her eyes are wet. "I… Griff…"

"Yeah, baby?"

"It's perfect. Thank you."

I wrap my arms around her. "Thank you."

"For what?"

"Loving me. Trusting me. Giving me time."

She nods. "Always."

"I'm going to hold you to that."

"I know." She presses her lips to mine. "I am too."

"You are what?"

"You waited for me too. You trusted me too."

"I love you more than anything."

"Me too. I mean, I love you too."

I do away with my gloves. Bring my hand to her cheek. Pull her into a slow, deep kiss.

It hits me slowly, then all at once.

My wife trusts me with her body, her heart, her soul.

That's everything.

She's everything.

Want more Inked Hearts?

Get to know cocky tattoo artist Dean in his (and Chloe's) book *Hating You, Loving You*, a smoking hot enemies to lovers romance. (It has all the banter, heart, and heat you loved in *Accidental Husband*).

Turn the page for a sample.

You can also sign up for my mailing list for an exclusive *Accidental Husband* bonus scene. (You'll see Griffin and Jules at a very special anniversary celebration).

Totally new to Inked Hearts?

Start with book one, *Tempting*, a featuring brooding tattoo artist Brendon and oh so off limits college student Kaylee. This forbidden romance has a dominant hero and a virgin heroine.

Already read Hating You, Loving You?

Chase's book, *The Baby Bargain*, is coming summer 2019.

Until then, keep scrolling for a sample from *Dangerous Kiss*, a sexy second chance romance featuring a dirty talking rock star hero and the math geek heroine who refuses to get out of his head.

Hating You, Loving You - Special Preview

CHLOE

Get *Hating You, Loving You* Now

Why do people drink?

This stuff tastes awful.

I force myself to swallow another mouthful of orange juice and vodka.

My throat burns.

My head spins.

I reach for something to hold onto. Find the white banister. It's smooth, ornate, pure money.

This entire house is pure money. Pristine carpet. Glass tables. Three-thousand-dollar leather upholstery.

Six-dollar Trader Joe's vodka.

The cheap booze ruins the aesthetic. It clashes with the skylights, the sliding glass doors, the glowing aqua pool.

Not that anyone notices. My classmates are used to expensive furniture and two-million-dollar mansions.

But cheap vodka and an empty upstairs?

That thrills them.

I've heard enough rumors to know the drill. Rich kids. Nice house. Cheap booze. Parents out of town. *I heard Dean fucked Judy...*

Not that it's always Dean.

It's just those are the only rumors I pay attention to.

A giggle cuts through the big, white room. It bounces off the high ceilings. It bounces right into my ears.

There's Judy, all blond hair and long limbs, standing at the table, running her red nails over Dean's forearm.

His smile lights up his blue eyes. They're bright. Full of energy and life and lust for torturing me.

He raises a brow. Runs his strong hand through his shaggy dirty blond hair.

Shrugs his broad shoulders. Those are swimmer's shoulders. He has a swimmer's everything. I've seen him in a Speedo enough times to know—the guys practice a few lanes over.

He's more than a hot body too. He's handsome. Charming. Funny.

Evil.

My head knows better. My head despises the cocky playboy. For calling me sunshine. For taking nothing seriously. For throwing people away.

But my heart?

My body?

It's impossible to get over a guy you see shirtless five times a week. That's a scientific fact.

He laughs at Judy's joke. Shoots her that trademarked Dean million-dollar smile as he blows her a kiss.

She paws at his chest.

He shrugs *maybe, maybe not.*

He's indifferent. Effortless. Aloof.

He has so much female attention he could give or take a knockout in fuck me heels.

That doesn't give a nobody in combat boots much of a chance.

I force myself to look away.

Watch Alan—this is his place—pound his red solo cup. He finishes. Crushes the cup. Watches it fall onto the pristine white carpet.

Drops of brown liquor catch on the fibers.

He shrugs like he doesn't care, but the worry in his eyes betrays him. The jocks around him laugh. Pound their drinks. Whisper some secret.

There are a dozen people here. Half in that circle. The rest on the couch or in the airy, stainless steel kitchen.

Everyone here is casual. Comfortable. Used to parties. To money. To cheap booze in plastic cups.

I…

This is way out of my comfort zone.

My gaze shifts back to Dean.

His eyes lock with mine. He raises his glass. Smiles.

My combat boots tap together. My hands go to my tank top. I play with its edge. Try to figure out what the hell that means.

Dean and I have shared two classes a day, every day, for the last three years.

He spends most of his free time teasing me.

Calling me sunshine.

Mocking how seriously I take art, math, and science.

Mocking my all black clothes, my thermos of tea, my tendency to gush about cartoons.

He turns to Alan. Whispers something.

Alan laughs.

Dean nods *hell yeah.* "Everybody come here." His playful voice bounces around the room.

Everyone turns his way.

Looks at him.

Hangs on his words.

Dean commands attention, friendship, respect. All he does is smile and a dozen girls fall over themselves trying to claim him.

A dozen guys want to be his friend.

The world is his oyster.

"Why should I listen to anything you say, Maddox?" Alan teases back.

Dean's shrug is effortless. *Why should I bother exerting a single ounce of energy on anything?* "If you don't want me to blow your mind, go ahead. Leave."

"Maddox, I don't want you blowing anything." Alan laughs.

I roll my eyes. How original.

Dean's eyes catch mine. He shakes his head *not great, huh?*

I fight my smile.

Every day this year, he turned our art class from my happy place to my *deal with Dean's constant teasing* place.

He doesn't get a smile now.

Even if my body is buzzing with nervous energy.

Even if my limbs are light and airy.

Even if my sex is aching.

I must be blushing, because he's smiling wider. Knowingly. Like he's sure I'm eating out of the palm of his hand.

He turns back to the group. "Truth or dare."

"I'm not fourteen," someone says.

"Sounds like you're chicken." Dean turns to me. "What do you think, Chloe? Are you chicken?"

"No." My heart thuds against my chest.

My head fills with ideas. Every dirty dare he could offer me.

His hands in my hair.

His groan in my ears.

His lips against mine.

God, those soft lips.

I want to slap them for all the stupid shit he says. For not giving a fuck about the classes his parents pay a fortune for. For calling me sunshine every three seconds.

But he's calling me Chloe.

He…

I…

My heart pounds so hard I'm sure it's going to break out of my chest.

It doesn't.

But a deep breath does nothing to help me calm down.

For three years I've been smitten. Ever since our first day in geometry, when he turned to me and asked to borrow my protractor. Then promised to make it worth my while with a wink and a smile.

Calm eludes me.

Sense eludes me.

Everything but a fangirl voice screaming *Dean Maddox* eludes me.

His lips curl into a smile. He holds out his arm. Motions *come here.*

My knees knock together.

Lightness spreads into my chest, neck, head. I'm dizzy. Like I'm going to faint.

Who knew swooning was a real thing? I thought Gia made it up.

My feet move of their own accord.

My combat boots sink into the plush carpet.

My hands slip from my pockets.

One finds his palm.

He wraps his fingers around my hand. Rubs the space between my thumb and forefinger with his thumb.

He looks down at me—he has to, he has a foot on me—like I'm the only thing he needs.

Like I'm *everything* he needs.

His voice is soft. Sweet. "Nice of you to join, sunshine."

The nickname breaks my trance.

Dean doesn't need me. He needs to push my buttons.

Gia insists he's teasing because he likes me, but what does Gia know about guys like Dean? She met her boyfriend at a comics shop. They read *Spider-Man* and play video games together.

Gia doesn't know Dean, but I do.

With him, you have to bite back.

I shoot him my best *fuck you* smile. "Nice to see you, dick face."

He chuckles. "You know I take that as a compliment."

I shrug *do you?* People mill closer. Take seats on the couch, at the table, on the ground.

"If you'd seen my dick, you'd know why." He steps forward to let someone pass. His hand brushes my arm. His chest brushes my shoulder. His crotch brushes my outer thigh.

My body responds with gusto.

Any sense of calm, of upper hand, of any hand, dissipates.

My body goes into overdrive. Every molecule screams the same thing: *more Dean please.*

A jock's voice pulls me from my thoughts. "Damn, Maddox. Stop bragging. We're playing a game here." He pats a spot on the packed couch. It's all designer jeans and BCBG dresses and pretty girls in hot guy's laps.

I take a step backward, but there's nowhere to go. My ass hits the glass table.

Dean turns to his friend. "Should I whip it out instead?"

A girl sitting on the couch claps with glee. "Hell yeah!"

The five girls sitting on the ground clap with her.

"There's a demand." Dean shrugs, effortless. He reaches for his jeans. Pretends to undo his button. "I can't let my fans down."

"Save it for the game," the friend says.

A dozen *awwws* and *no fairs* bounce around the room.

Dean turns to me. Winks. "Fair is fair." He offers his hand. "Sit with me, sunshine."

He leads me to the couch. Rests his ass on its arm.

I stand next to him. Shift my weight between my feet. Tap my toes together. Listen to the hollow sound the synthetic leather makes.

His hand brushes my hip.

My body responds immediately.

My pulse races. My nipples perk. My sex clenches.

I want him touching me. I think about it all the time. Too much.

He's everything I hate.

He's someone I hate.

But I still want him touching me.

I still stroke myself to orgasm thinking about him every fucking night.

"Why don't you start, Romeo," Dean's friend calls.

Ooohs and *ahhs* bounce around the room with *do its* and *Oh my Gods!*

The room wants Dean.

The entire world wants Dean.

He wants…

Who knows what the hell the manwhore wants.

He smiles, reveling in the attention. "With pleasure." He turns to me. "Chloe, truth or dare."

My head fills with ideas.

A dare to kiss him.

To flash him.

To touch him.

God, I want to touch him.

And to slap the smarmy smile from his face.

He did call me by my name.

Maybe there's some shred of decency behind his party boy façade.

Or maybe that's my hormones talking.

Either way.

I adopt his aloof posture. Watch clouds roll over the skylight. Watch the wavy lines of the pool bounce off the sliding glass door. Watch a dozen people turn their attention to me.

Deep breath. Slow exhale. "Truth."

His blue eyes sparkle as his smile spreads over his cheeks. "Are you a virgin?"

My cheeks flush.

My chest too.

Fuck Dean.

He must know I am.

Everyone at school knows.

I'm the weird loner who spends lunch drawing in her sketchbook.

Guys aren't interested.

Not that any guys appeal. The guy who tortures me is the only one I want.

Why am I here?

I step backward. Dig my heel into the soft carpet. My instincts scream *leave*, but I can't do that.

I'm not embarrassed of my inexperience.

I'm not letting him rattle me.

I'm not letting his friends think I'm some loser ashamed of her decisions.

"Yes." I shoot Dean my most serene smile. "I have standards. I'm sure that's hard for you to imagine."

He scratches his head. "Standards. Never heard of those."

His friends laugh.

Someone calls out, "It's when you need more than a pulse and two legs."

"Two legs? Look who's Mr. Picky." A jock laughs.

"I'd never discriminate against a woman with one leg. Or no legs." Dean's eyes find mine. "I don't need a smile either. A million-dollar scowl is better."

I fight my scowl. I'm playing Dean's game. Indifference. Aloofness. Utter coolness. "Unfortunately for you, I do have standards."

Someone makes that *ooh, burn* sound.

The girls on the floor giggle. Whisper something. No doubt it's *who does she think she is? No way Dean wants her.* But I don't care about them.

They're seniors. They're graduating. In two weeks, they'll be out of my life forever.

Dean looks up at me with a wicked smile. "Your turn."

Oh. So it is. I scan the room.

Fuck the girls trading rumors.

Fuck the guys looking at me like they're deciding if I meet their standards.

Fuck this whole party.

My gut churns. Why did I let Gia talk me into this? Why did I think an invite from Dean could lead to anything but teasing and embarrassment?

I need to get out of here. Fast.

I look to Alan. He's a wannabe Dean. Not quite as cute or tall or blond. Not as funny or charming or attention grabbing. "Alan, truth or dare."

Everyone turns to him.

He leans back in his black chair. Revels in the attention. "Dare."

I have to fight fire with fire. "I dare you to streak around the neighborhood."

Alan jumps to his feet. Holds up his hand in salute. "I hope you ladies are in for a show." He sends winks in every direction. Even mine.

Then he marches over the carpet, the white tile foyer, the mat. All the way out the door.

It slams shut with a thud.

"Let's set up on the porch." Dean motions to the door. Leans in to whisper something to the girl next to him.

Even though she's sitting on some guy's lap, she giggles at Dean. "Sure."

She slides off her boy-toy's lap. "Follow me." Her red heels sink into the carpet, then they click against the tile.

She turns back. Motions *let's go*.

And everyone does.

One by one, people stand. File out of the room.

Someone, a guy about Dean's height, with a letterman jacket and dark hair, whispers something in Dean's ear.

Dean shakes his forehead. "Got something else to do."

The friend laughs.

Dean watches him leave.

It's just us in this giant house.

I move to the table. Fill my glass with more orange juice and vodka. Pray for it to erase that *you don't belong here* voice completely.

This is supposed to be the best time of my life. Parties. Boys. Fun.

I'm having fun, dammit.

Dean follows me to the table. "You don't want to watch?"

"Alan isn't my type."

"What is?"

"Smart guys." I take a long sip of my drink. "You know any?"

"Not one. But I can help with that drink." His hand brushes mine. Slowly, he peels my fingers from my cup. "Grenadine." He picks up a bottle of candy red liquid. Pours it into my glass. "Goes down smoother."

"Thanks." My stomach flutters as he hands the glass back.

This is intentional.

He's touching me on purpose.

He's helping me on purpose.

He's alone with me on purpose.

He fills his cup with Jack and Coke then lifts it to toast.

"To?" I ask.

"Good friendships."

"We're good friends?"

"Of course." His voice is earnest. Honest.

"I hate you."

"I know."

"That doesn't bother you?"

"Fuck no. It's what I like about you." He clinks his glass with mine. Takes a long sip. Lets out a low sigh of pleasure. "You keep me on my toes."

"You live on your toes."

"Should take up ballet." He makes a show of rising to his tiptoes. It's nowhere close to a ballet move. But it's Dean all the same.

Charming *and* irritating.

Gia says he reminds her of Han Solo.

But Gia isn't the one taking his constant insults. (And Gia needs to learn that *Star Wars* isn't the answer to all of life's questions).

"I do like you, sunshine." His eyes find mine. "Have for a while."

"So that virgin question?"

"I wanted to know something. So, I asked."

"What did you want to know?"

He moves closer. Until I can feel the heat of his body. Smell his cologne. "If I'd be your first."

What? My cheeks flame. There's no way he…

There's no…

I…

"Chloe?" His fingers brush the inside of my wrist.

"Huh?"

"I want to fuck you."

"But—"

"Let's go upstairs. I'll show you the night of your life."

My defenses crumble.

Dean wants me.

He's offering to fuck me.

He…

How is this possible?

My heart screams for him. My body aches for him. My head—it's still reasonable.

I throw up the only defense I know—sarcasm. "Of my entire life?"

"Yeah."

"Doesn't speak well for your future performances."

"You already thinking about round two?"

"No. I…" My cheeks flame. "I meant—"

"I know what you meant, sunshine. Round two will be just as good. But nothing is as special as your first time."

"Yours?"

He shrugs, effortless. "Wasn't lucky enough to have someone like me showing me the ropes."

"You're going to show me the ropes?"

He nods. "Yeah." His fingers trace circles over my skin. "If that's what you want."

"Judy offered to fuck you."

"And?"

"Why me over her?"

"I told you, sunshine. I like you. It's that simple."

"You're about to graduate."

"You will next year."

"But you're… you're leaving."

He shakes his head. "Not going anywhere."

"Where will you be?"

"Ryan is gonna get me a gig as an apprentice."

"Yeah?" I bite back my enthusiasm. Dean's older brother is a tattoo artist. It's the coolest thing ever.

"Yeah." He nods. "Just got this one." He pulls his shirt up his torso, showing off inches of taut abs.

He pulls it higher.

All the way to his side.

He turns to show off a tattoo on his ribs—the state of California, adorned with grey and red roses.

"How much did that hurt?" I ask.

"Like a bitch."

"Guys usually say it doesn't hurt."

"Liars."

"Can I?"

"Of course."

My fingers go to his skin. It's soft, but he's bone and muscle beneath it.

God, the feel of him against my fingertips…

My knees knock together.

"Didn't think you were the ink type," he says.

Words dissolve on my tongue. He's so close. And so undressed. And so hot.

My hand knows what it wants.

It traces his ink again and again.

I look up at him. He's so tall. I'm short, yeah, but he's on some other plane of height.

"Can you keep a secret?" I ask.

He pulls an imaginary zipper over his lips in a *my lips are sealed* gesture.

"I got one last month." I roll my jeans over my right hip to show off my new tattoo. A star. It's a little lopsided, but it's mine.

"Badass." He flashes me that million-dollar smile. "I have another one to show you." He offers his hand. "Upstairs."

There's weight in the word.

Upstairs isn't for conversation. It's for what I've been dreaming about for the last three years.

"Okay." I down half my drink. Pray for the liquid courage I hear so much about. "Upstairs."

I take his hand and follow him to the bedroom.

Dean presses his lips to mine.

He strips me out of my clothes.

He lays me on the bed and warms me up.

Pulls a condom from his jeans. Tears it open. Slides it on.

Then he's on top of me, easing into me, whispering dirty promises in my ear.

It hurts, but not as badly as Gia told me it would.

The pain fades to discomfort.

To pleasure.

To the thrill of knowing that Dean and I are one.

He takes care of me. Makes sure I come.

It feels like we go forever.

We finish. He helps me dress. Promises to stay in touch.

Never does.

He doesn't text, or call, or email, or IM.

The next week, he graduates.

And I spend seven years without hearing a peep from Dean Maddox.

Get *Hating You, Loving You* Now

Dangerous Kiss - Special Preview

VIOLET

Get *Dangerous Kiss* Now

The manila envelope is thick. It's *Violet Valentine, we are delighted to offer you admission to the New York University master's degree in mathematics* program thick.

For the first time in two months, my stomach isn't weighed down with dread. It's light. Airy.

I take a deep breath then exhale slowly. I should call Ethan for this. He can share in the moment. He needs the lift in mood as much as I do.

But my phone is up in my room and he's at practice. This *is* the band that is going to launch him to the stratosphere. It's not a line he uses to get me on board. I love the way he plays guitar.

I love the way Dangerous Noise sounds together.

Fuck it. I tear the envelope open. Shreds of manila flutter to the concrete path that cuts through my parents' perfectly green lawn.

There's something with thick, heavy paper in here. It's

got to be a welcome booklet. It's got to be NYU enticing me to study in the middle of New York City, in a glorious purple sweatshirt, surrounded by life and energy.

It's three thousand miles away from here, yeah, but the only thing I care about here is Ethan and he's spending six of the next eight months on tour. What's it matter if he visits me here or in New York City?

One more deep breath and I can look.

Inhale.

Exhale.

I press my heels against the ground until the concrete is boring into my bare feet.

I'm ready for this.

I pull the papers out.

Ms. Valentine, we are excited to invite you to join our master's degree in mathematics program starting in the fall. Your financial aid and scholarship information is enclosed.

I'm in.

I'm in and I have a partial scholarship. Between loans and a part-time job, I can make this work.

For the first time in two months, life is full of possibilities. This is everything I want. It's much better than the actuary job I have lined up. It's much better than staying at my parents' house to save money while I commute from Huntington Beach to Irvine for another few years.

It's the first piece of good news since Asher died.

I need to tell Ethan right away. I need to share my happiness with him. And I *need* us celebrating properly after.

The front door of Ethan's place is already open. I knock and step inside.

There's music coming from the practice room. I listen until I can pick out the sound of Ethan on lead guitar. My smile gets wider.

He has everything he wants. Now, I'll have everything I want, too.

I listen until I can't take it anymore. The song is amazing but I need his arms around me. I need him throwing me on the bed, peeling off my clothes, and reminding me how well we fit together.

"Hey." I knock on the practice room's open door.

Ethan steps into the hallway, his smile already at his cheeks.

He slides his arms around me to scoop me up then he's spinning me around.

I squeal, holding onto his strong shoulders as tightly as I can. This is how things are supposed to feel. And I haven't even told him yet. It can only get better.

Ethan and I are a team. It might be tough doing long distance, but a master's is only two years. That's nothing compared to us having the rest of our lives together.

"Let's go to your room." I press my lips to his. The peck isn't enough. My hands go to his dark, wavy hair. I pull him closer and I suck on his lower lip until he's groaning in my mouth.

"What the fuck did I do to deserve this, Vi?" He sets me down. His eyes are on fire, that look that screams *I need you naked immediately.* "You look hot as hell in that skirt."

"Do I?"

"You teasing me, honey? I'll get you back for that." His blue eyes light up as he smiles. He slides his hands to my ass and pulls me closer.

Then his lips are on mine and his tongue is in my mouth. This is the first time we've really kissed since it happened. This is the first time it's felt like everything really is going to be okay.

I soak in the feeling of his tongue dancing with mine. Then his hands are under my skirt. He presses his palm against my sex, over my panties.

His breath is heavy when he pulls back. "You're wet."

"Why do you think I want to go to your room?"

His smile widens. It's earnest. It's without defenses. The pain and distance of the last two months is already melting.

It's all in his eyes. I'm back. Grief isn't drowning me any longer. It hurts, yeah, but I can feel pleasure too.

God, the pleasure I can feel.

I take his hand and lead him to his room—Ethan lives with his parents too. He has other options, but he prefers it this way. His parents are always out of town. He and his older brother don't want their teenage sister stuck in the big house all by herself.

His room is clean and bright. With the window open, the whole place smells like the ocean.

Ethan slides his hands to my hips. "How about you come on my face before we talk?"

"How about after?"

"How about you come on my hands then my face after?"

"You drive a hard bargain, Mr. Strong."

He smiles and presses his crotch into mine, so I can feel his erection. "You have no fucking idea how badly I want you right now."

"Ethan…" I'm buzzing everywhere. I stare into Ethan's gorgeous blue eyes. This is an important moment. I want to remember every second of it.

"You gonna tell me or you gonna give me blue balls?" he teases.

He has an excellent point. I need to tell him so we can move on to the celebrating properly part.

"I got in." I pull my letter from my pocket, unfold it, and offer it to him. "I got into the master's program at NYU."

He's not smiling.

He's not scooping me into his arms and spinning me again.

He's not happy. His eyes are turned down and his brow is furrowed.

He takes the paper and reads it slowly. "You're moving to New York City?"

"It's only for two years." I reach for his bicep but he pulls his arm away. "I told you I applied."

"You said there was no chance you'd get in."

"I thought there wasn't."

"You're supposed to tour with us all summer. You're supposed to start that job here in November." His eyes fill with frustration.

But that doesn't make any sense.

I reach for him again. This time, he lets me touch him. But he stares at my hand like it's doing him wrong.

What the fuck? I expect this shit from everyone else. I get that it's weird that I love math. Everyone acts like it makes me a freak. Everyone except Ethan.

He gets it.

He always has.

Why isn't he happy for me?

Maybe he's still surprised. Maybe he doesn't realize that this is a beginning and not an ending.

"Things will be the same as they are now. Only I'll be in New York." I stare into his blue eyes. "You can stay with me when you aren't touring. I can fly out on weekends."

His eyes bore into mine. "You already decided?"

What? This is what I want, what I've always wanted. He knows that.

"You're just leaving. Like that?" He takes a step backwards.

"School doesn't start until late August." I… I don't get it. I go to all his shows. I do everything I can to support Ethan's band.

It's not an obligation.

We're a team.

Violet and Ethan against the world. That's our fucking motto.

He's still staring at me like I'm betraying him. "If you want to leave, then leave."

"It's not like that."

"What's it like? You're leaving cause you're so crazy in love with me you need to be three thousand miles away? You've been pushing me away since Asher… you don't want to talk, fine. You don't want to be in the same state as me, fine. Go."

I grab the paper from his hands. "It's not like that, Ethan."

"Then explain what it's like."

"We're a team."

"Teams don't make unilateral decisions." He pulls his door open and takes a step into the hallway. "You've already decided to leave. Why drag it out?"

"Ethan…"

"If you want to walk away, do it."

His eyes flare with frustration.

He…

This doesn't make any sense.

We need to talk later. We'll have cooler heads. He'll apologize. He'll realize that this is for us.

I grab the paper from him, crumple it, and shove it back in my pocket. "Fine."

"That's it, Vi. You walk out that door, it's over between us."

He stares at me with those gorgeous blue eyes of his.

"Things don't have to change." I stare back at him. "I can still come on tour with you this summer."

He shakes his head. "You've already decided to leave. Don't bullshit me about it now."

But this isn't bullshit. Things *can* stay the same. Why can't he see that?

His expression gets intense. "If you want to leave, do it."

My brow furrows. I hate to leave things like this. But I don't see what other choice I have. "Fine. I'm glad your dreams are more important than mine."

I stare back at him, waiting for a response.

Nothing. He just looks at me like I slapped him and told him I slept with his friend.

I can't talk to him right now. Not like this.

I walk out the door, sit in my car until I'm calm enough to drive home, and wait for him to apologize.

All night, I wait for him to apologize.

All week.

All month.

All fucking semester.

He never does.

Stay In Touch

Thank you for reading *Accidental Husband*. I hope you loved Griffin and Juliette's story as much as I did, and I hope you look forward to Chase's book *The Baby Bargain*, coming 2019.

If you enjoyed this novel, please help other readers find it by leaving an honest review on Amazon or Goodreads.

Want news about new releases and sales before anyone else? How about exclusive sneak peeks and bonus scenes? Sign up for the Crystal Kaswell mailing list.

Want to talk books? I love hearing from my readers. You can find me on Facebook or join my Facebook group.

You can find more of my books here.

Author's Note

This one is long. You'll have to forgive me <3

I try to keep art and business separate. It's hard as an indie publisher—the job is half art, half business. The sides fight sometimes, but, ultimately, they have to compromise. What good is an empty book everyone reads? Or an amazing book no one reads?

For the most part, I'm lucky on the art meets business front. If you found me in high school and asked me what I wanted to write, I would have said something about how I wanted to *be* the tortured lyricist I was completely in love with. I wanted people to see my pain as something beautiful, to read my words and understand and accept me, and understand themselves. (I was an angsty teen. Though I'm not sure exactly how far I've come…)

My second answer would have been something about dramas that showed people how beautiful and fragile relationships are. That good intentions and love aren't always enough to make connections work.

Really, is there anything more tragic than wanting and

failing to understand someone else? Or wanting them to understand you?

Fundamentally, writing is a way of seeking—and offering—that understanding. Just as I took solace in my favorite album. Hell, just as I still take solace in my favorite album, as I hold onto that belief that someone out there could understand my pain, I offer up my own dose of understanding.

Sometimes it goes well. A book soars, people love it, they *get* it, they *get* me. Sometimes… it doesn't. I try not to talk about this with readers. I don't want readers to worry about business, or about my feelings, or about what I want them to read.

But the reality of this gig is that some books do better and some do worse. And sometimes a book that's intensely person is the one that does worse and it feels like someone took all that understanding and vulnerability and tore it into pieces.

When I started writing *Accidental Husband*, I was there. Reeling. Whining. Kicking and screaming. The book in my soul had flopped. What the hell was I supposed to do? Sure, I could write another book. I could put on my business hat and write a commercial book. But I couldn't find my inner artist. She was back to moody teen, hurt and defensive and unwilling to come out. There was no way I could pour my heart into another book.

That wasn't ideal, but it was fine. After nearly five years of indie publishing, I'm a pro. I started *Accidental Husband* with plans of a fun, easy romp. Something that wouldn't risk my heart and soul. Only my heart had a mind of its own.

I was halfway through this book when I realized *holy fuck, this is exactly the book I want to write, in my head, my heart, and my soul.* It was personal in a different way. Honest in a different way. Raw in a different way.

Griffin and Juliette surprised me. Yes, they were funny and sexy and dirty, but they were also broken, hurt, vulnerable. Yes, they'd been best friends since forever. They had a deep connection and a bunch of unsaid expectations. They'd both screwed up in the past, and they were trying to move on, trying to get past the ways they'd hurt each other by accident.

It was perfect. Two people who loved each other, who couldn't get out of their own way. One relationship so strong and so delicate at the same time. Because, really, what hurts more than offering someone your heart and finding out it's not enough?

It hurts. It hurts like hell. But there's only one thing to do. You lick your wounds and find someone who deserves it.

I can't say I have my mojo back just yet. Every book is different. And I'm at a new stage in my career, a more intellectual one, driven my ideas rather than raw need. It's hard to explain, even to myself. Sometimes, I try to put on both my business and art hats, and I sit around asking myself "what is it I want to write? What is it readers love about my books? What do readers want?"

I haven't quite figured it out. Hopefully, I'll fall in love with my next couple. Even after twenty-something books, I'm never sure I'll figure out the next one. I start every book with a blank page and a deep fear I won't figure out how to write a single word. Eventually, I get something down. Then a little more. I stumble in the dark for half a draft or so, then eventually something clicks, and I figure out what the book was about. (It's not the most streamlined process).

Hopefully, the next book comes.

Until then, I'm enjoying the moment of finishing this

book and releasing it into the world. It felt good, letting the fire take over, letting Griffin and Jules steal my heart.

I hope they stole yours too.

I hope to see you soon for Chase and Ariel's story. I think *The Baby Bargain* will be a reader favorite. Chase is so deliciously damaged. The poor guy has issues with EVERYONE in his life. He wants so badly to trust again, to trust his friends, his family, himself, but he can't.

Until then,

Crystal

Acknowledgements

My first thanks goes to my husband, for his support when I'm lost in bookland and for generally being the sun in my sky. Sweetheart, you're better than all the broken bad boys in the world.

The second goes to my father, for insisting I go to the best film school in the country, everything else be damned. I wouldn't love movies, writing, or storytelling half as much if not for all our afternoon trips to the bookstore and weekends at the movies. You've always been supportive of my goals, and that means the world to me.

Thanks so much to my amazing audio narrators, Kai Kennicott and Wen Ross. You always bring my characters to life in a way that blows my mind.

A big shout out to all my beta readers. You helped give me the confidence to put out a book a little more heartbreaking than usual. And also to my ARC readers for helping spread the word to everyone else in the world.

To all my writer friends who talk me down from the ledge, hold my hand, and tell me when my ideas are terrible and when they're brilliant, thank you.

Thanks so much to my editor Marla, my designers Okay Creations and Tempting Illustrations, and to Wander Aguiar for the amazing cover photo.

As always, my biggest thanks goes to my readers. Thank you for picking up *Accidental Husband.* I hope you'll be back for Chase's book *The Baby Bargain*.

Also by Crystal Kaswell

Sinful Serenade

Sing Your Heart Out - Miles

Strum Your Heart Out - Drew

Rock Your Heart Out - Tom

Play Your Heart Out - Pete

Sinful Ever After – series sequel

Dangerous Noise

Dangerous Kiss - Ethan

Dangerous Crush – Kit

Dangerous Rock – Joel

Dangerous Fling – Mal

Dangerous Encore - series sequel

Inked Hearts

Tempting - Brendon

Hooking Up - Walker

Pretend You're Mine - Ryan

Hating You, Loving You - Dean

Breaking the Rules - Hunter

Losing It - Wes

Accidental Husband - Griffin

more coming in 2019

Standalones

Broken - Trent & Delilah

Come Undone - A Love Triangle

Dirty Rich

Dirty Deal - Blake

Dirty Boss - Nick

Sign up for the Crystal Kaswell mailing list

Made in the USA
Middletown, DE
10 September 2019